INTERSECTION

Nancy Ann Healy

ISBN: 0615934188
ISBN 13: 9780615934181
Library of Congress Control Number: 2013922511
Bumbling Bard Creations, Manchester, CT

Chapter One

Agent Alex Toles sat at her desk wiping the sweat from her brow. "What the hell is it with this place? The air conditioning never works."

"Guess they'll just have to raise taxes again," the man across from her joked.

"As long as it's not MINE they are raising," the woman answered raising her eyebrow. She pushed out her chair and stretched her back, rising to her feet.

"Your back again?" her partner inquired.

She sighed and turned her side back and forth attempting to release the knot in her back. "Nah...it's fine, Fallon, just stiff."

"You working out too much, or just working out too much with that new redhead down the hall?" he goaded.

"Jealous?"

"A little," her partner conceded with a grin.

Alex walked to the water cooler and started to fill a cup. She raised the cup to her lips and shook her head in disgust, "Uck....it's like freakin' bath water." Her partner laughed. "Listen, Fallon," Alex began, "I would love to find a nice woman like Kate. You're the lucky one."

"Yeah? You settle down? Who are you kidding?" He rolled his eyes.

"What's that supposed to mean?"

"Well, even if you could sit still long enough to actually have a relationship, no woman could ever put up with all your antics."

1

"Antics?" she asked, feigning surprise while her partner just shuffled some papers and laughed.

"Hey...Toles...Fallon," a voice called from the hallway outside the office. "My office – now."

"Great. See that?" Alex pointed to the door and tossed her cup in the trash. "You insult me and now we have to work. Karma's a bitch, huh?"

Fallon stood and walked to the door opening it for his partner to walk through. "Well, at least you'll get that air conditioning," he offered as they began walking down the hall.

"Hey Toles," a woman greeted.

Alex smiled seductively. "Brackett," she acknowledged.

"See you later," the redhead flirted as the pair of senior agents passed by.

Alex smiled to herself and took a short breath of satisfaction. Her partner scratched his head and smirked as he opened the door for her. "Let's get you cooled off," he joked.

Walking through the door, agents Fallon and Toles were immediately met by the cold stare of FBI Assistant Director Joshua Tate. Tate was a veteran of the agency and had mentored both Agent Toles and her partner Brian Fallon. "Sit," he instructed. The partners took their seats in front of the large pine desk. Alex shifted in the chair to make room for her legs. "You all right there?" the director inquired.

"Yep."

"Okay then," he looked at the pair and sat back in his chair. "I've got a case for you."

"What kind of case?" Fallon asked as Alex continued to squirm about.

The director rubbed his chin and frowned. "Look, this case is sensitive."

Alex stopped her movement and looked squarely at her boss, "Serial killer?"

The director pushed his chair out with some force and paced to the window behind his desk. He rubbed his chin again and sighed so heavily that both Alex and Fallon saw his shoulders rise and fall. "No," he answered flatly before turning to face the pair. "Are you both familiar with Christopher O'Brien?"

"The congressman?" Alex asked.

"That would be the one, yes."

Fallon looked at Alex and then at the director. "He's New York's new golden boy."

Assistant Director Tate frowned. "Yeah. And, in spite of his very public divorce, he is indeed a golden boy. So much so that the president is aware of this case."

Alex and Fallon were puzzled. "Should this be under Secret Service jurisdiction?" Fallon asked.

"Mmm," Tate stood behind his chair gripping it. "No. The president specifically requested *your* assignment." Fallon's shocked look prompted further explanation as Alex placed her hand over her mouth thoughtfully. "The president and Toles here go back quite a long way."

"You never told me you knew the president," Fallon said with some resentment.

"It never came up," Alex said plainly. "So, why me? Why us?"

"He trusts you," Tate sat in his chair and grabbed a large manila envelope, pulling out a small stack of photos. "The congressman started receiving these earlier this week."

Alex began thumbing through the photos slowly. Each was of a letter. Some of the letters appeared to be handwritten and some were pieced together from clippings but all had a similar tone. Alex stopped and brought one up to her face, studying it carefully while Fallon began exploring the pile left behind.

This and that
I know you
Can you find me?
Back and Forth
Hide and Seek
I'll find you
Before you see.

Alex studied the picture carefully. Her partner sought more clarification from their director. "Does he have some idea? Enemies? Some legislation," Fallon began asking.

"No," Alex shook her head. "This isn't political."

Tate's jaw tightened. "Why do you say that?"

Alex kept her eyes on the picture. "Whoever it is… There is something personal here, an obsession. 'I'll find you before you see'. It's a game, cat and mouse, a challenge."

Tate scratched his head and smirked. "Well, this needs to stay quiet."

"We need to talk to the congressman," Fallon said.

"Yes, and you will but not as FBI agents, at least not to the rest of the world."

Alex set the picture down. She was well versed in the issues of the day and clearly understood why the president was concerned about keeping this quiet. The congressman was a point person on several key pieces of legislation for military funding initiatives and domestic policy. He was also a likely senatorial candidate in the next election. The president certainly did not want any public distractions. "So, you want us undercover," she said. Tate nodded.

"As what?" Fallon asked.

"Well…This will be an easier one for you Fallon."

"Why is that?" Fallon asked while Alex began exploring the other photos.

"You, Fallon, will go in as Secret Service and liaise with the Secret Service and the D.C. police. All of the letters have been received here in his Washington office…All except…"

"This one," Alex said as she read it aloud:

This time apart
Breaks a heart
Who takes mine
I'll take his
I'll keep watch
Until you see

4

What you have
Belongs with me

"What the hell does that mean?" Fallon asked in complete bewilderment.

"It either means he is infatuated with the wife or in love with the congressman," Alex surmised, slowly placing the photo back on the pile and looking directly at Tate. "And me?"

Tate poked his cheek with his tongue and scratched his nose. "That came to his house. You're going to New York, The Big Apple as a P.R. Assistant to the congressman's ex-wife. Who is quite popular in the press these days, I understand."

"A P.R. assistant?" Alex questioned.

Fallon's eyes bulged. "That'll be great when she drop kicks some poor paparazzi dude," he joked, receiving an icy glare from his partner.

"Well, it was either that or a nanny to their six year old. Take your pick."

"Great," Alex sarcastically agreed.

"Hey…I'd pay to see you play nanny," Fallon laughed. "Looks like you're trading in Brackett for servant to a school teacher," Fallon gloated. "Guess everybody's luck runs out sometime, Toles."

"Funny, who's the comedian now?"

"Well, it's not funny," Tate said breaking up the partners' banter. "And for what it's worth Fallon, Mrs. O'Brien has a reputation for being…well…"

"Opinionated," Alex said standing up and placing the pictures back in the envelope.

"Yes, exactly."

"Great," Alex said again. "How do we communicate?"

"The congressman picks up his son on Saturday mornings. Fallon will be assigned to travel with him. Until then secure lines across the boards. Understood?" The two nodded their understanding and began to head out the door. "Toles," Tate called and the agent turned. "Do me a favor, will ya'?"

"What's that?" she asked holding the door slightly ajar.

"Don't corrupt Brackett."

Alex laughed. "Doesn't look like I'll have time for much corruption, Assistant Director." She winked and closed the door behind her.

***

Alex rolled over and out of the bed leaving the tall redhead entwined in the sheets. She walked slowly to the large chair in the corner of the room to gather her clothes. The redhead watched the senior agent as she made her way across the room. Alex was an amazing specimen. She was tall and muscular but still feminine in a way that was almost indescribable. Her skin was neither olive nor fair and her long black hair seemed to cascade perfectly over her shoulders when she allowed it to fall freely. "Where are you going?"

Alex stepped into her pants and put her arms through her white blouse. She turned to face the woman in the bed, buttoning her shirt at the same time. "Assignment."

"Just....assignment? What kind of assignment?" the woman asked.

Alex kept her eyes on the buttons of her blouse. "Just assignment, Brackett."

"Claire....how about Claire?"

Alex looked up at the younger woman in the bed. "I'm not sure we're ready for THAT," she teased.

"Well, why don't you delay your flight to wherever you are headed and come get better acquainted?" The redhead patted the bed. "Unless, of course, you have a *better* offer?"

Alex laughed as she fastened the holster for her sidearm and reached for her blazer. "Oh, I don't think there's much danger of that where I am headed."

"When are you going to be back?"

Alex shrugged, "no idea."

"Call me."

Alex pursed her lips. "Yeah....listen, Brackett....you know....
I'm not really…"

"Yeah, I've heard," the redhead climbed from the bed and
stood in front of the agent. "I didn't ask for a ring, just a phone
call."

Alex laughed. "If you talk to Fallon he'll tell you it's the
same thing." She kissed the redhead and smiled. "I gotta' go."
With that the agent headed for the door.

***

"Are you kidding me? Chris...this is not.....No... I do under-
stand...I don't want some agent hanging around here...
around Dylan…...What? Don't tell me that you…...Unbelievable,
Christopher....fine....yes.... yes...I do hear you...I said fine...
No, Chris, fine actually means fine. I should know, I do teach
English....When?.....Great.....yep.....Yeah… Saturday…...okay...
….I will....you too," Cassidy hung up the phone with a sigh.

"What was that all about?" Rose McCollum asked her
daughter.

"Oh, Chris is worried, you know him. Some FBI woman is
coming here tomorrow, to watch over us, I guess."

"Cassidy, I know things are not exactly, well, happy between
you two, but I'm sure it is to protect you and Dylan," the woman's mother offered.

Cassidy walked to the kitchen island and opened a bottle
of wine. "I'm sure that's true, Mom, but I hate this. I want my
own life."

"Well, you married a politician."

Cassidy poured two glasses and handed her mother, who
was seated on a bar stool, one of them. "Yes, and I divorced that
politician."

Her mother took a sip of her wine and set the glass down
slowly, "Mhmmm...but the public did not divorce YOU."

"Please don't remind me," Cassidy said as she took a rather large sip from her glass.

"Mommy...."

Cassidy turned to see a small toe headed boy looking up at her and rubbing his eyes. She squatted down to meet his gaze and brushed his bangs out of his face, "What is it sweetheart? Did you have a bad dream?" He nodded his head and kept rubbing his eyes. A floppy stuffed rabbit lay tucked under his left arm, its ears drooping toward the ground. Rose smiled as she watched her daughter pick up the boy who willingly wrapped his legs around her waist and his right arm around her neck. "Do you want to sleep in my room tonight, buddy?" Cassidy asked. He nodded and put his head on her shoulder falling asleep again.

"Still having nightmares?" Rose asked.

Cassidy sighed. "Not as much. He's over tired. I'm going to go put him down. Mom, are you staying?"

"No," Rose answered taking one last sip from her glass and leaving it half full. "I'll clean this up and show myself out."

"So much for a relaxing evening with a glass of wine, huh?" Cassidy laughed.

Rose smiled. "Good night, Cassie."

"Night Mom...I probably should get some rest anyway. Company tomorrow, you know!"

"Cassie," her mother cautioned. "Play nice with the FBI," she laughed.

"Yeah... I love being told what to do. Can you pick Dylan up tomorrow? Maybe bring him home around dinner, just let me get...."

"Of course," Rose stopped her daughter's thought. "Get some rest," she advised watching her daughter walk away. "I hope this FBI woman does too. God knows she'll need it," she mumbled as she set about cleaning the kitchen.

"I heard that," Cassidy called back.

"How does she do that?"

"That too....Night Mom."

***

"I hate planes," Alex mumbled as she hurled her baggage into the trunk of her rental car. She cracked her neck and climbed into the Toyota Corolla, stretching her long legs as best she could. She reached into her briefcase and pulled out her GPS and typed in the address. "Cherry Circle? This oughta' be GREAT." The ride to New Rochelle was irritating the agent. Traffic was slow and Alex liked to travel fast. She fiddled with the radio, the windshield wipers, the defroster, the overhead lights, anything to break up the monotony of sitting in stand still traffic. A short distance away her irritation was shared by her soon to be host.

"This is ridiculous," Cassidy griped at she picked up a toy truck and put it in the large wooden toy box that sat behind the living room couch. "Ouch!" She cried stepping on a Buzz Light Year action figure. "Ohhhh….FBI and a six year old… yeah….This should be FABULOUS."

Alex took a right onto Cherry Circle and was met with the sight of what she considered mini-mansions. "What the? Big Apple my ass….1215…"

The GPS spoke, "You are nearing your destination."

"Holy crap." Alex looked out the windshield as she slowly pulled into the driveway of 1215 Cherry Circle. It was a large white colonial style home on the end of a cul-de-sac. "How many people live here?" she muttered to herself as she turned the key off in the ignition. She pulled a file from the passenger seat and opened it. Clipped to the top was a small picture. She slid it out from underneath the paperclip and studied it for a moment. The picture showed the congressman, on his hip sat a small boy with blonde hair smiling broadly. Next to him stood a shorter woman with blonde hair similar to the boy's, a stark contrast to the congressman's dark brown waves. She was attractive and there was a gentleness in her smile that made Alex sigh unknowingly. "Here we go, Cassidy O'Brien."

The agent stepped out of the car, grabbed her briefcase and headed for the front door. She took a deep breath and let it out before letting her finger press the doorbell. As the door opened the agent caught sight of the short blonde woman who was immersed in the task of peeling a chunk of what appeared to be blue Play-doh from her bare foot. "Uhh….Dylan…" the woman grumbled. She picked her head up and her hair fell slightly in her eyes before she finally extended her right hand to greet the agent. Alex looked at the woman before her as she offered her own hand, suddenly finding it difficult to move. Cassidy O'Brien was beautiful. As their eyes met, the agent felt the breath leave her body. "Sorry, about that," Cassidy said shaking her head as she crumpled the Play-doh in her left hand. "Kids….Please, come in."

Alex smiled finding herself momentarily stunned by the woman's piercing green eyes. Cassidy tilted her head slightly, looking at Alex curiously. The agent had a presence that Cassidy could not describe. Her eyes seemed to sparkle as the afternoon sun hit them. "Oh Lord, where are my manners! I'm Cassidy," she said leading the agent through the door. "You'd think I'd be better at that after being married to a politician," she mused.

Alex smiled at the earnest statement. "Alex, Alex Toles… nice to meet you Mrs. O'Brien," she said as they entered the home.

"Please, anything BUT Mrs. O'Brien," Cassidy laughed leading the agent into the large living room. "I get to hear that all day at school. Cassidy, please, if you are going to be here….just Cassidy." The agent nodded and took the seat offered her on the couch. She watched the woman continue to pick up several toys and stow them, still chatting as she moved. Alex could not help but smile at the way this woman moved about with seemingly never-ending energy. Cassidy threw a couple of toys into a small box near the fireplace. "Dylan….my son," she explained, finally taking a seat across from the agent in a large chair.

"Look, I know this is probably uncomfortable," Alex began. "But I think it's a good idea...at least now."

Cassidy looked at the agent. "Chris tells me you are a friend of the president." She shook her head as though having some epiphany, "God. I AM sorry...you've been traveling. Did you want some coffee or," the woman said motioning toward the kitchen.

"Oh...no," Alex smiled. "Thanks, though." Cassidy looked at her and their eyes met again. Both sat frozen for a moment, what each had expected from their meeting was a far cry from what the other's eyes seemed to convey. Alex bit her lip gently and mentally snapped herself back to reality. "The president and I have known each other a long time, yes. I served under him in Iraq." Cassidy listened intently as Alex continued. "I was assigned to work with the locals...to determine threats. We got to know each other very well."

"I see... Do you speak the language?"

"I do."

"So...what do you do at the FBI? I mean when you're not forced to go play bodyguard to some high school teacher and her six year old?"

Cassidy was a bundle of questions and Alex was surprised at how willingly she seemed to be answering all of them. "I am a profiler."

Cassidy stood up and looked toward the kitchen. "I think I could use some coffee," she offered beginning the short trek to the kitchen with Alex following behind, surveying the detail in her surroundings. "How does one become a profiler?" Cassidy asked with genuine curiosity as she grabbed a bag of coffee from a cabinet and began the task at hand.

"Well, I am a forensic psychologist, at least that's what my degree says," Alex joked.

Cassidy filled the coffee maker with water and sat on a bar stool across from the agent. "So, you think these threats are serious?"

Alex saw the sudden concern in the woman's eyes. She tightened her lips and spoke cautiously, "I don't know, but I think it's safer to consider them dangerous than to discount them as a prank."

Cassidy sighed. "Do you think this is someone with some grudge….I mean after the divorce…well…to discredit Chris?"

Alex looked over the woman's shoulder at the coffee maker as it began to drip. "No."

"Really?" Cassidy sounded surprised. "He's gotten letters and pictures ever since he started in public office….I guess I just…"

The agent looked back at the woman seated across from her. "That is normal, but not so many from the same person."

"How many?" Cassidy's expression and voice took on a stern tone. Alex stumbled realizing suddenly that the congressman may not have conveyed the seriousness of the threats to his ex-wife fully. "Well?" Cassidy asked again. Alex stared at her. Cassidy stood and turned to the cabinet trying to calm her rising temper. She pulled two mugs down and looked back at the agent, "Look…Agent Toles…"

"Alex…just Alex."

"Alex….if you are going to be here, I need to know why. How much danger are we in?"

Alex examined the woman who held her gaze firmly. "I can't say that… maybe none…but eleven letters in a week is a lot; all from the same person."

Cassidy poured them each a cup of coffee and set them down on the island. She silently made her way to the large stainless steel refrigerator, "cream or milk?"

"Black is fine," Alex said. "Listen, it may be nothing."

The woman walked back to her seat with a small carton of milk. "Or it might be something," she raised an eyebrow.

Alex shrugged slightly. "I am here to make sure that it does not become anything." She was mesmerized by the teacher's stare. Cassidy O'Brien was not what she had imagined. She was chatty and personable. Opinionated? Perhaps, but she was also extremely likable. Alex immediately understood why the public seemed to have fallen in love with the woman. "Alex...." She cautioned herself in her mind. "What the hell are you doing?"

Cassidy's gaze narrowed but a slight smile began to creep onto her face. Something about Alex made her feel safe. She watched the agent sip her coffee. Alex's stare had drifted into the cup and she appeared to be lost in some private thought. "So...what do we do?" Cassidy chimed.

Alex nearly choked on the coffee as she processed the question; her mind preoccupied with her study of the congressman's ex-wife far more than the situation at hand. Cassidy giggled slightly and handed the agent a towel. "Long day, huh?"

Alex gave an embarrassed smile, "something like that... yes." Cassidy nodded. "Look...Mrs. O'," Cassidy raised an eyebrow at the agent. "Cassidy...is there anyone, anyone that you have noticed hanging around more than usual...someone you don't know... at work or here....Your son's school?"

Cassidy's body shuddered at the last part of the agent's question. "Are you worried about Dylan?"

Alex saw the fear that she knew only could appear in a parent's eye and immediately set out to calm it. She reached across the island and touched Cassidy's hand. "I'm just covering the bases," she said with an encouraging glance.

Cassidy inhaled and stared at the table top. The thought of Dylan in danger shook her to her core and the feel of the agent's hand on hers produced what felt to her like a surge of electricity. Alex removed her hand and continued. "Anyone at all?" She asked gently.

The woman across from her swallowed hard. "I must just be reacting to the possibility of Dylan in danger," she silently assured herself before looking up to answer the agent. "No... no one...well, except the endless parade of photographers and reporters. They can change from one minute to the next. Their faces just sort of blend after a while, you know?"

13

"I'm sure," Alex said. "Try and pay more attention to them… if you can…if anyone seems more consistent than the others." Cassidy nodded her understanding.

Just then she heard the front door open. "Cassie?" Rose called.

"In here, Mom."

In an instant a small voice broke loose, "Mom! Look!" Alex looked over the island to see a small boy holding up a blue ribbon of some sort.

"What's this?" Cassidy asked, taking it and looking at it.

"First Place," he said with a decided nod.

"He won the fifty yard dash at Field Day," Rose said, now entering the kitchen and catching sight of Alex. "Oh…hello," she greeted.

"Oh…Alex Toles…meet my mother, Rose McCollum."

"Nice to meet you," the agent greeted, extending her hand. Rose smiled and accepted the gesture.

"And this," Cassidy said lifting the boy onto her lap, "is my famous sprinter, Dylan."

Alex watched as the woman brushed aside the boy's short bangs and looked on him with pride. Her eyes seemed to dance as she looked at him. What was it about this woman; she wondered to herself. "Well, hello Dylan," the agent said.

"Ms. Toles is going to stay with us for a little while to help Mommy with some things," Cassidy explained.

"Like the dishes?" he asked looking at the agent.

Cassidy laughed. "Not exactly." He looked at his mother, puzzled, and then at the agent who rose to her feet.

"Actually," Alex smiled, "I'm very good at dishes." She picked up the mugs and brought them to the sink.

"Oooo…I like her," Rose joked.

- Cassidy shook her head. "You don't have to…"

Alex smiled as she rinsed the mugs. "I actually have many talents…including the knowledge of dishwashers," she kidded.

Cassidy laughed. "Well, I look forward to learning exactly what those are," she quipped back. Alex smiled. This assignment was not turning out at all as she had expected hours ago.

Chapter Two

The newspaper leaned slightly on the bar as the news played a reel of Congressman Christopher O'Brien in the background. The congressman was walking with the president and some other dignitaries. The hands holding the paper trembled slightly as the man pulled his glance to the monitor above. His eyes became almost slits as he watched the short reel play and he returned his attention to the photograph on the page.

"He's a fool," the bartender noted looking at the picture and then at the monitor himself. "Beautiful woman like that... what an idiot." The man leered at the bartender. "What? You got something against beautiful women," the bartender cracked, "or just politicians?"

The man returned to the photo and reached for his glass, downing the final sip of his whiskey. He looked at the photo for another long moment before reaching in his pocket and placing a five dollar bill on the counter. He traced the photo with his index finger longingly and stood to make his exit. He was tall and well-built with a military style haircut and deep brown eyes. He sauntered toward the door, apparently aware of his good looks. A young woman at the far end of the bar reached out for him as he began to pass by, paper in hand. "Hey," she said. "Buy you a drink?"

He clutched the paper tighter and looked at her severely. "Not interested," he answered, pulling away from her touch and exiting the bar.

"What's with him?" the woman asked the bartender.

The bartender just shrugged. "Guess he does have something against beautiful women."

"Weirdo," she said with some disgust.

***

Alex excused herself to answer her cell phone and walked into the other room. "She seems fine, Cassie," Rose said as Cassidy pulled some vegetables out of the refrigerator and started chopping them.

"Yeah....Well she's only been here an hour."

"Cassie…"

Cassidy laughed. "Dylan, go easy with that truck," she cautioned as her son crawled across the floor swiftly crashing his toy dump truck into various pieces of furniture and making his own crashing sounds. "I'm just saying…it's not a question of whether or not she is nice, Mom. I just want some normalcy."

"Good luck with THAT," her mother retorted as she moved to help herself to a pepper from the cutting board, soliciting a playful slap from her daughter.

***

"Yeah…so…what's the story there, Fallon?" Alex asked her partner through the phone.

"He says he has no idea. Lots of people have issues with him politically but he seems like he is kind of a likable guy. I don't really see him as having a lot of personal enemies."

"You figured that out in one day?" Alex said.

"Yeah…actually."

Alex held the phone away from her and shook her head at it before returning it to her ear. "Everyone has enemies, Fallon. They just don't always know it."

"Always the optimist, Toles," he said.

"Yeah well…comes with the territory."

"What about you?" he asked.

Alex looked toward the kitchen. "Seems pretty normal here. I don't know yet. Jury's out."

"On what? You suspect the wife?" Alex paused. For some reason Fallon referring to Cassidy as 'the wife' bothered her. "Toles...you there?"

"No...I mean yes, I'm here...no I don't suspect Mrs. O'Brien...but I do wonder who the target is."

"Maybe there is NO target, Toles."

Alex gave an uncomfortable chuckle as she headed back toward the kitchen and saw Cassidy working on dinner and reprimanding Dylan again. She watched at a distance as Cassidy laid down her knife, wiped her hands on a towel and calmly but deliberately walked to the boy and removed the truck from his hands. "That is enough, Dylan. Go to your room for a little while and play until you can calm down." Alex suppressed a laugh as the boy stood and pouted at his mother. Cassidy was unflinching, "Think again, little man...get marching."

"Toles? What the hell?"

"Sorry," Alex couldn't help but snicker as the boy stomped past her in the hallway, briefly looking up at the agent to convey his six year old dissatisfaction with his mother. "There is, Fallon...I feel it." She started to head into the kitchen when Cassidy noticed her and she cut off the conversation abruptly. "It's fine...I'll see you Saturday...talk to you then." Alex hung up the phone and put it back in her pocket.

"Everything okay?" Cassidy asked.

"Sure...just my partner," Alex explained. "You need some help?"

Rose smiled from the kitchen table. "Be careful what you offer her," she cautioned.

"Nice," Cassidy laughed turning back to Alex. "No. You traveled all day and you are a guest. Perhaps Joan Rivers here can show you where your room is," she glared playfully at her mother.

19

"Oh...whatever...don't listen to her," Rose laughed. "Though you probably won't have much choice," she whispered to the agent just loud enough that her daughter could hear. "You'll be lucky to get a word in edge wise with that one."

"I heard that," Cassidy said returning to her dinner preparation.

"Ears like a bat, that one," Rose offered quietly as they headed out of the kitchen.

"That too," Cassidy called playfully. Alex followed Rose up the stairs to the bedroom that had been readied for her arrival.

"Do you really think someone is trying to hurt Chris or Cassie?" Rose asked as Alex stepped into the spacious room.

Alex gave the woman a comforting smile. "I hope not," she said.

"That's not very convincing," the older woman said.

Alex sighed. "Well, I would rather be careful and hopeful then hopeful and careless."

"Huh." Rose released a sigh. "Well, I'm glad you are here." Alex smiled. "Don't you have a bag?"

"Oh...yeah...it's in the car. I'll get it later. Might rouse less attention when it is dark."

"I see," Rose said. "Well, the bathroom is right there if you want to freshen up. I'm sure Cassie will have dinner ready soon."

Alex smiled, "thank you." Rose left and closed the door and Alex immediately collapsed back onto the queen size bed. She rubbed her hands over her face and thought about the letters. Something was keeping her unsettled, a gut feeling, one she had experienced before. For some reason, though, being here with this woman, it seemed to be affecting her emotionally. She feared the congressman might not be the target. She pulled herself up, stretched out her back and winced at the twinge of pain running the length of her body. Stretching gently, she walked to the bathroom to splash some cold water on her face. She looked in the mirror and took a deep breath. "Concentrate, Toles."

Heading back down the hallway she watched the small boy slide down the stairs on his butt. Alex laughed out loud wondering what Cassidy would have thought of that. She thought about her nephew who was close to the same age. "Typical," she mused to herself. The smell of taco night seemed to permeate the entire house and it was a welcome sensation for the agent. Her life tended to consist of frozen dinners, macaroni and cheese and take-out. She entered the kitchen to a sight she only saw on her trips home to New England. That was one thing she was happy about with this assignment; if all went well she might have a chance to see her brother and his family.

"Hey," Cassidy greeted the agent's return. "Have a seat." Alex smiled. "Help yourself... Crazy I know, but we don't stand on any ceremony here."

"Works for me," the agent said.

The dinner conversation was surprisingly easy for Alex. Dylan had a bunch of stories about field day and the agent found him amusing. She watched him and listened intently, laughing as he acted out the day physically with his tacos. "Did you ever run a race?" he asked the agent.

Alex took a sip of her iced tea and answered. "I have, actually. I was on the track team at West Point. I ran hurdles."

"What are those?" he asked.

"Those are things you have to jump over while you run," Cassidy explained and looked at the agent. Alex had the most stunning blue eyes she had ever seen. She found herself drawn to them somehow. The agent held the woman's gaze for a minute and felt her heart begin to quicken as they exchanged a smile.

"West Point?" Rose said. "Wow, not a lot of women still."

"No," Alex conceded breaking the exchanged glance with Cassidy and turning toward the woman's mother.

"Did you ever win a ribbon?" Dylan asked now.

"A few," Alex said modestly. "But none as nice as that one," she gestured to the ribbon now attached to the large refrigerator. The boy beamed with pride and his eyes flew open wide at her compliment. Cassidy was surprised when she felt her heart skip at the agent's interaction with her son.

"Well," Rose said, beginning to collect the empty plates, "I am going to get going after I clean this up so you can all get settled."

"Let me give you a hand," Alex offered.

"No, no...You go get your things. Sun is setting...next time." Alex nodded her appreciation.

"Do you need some help?" Cassidy asked the agent.

"No, I've got it."

"Well, Dylan...Why don't you and I get you washed up?"

The boy moaned and Alex smiled. "I'm going to do the same thing," the agent winked.

He pondered her statement. "Will you teach me to jump over hoidles?"

"Hurdles," Cassidy corrected with a slight snicker at his mispronunciation.

"We'll see," the agent said pretending to think carefully about the request.

"Okay," he said running for the stairs.

The two women reached the foyer as Dylan half ran, half crawled up the stairs. "If you need anything," Cassidy offered.

"Thanks," Alex said turning to head out the door to retrieve her luggage. "I promise I will do my best not to interrupt your life too much."

Cassidy stopped on the bottom stair and looked at Alex. "Well, if any of those many talents you mentioned include fixing clogged sinks from action figures or clogged vacuums from Play-doh...it will be a welcome interruption," she jested.

"Mmmm. Agent Fix-it at your service," Alex joked.

Cassidy sighed with a smile as Dylan screamed for her, "MOM!"

"Duty calls," Cassidy said. "Hold your horses...I am coming."

"Yes it does," Alex said to herself. "Yes it does."

Intersection

The door to the apartment opened slowly and the man threw the newspaper on a small card table at the center of his living space. He silently walked to a large roll top desk and picked up a pair of scissors. Then he made his way to the kitchen and poured himself a small glass of whiskey, straight up. Walking back to the table he spun the scissors around his finger while he sipped his drink. The folding chair at the table had bent legs, but he seemed unconcerned about its ability to support his weight. He set the whiskey down and spun the scissors one final time. Unexpectedly, the blade slipped and poked his palm. A small trickle of blood fell onto the paper. He frantically grabbed a napkin and wiped the blood from his hand while swiftly turning to find the photo that commanded his interest. There was a tiny, barely visible drop of blood on its corner. His face grew flushed and he pulled at the very short hairs on his head as though his world were ending. He took a deep breath, licked the napkin and dabbed the spot on the picture.

The spot became slightly darker, but in his mind it seemed to erase the evidence of any transgression. He traced the outline of the face in the picture with his finger and his breath quickened. He picked the scissors back up scolding them with his eyes. Deliberately, he looked back at the face on the paper and inhaled, closing his eyes to calm himself. His hands shook but he remained determined to cut the picture out with perfect symmetry. He slowed his pace and methodically removed the photo from the page before walking to the large wall across from him. He stood and studied his work, found the perfect place and put a small tack in either corner to secure it.

***

Alex paced across the living room and looked at the photos displayed on the tables and mantle in frames. There were photos everywhere. Most were photos of Dylan; Dylan with Cassidy, Dylan with Rose, Dylan with the congressman, Dylan. Alex stopped and looked at one that sat on the mantle. It was Cassidy. She was younger in the photo, Alex thought perhaps eighteen or nineteen. She was smiling and holding a Stanford banner. Cassidy reached the large doorway to the room and stopped, taking a moment to watch the agent as she studied her new surroundings. "Yeah…hard to believe I was ever THAT young," she acknowledged.

Alex turned and looked at the woman as Cassidy made her way into the room and plopped onto the couch. "Stanford?" the agent questioned.

"I guess I figured you would already know that," Cassidy said.

Alex shrugged, "I did…I just wondered."

"How a Stanford grad ends up teaching school in Harlem to at risk teenagers?" She laughed. "Well," she said kicking the shoes off her feet and heaving them onto the coffee table. "I always hoped to write a novel, but I also wanted to teach. When we moved here…well…"

Alex sat down on a chair. "What did the congressman think?"

"Of me teaching or of me teaching in Harlem?"

"Either."

Cassidy laughed. "We may need wine for this conversation." Alex smirked. "Ohhh… well, as long as it worked for his image, I guess. He's always worried about how people perceive him… you know, his *image*."

"I'm sorry," Alex said unsure of what else to say.

Cassidy chuckled. "Don't be. It goes with the territory and that is just Chris. He's like that guy who admires anyone who can do anything better than everyone else. Like, for example, he loves that movie *The Italian Job*–you know the prefect heist? That's just the way he's always been. Bigger is better and if you give him a lot of attention along the way, well, that's heaven."

Alex knew the type well. Her career had been littered with men who craved more attention, more power, more everything. "So, anyone come to mind at all?" Alex asked. "You know, that might be out of place?"

"You really think this might be something, don't you?" Cassidy asked looking at the agent for some reassurance.

"I've learned to be careful, Cassidy. Some people might accuse me of being too careful."

"Well, I just can't understand why anyone would want to hurt Chris...or us."

Alex looked at the woman and shrugged slightly. "Unfortunately, there are some people in this world that just...well they can be dangerous. You are all in the public eye. That increases your risk."

"Yeah...great," Cassidy chimed.

"You didn't want a public life?" the agent inquired.

Cassidy rubbed her face and then answered. "Well, it's not that so much, but I don't want to change who I am for that life." Alex looked at the woman intently as she continued. "You know, I just am not good at pretending to...Saying one thing and thinking another...or...if you ask Chris, saying nothing at all. Be 'seen not heard'. I don't want Dylan growing up with that model of his mother."

"Sounds like the military a bit," Alex said in jest.

"Maybe," Cassidy confessed. "What about you? West Point, runner, Iraq...FBI? No one special in your life?" Cassidy choked slightly at her need to ask the last question. She was curious about this woman, and it was certainly personal.

"No...not really."

"Never?" Cassidy asked curiously.

Alex shrugged, "I lead kind of a fast paced life...always have."

"So," Cassidy asked now, "did you like the military?"

"I liked the challenge. Just like the FBI....And I liked the travel."

"Nomad, huh?"

Alex laughed at the analogy. "A bit, I suppose."

"So then this must be culture shock," Cassidy looked around the room.

"Well, let's just say it's a lot bigger than what I am used to."

Cassidy shook her head with obvious agreement. "It's too big for two people...it's too big for five people, who am I kidding?"

"It's nice," Alex complimented.

"It's ginormous," Cassidy conceded with a giggle. "Seriously, it's ridiculous. I work with kids who are lucky if they have a bed to sleep in some nights. I come home to THIS. Not me."

"Do you think you'll stay here...I mean for a long time, then?"

"It works for right now," Cassidy said. "Another argument for us. Chris wants Dylan to have *everything*. I guess we have different ideas about what that word means." Alex watched as the woman pulled herself off the couch and gathered her shoes. She was amazed by Cassidy. She expected a privileged snob. Cassidy was the opposite. It was refreshing to Alex. "I'm going to turn in," Cassidy smiled. "5:30 a.m. comes quickly. You help yourself to whatever you need," she offered as she started out of the room.

"Cassidy?"

"Yes?" Cassidy turned back.

"I will figure out what this is."

Cassidy squinted and curled her lip into the hint of the smile. "I know you will," she said.

Alex watched the woman walk away. She looked around the room and took a deep breath. Somehow she would put these pieces together. It had been years since she had felt so at ease with another person so quickly. And, she was determined that she would protect this family no matter who sought to do them harm. Whatever the reason, Cassidy O'Brien seemed to stir something within the agent. "What is it about you, Cassidy O'Brien?" she asked herself out loud.

Chapter Three

Cassidy stood at the kitchen island sipping a coffee and leafing through the morning paper. The sky was still dark, just beginning to transition from black to indigo as the sun started its journey back to light another day. She heard the door close and looked up, "Mom?"

In what seemed like an instant Alex was in the kitchen. She bent over with her hands on her knees. "Morning."

"I thought it was early for my mother," Cassidy laughed. "You were out early."

"Yeah," Alex stretched her back a little and winced. "Force of habit." Cassidy caught the grimace and realized that her own face must have expressed some concern. "Yeah…gets stiff when I run now. Not getting any younger, I guess," Alex joked.

"Want some coffee?" Cassidy offered.

"Coffee is great."

Cassidy went about the task of getting the agent some coffee. "You always up this early?" Alex asked taking a seat on a bar stool.

Cassidy snickered a bit, "unfortunately, yes."

"Not a morning person?"

"Hardly," Cassidy said pouring the coffee into a tall mug. "Black, right?"

"Yeah, thanks."

Cassidy sat down. "When I was in college Chris used to joke that he was surprised I made it to class. I've always been a bit of a night owl…and a noon sleeper. But, with this job, well

I've got to drive to the train station, catch the train and walk 8 blocks….so…"

"Ahhh…what about Dylan?"

"Mom usually gets here just about 6:30 and gets him ready. I swear she should just move in here, but she likes her *space*," she laughed. Alex sipped her coffee and glanced at the paper. Cassidy had apparently been reading the calendar section for the weekend. She wondered what the congressman's ex-wife was contemplating for her free days. "So…what will you do today, as a press advisor?" Cassidy asked.

"I actually am going to check out both schools."

"You mean Dylan's?"

"Yes, but I will be careful. Don't worry. Just going to talk to the principal," Alex explained.

"As an agent?"

"No. Just to advise him that the congressman's staff is aware of the increased attention surrounding the family and that I am assigned to help liaise with the press and arrange security should the press become overly intrusive."

"I see," Cassidy said.

Alex noted the apprehension in the woman's voice. "He may offer something without even knowing it. That's often how we get information. And…I will have a chance to look at the building from a security standpoint; get a feel before I have to start looking at personnel profiles."

"What do you mean? Are you telling me you are looking into the teachers?" Cassidy was clearly becoming frustrated by the conversation.

"Yes," the agent answered plainly.

"Teachers?" Cassidy put her mug in the sink with some force. "This is insane." Alex pinched the bridge of her nose as Cassidy continued. "Isn't anyone above suspicion in this world? What's next, my mother for God's sake?" Alex just looked at her and remained silent. "I know it's your job, but…so you will be looking into the teachers I work with? My friends?"

"Yes." Alex was direct and firm in her answer. It was strange to the agent but this felt somehow very familiar; like an episode of déjà vu. Something instinctively told her that no rational argument she could make would fully satisfy Cassidy.

Cassidy stood across the counter practically glaring at the agent. She was frustrated by the entire situation. The door opened again and Rose entered. She immediately noticed the tension in the glance that was exchanged between her daughter and the agent. "Good morning?" she phrased her greeting as a question.

Cassidy just shook her head with irritation at the agent. "I'll get Dylan up," she said still looking directly at Alex who did not avert her glare. "Should I arm him first? It is the first grade after all?" She asked the agent sarcastically. Alex's unflinching demeanor frustrated Cassidy. She looked briefly at her mother. "I hope you have your passport with you," she said as she left the room. Alex let go a sigh and pressed her thumbs to her temples.

"What was that all about?" Rose asked. "I thought you two were getting along fine."

Alex took a sip of her coffee and folded the paper. "Well, she sees the best in people. I have to look for the worst."

Rose grinned. "I see. Cassie can be…Well, she has always been very idealistic."

Alex nodded. "I got that."

"She'll get over it."

Alex looked toward the hallway and shook her head. There were things about her job she truly hated and this was one of them. Cassidy was right and Cassidy was wrong at the same time. Sometimes the people you trusted the most could be the people you should trust the least. Experience taught Alex that. And, it was her job to make sure nothing happened to Cassidy or Dylan; to find out what exactly these letters were all about. Whatever that took, that was her job. "I should go get ready," Alex said turning her attention back to Rose.

"Alex," Rose called after her, prompting Alex's turn. "Do whatever you need to. Just keep them safe." Alex nodded and made her way up the stairs.

Cassidy waited until she heard Alex's door shut to make her way back down the stairs. Dylan ran into the kitchen and gave his grandmother a hug. The teacher gathered her things in silence, her temper still simmering, while Rose set a bowl of cereal in front of Dylan. Silently, the younger woman began walking toward the foyer. "Eat your cereal, Dylan," Rose instructed following Cassidy to the door.

Feeling her mother's presence Cassidy piped up. "Don't even say it."

Rose gave her daughter a motherly look of caution. "I understand, Cassie, but she is here to keep you SAFE. I don't care if she literally goes through my dirty laundry. Whatever that takes."

Cassidy sighed and smiled. Her mother was right. She looked up the stairs and sighed again. "I'll talk to her later," she said. The fact was that she could not help how she felt. She knew this was what the FBI agent was here for. Their conversations had flowed more like that of friends until this morning and she found the new reality that was now surrounding her unsettling. She smiled at her mother, "I have to go."

Rose nodded as she watched Cassidy walk through the door. "Oh Cassie," she mumbled to herself.

***

Alex sat quietly on a chair in the hallway looking at the bulletin boards that lined the walls. She examined every detail, where the doors were, where most of the people entered, the closets, lockers and the people, even who entered which room and when. "Ms. Toles?" a woman's voice beckoned. "Principal Scott will see you now."

Alex stood, offering a cordial smile and followed the woman through double doors into a large office area. She stepped through the thick oak door and was immediately greeted by a strong hand. "Ms. Toles."

She accepted the hand and returned its grasp. "Thank you for taking the time to see me," she greeted the principal.

"Not at all," the principal answered. He was fairly young, she surmised in his mid-thirties. "So, what is it that we can do for the congressman's office?" he asked, motioning for her to take a seat.

Alex nodded her appreciation and sat across from his desk. "Actually," she began, "I am really here to assure you of the congressman's commitment to keeping the press at bay from the school. I know that the attention to the family has been quite high of late. I will be helping Mrs. O'Brien navigate this time. I am also here to help with Dylan's exposure to the press and I am available to you at any time as well."

The man smiled. "I appreciate that," he answered. "So far we haven't had any issues dealing with the press effectively, but it is certainly nice to know we have an actual face to reach out to if needed." Alex watched him as he spoke. She studied his mannerisms and searched for signs as to whether he might be single or married. If Cassidy was somehow the center of these letters, a single, younger man would fit the profile. He continued his thoughts. "You know...it's hard enough for children and teachers," he said. "And it has been hard enough on Dylan already." Alex looked at him curiously.

"I don't mean to speak out of turn," he continued, "I realize you work for the congressman."

"No...please...I assure you, my goal is to keep the family protected from the press...sometimes the strangest things can matter....please continue," she urged.

"Divorce is hard...but you know, as a congressman he was not home much anyway and when he was it was always with a lot of attention from the press. We did have a brief time when there were reporters outside waiting for Mrs. O'Brien to pick Dylan up. He used to go to the afterschool program, but the press seemed to unsettle him so Mrs. O'Brien began having Mrs. McCollum pick him up after school. Anything you can do to keep the press away would certainly help Dylan."

Alex could hear his genuine concern for the boy and her heart sank as the morning tension with Cassidy entered her mind. Here she was sizing him up, just as Cassidy had suggested, mistrusting everyone. That was just the nature of the beast. She tried to quiet the thoughts in her mind now. "You say that there were reporters waiting for Mrs. O'Brien. Was that during the divorce?"

"Yes, but there have been quite a few photographers on and off all along."

"Recently?" Alex asked, trying to keep her questions light and avoid her agent tendencies.

"As a matter of fact, yes…but not for a few weeks now, three or four. Our assistant principal had some words with them one afternoon and it has been fairly quiet since."

"Well, that's encouraging," Alex said. "I will make certain that I speak with the powers that be at the papers to be sure they understand their boundaries." She handed him a mock business card, "but please feel free to call me anytime."

"Thank you…You know…Ms. Toles…."

"Yes?" Alex answered.

"I hope you can get this all quieted down. Mrs. O'Brien is a terrific lady and a great teacher. Her students, well…people talk, those kids love her. She deserves some peace."

Alex smiled. The principal's compliment of Cassidy was clearly heartfelt. "Yes, she does."

***

Cassidy paced behind her desk waiting for her next class to arrive. She looked at the old fashioned chalk board behind her and stepped up to it to write. *How do you tell a GREAT story?* She wrote the words and set the chalk back in its place. She looked out at the empty desks and sighed. How did her life get so complicated? A head poked around the door, "Mrs. O.?"

"James...come in."

"Hey...ummm," the boy was about fifteen but nearly six feet tall already.

"What is it, James?" He walked up to her desk and put a paper on it. "What's this?" she asked. Alex had just reached the doorway. It was time for her to visit Cassidy's school to assess the risk and she was dreading it. She watched silently, staying just behind the classroom door that lay ajar.

James looked up at the words she had scrawled on the board. Several days earlier she had written the words; *why should you tell your story?* "I was thinking," he said, "about what you said."

"What was that?" Cassidy asked the boy.

"That sometimes, if you tell your story it helps you understand your feelings....and sometimes it can even help someone else."

Cassidy picked up the paper and glanced at the title, *I Am Happy I Have Two Moms.* She smiled and looked at him.

"I thought...well, I wanted you to read it."

Cassidy looked at the boy to convey her pride. "Of course I will read it."

"I don't talk about it, you know... I mean the team knows, but maybe I should... you know... so I thought I would write about it... you know...first."

Cassidy took a gentle hold of the boy's arm. "I think that's a great idea, James. I will read it tonight."

"You can keep that one," he said with a smile. "But...will you tell me....What you think?"

"Sure I will...but what really matters is what YOU think, James...how YOU feel about it. Just remember that."

"Thanks, teach," he left with a bounce in his step.

Alex smiled as the lanky boy nearly skipped past her. She watched as Cassidy picked up the paper again and saw the woman's face light up. 'My God, she is beautiful,' Alex thought silently. Cassidy had started sifting through some other papers as Alex entered the room. She stood still and tried to catch her breath. "Hey," was all she could summon.

Cassidy looked up and saw the agent looking back at her. She wanted to be angry. She was angry, but Alex wasn't the reason and she knew that. She just didn't know how to say it now. "Hey yourself," she said, unable to contain the grin that Alex seemed to provoke. She hated this whole situation, but her mother was right, Alex was there to help. This was her job.

"I wanted you to know I was here," Alex said as a bell rang and the halls immediately began to fill.

"Thanks," Cassidy said. "I appreciate that."

"I promise, no inquisition," Alex crossed her heart as students began to poor in.

Cassidy tried not to laugh. "I'll hold you to that," she said. Alex nodded and headed out the door getting knocked by several students in the process. Cassidy watched her leave, and suddenly realized that she was looking forward to going home.

***

The lens was not fitting on the camera properly. "DAMMIT!" The man yelled in frustration. He held his breath and tried again, attempting to steady his hand. He carefully and slowly turned the lens until he heard a click and then exhaled. He picked up a pack of Marlboro's and fished out a cigarette, lighting it and taking a long drag. He put the camera in its case and then caressed the case lovingly. The phone began ringing on the desk behind him but he seemed lost in his exploration of the camera case. The ringing continued and he looked over at the desk. He released his grip from the case and made his way to pick up the receiver of the old fashioned rotary phone.

"Hello…..No…No…an assignment…yes, to take some photos…fine…..not tomorrow…..Sunday….fine." He hung up the phone and went back to retrieve his camera case. "Assignment," he said to himself with a sly smile.

***

Cassidy walked into the living room and greeted her mother. "Hey, Mom," she said tossing her bag down and flopping onto the sofa, exhausted. She looked around a bit, wondering if the agent was still out.

"How was your day?" Rose asked.

"It was all right. I am glad it's the weekend," she confessed. "Alex here?"

Rose smiled and put a toy in the toy box. "No, she was…said she would be back shortly…..seemed a bit mysterious about it," she laughed. "Must be the FBI thing."

"Maybe," Cassidy said pulling off her shoes. "Are you staying for dinner?"

"Why? What are you making?" Rose joked.

"As tired as I am it might be macaroni and cheese and hot dogs…a Dylan delicacy."

"Think I'll pass on that one. Let me know when it is caviar," Rose suggested.

"Second Tuesday of next week…be here," Cassidy offered.

***

Alex stood at the counter waiting patiently and sipping a glass of water. "Sure you don't want a drink while you wait?" the bartender asked.

"No, thanks." She was swirling an ice cube around in her glass when something caught her attention.

Big vote coming in the house next Tuesday. Congressman Christopher O'Brien has been working overtime to muster support for the bi-partisan initiative, but with his private life tarnished does he have the influence?

Alex looked up at the monitor and saw the congressman and Cassidy during the last election.

"Crazy," the bartender said.

"What's that?" Alex asked.

"Tarnished...Hell they've practically sainted the man. Personally, anyone who lets that woman go has a screw loose." Alex looked back at the monitor as the image was just changing and felt the bartender's comment lodge in her chest. She agreed. "All set," the bartender said as he handed the agent two large boxes.

Alex started to reach for them when she felt a strong bump in her back. "Hey!" She yelped as a matter of reaction. The man did not speak. His eyes were focused on the ground where a beer had crashed and spilled from his clumsy collision with the agent and another customer. Alex bent over and picked up the case that was lying in the small puddle and handed it to the man. He glanced at her for a second and immediately looked away, swiftly heading for the exit. "You're welcome..." Alex called after him. She turned back toward the bar to retrieve her boxes shaking her head.

"Nut," the bartender said watching the man leave.

"Thanks again," Alex said.

"Next time, stay a while," the bartender winked.

"I'll think about it."

***

"You're sure you don't want to stay for my improvisational cooking?" Cassidy asked, not wanting to move from her current position on the sofa.

"Tempting, but no," Rose laughed. "I have a date with a nice glass of wine and some takeout sushi."

"You're back!" A small voice yelled as the front door closed.

"Looks that way, huh?" Alex replied.

"What's that?" the boy asked.

Alex stepped into the living room holding two large pizza boxes. Cassidy looked over at her and cocked her head with an inquisitive squint. Alex held out the boxes, "peace offering."

"Well...you certainly have good timing," Rose laughed. "You just saved yourself from starvation, I think." Cassidy shot her mother a playful look of disdain. Rose just shrugged. "I'm off kiddos."

"Are you leaving?" the agent asked.

"I am. I have a hot date with some cold sushi. I'll see you Monday."

Alex looked at Cassidy as Rose left and noticed that she looked a bit pale. "You feeling all right?" she asked with genuine concern.

"Yes, just tired. Long few days, I guess."

Dylan was standing under the pizza boxes attempting to determine what they might be. Alex looked underneath them at him and then back at his mother. "Well, I'll tell you what... why don't you go change and Dylan and I will get these all set."

Cassidy could hardly believe Alex's gesture. "You don't have to do that...I mean Dylan..."

Alex interrupted her. "Dylan and I, we got this, don't we?"

The boy peeked out and nodded at his mother who laughed. "Okay, then."

"Good...Just come on down when you are ready," Alex said.

It was such a welcome surprise for Cassidy. She couldn't believe it as she climbed the stairs. She couldn't remember the last time she was able to just relax for even a few minutes, unless she was asleep. She put on a pair of gray sweat pants and a sweatshirt and sighed at the relief she felt in them. She heard Dylan laughing downstairs as she entered the hallway and she stopped to listen. "You see... if the pepper is the hurdle and the hamburger is you....You have to run really fast and make sure you take big steps so you can make it over the pepper. I mean the hurdle...if you don't, well then you have pepper and hamburger on top of each other...and that is just NOT good."

Cassidy shook her head and laughed. Alex was actually illustrating hurdles with their pizza. Dylan was still laughing and she could only imagine what the agent's demonstration had looked like. She made her way down the stairs and into the kitchen where she was greeted by a small boy with a towel draped over his arm. He looked back at Alex who gave him a nod. "Dinner is served," he said to his mother who fought to contain her laughter.

"Why thank you, Sir," she said as he led her to the table. She looked at Alex who was watching with great satisfaction and found herself locked momentarily on the agent's blue eyes.

Alex caught herself and looked at the pizza. "I didn't know what you liked so…one is half veggie and half meat and the other is half Hawaiian and half cheese. Figured that covered most of the bases."

Cassidy sat down at the table. "It's perfect…and not necessary." Alex opened her mouth to say something but Cassidy continued before she had the chance. "But it is appreciated," she looked back at Alex. "So…how was YOUR day?" Cassidy asked the agent.

"Other than the klutz who ran into me where I got the pizza, uneventful, I am happy to say."

Cassidy smiled. "And you, Dylan?"

The boy was eating a piece of Hawaiian pizza and seemed completely consumed by the task. He shrugged, "unementmul."

Cassidy laughed. "Looks like you have a fan," she said to the agent who just smiled. 'Maybe more than one,' she thought to herself.

***

"I don't want to go to bed," Dylan griped.

"Well, I'm sorry, buddy….Your dad will be here early and it's bed time," Cassidy directed. He looked over at the agent who was wiping off the table. Cassidy could tell he was wondering if

Alex would still be there when he got up. "Alex will still be here in the morning." Alex smiled at the boy and he sighed heavily. "Say good night, Dylan."

He walked over to the agent and put his arms around her waist. "Good night," he said with a squeeze.

Alex was taken aback by his affection at first but quickly responded with a pat on his head. "Good night, Speed Racer," she smiled.

Cassidy looked at them and wondered if that nickname had come from the agent's earlier pizza slash hurdling lesson. Dylan ran past Cassidy and up the stairs. "Thanks," Cassidy grinned at the agent.

"Least I could do."

"No...it was far more than you had to do," Cassidy said. She suddenly felt her heart begin to quicken as the agent held her gaze. "And, I owe you an apology."

Alex shook her head. "No...seeing the good in people is not something to apologize for."

"Well, I am sorry for taking my frustration out on you."

"No apology necessary," Alex smiled.

Cassidy stood frozen for a moment looking at the agent before she pulled her stare toward the hallway. "I'll take care of all of this once he is settled in bed."

Alex raised an eyebrow. "I told you; I got this. I can handle empty pizza boxes and you already know I am dishwasher savvy. Get some rest."

"Alex, you don't have to..."

"Yeah...I do...and I want to...least I can do for intruding in your life."

Cassidy nodded at the sentiment and started to leave before she stopped herself. "For the record, Agent Toles," Alex looked at the woman staring back at her as Cassidy finished her thought. "It's a welcome intrusion. I'm glad you are here," she said as she continued on her way out of the kitchen.

'Me too,' the agent thought to herself, 'me too.'

Chapter Four

Alex stood in the kitchen drinking a cup of coffee and reading a file at the counter. She was in jeans and a white blouse, her hair no longer pulled back in a ponytail, but falling freely on her shoulders. Cassidy entered the room and felt her entire body freeze. Alex was gorgeous and Cassidy was noticing it. "Good morning," Cassidy said trying to process whatever this was she was feeling.

"Hey, there," Alex smiled. "Did you get some sleep?"

"I did, actually. Dylan slept through the night for a change." Alex looked at the woman curiously while she reached into the cabinet and pulled down a mug for Cassidy. "Thanks... yeah... he's been having some nightmares."

Alex never dismissed anything as unimportant. She searched Cassidy and saw her concern. "What kind of nightmares?" the agent asked cautiously.

Cassidy's gaze narrowed for an instant but then she let the hint of a smile show. She had fallen asleep thinking about how Dylan had laughed harder than she had heard in a while with the agent and she knew whatever Alex was asking it was out of concern. "I don't really know...he's six, but he says he sees lights in his room...red lights and white lights and he gets scared." Alex sipped her coffee slowly. Cassidy noted that the agent's expression seemed to tighten. "What is it?" Cassidy asked nervously.

Alex set down the mug and shook her head. "Nothing.... Just something his principal said."

"What?" Cassidy said, growing worried.

"Sounds like cameras...you know...flashes," she explained. "Obnoxious," she muttered.

"Oh my God...I never put that together...I can't believe..."

Alex looked at the woman with reassurance. "Why would you? It's what I do.....just seems unfair...he's just a kid."

Cassidy grinned. Alex was clearly irritated by the idea that the press had upset Dylan and she found that incredibly endearing. "He likes you," Cassidy said.

"He's a neat kid," Alex responded taking another sip of her coffee and straightening the papers in her file.

"Always working?" Cassidy inquired.

Alex shrugged slightly, "well, let's just say I always have homework."

Cassidy laughed at the explanation. "Understood." She started back out of the kitchen with her coffee in hand. "I have to go get Dylan ready....Chris will be here in an hour. Guess that means I will get to meet your partner too."

"Lucky you," Alex kidded. Cassidy just smiled. She was curious what she might learn about the agent during the brief visit.

***

Alex was sitting on the floor with Dylan who was busy explaining how his trucks could be superheroes when the doorbell rang. Alex watched as the blonde woman's posture stiffened and she took in a deep breath. Cassidy dreaded Saturday mornings. She hated being apart from Dylan and seeing her ex-husband was still uncomfortable. They had been together since Cassidy was a freshman in college. He was a graduate student and a TA for a class she was taking in Political Science. He was handsome and intelligent and passionate. He had noticed her immediately and she loved his attention. He made her laugh and she was drawn in by his charisma and intellect. The truth was that she loved him, in her own way, but she wondered if she had ever been in love; with anyone. He showed her a whole new world and she reveled in that, but she never felt connected to him in the way she imagined real love would feel. Perhaps it was just the romantic in her; that's what she told herself for many years. Over time, and after Dylan, she just couldn't keep up the facade. He was away most of the time, always worried about moving up and frequently seen in the company of other women. She enjoyed the adventure of meeting new people and travel, but she had grown tired of feeling like an afterthought in his life and she needed to be herself. With a deep breath she opened the door and smiled. "Chris…"

"Cassie," he said. "How are you?"

"Fine," she answered as she watched him head into the living room. She noticed the man walking behind him. He had a kind face, she thought, as he extended his hand.

"You must be Alex's partner," she said. "Nice to meet you," the teacher offered her hand.

"And you, Mrs. O'Brien."

"Just Cassidy…come in…please…I think my son is torturing your partner with Tonka trucks in the living room," she giggled.

"Fallon, Agent Brian Fallon," he answered following her through the large doorway.

Alex had managed to reach her feet and Dylan was chatting up his father. "Daddy…I won a ribbon, but Alex…she won ribbons too," he said turning to point to the tall woman standing behind him.

The congressman smiled. "I've heard a great deal about you, Age…I mean…Ms. Toles… you have a very powerful fan base," he extended his hand.

Alex nodded her appreciation. "Don't believe everything you hear," she commented, beginning to make her way across the room to Fallon. Cassidy looked on unaware of the smile that completely overtook her face. Dylan was acting out Alex's hurdle scenario to his father with his trucks. As Alex approached, the two women locked eyes. Cassidy's smile grew a little wider and she made her way toward Dylan and his father to give the partners some space. "Fallon," Alex said.

"Playing with Tonka trucks? You feeling okay?" he jested.

"Funny," she said. "Anything to report?"

"No...not really...not yet... but I think you're right...I mean about it being personal." Alex looked over at the family that had gathered in the center of the room. She unconsciously bit her bottom lip and scratched her head with her thumb, a signal to Fallon that she was worried. He had seen that before. Agent Toles was watching the group very closely and Fallon noted that her gaze focused squarely on Mrs. O'Brien. "So, is she as difficult as they say?"

"What?" Alex snapped back.

"The congressman's wife....I mean is she the backbreaker they say."

"Ex-wife," Alex said dryly, "and I don't know who 'they' are...but no."

Fallon looked at his partner quizzically. "Easy there... killer....you're not.....no way..."

Alex shot her partner a look of stern warning. "I'm just concerned, Fallon. They're a nice family."

"OOOkayy...Well, that's good because Brackett would be heartbroken."

"What the hell are you talking about?" Alex was clearly annoyed by the entire exchange. As she turned to face her partner, Cassidy looked over and saw the agent's obvious irritation. She gently pried a truck from Dylan's hand wondering what the pair was discussing. "Fallon...I am not interested in anything with Brackett, let's just stick to the case, okay?"

"What's with you, Toles? You're taking all this kind of personal."

"I'm not. I just have a bad feeling, Brian," she looked back at Cassidy.

"You're sure that's all?"

"Of course," she turned back to him. "Can you run some background on the reporters that have filed stories and the photographers with photo credits of the family?"

"Sure," he said. "Why?"

"Just a feeling." Fallon swallowed hard. There was one thing the senior agent had learned in his three years with his partner; her *feelings* usually were right and that usually meant trouble.

The congressman was headed toward them now as Cassidy scooted Dylan along in front of her. "You apparently have another fan," the congressman said to Alex. "My son is determined to become a hurdler," he smiled. Fallon felt his own eyes widen. Alex somehow had managed to be personable with this family in less than three days. He had been with the agent nearly every day for three years and they seemed to know as much about her personally as he did. "Thank you," the congressman said earnestly to Alex.

Alex nodded as Cassidy came even with her stance. "Not at all, Sir."

"Call me, Chris," he said warmly. "Come on, bud," he said to Dylan who stopped and looked up at the two women before him.

"Have fun with Daddy," Cassidy bent over and kissed her son.

"I will," he hugged her tightly, not letting go for several seconds. Cassidy kissed his head and whispered something in his ear prompting him to slowly release his grip on her and look up at Alex. Before she could speak he had grabbed her waist. "I'll bring home my big truck to show you," he said.

Alex smiled. "I will look forward to that, Speed Racer," she whispered to him.

"Keep her safe," the congressman instructed looking at Cassidy. Cassidy inhaled a sad breath, feeling his concern was genuine.

Alex nodded her understanding as he passed through the door with Dylan nearly tripping him. She walked side by side with Fallon. "Send me everything you can get on those press folks," Alex said.

"Toles?"

"Yeah?"

"You're really worried," Fallon said.

The agent sighed watching the congressman climb into the waiting car with his son. "I am."

***

Cassidy had poured herself another cup of coffee and was headed to the kitchen table where Alex was scanning through some files. "What you got there? Or is it top secret, Alias stuff?"

Alex laughed and looked at Cassidy teasingly, "Alias is CIA…this is more you know…Gillian Anderson than Jennifer Garner."

"Ohh….I see," Cassidy quipped back. "Not into that whole disguise thing? Prefer the little green men?"

"Not so much for the little green *men* either," Alex joked and then felt her cheeks flush, realizing what she had just unwittingly revealed.

Cassidy felt a slight lump in her throat and was amazed by her own response. "So… Gillian or Jen?"

Alex looked at the woman with surprise and gave a slight nervous chuckle. "MMM… tough call….Gotta' go with Gillian."

"Interesting," the small blonde woman mused with a smile.

Alex changed the subject. "So, what's on your agenda today?"

Cassidy saw the name on the top of the file and sighed. Alex winced a bit. "I'm sorry Cassidy…it's…"

"You don't have to explain Alex. I get it. I just hate it."

Alex's lips wrinkled. "So…really, what are your plans?"

Cassidy took a sip of her coffee, "I was thinking of taking a drive, actually."

"Really?" Alex's phone rang, "sorry," she said as Cassidy shook her head indicating it was fine. "Hello? Hey...What? When?...Yeah.... can you scan it.....send it...yeah, now," she looked at Cassidy and then continued with the conversation. "No, I'm here...send it to my email...Does Tate know?.... Okay....Fallon? Get on those backgrounds." Alex hung up the phone and saw Cassidy looking at her with great apprehension over her coffee mug. "Another letter," she said softly. "Look, Cassidy...."

"What did it say?"

"I haven't seen it yet. Fallon is sending it now." Cassidy set down her mug and let out a nervous sigh. Alex opened her laptop on the table and logged on. She could see Cassidy's anxiety as she opened the attachment. She tried to remain stoic as she read it to herself.

I see her
Every night
You left her
Out of sight
I'll take mine
She'll have me
Before you know
What you can't see

Alex felt a chill rush through her body. She looked over at the woman across from her. This was no simple game and Alex knew it. It wasn't a prank and it wasn't about the congressman. Someone was obsessed with Cassidy and his rhetoric was increasing.

"Well?" Cassidy urged.

Alex took a deep breath. There was no point in lying or hiding anything from Cassidy. "It's about you."

"Me?" Cassidy thought she might throw up.

"Listen, Cassidy..."

"What the hell? Why would anyone want to hurt me? To get at Chris?"

47

"I'm not sure…and I don't think this is about the congress-man really, other than resentment toward him….I think….well, I think you have a stalker."

"That's insane."

Alex filled her cheeks with air and released it. "Look, I need call Fallon back. Just give me a minute, okay?" Alex picked up her laptop and carried it into the other room. She studied the document again and picked up her cell phone. "Hey….yeah I'm looking at it now…..I don't know….I think she needs some pro-tection…..what? Yeah, well…..I know…..is Tate on the line? … Yes, Sir… I know…I realize that, but…you and I both know this will likely escalate, no…that's not…yep….yes, Sir…I under-stand…Fallon?...yeah…just get those damn work ups done." Alex hung up the phone and rubbed her temples. She looked at the words on the screen one more time and then logged off, closing the laptop slowly. "Oh shit, Toles," she said quietly to herself. Her stomach was in knots. Fallon was right, she was taking this personally. The thought of anyone harming Cassidy terrified her. "What the hell is wrong with me?" she said aloud softly again. "Not even three days, Toles…get a grip."

Alex took a few deep breaths to calm herself and then walked back into the kitchen. Cassidy had her face in her hands; her long blonde hair falling over them and resting on the table. Alex fought to breathe. She pinched the bridge of her nose hard. The agent's emotions felt foreign to her. She didn't understand how this woman could be affecting her so deeply and in such a short time. It wasn't just an attraction, although as Alex approached the kitchen she could not deny that she found Cassidy alluring. It was more than that, not just the job; she felt an overwhelming need to protect the woman. "Hey," Alex said very softly, setting down the laptop and putting her hand on Cassidy's shoulder. Cassidy lifted her gaze and Alex immediately saw that she had been crying. Her heart sank. She gave the woman a gentle smile. "Listen, let's take that drive…okay? Get away from here for a while, what do you say?'

"Alex, you don't have to babysit me…I…"

"Actually, I do," the agent said and saw Cassidy look down. "But I really wouldn't mind a drive….or the company."

Cassidy looked back at her. "That's nice of you to say."

Alex looked into Cassidy's green eyes, eyes that had turned slightly red from tears. "No…it's not," she was overcome by the need to comfort the woman before her and touched her cheek. "It's just true."

Cassidy looked at her. 'Oh my God,' she thought to herself as she found herself wishing Alex would kiss her and somehow make all the fear disappear. She caught her breath, "I'd like that."

Alex pulled back trying to regain control of her own emotions. "It's settled…you pick the place and I'll drive."

Cassidy shook her head. "Actually…I can't even think right now, Alex."

"Well, then…I'll pick the place and I'll drive." She laughed. "Why don't you go ahead and get yourself…"

"Together?" Cassidy chuckled.

"Your words, not mine," Alex winked. "I'm going to put this all away…and I'll figure something out…okay?"

Cassidy pondered the agent's offer silently for a moment watching her put her files neatly in her briefcase. "Alex?" The agent looked up. "I'm glad you are here."

Alex smiled as Cassidy left the room. "I hope you remember you said that," Alex said quietly to herself.

"I will," Cassidy called back.

Alex looked up in shock. "She really does have ears like a bat."

"Yes, I do." Alex snickered. She was going to find something to take Cassidy's mind off things, something.

***

"Okay... thanks.... Perfect... no...I will...about four o'clock or so." Alex hung up her phone and grabbed her wallet, her badge and her side arm. She knew Cassidy would hate that, but she couldn't take any chances. She would put it in the glove box for the drive and then she would gauge whether or not she needed it. The truth was that she was beginning to think the undercover scenario was foolish, but that was not her decision to make. Cassidy walked back into the kitchen after deciding to take a quick shower. The teacher thought it might help settle her nerves about everything. Alex looked up and saw Cassidy and thought she might have stopped breathing. Cassidy was wearing jeans and a black sweater that seemed to cling to her perfectly. The teacher smiled noticing that Alex was staring at her.

"So...find something?" Cassidy asked.

"I did...listen before we go..."

Cassidy suddenly felt sick. She wondered if Alex was a having second thoughts about leaving or worse that she had noticed Cassidy was looking at her. And why, Cassidy wondered, was she looking at her? Her head was spinning. "Alex, we don't have to go..."

Alex shook her head. "No...no...I just...I'd feel better if I brought some protection," she pointed to the pistol.

Cassidy sighed partially from relief and partially from the gravity of her new reality. "I understand."

"I promise, I won't wear it unless I think..."

"Alex, it's okay....really."

Alex was the one to breathe a sigh of relief now. "Good. Enough of that...you ready? First question; are we on a timetable?"

Now Cassidy was curious. "I haven't had a curfew in at least six months," she joked.

"Good." Alex was surprised by the butterflies she felt in her stomach. She felt a bit like a teenager on her first date, but she had a good plan mapped out to take Cassidy's mind off things, at least she hoped she did. "Well...let's go."

Alex put on her long black leather jacket and watched as Cassidy slipped on her short denim jacket. They walked out the door and Cassidy turned to lock it. When she turned back Alex was holding the car door open. Cassidy walked to the car with a flirtatious grin. She stopped at the door right in front of Alex. Inches away from each other, Cassidy looked directly into the agent's eyes. "Are you going to tell me where we are going?"

Alex raised an eyebrow. "Nope."

Cassidy held her stare for a moment not wanting to look away. There was a feeling running through her body that she could not explain. What she did know was that Alex made her feel safer and more appreciated than she could remember. "Hummm," she groaned her curiosity as she got into the car.

They had been driving for a while, talking about everything and nothing and laughing at nearly all of it. Alex had started singing a song to the radio and Cassidy was struck by her voice. "You should have been a singer," she remarked.

"Ah...maybe if hip hop had been popular in the eighties and nineties," Alex joked. "What about you?" The question prompted Cassidy to tell Alex about her one attempt at playing a musical instrument and how she "fell flat." They just kept talking, Alex breaking into a harmony to some song on the radio every now and again. The agent had shared a bit about her first days at West Point and how she almost got kicked out for punching an obnoxious cadet. The conversation was easy and natural and both women quickly forgot what had led them to be together in the first place. "Hey.... here we are."

Cassidy had not been paying any attention to where they were going, consumed in the conversation and in listening to Alex sing. "Where are we?" she asked. She wasn't even certain how long they had been driving.

Alex just smiled and got out of the car. Cassidy stepped out and looked behind the car to see the ocean as a backdrop. To the left was a large white building adorned with white lights. A covered deck with a large fireplace at its center sat overlooking the water. "You like seafood?" Alex asked hopefully.

"I do, actually."

"Well, good...not that they don't have other things," Alex began to lead Cassidy toward the building. "But they have the best seafood around...but I'm not exactly an objective party."

Cassidy wondered who the 'they' was until she reached the door and saw the name *Toles*. Alex opened the door and stepped through. "Ummm, Alex?"

"Alexis!" A handsome man walked up to the agent and gave her a hug. Cassidy was completely perplexed.

"I'm sorry...Cassidy O'Brien, meet my brother, Nick."

Cassidy was sure her eyes were as big as saucers. The resemblance was undeniable. "Nice to meet you," she said. He took her hand and squeezed it.

"I don't know what a beautiful woman like you is doing having dinner with this fool," he pointed to his sister. Cassidy laughed watching Alex roll her eyes. "Oh well, follow me ladies." Nick led them out to the patio to a table beside the fireplace. It was warm for March, but still cold enough that sitting outside was not normally an option. Nick handed them each a menu and whispered to Cassidy. "Make sure she leaves a big tip." Cassidy giggled and nodded.

"Alex..."

"Oh...well...you said you couldn't think..."

"Where are we?" the teacher asked curiously.

"You really weren't paying attention, were you?" Cassidy gave the agent a look of mock annoyance.

"Okay...okay...we are in Connecticut...Stonington to be exact," Alex answered.

"Are you from here?"

"No....Massachusetts actually, but my brother, he moved here right after college and opened this place. I haven't been here in a couple of years, it's great though...only place you can sit outside almost year round…and I promise the food is excellent…the service…eh."

Cassidy laughed. The view was beautiful, almost as beautiful as the agent with the fire light reflecting in her eyes. "It's beautiful," Cassidy remarked unable to look away from the agent.

"Yes…It is," Alex responded looking into the green eyes that seemed to captivate her.

A young waiter interrupted their moment. "Mr. Toles asked red or white?"

Alex looked at Cassidy; silently directing the question to her. "White?" Cassidy answered a bit unsure.

"White it is," Alex directed the young man who smiled and headed off.

Cassidy was looking out at the water. The sun was still up but it had begun its slow progression downward. She took a deep, cleansing breath, filling her lungs with the ocean air and closed her eyes drinking it all in. Alex just watched, mesmerized. The waiter returned and Alex silently directed him to leave the wine and the plate of shrimp on the small table that was next to her. Cassidy opened her eyes to see Alex pouring her a glass of wine and moving the plate of shrimp cocktail to the table. "Alex…this is…"

Alex gave Cassidy an impish grin. "How are you feeling?"

Cassidy had to laugh, "relaxed…but you don't…"

The agent poured her own glass of wine and then looked across the table. There was an ease and gentleness about this woman that she had never experienced. She felt as if they had known each other forever. Alex wore no masks, and even when she tried Cassidy seemed to strip them away with a glance. "There isn't any place I would rather be or anyone I'd rather be with," Alex said plainly. Cassidy felt her entire body go weak wondering who this woman across from her was.

Dinner progressed just as the car ride had. The sun set as they ate and they talked and laughed, the waves lapping the shore behind them. It was getting late and Cassidy had consumed her fair share of wine. She looked around the patio. "Alex, no one else has been out here all night."

"I know," Alex smiled. "I asked Nick to keep it closed...no side arms...no people... no press."

"You did that for me?" Alex managed a slightly embarrassed shrug, rendering Cassidy speechless.

As they were leaving Nick said his goodbye to Cassidy who walked ahead looking at a large saltwater fish tank in order to give Alex a moment with her brother. Nick saw the twinkle in his sister's eye. "She's a keeper, Alex."

Alex took a deep breath. "She's straight, Nick."

"Ohhh.... So you're not...falling in love with her then?" Alex was completely floored by her brother's insinuation. She was ready to give him a piece of her mind when Cassidy turned and directed a smile her way momentarily. The agent sighed. "Well, I may not know a lot Alex...but I know you...and I know what I see when I see it."

"Nick...I am assigned to protect her...for God's sake her ex-husband is a congressman."

"Huh?" he mused. "I thought she looked familiar....oh whatever, Alex...I saw you two out there. You want to fool yourself out of a good thing? Well, that's just stupid...but that's your business...you're not fooling me."

Alex gave her brother a hug. "What do I owe you?"

Nick shook his head and looked at Cassidy. "Nothing, sis... just kiss the girl already."

Alex laughed. "Thanks."

***

"Alex," Cassidy began as she listened to the agent humming away to a song on the radio. "What do I owe you for dinner...I was so caught up in..."

"Nothing."

"Ummm...no... Alex... really...you can't ...."

Alex glanced over and laughed. "You can't owe me anything because I didn't pay anything."

"What?" Cassidy was confused.

"Ahhh… that's just Nicky," Alex glanced over again. She could see that the woman's eyelids were getting heavy and smiled.

"I'm sorry," Cassidy offered, catching herself beginning to nod off. "I don't know why I am so tired."

"Good wine, good food and the ocean…always relaxes me," Alex said.

Cassidy looked over at the agent who was gripping the wheel with one hand and running the other through her hair. "Good company," the woman gently added fighting the sleep that was overtaking her. Alex glanced back and saw Cassidy's eyes had finally closed. She was pleased. The stress seemed to have temporarily left the small woman next to her. Alex turned the radio down slightly and continued the hour plus trek back to New York. Nick's words were still ringing in her ears. He knew her as well as anyone; he should. Their childhood had been strict and at times difficult. Their father could be unbending and their mother followed along. Neither Nick nor Alex followed the path that their parents had wanted; both left home for school after high school and both made their own lives from there. Alex had not felt comfortable around her parents for years. Nick was her true family, the one she felt comfortable with. They hid nothing from one another. He saw immediately what she could feel but could not comprehend.

Every so often Alex would catch a glimpse of Cassidy shifting in her sleep in the seat next to her. She tried to keep her breathing steady. She felt a mixture of confusion, excitement and fear just being near the woman. "Three days," she kept telling herself. "She's in your care," she would remind herself. "Christ, Toles …she's straight", she would scream in her head. Then she'd glance over and see the woman sleeping and the fight would begin all over again. What felt like the deafening sound of *Brick House* began to blare through the car, breaking one of Alex's many mental arguments with herself. Cassidy jumped and Alex realized it was the teacher's cell phone. The woman fumbled a bit, still groggy, and answered it while Alex attempted to suppress her laughter. She wasn't sure what amused her more, Cassidy's theatrics or her choice of ringtone. 'Does she know what that song is about?' Alex mused to herself, allowing a very hushed giggle to slip across her lips.

"Hello?" Cassidy answered still groggy. "Chris? What the hell time is it? Is Dylan…"

The voice on the other end of the phone cut her off, "Dylan is fine…I guess you were sleeping."

"Yeah…I guess I dozed off….Chris what is going on?"

"Ummm….I got called back to D.C., Cassie….I have to leave first thing in the morning."

"Oookay," Cassidy answered. "So you're going to drop Dylan off early then?"

There was a brief pause before the voice answered as the congressman prepared for his ex-wife's reaction. "Actually, Cassie, my flight is at 4:45 am out of JFK…..I would have to get Dylan up at 2:00 to make it in time…..I was kind of hoping…"

"You're serious right now?" Cassidy was now wide awake and simmering. "Isn't he asleep?"

"Yes…..You can always just stay here at the apart…."

Cassidy let out a disgusted chuckle. "No…Chris, I can't. Why can't you get a later flight?" Alex tried to concentrate on the road but she could feel the steam pouring off Cassidy.

"I have a 9:00 a.m. meeting at the White House."

"Of course you do," she said sarcastically.

"It's not my choice, Cassie…it's my job."

"Yeah…well you have a six year old too…in case you hadn't noticed… that is SLEEPING right now… that you see for exactly a day and a half every week."

"Well, whose fault is that?" he answered in frustration.

"Yes...Chris...it's my fault," Cassidy stopped herself and took a deep breath. She looked over at Alex quickly and sighed. "I don't want to argue."

"Me either," he said feeling suddenly guilty about everything. "Why don't I just bring him over now?"

Cassidy looked at Alex. "Where are we?"

"What?" He asked uncertain of her question.

"I'm not talking to you," she said simply as Alex began her answer.

"About twenty minutes from home," Alex answered.

"Where are you?" he asked.

Cassidy ignored his question and continued her conversation with the agent. "Do you mind if we stop and get..."

Alex had already surmised the situation. "Just tell me where to go."

"Cassidy!" He raised his voice slightly, "Who is there?"

She shook her head and replied with a tone of disgust. "Not that it is ANY of your business, Christopher...but I was talking to Alex...Agent Toles."

He sighed. "Oh....I can bring him..."

"No, I'm not home.....we'll be there in about twenty-five minutes. Just have his things ready," she hung up before he could answer. Alex could tell she was irritated. "Unbelievable," Cassidy muttered. "I'm sorry, Alex."

"For what?"

"Oh...subjecting you to that. Making you take me to pick up my son at...what is it? 11:30 at night."

"It's fine, really."

Cassidy was silent the rest of the drive to the congressman's apartment except for giving basic directions. Alex pulled in front of the building and put her car in park. "I'll be right back," Cassidy said.

"Do you need help?" Alex asked.

Cassidy looked at the agent and smiled for the first time since the phone call. She sat still for a moment, just looking at

Alex. There was something about the way Alex looked at her; it just made her heart sing. "It's okay," she finally said. "I'm used to it." She hopped out of the car and headed into the building. Cassidy had barely left when Alex saw her grabbing the backpack from the congressman with Dylan wrapped around her tightly, his legs hugging her waist and his arms draped around her neck. The sight filled Alex in a way she had never experienced. She jumped out of the car and opened the back door. "Oh shit," Cassidy remarked as Alex took the backpack and put it on the driver's side backseat.

"What?" Alex asked.

"I need his booster seat." Alex looked at the small woman that stood before her. The agent instinctively put out her hands and Cassidy did not even have a passing thought as Alex gently pried the sleeping boy from his mother and shifted him onto her. He mumbled something and then just wrapped himself around the agent. He settled his small head on her broad shoulders as his mother made her way to the front door again to get the seat. Alex felt the boy nestle against her. He sighed a little and mumbled again in his sleep and she couldn't help but think how adorable he was. Cassidy emerged in another moment looking at the ground with a miffed expression. As she hit the bottom stair she looked up and saw the sight before her. Alex didn't realize it, but she was swaying instinctively with him and humming softly every time he seemed restless. The teacher stopped dead in her tracks. The sight of Alex holding Dylan so tenderly melted her. She caught her breath and headed to the car.

Cassidy leaned past Alex to put the seat in the car and brushed up against her slightly. Her mouth went dry momentarily from the contact. It did not go unnoticed by the agent either. Just the sensation of Cassidy brushing up against her accidentally made the agent's knees grow weak. Alex bent over and sat Dylan in the seat. He opened his eyes slightly and saw clear blue ones looking at him. "Sorry, Speed Racer," she said softly as she buckled him in. His drowsy eyes gave the hint of a smile to the agent but almost immediately closed again. Cassidy gave the agent a curious look. "What?" Alex asked.

"You're a natural."

Alex laughed and opened Cassidy's door. "Eight year old nephew," she said.

"Hmmmm," Cassidy climbed into the car. 'Some things can't be taught', she thought to herself. With each moment that passed she found herself more and more drawn to the agent.

Chapter Five

Alex pulled in the driveway and turned off the car. She sat incredibly still, squinting and looking toward the front door as if to try and bring something into focus. Cassidy saw her expression. "Alex....what is it?" Alex continued to focus for a moment. She silently reached across Cassidy into the glove box and retrieved the pistol. Cassidy felt her heart sink. "Alex?"

Alex kept her focus forward. "Stay here with Dylan," she instructed, "and lock the doors."

Cassidy suddenly felt an unbelievable rush of fear. She did exactly as Alex told her and looked behind her to see that Dylan was completely unaware that the car had even stopped. She watched as Alex held the pistol with both hands at her side, walking almost sideways toward the front door with a cautious confidence. Suddenly, her fear turned from an anxiety for Dylan and herself to an overwhelming fear for Alex's safety. Her stomach lodged in her throat as Alex reached the porch. Then she saw it. Something was taped to the front door.

Alex turned the handle to the front door. It was locked. The agent's stance relaxed slightly and she studied the item on the door. Cassidy couldn't completely make out her expression but she sensed that the agent was concerned. Alex studied the photo. It was a picture of her and Cassidy in the kitchen. In black marker the words, "I SEE YOU," were scrawled under Alex's face. She took a deep breath and grasped the pistol at her side tighter. Someone was watching them. The question now was who and how. She looked back at the car and held a finger up to Cassidy. "Oh God, Alex," Cassidy said aloud as the agent resumed her stance and began circling the house. Within a moment Alex was out of sight. The agent circled house, carefully looking to each side and in front of her. She continued slowly and methodically until she appeared on the other side. Cassidy felt her heart lurch inside of her. She looked back at Dylan again and closed her eyes tightly, trying to keep herself calm. Finally seeing Alex headed back toward the car, she felt her breath release.

"Give me the keys to the house," the agent instructed.

"Alex..." The panic on the teacher's face was evident.

Alex needed to stay focused. She looked at the woman she knew she was falling in love with and calmly continued in a professional tone. "Cassidy, I need to check the house. Get in the driver's seat and lock the car until I come back. Keep the keys in the ignition. If you see anyone BUT me coming, you drive back to the congressman's apartment and get Fallon. Do you understand me?"

Cassidy swallowed hard and nodded, getting out of the car and moving next to Alex before getting into the driver's seat. Alex started to turn when Cassidy grabbed her arm. The look on the teacher's face was transparent to the agent and she had to fight her own emotion. "Alex...please," Cassidy felt her heart dropping in her chest again. Alex flashed a reassuring smile and turned back repeating her earlier stance and motion. Cassidy shut the car door and locked it. She watched paralyzed as Alex unlocked the front door and pushed it open, gun drawn. She knew Alex was moving through the house slowly as lights methodically came on room by room. It seemed like an eternity before the agent emerged again holstering her weapon and walking toward the car.

"It's safe." Alex said, finally beginning to relax a bit herself. Alex opened the back door and Cassidy moved in to unbuckle Dylan but her hands were shaking so hard she couldn't keep a grasp on the buckle. She felt a strong hand cover hers, lingering for a moment and then unclipping the buckle. She stood back up straight and looked at Alex. She couldn't even cry. "I'll get him," the agent said. Cassidy didn't argue. Alex handed her the backpack and pulled Dylan up into her arms. Cassidy shut the car door and Alex followed her to the porch. The smaller woman froze as she started to enter and saw the photo. "Cassidy," the agent gently called from right behind her. "Don't. Let's just get Dylan upstairs." Cassidy took a deep breath and kept moving. Alex followed and carried the boy up to his room, lying him in his bed so that Cassidy could get him settled. "I'll be right back," Alex said.

The agent went to her room and retrieved a pair of gloves and an evidence bag from her things. She went back to the door and carefully removed the photo, placing it in the bag. She reached for her cell phone, pressed a number and waited. "Toles?" the voice asked.

"Fallon... listen things are progressing faster than we hoped....I don't want to get into the details now. Is the congressman all right?"

"Yeah...why?" he asked in confusion.

"Okay. Do me a favor. Check the perimeter of the apartment."

"Now?" he responded.

"Yes...now."

"Okay I'll..."

Alex interrupted her partner in frustration. "No, while I am on the phone."

Fallon complied and the phone was silent for a few moments, "What am I looking for, Toles?"

"I don't know...it's just a feeling."

"Another *feeling*? Christ, Toles....wait.....wait...shit...."

"What is it?"

"What the hell is this?" Fallon began.

"What?"

"Christ, Toles.....There's a photo on the back door...."

"Of what?" she asked.

"Me....Me and the congressman."

Alex huffed. "Jigs up, Fallon...someone knows who we are."

"What?"

"Same thing here. Anything written on yours?"

"No..."

"All right.... Bag it." She paused and looked up the stairs, her thoughts suddenly turning to the woman she had left there moments ago. "Fallon?"

"Yeah?"

"Will you call Tate?"

"Sure....you don't..."

"I have to finish some things here," Alex explained.

Brian Fallon pulled the phone away from his ear and looked at it. There was something in his partner's voice that he had never heard before. Alex was always focused. He knew when she thought there was danger by the tone in her voice, but this was different. She was worried, maybe even afraid. "You okay, Toles?"

"Yeah...just..."

He finished her thought, "a feeling....I know....all right. I've got Tate covered. I'll call you when I get back to D.C."

"Okay." She stood at the bottom of the stairs for a moment and swallowed hard. She felt sick and she had to face Cassidy now. For the first time in the agent's career she was truly afraid, not that there was imminent danger in the moment, but that one look at the woman who waited up the stairs and all of her secrets would be instantly revealed. She tried to force herself forward, her thoughts racing. Days didn't matter, facts, places; none of it mattered. Alex felt something for this woman and she wasn't certain she'd change that even if she could. When Alex reached Dylan's room Cassidy was standing over his bed, stroking his hair while he slept. The agent couldn't separate one emotion from another. "Cassidy?" The teacher turned to look at the agent who was moving toward her now. Cassidy's eyes silently confessed her fears and Alex held her gaze, attempting to convey her own understanding. When Alex finally reached the woman across the room, Cassidy's feelings completely consumed her. Her tears began to fall and her knees gave way. Alex grabbed hold of her and pulled her close, holding her while Cassidy wept. "It's okay," Alex said gently. "It's going to be okay." The agent looked over the woman's shoulder at the sleeping boy and closed her eyes, feeling Cassidy in her arms and wanting only to take her pain away.

Cassidy tried to calm herself, but feeling Alex's arms around her brought on a whole new flood of sensations and emotions. She didn't want the agent to let her go. It was such a wonderful sensation and it terrified her almost as much as what had just transpired. Alex held her tightly and spoke softly, trying to tame her own heartbeat. "Cassidy...I promise you.....I promise...I am not going to let anyone hurt you or Dylan." Without thinking she kissed the top of Cassidy's head. When she realized her own action she felt a burst of fear expecting Cassidy to pull away, but instead Cassidy instinctively clasped the agent's waist and held on.

"I know you won't." Alex closed her eyes and took a deep breath. She had no idea what was next, but she knew one thing, even if it was impossible for her to fathom. 'I think I love you, Cassidy O'Brien,' she silently admitted to herself.

Cassidy was reluctant to leave Dylan's room. Once she had managed to let go of the agent she turned back to her sleeping son. "Alex...how am I?" She couldn't finish her thought, overwhelmed by the array of emotions coursing through her. Why was this happening to them? All she wanted was for the agent to hold her and never let go. She tried to breathe but Alex could see that she was struggling to process things. The agent felt more helpless than ever before in her life. She wanted to take Cassidy back into her arms and tell her what she felt; that she would sooner die herself than to see this woman in any pain.

Alex spoke softly and placed her hand on the woman's shoulder. "I know you don't want to leave but you need to get some rest, Cassidy."

"How can I leave him...even here?"

"You can't stand here all night."

"I can't leave him." Cassidy's tears began to fall again as she stroked his head. Alex sighed and looked upward. She moved past the woman in front of her and lifted the boy into her arms. "What are you doing?" Cassidy asked.

"I'm putting him in your room so you can sleep...or at least rest." The agent walked out of the room and down the hallway.

Cassidy stood still, watching the woman leave the room. She cupped her face in her hands and tried to process everything she was feeling. "Deep breath," she said to herself and headed down the hallway. Alex was covering Dylan with a blanket when Cassidy reached the doorway. She stopped for a moment and forgot everything that had just happened. Alex had a concerned smile on her face as she slowly pulled the blanket over the boy. She was looking at him with such compassion and, 'love', Cassidy thought. Alex took a deep breath and moved to face Cassidy, both finding it difficult to move. Finally Cassidy smiled and walked to the far side of the bed.

The agent bit her bottom lip gently and forced a smile. "Get some rest," she said beginning to head for the door. Before she could make her exit, she felt a hand on her arm.

"Alex..." Cassidy's voice was barely a whisper. The agent closed her eyes and struggled to compose herself before facing the woman. Slowly she turned and took in the sight before her; green eyes pleading for some type of comfort. "I," Cassidy fumbled her words. "Can you just stay here....for a while?"

The agent thought that her heart had stopped beating momentarily. Cassidy looked at the floor and Alex inhaled as much air as she could handle. Emotions filled her so deeply that she felt as if there was not enough room inside of her body for even air to breathe. Cassidy kept her gaze down until the agent tenderly prompted her chin to rise with her finger. "Come on." The agent slowly led the woman to the bed and turned down the covers. Cassidy just looked at her. She knew that this was no time to be having the thoughts that seemed to be filling her head. They were thoughts she had never had before. She looked at the agent, afraid that her heart and mind were written across her face. Alex gently coaxed the woman's jacket off her shoulders. She patted the pillow, "go on," she instructed quietly. Cassidy climbed in, still in her clothes and too emotional and exhausted to care. Alex pulled the covers up over the woman. "I'll be right here," she assured. She grabbed the large chair from the other side of the room, pulled it next to the bed and draped the jacket over it. Cassidy watched as the agent sprawled in the chair and gave her a smile. "Sleep now," Alex said sweetly.

Alex watched as Cassidy drifted off slowly. She could not sleep, only watch. Cassidy had captured her heart and Alex was sure now it had been from the moment she saw her. The teacher's jacket hung behind the agent's head, and as she shifted in the chair the scent of Cassidy's perfume was unmistakable. Alex closed her eyes as her heart raced. If she had worried that her heart had stopped beating earlier, there was no doubt now that she was very much alive. She wondered as she began to fight her own exhaustion how she would handle this. She had a job to do; maybe she should recuse herself. No. She didn't want to leave and she didn't trust anyone else to keep Cassidy safe. Somehow she would fight the urge to confess her feelings, somehow.

***

Cassidy struggled to open her eyes. She rubbed them and sighed in relief when she felt Dylan pressed up against her. She gently maneuvered away from the sleeping boy and looked over to see the agent in the chair, asleep. Alex had Cassidy's jacket under her head like a pillow. Cassidy rolled to face the agent's position and studied her. In spite of her discombobulated position in the chair, her hair falling slightly in her eyes, Alexis Toles was stunning, even as she slept. Cassidy felt an incredible sense of happiness penetrate her as she finally rose to her feet. Alex was in a ball in the corner of the chair. Cassidy stood in front of her for a long moment. She grabbed a blanket off the bottom of the bed and carefully put it over Alex, making every effort not to disturb the sleeping woman. As she bent over the agent and the blanket reached her chest, she contemplated the face before her. Unconsciously, her hand moved to brush the hair aside from Alex's eyes. Lost in her emotions, she forced herself to step back and gather her thoughts.

In the few days they had been together, the agent was always up before the sun. Cassidy would hear Alex as she left out of the front door for her morning run, just as Cassidy was about to rise. She was pleased that Alex was asleep now. The agent had done so much for her in just a couple of days. Cassidy thought the least that she could do now was head downstairs and make certain everyone had a nice breakfast. There was nothing she could do about the picture or the letters and she trusted Alex implicitly. As she reached for the bag of coffee in the cabinet she pictured Alex handing her a mug just a couple of days ago. She was beginning to realize that, whatever she felt for this woman, it was powerful and as much as it surprised her; she had no desire to escape it.

***

Alex stirred in the chair. The room was still fairly dark with the blinds closed and she squinted to bring everything into focus. Dylan was sprawled across the bed, but Cassidy was gone. Her heart stopped. She was so panicked that she failed to notice Cassidy had covered her up. She sprang to her feet and headed swiftly into the hallway. When she reached the stairs the familiar smell of coffee brewing was apparent. She slowed her pace slightly and made her way into the kitchen. Cassidy was at the counter. The teacher was in jogging pants and a T-shirt and her hair was wet from the shower. Alex instinctively closed her eyes in relief and put her hands over them. When Cassidy turned, Alex still had her face in her hands. Immediately, the teacher realized that Alex had been alarmed by her absence in the room. "Alex," she said very gently. Alex opened her eyes and Cassidy was amazed at what she saw there. The strong and assertive agent had tears in her eyes. The teacher set down the knife in her hand and walked directly to the agent. "I'm okay."

Alex looked at the woman before her. She had no control of her feelings. There was no logic to be had. Cassidy looked up at the woman as Alex stuttered, her hands trembling as she took Cassidy's face in her hands, "I thought..."

Cassidy stood contemplating the blue eyes before her. They seemed endless and her heart seemed to be telling her what her mind was not yet ready to process. Alex loved her, and perhaps that was exactly what she was feeling for the agent. "I'm sorry," she said, never breaking their gaze. Her breath left her as Alex began to lean toward her and she anticipated her kiss.

"Mom!" A small voice called from the bottom of the stairs snapping both the women back to their senses.

"In here, Dylan," she called back still looking at the agent who was trying to conjure a smile. Cassidy slowly broke the exchanged glance and returned to her task as Dylan entered. Alex took a deep breath and headed to the cabinet for a mug; desperate to do anything that seemed 'normal' to help her regain control.

"Can I watch cartoons?" the boy asked standing behind his mother.

"Yes, you can go watch some cartoons, Dylan."

"Alex!" He said excitedly, "wanna' watch Kung Fu Panda?"

Alex looked over at Cassidy who shrugged. "Go on," Cassidy smiled now. She squinted slightly at the agent. "Kung Fu Panda and banana pancakes, what do you think?"

Suddenly all of Alex's fear vanished. She didn't know why, but something in Cassidy's eyes was telling her that everything would be all right. She didn't know how and she didn't know when, but in that simple moment she understood. She was not recusing herself from the case, not running away. Dylan pulled on the agent's hand. "Be right there, Speed Racer," she said. She walked back across the kitchen and stood in front of the woman who had unexpectedly captured her heart. Cassidy looked up at her and Alex smiled. There was nothing to say now. Alex kissed Cassidy's forehead and Cassidy closed her eyes reveling in the loving gesture. As Alex pulled back, slowly her gaze narrowed a bit. "No matter what," she began searching the smaller woman's eyes, "I will make sure you are safe." She brushed some flour from Cassidy's forehead.

The smaller woman's lips crinkled into a knowing smile. "Where did you come from, Alex Toles?"

"ALEX!" A small voice beckoned. "It's starting!"

Alex raised her eyebrow playfully and shrugged. The agent grabbed her coffee off the counter and headed for the next room. She jokingly answered Cassidy's question to herself, "I would have thought Rose would have given you THAT lesson."

"I heard that," Cassidy called back playfully.

"I know," Alex quipped, making her way into the living room.

"That too!" Cassidy called as Alex smiled taking a seat on the couch with the boy.

"She hears everything," he offered, never turning his attention from the television.

"I'll remember that."

***

Chapter Six

C assidy had stepped out onto the deck to take a phone call and Alex was absorbed in observing the woman's mannerisms. "She's mad," Dylan offered in his typical matter of fact way. Alex smiled at the boy as he continued to shovel the pancakes into his mouth. Looking back at the display unfolding just beyond the sliding doors, the agent knew the boy was right. There was no mistaking Cassidy's disapproval of whatever conversation was transpiring. She was pacing back and forth shaking her head. The grimace on her face occasionally changed to a sarcastic smile as she would close her eyes and grab her bottom lip with her teeth. The agent wondered what was transpiring, though she could guess it was the congressman by Cassidy's demeanor.

"No!" Cassidy pressed her tongue against her cheek with force in an attempt to quell her anger. "This is crazy, Chris... of course I understand that.....I can't do that...what about Dylan?"

Alex's phone rang. She pulled it from her pocket, still focused on the woman outside, "Toles," she answered. "What's up Fallon?....What?" The agent took a deep breath and let out a slight groan as she watched Cassidy's reactions move from what seemed to be frustration to unmistakable anger. She took another deep breath and stood. Dylan questioned her with his small eyes and she gave him a sideways smile. "Finish those pancakes," she said.

"What the hell?" the voice on the other end of the phone asked. "Are you listening to me?"

"Yeah….I heard you, Fallon," Alex answered as she made her way into the living room where she had the perfect vantage point to keep an eye on Cassidy.

"Tate wants you here tonight…all of you." Alex now completely understood the conversation that was transpiring outside. "Toles?!" Fallon called over the phone loudly causing the agent to wince.

"I heard you," the agent answered taking a deep breath. "So, what then? Why D.C.?"

"It isn't him, Toles. It's the congressman. You know…he has the president's ear…and when the president calls… well…"

"She's not going to agree to that," Alex said with a slight chuckle.

"It's only for a couple of days, Toles. Tate says they want to…"

"Yeah, listen, Fallon…I gotta' make a call…."

"Toles…." Brian Fallon took a long time to say his partner's name, cautioning her interference.

"Fallon, it's a bad idea and we both know it." Alex looked out to the deck where Cassidy was still in the midst of an argument.

"Doesn't matter what we think…if the pres…"

"Yeah… look…I'll call you back." Alex hung up the phone and rubbed her forehead. She knew exactly what was happening. The congressman wanted his family nearby and the excuse to make that happen would come in the form of a need to fit the house with some type of surveillance. The cover would be a simple maintenance issue, perhaps a burst pipe, and the family needed to vacate. A team would come in and fit the outside with hidden cameras. The problem was there was no reason for Cassidy to leave New York. For the sake of the case, and even of her safety, this was a mistake and Alex knew it. She had never called in her relationship with John Merrow, but now it was time. The agent dialed the number and waited, exhaling slowly. "Mr. President…"

"Alex...How are you?"

"I'm fine....I need to talk to you."

President John Merrow smiled at the sound of the agent's voice. He had always loved Alex. He was engaged by her strength and intelligence, and of course her beauty. Over the years the two had remained friends, quietly. He admired her and she respected him. "I assume this is about Mrs. O'Brien then?"

"Listen, Mr. ..."

"Alex," he said softly, "drop the formality, will you?"

The agent pinched the bridge of her nose. She hated doing this. "John...moving the family to D.C. right now...it doesn't make sense....and it isn't best for the case....at all."

John Merrow sat down on the love seat in the corner of his private office. "Alex... the congressman is worried about his family....you can understand...."

"Of course I do but there is no reason why Cass...Mrs. O'Brien would leave her job, pull Dylan out of school so abruptly....We are already exposed to some degree..."

"I heard," he interrupted.

"You know this makes no tactical sense. If the house needs to be addressed, let's move them to a hotel or a rental of some kind for a few days."

The president was silent for a long moment. "I know.... look....I'll tell you what...the congressman and I have a joint appearance with my family Wednesday.... How about we agree that he flies home tomorrow and takes Dylan for the week?"

Alex shook her head. This wasn't even about worry; it was about politics. "She's not going to like that."

"I suspect not, knowing Cassidy," the president chuckled with a hint of affection for the woman. "Listen, Alex, I promised him. You're really worried about this guy, aren't you?"

The agent licked her lips, "I am."

"All right...look ....I will talk to the congressman." Alex remained silent. "I will talk to Tate, but Dylan needs to come here…and maybe that's best, Alex…just for the week. It's less distraction for you." Alex laughed inside at the president's assertion. Dylan was a distraction, but he certainly wasn't the source of any interference with her *job*. "But, Alex," he continued, "she needs to stay safe…if that means she…"

The agent knew exactly what her former commander was saying. "I know," she answered plainly. Cassidy might *have* to leave work for some time if things continued to escalate or they didn't locate the source quickly. The teacher might have to agree to constant protection, even in the classroom, and Alex already knew that was a battle she did not want to fight. The truth was that a personal family appearance did give a good cover story for Dylan going to Washington with his father, and with Dylan away she would not need to relocate Cassidy. She looked toward the deck as Dylan was just making his way back to the living room.

"Alex? You there?" the president asked.

"Yeah…sorry….look, John…I can call Tate…I know that…"

John Merrow laughed. "No…no Alex…I will tell him that I called you…besides…you are right about moving both of them…it might embolden whoever this is…..just promise me you will keep me in the loop."

Alex was puzzled. It was neither her habit nor her place to update the president on any case. "I'm sure A.D. Tate…"

"Yeah….well, Tate's not there, you are. It's between us. If you're worried then I know there is something to worry about."

"Are you worried about the congressman?"

The president scratched his head and moved the phone to his other ear, "I'm worried about a lot of things, Alex…a lot of things." One thing Alex knew about John Merrow was that he was cautious in his assessments and deliberate in his actions. The congressman was an important part of many public initiatives, but she suspected there was more to this. Whatever it was that was driving her friend's interest; that was the least of her own concerns. "Alex?"

"Yeah?"

"Just....Well...Cassidy can be...well...good luck," he said with a hint of levity.

Alex laughed. "I understand....Thank you 'Mr. President'." As she hung up small eyes peered at her.

"You wanna' watch Batman?" Dylan asked hopefully.

Alex smiled and looked over him at the woman outside. Cassidy was gripping the railing with both hands, her face pointed toward the sky. "Maybe in a little while. I gotta' go talk to your mom." He shrugged his small shoulders and headed back to his spot on the couch grabbing an action figure on the way. Alex began the short trek to the sliding glass doors, taking a deep breath as she opened them and walked through.

Cassidy made no movement. "He wants us to come to Washington," she said with disdain.

"I know."

"I can't believe this....I can't just leave...I mean this is..." Cassidy rambled with frustration but continued to look out over the back yard. Strong hands now placed themselves on her shoulders and she closed her eyes. The feel of Alex touching her calmed her anger and replaced it with something that was almost equally unsettling, yet somehow welcome.

"You're not going to D.C.," the agent assured. Cassidy turned to face her, searching the agent's blue eyes for an explanation. "But, Cassidy....Dylan..."

"So, not me...but Dylan has to go...that's what you are telling me?" Cassidy's anger began to rise again.

Alex took a deep breath. "Yes."

"Why? Alex...Why? For what purpose...and don't tell me it's for his *safety*." Alex continued looking directly at the woman before her. This conversation was unraveling exactly as she knew it would. It was strange; she barely knew this woman; yet Cassidy O'Brien was no mystery to the agent. She could anticipate in just a glance what the teacher was thinking. "Well?" Cassidy urged Alex's response.

The agent released her breath in a rush. "I can't tell you all the reasons why. I suspect you might know that more than me." Cassidy closed her eyes and pressed her lips together trying to calm the anger that was rising within her again. Alex wanted so badly to make everything all right for Cassidy that she spoke without thinking, "That's the best John would..."

Cassidy's eyes flew open. She looked at the agent in disbelief, "you spoke to the president?"

A heavy sigh escaped the agent now as she realized what she had revealed. "Yes."

"How? When?"

"I called him after I got Fallon's call."

The teacher placed her hands over her eyes and turned away from the agent again. "This is insane. I can't even..." Alex felt the frustration pouring off of the teacher from all of the reality pressing in on her life. Cassidy's voice quivered. "I can't do this."

Alex moved her hands to the smaller woman's shoulders again. She whispered softly as she leaned into Cassidy's ear. "Yes, you can."

Cassidy felt Alex's breath on her neck and it sent a rush through her body. She felt her heart skip and struggled to maintain her breathing. "Alex...I'm so...my life is..."

"I'm not leaving you. I promise," the agent said, her body now against Cassidy's. Cassidy closed her eyes, feeling the warmth of Alex's body against her.

"Alex....I'm so..."

Alex turned the smaller woman to face her. The agent lifted the smaller woman's chin and smiled at her. "You're so what?"

Cassidy could feel her heart pounding. She felt Alex's thumb caress her cheek. So much was happening all at once. She didn't know how to process it. What she felt in this moment, it was something she had never experienced. In the midst of all this fear, anger and resentment; here, Alex looking at her; she felt so safe and so afraid at the same time. Alex's eyes smiled at the green ones before her as Cassidy finally gave her answer, "afraid…I'm afraid…"

The agent tucked the woman's long blonde hair behind her ear, never averting her gaze. "What are you afraid of, Cassidy?"

Cassidy felt her heart quicken again. She fought to swallow. Her mouth had gone dry and her head was suddenly spinning. As she tried to coax an answer, her voice cracked and hovered barely above silent thought. She dropped her eyes to the ground, "you."

Alex had expected that answer and she knew exactly how to resolve the question. She gently propelled Cassidy's face upward and leaned in slowly, stopping just before their lips would meet. "I know," she said as she finished her progression, her lips softly touching the smaller woman's. The kiss was tender and loving. The agent gently coaxed Cassidy's lips to part and felt her entire body ache from the connection as her tongue softly brushed against the smaller woman's. It was such a simple kiss, and yet there was a passion surging in her that she could not describe.

Cassidy felt the agent begin to pull back. She was breathless. The feel of Alex against her, the way she tasted, the warmth of her kiss, the sound of her own heart pounding in her chest, Alex's hand lovingly caressing her cheek, all at once, overwhelmed her senses. It was as if in one simple kiss Alex had encompassed her entire being, her very soul. Alex looked at the woman before her. Cassidy was still standing with her eyes closed and the agent knew there was a part of the woman terrified to look at her now. She touched Cassidy's cheek again. Cassidy sighed and tugged on her bottom lip with her teeth, "Alex, I…"

"Don't say anything," Alex reassured her. The agent leaned over and placed several small kisses on the woman's forehead as Cassidy's arms wrapped around her. "You don't need to say anything…I already know." Somehow Cassidy knew that was true. She thought for just a second that she should run from this, but the sound of Alex's heart in her ear as she placed her head against the agent's chest erased all of those ideas immediately. She could scarcely comprehend what she longed to say. Silently, the woman thought, as the agent held her close, 'I think I'm falling in love with you, Alex.'

***

Alex broke the embrace when the sound of her cell phone startled Cassidy. She gave the petite blonde a smile and placed the palm of her hand on the woman's cheek as she slowly brought the phone to her ear. The last thing she wanted was to leave Cassidy feeling any more uncertain. "Toles," she identified herself and listened for the response. "Yeah," she said quietly, not wanting to remove herself from the woman before her. Cassidy finally gave just the hint of a smile and Alex removed her hand to engage her partner on the phone.

"You okay?" Agent Fallon asked sensing that his partner was not paying attention. The pause lingered for another moment.

"Yeah...what's up?" Alex answered turning to see Cassidy gripping the railing again.

"Tate called....I guess you get to stay there," he said.

"Yeah...I heard."

"Well, I guess I will see you tomorrow then," Fallon said.

"Are you coming with the congressman to pick up Dylan?"

"Just me, I'm afraid...apparently the congressman is going to be at the White House, so I get the honors."

Alex kept a watchful eye on the blonde woman whose grip had loosened on the deck railing, but whom she knew was still in the throes of many questions. "Do you know when?" Alex asked softly.

"Geez...what is with you?" It was not customary at all for his partner to be so reserved in her dialogue.

"Nothing, don't worry about it...Do you know what time?" Alex asked again.

"Yeah…Tate said it's a 7:30 a.m. flight direct to JFK. I should be there around 10:00 if all goes well."

The agent rubbed her temple knowing that this would be the next piece of news that she would have to deliver to the woman she was falling in love with. And, she knew that Cassidy would not be happy about Dylan's early departure and his absence for a full week. "All right," she said with more than a hint of strain in her voice.

Brian Fallon listened carefully to the drop in his friend's tone. "Alex," he said, "is everything all right there…really?"

Alex took a deep breath. Everything was better than all right yet it was far from settled. "Yeah."

"Ooookayyy…I'll see you tomorrow then…by the way I emailed you those files – you know on the media folks…"

"Hey, Fallon…"

"Yeah?"

"Thanks." Alex hung up the phone quietly and stood still for a moment.

"So?" Cassidy said continuing to face the yard.

"Fallon's picking up Dylan tomorrow morning."

The blonde woman let out a sarcastic chuckle. "Of course he is… Jesus, he can't even pick up his own son."

Alex knew the woman was angry by both her choice of words and the brashness in her voice. "Hey," she began, gently putting her hand on Cassidy's shoulder.

Cassidy interrupted her with her own thought. "He just…I just don't understand."

Alex understood. Her father had been the same way; away much of the time and when he was around he had very definite ideas about how his children should behave and who they should be. "Listen," the agent stroked Cassidy's hair lightly. "Why don't you call your mom? I have some things I have to look at, but maybe we can all just get out of here for a while this afternoon. You know? Go grab a pizza or something."

Gradually Cassidy began to turn to face the agent. Alex was looking at her intently with such an expression of love and concern it somehow seemed to penetrate her anger and coax a smile. "How do you do that?"

"What?" Alex asked.

Cassidy shook her head. "Make me feel better when I wanted to punch something two seconds ago?"

"Go call Rose." She was tempted to kiss the woman again. Cassidy was looking at her in a way that no one ever had. It wasn't something the agent could put words to. It just felt natural. It felt familiar somehow and Alex reveled in the feeling, but she didn't want to push. Cassidy grasped Alex's hand lightly wondering how this woman could affect her so deeply. She gave the agent a sweet smile as if she wanted to say something but couldn't. Slowly she let go of the agent's hand and headed into the house.

***

Alex sat at the dining room table with her computer combing through profiles of reporters and photographers methodically and thoroughly. There were nearly a hundred for her to review and in the last two hours she had barely managed to make a cursory analysis of them. She was convinced somehow this is where she could find the answer, but finding it would mean painstaking analysis until something jumped out at her and so far nothing had. She was frustrated and worried about Cassidy's safety. The more time she spent with Cassidy O'Brien the greater her need to protect the teacher became. She heard Cassidy yell to Dylan to "get a move on" upstairs and put her forehead in her hands.

Cassidy reached the corner of the stairs and saw Alex sitting with her face in her hands. She could feel the tension rising from the agent and she knew what its cause was. In their few short days together Cassidy had learned a few things about the agent. She loved her coffee and she loved her Diet Coke with crushed ice. She wouldn't have wanted to admit it to the agent, but the teacher had closely observed nearly everything about Alex Toles. She already knew how she held the steering wheel, how she pulled her hair back into a pony tail with only her right hand, the way she pinched the bridge of her nose when she was frustrated and the way she rubbed her temple when she was worried. She filled a glass ½ way with crushed ice, cracked open a can of Diet Coke and headed back to the dining room. Alex was rubbing her temple and Cassidy bit her bottom lip to quell the smile that had begun to take shape. "Hey," she said walking toward the table and placing the glass next to the agent.

Alex let go of her temple and looked back at the small woman standing slightly over her shoulder now. "Thanks," she said squinting as if in a bit of pain. Her constant focus on the computer screen had brought on a headache.

Cassidy's right eye closed slightly and her lip curled as it always did when she grew concerned. "I think it's time for a break," she said putting her hand lovingly on the agent's shoulder.

"I have to get through as many of these as I can." Alex closed her eyes and rubbed them gently.

"Well, that will be a little hard if you can't SEE them," Cassidy said picking up the glass and placing it in the agent's hand.

The agent shook her head as a smile unexpectedly swept over her. "Mmmm…I guess so." The sound of the front door opening did not seem to startle either woman; the teacher standing now next to the agent's chair and the agent looking up at her, both with a crooked smile.

Rose McCollum reached the doorway and looked curiously at the two women. "Aheemmm," she cleared her throat with some theatrics.

"Hey, Mom," Cassidy turned to her mother still smiling as Alex sipped on the drink and closed her computer.

"So…" Rose started. "What is all this I hear about Washington and….pizza?" Cassidy looked down at the agent for a brief second as if to insure she was complying with the teacher's instructions. Seeing that the agent had in fact taken her advice, she gently touched Alex's shoulder and led her mother into the kitchen.

"Is Alex okay?" Rose asked with genuine concern.

Cassidy looked out over the counter and down the hallway toward the agent's location. Rose could tell that her daughter was worried. What she wasn't sure about was who the worry was for, herself and Dylan or the FBI agent. Cassidy sighed and shook her head turning back to her mother. "Yeah, she's been at that computer for hours. I think she has a headache. She won't stop, though," she paused and looked down the hallway again and sighed. "I'll bet she opened it back up as soon as I left."

The woman's mother studied her carefully. There was something different in Cassidy's voice. "You think she's worried? I mean…do you think she's worried about Dylan going to D.C.?"

Cassidy shook her head and made her way to the refrigerator to get them each a soda. "No….no….she's worried about me," Cassidy said popping open the cans and placing one on the counter in front of her mother.

"Why? Did something happen?"

Cassidy took a sip of her soda and rubbed her chin. "A picture…just a picture."

"Of what?" Rose asked as her volume increased slightly.

"Mom…it's all right. Honestly, I am more annoyed at Chris right now than I am worried about some stupid picture." That was only partly the truth. She was extremely angry with her ex-husband but she was equally troubled by the picture that Alex had found taped to the front door the night before. In a few days her life had been turned upside down and her emotions followed suit. She was trying to carry on the conversation with her mother, but she was preoccupied thinking about the agent down the hallway. Alex's demeanor told her everything she needed to know. The agent was determined to find out what was going on. And, Cassidy did not need any more time with Agent Toles to know that meant Alex was going to be relentless in her pursuit of this person; whoever it turned out to be. She heard her mother talking to her but it felt as though the words were traveling through a tunnel. Her mind was still trying to process everything and the reality that she seemed to know Alex far better than three days would warrant, not to mention the fact that she had an increasing desire to be closer to the woman.

"Cassie?"

"What?" Cassidy said snapping out of her momentary haze.

"Did you sleep last night?"

"Some, not a lot, no."

"I can tell," Rose said chalking up her daughter's absent mindedness to fatigue.

***

Alex felt a gentle tug on her shirt. She turned slightly to bring the small face into focus. "Hey there, Speed Racer."

"I don't want to go to Daddy's," he said plainly.

Alex shut the computer again and pulled him onto her knee. "Why not?"

He shrugged. "I don't like it there."

Cassidy looked down the hall again. "Dylan must still be playing upstairs," she said to her mother.

"Do you want me to go get him?"

"No, I'll go…but can you do me a favor? Call George's and see if they have seats in one of the cars for lunch." Cassidy had decided that lunch at one of Dylan's favorite places was in order and she suspected that Alex would enjoy it as well. She made her way down the hallway and stopped just short of the stairs at the sound of familiar voices.

"Dylan, I'm sure your dad just misses you."

"No he doesn't," Dylan said plainly. "He's never even home. Cheryl will be there."

"Cheryl?"

"Yeah…and she's no fun. She hates Kung Fu Panda and she thinks superheroes are stupid," the boy explained. Cassidy listened from the bottom of the stairs, her irritation with her ex-husband growing as she listened to Dylan confide in the agent what he had never confided in his mother.

"I see," Alex said.

"She's not like you," he continued. "I want to stay here with Mom and you."

The agent tried not to smile. She was growing very fond of the young man who had now taken up residence in her lap. "Well, let me ask you something." He looked up at her inquisitively as she continued. "What does Cheryl, that's her name right?" He nodded. "What DOES Cheryl like?"

He shrugged his shoulders all the way up to his ears. "I dunno!" He confessed.

"Hmmmm….Well…maybe you could ask her what she likes to do and try that," Alex smiled.

"It'll probably be picking flowers or some girlie thing," he said crinkling his nose with displeasure. Rose was headed toward Cassidy and began to open her mouth when Cassidy stopped her. The teacher silently put her finger to her lips in a sign to hush and directed her mother to listen to the dining room conversation.

"So, Cheryl's kinda' girlie, huh?"

"Yeah, and I'm not playing with Barbie dolls."

Alex tried to suppress her mounting amusement, knowing that Dylan was confiding in her. She was accustomed to these sort of conversations with her nephew when they spoke over the phone about Alex's mother. "Well, maybe if you ask her you two can find something you both like."

"Like picking flowers?" he said with a degree of young sarcasm.

Alex shook her head, "like maybe, pizza...or games...or maybe drawing, something like that."

He huffed and looked at her with a serious face. "Okay... but can't I just stay here with you and Mom?"

"You know what, Speed Racer, I have a feeling that we will see each other soon, and then you can tell me and your mom all about what you did at your dad's. Think about it like an adventure. Maybe you could pretend you are Batman...you know...on a mission and when you come home it'll be like landing in the Batcave."

"Okay, but The Batcave is way cooler," he said.

Cassidy scurried her mother back down the hallway and the two began to laugh when they entered the kitchen. It was only a few seconds before Dylan came strolling in with Alex following close behind. Alex was still sipping the soda Cassidy had poured her. "Feeling up to pizza at George's?" Cassidy asked the group.

"Yep!" Dylan answered. "Alex...George's has cars you can eat INSIDE!" Alex nodded her approval with wide eyes, trying not to choke on the ice in her mouth.

"Yes, and they have a CAR for us in half an hour, so we'd better get moving," Rose said. "Come on Dylan, let's get your jacket." He followed his grandmother dutifully down the hall.

Cassidy stepped squarely in front of the agent and looked up into her eyes as she was bringing her glass to her lips a final time. "Batcave, huh?" Alex nearly choked on the ice at the realization that Cassidy had overheard her conversation with the boy and soda dribbled over her lip. Cassidy just looked at the agent and wiped the soda away with her thumb. She leaned up and planted a light peck on the agent's lips, smiling at Alex's obvious shock. "Get your jacket, Alfred. We wouldn't want to keep the Dark Knight waiting," she said as she walked away, leaving the agent speechless.

***

Lunch went by too quickly for Cassidy's liking. She was enjoying watching her son chat up the agent and found that her emotions welled inside of her every time Alex managed to divert a glance her way. When Dylan grabbed the agent's hand and pulled her across the restaurant to an empty truck cab that had a driving game in its dashboard, Rose finally spoke. "Cassie...."

"Yeah?" Cassidy answered smiling broadly as she watched Alex lift Dylan to the driver's seat that sat in the front of the cab.

Rose smiled to herself as she heard Dylan scream Alex's name in delight. She took a deep breath. "She's great."

"What?"

"Alex....she's great," Rose said.

"Yeah...she is."

Rose licked her lips. She was not going to dive directly into these waters just yet, but she did know her daughter better than anyone and the look on Cassidy's face told Rose every single thing that was in her daughter's heart. "So, what did you do yesterday?" Rose asked. "Did you go for that drive you were talking about?"

Cassidy was still engrossed in the display that was unfolding across the room. She couldn't see Dylan but she could hear him laughing and she could see Alex standing over his shoulder. It was a sight she had seldom seen with her husband and it filled her with happiness to hear her son's laughter and to know that Alex was its cause. "What?" she asked, realizing her mother had spoken but having missed the words.

"I asked if you went for that drive yesterday."

"Sort of."

"How do you sort of take a drive, Cassie? Either you are in the car driving or you are not," Rose kidded.

"Ha ha...I did, but I didn't drive, Alex did."

"Ohhh....what did you two do?" Rose was truly curious now.

"Well, you know...after Agent Fallon called about the letter..."

"I thought you said it was a picture?" Rose was confused.

"No...well, yeah, but that was when we got home."

"Are you telling me there was a letter and a picture?" Rose's voice began to tremble.

"Mom....Yes...just....can we just not talk about that today?"

Her mother took a deep breath and let it out with a groan, "Fine, so tell me about this drive."

"Well...You know...I was a little upset with Dylan leaving for the weekend and Agent Fallon's call...so Alex took me for a drive."

"And...."

"Oh...well, we went to her brother's restaurant in Connecticut," Cassidy explained.

"Alex is from Connecticut?"

"No. Massachusetts, but Nick has a restaurant in Stonington by the ocean."

Rose looked down at the table and toyed with her napkin trying not to be too obvious about her suspicions. "So...was it nice?"

Cassidy really wasn't thinking about her answers. She had long considered her mother her best friend and she did little to censor herself in front of the woman. A very subtle glow seemed to wash over the teacher as she spoke now. "It was wonderful," she said as if transported back to those hours. "We sat outside for hours and talked."

"Cassie...it was about forty-eight degrees last night."

"Oh yeah...there's this awesome fireplace outside that we sat next to... It was beautiful, actually."

"Hmmm....Sounds like you had a good time," Rose continued playing with her napkin beginning to suspect that her assumptions were correct. Her daughter was falling for the agent.

Alex appeared walking behind Dylan who was still pretending he had a steering wheel in his hands. Dylan jumped onto his mother with excitement. "Alex and I made it all the way to level 32!"

Tomorrow would not be an easy day for the teacher and she knew it. Dylan often got emotional when he had to leave for more than a weekend and she knew more about the reasons why now; thanks to his conversation with Alex. Right now he was happy and so was she. He was demonstrating their victory to his grandmother excitedly with Rose laughing at his theatrics. Cassidy looked at the dark haired woman who seemed to be able to calm her with just a glance and mouthed the words 'thank you.' Tomorrow was a problem that could wait.

***

The man watched out of his car window as the women walked slowly to the SUV that was parked across the street. The clicks of the camera rattled off almost like the sound of crickets chirping on a summer evening. He peered through the lens and focused it, zooming in; click, click, click. He turned the lens to the right as the sun reflected off the rear view mirror, momentarily blinding him. He flung his hand wildly at it, knocking it to one side and resumed his task. The face was clear now. He could even see the green of her eyes; tick, click, tick.

He jostled himself in his seat as the tall woman held the door open for her. A sound like the grunt of a wild animal stalking its prey escaped his lips as he watched her close the door and he zoomed in closer on her face; click, click, click, click, click. He cringed at the constant sound wanting to will it away, but he continued. His breath was heavy and his eyes narrow. Carefully, he focused on his subject. He looked through the lens, wanting to feel closer as he watched them drive away. He breathed a heavy sigh and grabbed the cigarette that had half burned away in the ashtray during his brief escapade. Smoke filled his lungs and he inhaled fully, holding the smoky air in as long as his body would allow before releasing it. On the passenger's seat sat a manila envelope. He touched it with his gloved fingertips as if he were exploring a lover. Carefully he picked it up and brought it to his nose, inhaling its papery scent as though it were a fine cigar. His eyes closed with satisfaction and he opened his door. He walked three or four yards to the blue box at the side of the road and stopped to ponder it. The door squeaked as he pulled its handle and it opened. It reminded him of a mouth and he tipped his head to the side considering it again. Again he brought the envelope to his face. He longed to feel it, but the black leather that covered his hand prevented the sensation he so desired.

Slowly he allowed it to slip from his grasp into the awaiting blue mouth before him. He stood as it was swallowed and he waited, staring blankly at the vacancy in his hand. A slight shudder ran through him as he made his way through the truck's door. Another long drag from his cigarette and an exhale of satisfaction. His hands gripped the wheel and he straightened the once offending mirror. Looking over his shoulder he saw the red duffle bag and smiled. "Assignment," he mumbled as he drove away.

Chapter Seven

C assidy walked into the kitchen to find Alex at the stove and coffee on. "Whatya' doing there?" the woman asked pulling up a bar stool at the island facing the agent's back. Alex reached up and pulled down a coffee mug for the woman now across from her.

"I'm making breakfast. Isn't that what Alfred does?" she jested.

"Uh huh...I don't know. I haven't had any invitations to Wayne Manor since I divorced the social circuit," Cassidy quipped.

Alex chuckled. "I see...well, lucky for you I double as a butler when necessary."

"So you cook?"

"Ummm...not as well as my mother would like, no. I'm afraid that skipped right through me to Nicky....BUT, I can make a mean omelet. That's about the extent of it, unless you love macaroni and cheese," the agent confessed lightheartedly as she added eggs to the pan.

Dylan entered wiping the sleep from his eyes and looked curiously at the scene before him. Cereal was the normal morning feast in this house unless it was the weekend. He walked next to the agent and strained to look into the pan. He rubbed his eyes again and spun on his heels to face his mother. Cassidy watched him closely wondering how he was going to react this morning. Alex had explained to him that her friend, Mr. Fallon, would be taking him to his dad. She said Mr. Fallon was silly and that Dylan would have a lot of fun with him. Cassidy hoped that might help to ease the boy's stress. "Can I have juice?" Cassidy got up and poured the boy a glass of juice. "Can I watch Batman?" he asked with a yawn.

"Yeah, go ahead...but we have to get you ready in an hour, all right?' He didn't respond, just walked off into the living room.

Alex moved the eggs in the pan gently. She could sense that Cassidy was stressed. "He'll be fine," Alex said reassuringly. One thing the agent understood about this woman was that Cassidy was dedicated to both her family and her students. She had prattled on and on about both with pride during their car ride the other night and it was evident every time she looked at Dylan or mentioned a student. Today she was forced to step away from both.

"I hate this," Cassidy offered bluntly.

The agent grabbed a plate down and flipped the omelet onto it. She moved the two steps required and placed it on the counter in front of the small blonde woman. The tall dark haired agent studied the smaller woman before her. Cassidy was adorable in her sweat pants and T-shirt with her hair still slightly ruffled from sleep. "Eat your omelet," Alex said plainly.

"Is that an order?" Cassidy laughed.

"Butlers don't give orders," Alex scoffed playfully. "You have some serious superhero etiquette to learn."

Cassidy laughed out loud which prompted Dylan to poke his head around the corner in curiosity. "Let me guess," Alex said looking at the boy. "Batman wants cereal for breakfast." Dylan nodded and headed back for his spot on the couch. "That's what I like," Alex looked at his mother. "Low maintenance superheroes." She walked across the kitchen and grabbed the cereal, then the milk and put it in a bowl. Cassidy sat toying with her eggs. "Ummmm..." Alex looked at her from across the counter. "Are you afraid to eat my cooking?"

"No...I'm sorry, Alex."

"Mmmhmm…come on," Alex grabbed the plate out from under the woman and the bowl of cereal.

"Where are you going?"

"We are going to watch Batman over breakfast," Alex said already out of the room. Cassidy grabbed her coffee and shook her head. When she reached the room, Dylan already had his bowl of cereal on the coffee table. He was engrossed in the images of the caped crusader on the television while the spoon unconsciously entered his small mouth over and over. Alex patted the couch and Cassidy took her seat silently. The agent seemed almost as focused on the cartoon as the boy and watching them both completely lost in the adventure; Cassidy suddenly felt a bit of relief. "Awww…." Alex let out an audible cringe as the Joker hit Batman with a ray gun. "That's not right."

"He's gonna' get the Batmobile….watch, Alex…here …. look," Dylan pointed to the television. Cassidy looked at the woman beside her. Alex was already showered and dressed, as always. She had her hair pulled back in her signature pony tail and her white blouse buttoned just to the top of her cleavage; which Cassidy was surprised she seemed to be noticing with some intensity. She was beautiful. Alex felt the woman's gaze and it sent a burning sensation through her. Everything about Cassidy O'Brien intrigued Alex, everything. But, for the first time in her life the agent was not on a mission of seduction. She was fully aware that she loved Cassidy. It was a feeling she wasn't certain she was capable of, but any doubts she had ever had were erased within a few minutes of being in this woman's presence. As the last scene unfolded Cassidy prepared to call Dylan to get ready, but before she could speak her ears were met with the thunderous sound of two voices in unison, "Dundah dundah…BATMAN."

The teacher shook her head, "all right you caped crusaders…let's go." To her surprise Dylan rose to his feet quickly. He smiled at Alex and headed up the stairs.

Cassidy looked at the agent and bent over to pick up the boy's bowl. "Just go get him ready. I'll get these. I need more coffee anyway." Cassidy nodded her agreement and followed her son up the stairs.

***

Alex looked at the paper and groaned at the picture. There she was with Cassidy in the driveway, the same day the other photo had been snapped:

FBI guarding Cassidy O'Brien or Congressman O'Brien's Secrets?

"I hate the press," she mumbled as she tucked the paper under her laptop on the kitchen table. She had no intention of allowing Cassidy to see the headline until after Dylan was safely away. The teacher was upset enough already. Alex had been on the phone with A.D. Tate and the president at the crack of dawn. John Merrow had apologized to the agent for the miscalculation. Alex had expressed from the beginning that this was a silly assignment to take undercover. She had to admit, for her part, this was one weight lifted off her. She no longer had to pretend she was someone else and that made her feel more confident about protecting Cassidy. At the same time, Alex was certain that the woman who commanded her affection would find the article unsettling. The doorbell rang and the agent moved to the hallway. Cassidy called from upstairs to her as she opened the door, "we'll be right down, Alex."

"Take your time," the agent called back, opening the door but looking up the stairs.

"So…Nice to see a celebrity first thing in the morning," Fallon greeted his partner.

"Shhh…" Alex whispered her warning to the man as she looked back up the stairs for any sign of the teacher and the boy.

"Why are we shushing?" Fallon crouched into Alex.

"She doesn't know," Alex motioned upstairs.

"You mean she hasn't seen the papers?"

"No...shut up already, Fallon."

"Well," a voice beckoned from a few paces away. "Looks like suburban life agrees with you, Agent Toles," a flirtatious redhead offered. Alex nearly swallowed her tongue. It was Brackett. "Aren't you going to say hello?" Brackett moved a little closer to the agent as Cassidy hit the top of the stairs and caught the redhead's seductive gaze toward Alex.

Cassidy felt her heart stop and then pound with such force she momentarily thought it might knock her down. She surveyed the interaction, watching the redhead's expression as she seemed to undress Alex with her eyes. The sight before her made her stomach flip and she froze. Dylan skipped past her on the stairs. "Come on, Mom," he said heading directly for Alex.

Agent Brackett greeted him. "Hello there," she said pulling away from Alex and extending her hand to the boy.

"Hello," he said turning to look at Alex for approval.

"This is Ms. Brackett, Dylan....I guess she's ...well...she's helping Mr. Fallon–and this is my friend, Mr. Fallon."

Brackett stared at Alex, her gaze unmistakable. Cassidy began making her way down the stairs. One thing Cassidy could do when she needed to was extend pleasantries. She hated it, but being in public life made it a necessary skill. Inside she was seething. She felt jealous and she hurt more than she was capable of understanding. She didn't even know if the redhead's actions meant anything, but she suspected they did and it was ripping her insides apart. "Sorry about that," she said sweetly as she stepped to the ground floor.

"Mrs. O'Brien," Agent Fallon greeted the woman. His eyes twinkled a bit as she held his gaze. "I promise we will take great care of Dylan."

"I know you will," Cassidy smiled. The knots in Alex's stomach suddenly felt more like fish swimming upstream. Cassidy was not acting like herself and the agent already knew why. She had clearly caught on to Agent Brackett's attention to Alex, and she almost certainly wondered what role the agent played in it all. Cassidy busied herself getting Dylan's coat on and making pleasantries with Fallon. She kept a watchful eye on the pair of female FBI agents that stood close to the door. Alex had her back to Cassidy and the teacher could not see the agent's expression, but she had full view of every suggestive smile the redhead offered Alex.

"So...Agent Toles," Brackett began with a raise of her eyebrow. "Now that you are *exposed*...what is your plan?"

Fallon closed his eyes tightly and Alex swallowed hard. She dared not face the teacher yet. First she needed to get Dylan off. The agent shot the redhead a look of cautionary disgust and then turned to look down at the boy. "Say goodbye to your mom, Dylan." Her heart was completely lodged in her throat as she attempted to avoid Cassidy's eyes.

The boy hugged his mother and Cassidy dropped all pretenses and all questions for a moment to encircle his small form within her arms. "I love you, sweetie."

He smiled at her. "Love you too," he said sweetly and then turned and ran to the agent that had become his hero. "Alex... when I get back make sure the Batmobile is ready...we might have to find that Joker," he said emphatically, preparing for his mission.

For a split second both Cassidy and Alex forgot the current situation as Alex bent down to accept his hug. "You got it, Speed Racer." He looked at her quizzically. "Oh...I mean BATMAN," she corrected herself.

Agent Fallon's eyes were wide. Alex had always been good with his kids, but the affection she seemed to have for the small toe headed boy was different somehow. He sensed there was something more to this case for his friend. Fallon accepted the backpack from Cassidy with a sideways grin and shuttled Dylan out the door in front of him. He stopped briefly to whisper to his partner, "I'm sorry...it wasn't my idea for her to...."

Alex patted his shoulder; she was sure she knew whose idea it was to send Brackett, Brackett's. She lingered in the doorway as the redhead came even with her, "Christ, Brackett...."

"What?"

Alex led her through the door and leaned into her ear, "just what the hell do you think you are doing?" Alex said attempting to control her temper.

Brackett smiled, catching the expression of the small blonde behind the agent. "Hmmm... *exposed?* Pretty good at that, huh, Toles?" She leaned into the agent. Alex felt her body twitch from the anger that was brewing within her. "It's all right... your secret's safe with me," the redhead winked.

"Do you have any idea how unprofessional you are acting?"

"Hummm...must be the rookie in me. I thought a seasoned agent would have changed that. Huh? See you in Washington," she nearly cooed as she walked away.

Alex shut the door and very slowly turned to face the teacher. The fish in her stomach had suddenly turned to whales and were flipping wildly. Cassidy stood staring at her. "What did she mean, *exposed?*"

Alex took a deep breath. "The picture made it to the papers...they know we are FBI...at least that I am...that's all."

"That's all?" Cassidy said flatly. "I see...and when did you discover this little *exposure?*"

"This morning."

"Uh huh. This morning before breakfast or this morning while I was upstairs?" Cassidy's tone remained amazingly the same.

"I got a call from A.D. Tate early that the story was running."

"Of course you did...so Batman and eggs...no exposure?"

"Cassidy...I was going to tell you as soon as they left...you were already upset..."

"When they left? Yeah...so, a little more *exposure* than you bargained for, Agent Toles?"

Now Alex was getting annoyed. Brackett meant nothing to her and it was something that happened before she even knew Cassidy. "That's not fair," Alex answered.

"Well, I'll tell you what," Cassidy said as she struggled to hold back tears. "I'm not so easily *exposed*, Agent Toles."

"What the hell? Brackett is a coworker."

"Really? Pretty friendly at the FBI…"

"I'm not doing this," Alex said. She was feeling both guilty and defensive and neither was an emotion that she cared for.

"Well, good then," Cassidy said. "That makes two of us." The teacher turned and walked up the stairs slamming her bedroom door. Alex bit her bottom lip so hard she drew blood. She rubbed her temples and headed up the stairs, closing her own door with some force. She threw on her running clothes and headed out the front door with a thud.

*****

When Alex Toles was upset she ran. When she was angry she ran. When she was confused she ran. When she was scared she ran. She was all of those things now and she ran hard, as hard as she could, trying along the way to clear her mind. At first she muttered to herself that Cassidy had no right to be upset and that Brackett was a bitch. Then she tried telling herself that she was being foolish, Cassidy was just a conquest that had gotten out of hand. Then she ran harder. Then she pictured the small blonde woman sleeping in the car, the mother who gently caressed her little boy's hair while he slept, and the beautiful woman who looked into her eyes so deeply when they kissed just a day ago. She stopped running and bent over with her hands on her knees.

"Oh, Christ, Toles…." She scolded herself. "When are you gonna' stop running?" The truth was pressing in on her chest like heavy stones in a wall. She always ran away when things got tough emotionally. A fight she could handle, a case, a project, but love? She regulated her breathing and started to walk back toward the house. She had no idea what she was going to say. All she could think about as she walked was how Cassidy must be feeling. Was Cassidy okay? Could Cassidy love her? Just Cassidy. So much was upside down in the woman's life and although Alex had not asked; she suspected that Cassidy had never been with another woman; perhaps never even entertained the idea. She should never have left. Never have run away. The agent started toward the door when she saw a photographer. Immediately she thought of Dylan and her anger began to churn. She glared at the man and he shied away. "Smart move," she thought. She reached the porch and stood there for a long moment trying to build up the courage to enter. She quietly climbed the stairs and stood in the doorway to her room. Cassidy's door was closed. She let out a long sigh and headed for the shower.

Cassidy had heard the front door close. She had spent the last couple of hours in tears. At first she was furious with Alex. She felt stupid; of course she was just another of the agent's conquests. Brackett was beautiful and she was certain that the attractive agent was far worldlier in certain ways just by her demeanor. Here she was thinking she might be falling in love with Alex and all she was to the agent was a booty call. But after a while she started thinking about Alex buckling Dylan in, Alex's expression when she found Cassidy safe in the kitchen the day before, Alex's face as the soda dripped down her lip, Alex's kiss. She should have given the agent a chance to talk. She was so hurt and so scared. She told Alex that; after all. She could scarcely comprehend what she was feeling for the dark haired woman. Right now as her tears fell all she wanted was the agent's arms around her and the reality of what that might mean terrified her. Cassidy got up and washed her face. She did her best to steady herself as she began the walk down the short hallway to Alex's room. The door was open. Alex was bent over the chair in the corner in sweats and a T-shirt, her hair wet from the shower. Very gingerly Cassidy stepped into the doorway. "Alex," she called so softly Alex barely heard her. Alex didn't move. "Alex," she said a little louder. "Would you please look at me?"

"I can't," Alex said.

"Alex...I..."

"No, Cassidy, I mean I really can't...my back..."

Cassidy moved across the room and found that the woman she was just admitting she might actually love was doubled over the chair. Cassidy's hands gently touched the agent's arm and she tried to look into Alex's eyes. "What happened?"

"It'll pass," the agent said but Cassidy could hear the pain rattling in her voice.

"What can I do?" Cassidy asked. Alex tried to inhale a deep breath and winced as her back twitched. "Okay...I'm going to call somebody..."

Alex clasped the woman's hand, "no, Cass.....no... don't call anyone...please..."

"Alex, you can't even..." Every trace of anger had vanished from them both. Cassidy's only concern was Alex right now.

"It could affect my work, Cassidy...just help me stand up straight." Cassidy helped the agent brace herself until she was finally erect. Her green eyes were red from the tears that had fallen for so long just shortly before. Alex looked in them now and knew instantly. She reached for the woman's cheek. "I'm so sorry, Cassidy...I should have told you....Everything...I didn't mean....and Brackett–that was just..."

Alex was rambling faster than Cassidy could keep up. "Stop," the blonde woman who stood a head shorter than the agent said. "It doesn't matter right now...let's just get you..."

"It does matter," Alex touched the woman's cheek. Cassidy closed her eyes and kissed the hand that caressed her.

"Alex...I'm serious. We can talk about this later."

"Cass...."

"It's okay," Cassidy looked at the agent who had a tear falling down her cheek. "Is it your back?" Alex just kept looking at the woman silently. She closed her eyes as the pain in her back began to slowly subside and a wave of raw emotion replaced it. "Alex…"

"Cassidy…I just…I…" Cassidy looked into the woman's blue eyes as they looked back into hers. Alex wanted to tell her, right now, that she loved her, but she was afraid it would be too much. "I would never hurt you, Cassidy…never."

Cassidy knew that was true. She knew it the moment she met Alex Toles. "I know that," she said. "Let's get you to the bed."

"No…I need to walk…maybe the couch."

Cassidy nodded and the two made their way one step at a time down the hallway, and then down each stair slowly, repeating each action as carefully as possible; the small blonde supporting the weight of the strong, muscular agent until they finally reached the couch. Cassidy put a pillow behind the agent's back and scurried off to the kitchen. She filled a glass half way with ice and poured the Diet Coke over it. She reached into her bag and pulled out three ibuprofen and headed back to the living room. "Here, take these," she instructed. Alex complied. Cassidy sat on the far end of the couch and pulled the agent's legs onto her lap. They sat in total silence for what seemed hours before Cassidy spoke, "Alex?"

"Mmm?"

"Did you love her?" Alex was perplexed. "Agent Brackett, did you love her?" Alex could hear the fear in the woman's voice as it trembled slightly.

"Cassidy, I have loved exactly one person in my life." Alex had promised herself as they sat in silence that she would answer all of the teacher's questions honestly. Cassidy looked down and closed her eyes. Alex smiled and began to move her position.

"What are you doing? Alex you need to," but the agent was already in her forward motion and in almost an instant she was sitting beside the teacher. "Alex….you don't have to…" Cassidy fumbled through her words.

Alex took Cassidy's hand. "You…Cassidy, I don't even want to explain it…I don't love Agent Brackett… I love you."

Cassidy's entire body went weak. "Alex…"

"Don't say anything…please." Alex kissed the woman and felt Cassidy's lips gently part, her tongue searching softly for Alex's. The agent responded as gently as she could. She wanted so badly to make love to Cassidy; her entire body hummed with energy as their kiss deepened. There was one thing she wanted more; that was for Cassidy to trust her completely. She broke the kiss slowly and looked at the green eyes searching hers. The agent took the woman in her arms and gently laid her back on the couch, holding Cassidy firmly against her.

Cassidy felt her body shiver from the contact. It was all so much for her to believe. She could smell Alex's shampoo as the agent's damp hair brushed against her face. She closed her eyes and inhaled. How could this be happening? Her breath rattled in her chest as she tried to hold back the tears that were beginning to rise again. Her anger was gone, but her fear lingered. Cassidy was unsure of so much right now, but more aware of what she felt than she ever had been in her life. "I don't want you to let me go," she confessed with some apprehension. In spite of the agent's declaration the teacher feared pushing her away more than anything she ever had in her life.

Alex kissed the woman's head softly and held her tighter to reassure her. "Never."

Chapter Eight

C assidy woke up in the same position she had fallen asleep in. She was all but on top of the agent who had drifted off as well. Her head was nestled on Alex's chest and she could hear the steady thump of the agent's heart in her ear. The smaller woman opened her eyes and looked at the figure beneath her. Her arm was draped over the agent and she closed her eyes and inhaled all the feelings coursing through her as she tenderly caressed the agent's side. She allowed herself the luxury of just remaining close. The feel of Alex's warmth, the calming sound of the agent's heart; it all seemed to be whispering some truth to her now. She sighed when she heard the phone in the kitchen and slowly pried herself from the agent's grasp. Alex looked peaceful, almost like a child as she slept, and Cassidy paused to take in the sight. She let her finger gracefully roll across the agent's cheek and carefully lifted herself out of her position, ensuring that the sleeping woman remained at rest. She took a deep breath and let it out slowly as she placed her hand on the phone. The hours sleeping in the agent's arms had been the most at peace she had felt in a long time. She didn't want to leave that tranquility. "Hello," she said quietly, glancing into the room and smiling at the sight of the agent fast asleep on the couch; exactly the same as she had left her.

"Mrs. O'Brien?"

"Yes?"

"Agent Fallon....is Agent Toles there?"

Cassidy sighed at the knowledge she would have to wake the woman. "Yes, she is…hold on." She walked into the other room and softly touched Alex's cheek, trying to cover the phone with her other hand. "Alex," she called quietly. The agent stirred slightly and leaned into the woman's touch. Cassidy smiled. "Alex…"

"What?" Alex mumbled. "Where did you go?" she asked rubbing her eyes.

"Agent Fallon is on the phone," Cassidy said softly. Alex opened her eyes and saw the face before her, green eyes affectionately exploring her expression. She smiled as best she could through her sleepiness and took the phone.

In spite of Cassidy's attempt, Agent Fallon had overheard the tender exchange between the pair. "Fallon?" Alex asked trying to wake herself.

"Jesus, Alex…what the hell is going on? I've been trying to call you for over an hour."

"Sorry…I must have left my phone upstairs." Her voice was still groggy and she was yawning.

"Alex," he hesitated, sensing that what he was about to say was not going to be received well by his partner. "Listen…"

"Fallon, what is it?" Alex heard her partner's breathing become shallower and it seemed to wake her from her dreamy state. Something was wrong. "Brian…what…"

"There was an accident."

Alex felt her heart drop in her chest as her thoughts immediately traveled to Dylan. She tried to respond as quietly as she could, "Dylan?"

Cassidy caught the tension in the agent's voice and a look of terror swept across her face and she moved closer to the agent who swiftly placed an arm around her. "No," Fallon answered soliciting a heavy sigh of relief from Alex that told Cassidy she could relax. Alex released her from her grasp and the teacher took a seat back on the couch.

"Fallon, What? What's going on?"

"It's the congressman." Alex unconsciously began running her tongue over her lips as she listened to her partner continue. "It happened on the way back to his office from the White House; some idiot barreled through a light and crashed head on into their car." Alex's hand now reached for her temple and Cassidy knew something was very wrong. "Alex?" Fallon called cautiously, beginning to become concerned about his partner's uncharacteristic silence.

"How bad?"

"Bad...he's in surgery now."

"Fallon...how do you know this was an accident?"

"Well...Secret Service seems to think so. The kid in the other car is dead. Doesn't look like anything but a reckless kid...just wrong place, wrong time."

"Where's Dylan?" she asked still rubbing her temple.

"He's here with me in the lounge....I've got him watching a movie. I didn't tell him much...just that his dad was hurt."

Alex was relieved to know that the boy was with Fallon. Sometimes her partner drove her crazy but Brian Fallon had in many ways, become her best friend. He was a good man and a good father. She knew that he would take good care of Dylan until she could get Cassidy there. "Good...Brian..."

"Yeah?"

"I need to...."

"Yeah...I know." Brian Fallon knew Alex as well as anyone could. He had never seen the look in her eyes that was there earlier that morning when Cassidy saw Brackett. Alex was notorious for attracting all kinds of women but he could tell by his friend's painful expression something was different. Hearing their exchange as his partner took the phone; Fallon had begun to wonder if maybe, just maybe someone had finally tamed Agent Toles' reckless heart.

"Stay with him, okay? I'll call you back in a few." Fallon heard the deep concern in his partner's voice.

"Alex," he said cautiously.

"Yeah?"

"I don't know what's going on, but it really does look like an accident."

"Yeah. I'll call you in a few," she hung up the phone and her eyes were immediately met by the alarmed stare of the woman she loved. It seemed they had just found a moment's peace and here she was having to deliver more bad news. She covered her mouth with her hand and pulled her bottom lip with some force. She sat down beside Cassidy and took a deep breath.

"Alex... is Dylan..."

"Dylan's fine...he's with Fallon," she paused not certain of how Cassidy would handle the news. "It's the congressman, Cassidy.....There was a car accident."

"Is he..."

"No...he's in surgery. That's all I know."

"Was it deliberate?" Cassidy asked. Alex rubbed her temple again. She had heard all that her partner told her but somehow it just seemed too convenient. Something felt 'off' and she wasn't ready to discount any possibility; not particularly if Cassidy or Dylan might be at risk. "Alex..." Cassidy implored the agent to answer with her eyes.

"Secret Service believes it was an accident–some kid who ran a light at full speed."

The teacher studied the face of the woman before her. "But you don't think so, do you?" For whatever reason Cassidy seemed to be able to read Alex Toles like a book. It was uncanny, really. When Cassidy allowed herself to completely let go of her conscious thoughts, it felt to her as if she had always known Alex. The sensations, the attraction, it was new and when she was away from Alex her feelings could confuse her, but in the agent's presence she felt a unique sense of connection and comfort.

"I don't know what I think...All I know is we need to get you to D.C. and to Dylan."

Cassidy reached for the agent's hand, "Alex..." Alex was focused now and she was dialing Fallon back.

"Hey," she said. "Put Dylan on so Cassidy can talk to him."

Cassidy took the phone and Alex took the opportunity to head back to her room. She opened her cell phone and immediately made reservations for her and Cassidy to fly to D.C. that night. She took the liberty of booking a flight for Rose the next morning. She could hear Cassidy chatting with Dylan as she picked up the phone again to dial the woman's mother. Rose reacted as Alex expected, concerned for everyone involved and more than appreciative of Alex's thought. As she hung up, she felt Cassidy's gaze upon her. "Who was that?" Cassidy asked.

Alex turned and narrowed her gaze at the blonde woman in her doorway. "How is Dylan?" she asked, clearly worried about the boy that she had grown to adore in their time together.

"He's watching cartoons. I don't think he really knows what is going on," she answered, studying the agent's face carefully. "Alex...who were you talking to?"

Alex scratched her eyebrow, "your mom." Cassidy looked at the agent in disbelief. The agent just smiled. "I booked us on the 7:00 p.m. flight out of LaGuardia to Dulles....I thought....I thought your mom could help....I got her a flight tomorrow morning."

Cassidy couldn't move at first. "The FBI let you book a flight for my mother?"

Alex turned away slightly and started putting some things together. "Cassidy... don't worry about it."

The blonde woman slowly made her way to the agent and tugged on her arm until she turned. "You booked those tickets yourself, didn't you?" The agent shrugged, feeling a bit embarrassed by the woman's discovery. Cassidy reached up and looked at the blue eyes above her. She thought perhaps she could swim in them they were so blue. There was not one conscious thought passing through her mind as she guided the agent's lips to her own, only an understanding that this woman before her was sweeping her away. She heard a slight gasp escape from the agent and felt her body tingle at the response. As she pulled away Alex stood looking at her in a way that she was certain no one ever had. The smaller woman smiled. "Thank you," was all she could seem to summon.

***

Alex hated hospitals. They reminded her of a time when she had been helpless and that made her extremely uncomfortable. As they approached the lounge Cassidy noticed that the normally composed agent was fidgeting with her phone, her holster, her ponytail; constantly fidgeting. "Are you okay?" Cassidy asked.

"Yeah," Alex said, realizing that she was displaying her anxiety. "I just hate these places." Cassidy was curious but this was neither the time nor the place to start that conversation. The lounge came upon them suddenly and the pair caught sight of Dylan sitting on the floor watching the television. Agent Fallon rose from his seat on the small couch when he heard the slight rap on the window. He opened the door and Cassidy looked at Alex. The exchange was unmistakable to the senior agent. He couldn't imagine how it had happened, but he was certain now that Alex was in love with the congressman's ex-wife, and judging by the look in Cassidy O'Brien's eyes; the feeling was mutual. "Go on," Alex encouraged the smaller woman, feeling Cassidy's hand slip in and out of her own briefly. The agent made no attempt to censor her emotions in front of her partner as she watched the woman kneel beside her son. She gestured to Fallon to close the door and give them some privacy. "I don't like this, Fallon," she said very curtly, still focused on Cassidy.

"I told you, Alex…it was an accident."

"Doesn't that seem just a little bit TOO much of a coincidence to you?" Agent Toles answered abruptly.

"Are you sure your personal feelings aren't clouding your judgment?"

"My personal feelings?"

108

"Oh, come on, Toles...I saw how you looked at her just now...Christ, you can't keep your eyes off the woman."

Alex nodded. "Fallon, what I feel for Cassidy is not the point." He was stunned at her off handed admission. "It doesn't make sense." Before she could continue Cassidy was opening the door.

"He wants to see you," she said to the female agent with a heartfelt smile. Alex looked over at the boy and then at Fallon. She nodded and headed directly for Dylan, leaving her partner and the woman she had fallen so deeply in love with an unlikely pair of observers.

"Hey there, Speed Racer," she said. "Whatya' watchin'?" He didn't answer her. "Dylan..." she put her hand gently on his shoulder and began to bend down when he threw himself at her physically. Cassidy choked back a tear as she watched the agent gently scoop him up and pull him onto her lap. "Hey... what's this all about?"

"Daddy's gonna' die, Alex."

"What? Hey...Why would you say that?"

"You and Mom wouldn't come here if he wasn't."

Cassidy stood in the doorway with Fallon watching, both moved by Alex's response. "Your mom would be anywhere you needed her to be, any time...and I would be there for you and your mom no matter what, Speed Racer. We just didn't want you to have to be alone playing with Barbie dolls," she kidded him, encouraging a slight giggle through his young tears. Agent Fallon looked at the woman next to him. A tear was rolling over her cheek and he couldn't help but smile at the realization that, indeed, Alex had lost her heart.

"Excuse me?" a voice called from behind. "Are you Mrs. O'Brien?'

"Yes." Cassidy answered as she turned to see a tall man in a white coat.

"I'm Dr. Crenshaw. Your husband is out of surgery. He's pretty out of it, but he did ask for you. You can see him if you like." Alex looked over and saw Cassidy's face. The teacher suddenly appeared very emotional as she followed the doctor away, glancing only briefly at Fallon as she left. It occurred to Alex that this was not her family, this was Cassidy's and the congressman was an equal part of that. She set Dylan back in front of the television and approached her partner. He reviewed all the details of the accident that he could for Alex and she did her best to listen. She was suddenly feeling insecure about Cassidy. They had only just met and here was her ex-husband, the father of her child, a man she'd been with for fifteen years, the person she'd shared her life with until recently fighting for his life. Maybe this was not the agent's place. At the same, time she feared this had been no accident. Everything inside of her told her there was more to this, and no matter what she needed to figure it out, and quickly.

Cassidy had been gone a while and Alex needed to move. She walked down the hallway of the ICU with her badge on full display. On the right hand side of the hallway something caught her attention. There she was, Cassidy O'Brien. She had her face in her left hand as the congressman grasped her right. Alex thought her heart might have completely broken in that one moment. What else should she expect? Who was she to bring more upheaval into this woman's life? She was supposed to protect her. She felt a hand on her shoulder. "Toles?" Fallon said gently, noticing the scene in the room. He looked down at the boy that met his hip. "Here you go...right over there." Dylan looked up at Alex who just smiled at him as best she could.

"Are the original letters at the office?" Agent Toles asked in an extremely professional and direct manner.

"Yeah, but Toles..."

"Can you please get Cassidy and Dylan to the congressman's apartment? I know there is security there. I need to go look at the letters....send me that accident report too," she glanced back in the room where Cassidy had stepped closer to the congressman's head, his hand still holding onto hers. She closed her eyes momentarily and then started to leave.

"Hey," Agent Fallon grabbed hold of his partner's shoulder. "Alex...that doesn't mean..."

Alex just shook her head. "I'll call you later."

***

Alex sat at a long table in the back of the office with all of the letters spread out before her. Her laptop was open with a copy of the accident report visible on its screen. She needed to focus on this case. Her feelings for the congressman's ex-wife had deterred her and that had been a mistake on many levels she thought now. She sipped her coffee and studied one letter picking it up and holding it against another. She repeated it with two more, and again, and again. One letter kept sticking out to her.

> *There she is*
> *She'll be mine*
> *You don't know*
> *Give it time*
> *She wants me*
> *It's never you*
> *Now read this*
> *It's your clue.*

"Three words...all three words," she said to herself. She pulled out another.

> *This and that*
> *I know you*
> *Can you find me?*
> *Back and Forth*
> *Hide and Seek*
> *I'll find you*
> *Before you see.*

"Three words again...every line but one," Alex looked at them again. She picked up the letter that had been delivered over the weekend to the congressman's office.

Every night
You left her
Out of sight
I'll take mine
She'll have me
Before you know
What you can't see

"No...this isn't right." She combed through the pile. "The first came to the house... shit... shit...the first came to the house...three have...all three words." She picked up the picture with the handwriting scrawled under her face, "I SEE YOU...three words...Oh my God... they're not the same person." She reached for the phone.

"Tate," the voice answered.

"A.D.?"

"Toles? Where are you?"

"There's two...Tate...two...the letters they are not the same person."

"What the hell are you talking about? Where are you? Aren't you at the hospital?"

"Just listen...they are not the same. The first, the fifth, the picture on Cassidy's door... the same, the same person...all three words...every line, three words. The rest, they sound the same but the pattern changes. It's not the same person. It started with Cassidy...whoever is stalking her...but the others...they're only meant to look that way...they are not the same...Tate..."

"What are you saying?" the Assistant Director asked. Alex moved over to her laptop and started scrolling through the accident report. "Toles!"

"Right here. Why would anyone be going eighty down Pennsylvania Avenue, PENNSYLVANIA AVENUE?"

"Toles...What are you thinking?"

"I'm thinking you'd better reopen this accident case, Sir... and quick."

***

Cassidy walked into the congressman's apartment and sighed. Fallon had carried Dylan up the stairs for her to his room. Cassidy sat down on the large sofa and put her face in her hands. Her ex-husband's prognosis was extremely guarded. She was worried about him and she was worried about Dylan. He had told her he was sorry for everything in the visit, struggling to make sound. She wanted to believe that was true, but she also knew that he could never change. Christopher O'Brien was who he was and no accident would change that. Agent Fallon came back into the room and regarded the woman sitting quietly. He cleared his throat a bit and she looked up at him. "Are you all right, Mrs. O'Brien?"

Cassidy struggled to smile. "Yes...and just Cassidy, Agent Fallon...please." She closed her eyes again and looked toward the ceiling as if attempting to summon some type of answer. Fallon could tell that the day's events had taken their toll. The woman was exhausted.

"I should let you get some rest," he began. "Dylan's asleep and the Secret Service is outside, plus two of our agents. You'll be more than safe."

"Agent Fallon," she called after him.

"Brian," he offered, "Yes?"

"Where is Alex?" Agent Fallon had spent many years learning how to read people and right now Cassidy O'Brien was an open book. He didn't know what he should say or how much. What he did know was that he saw a vulnerability in his partner he had never seen before at the hospital. He loved Alex Toles like a sister. She had been there for him through a great deal over the last three years. She had been there for his family when he had been injured. More than any case ever could, his partner's happiness mattered to him. Cassidy saw the agent was wrestling with something. "Brian, where is Alex?"

He inhaled and nodded his head trying to muster the courage to say what he knew needed to be said. "She went to the office….to look at the letters."

"Okay…when? She hasn't called or…"

He sighed nervously still nodding and looking deliberately at the floor beneath his feet, "Alex…you know…she…"

"Just tell me…please," the woman implored him. "When did she leave?"

"After…well…you know, you were gone a while and we were waiting, and she decided to go, well, get something….and…."

Cassidy took a deep breath and released it upward. "Shit."

He looked up at her as she shook her head at the ceiling above. "She saw me…. with Chris; that's it, isn't it?"

He nodded. "But only part of it… I mean she was really worried ….about all of you… and when Alex gets…"

"I know…but that's not why she hasn't called…why she's still not here."

"No," he said plainly.

"Have you talked to her?"

"Only for a minute."

"Do you know where she is?" Cassidy hopped to her feet. She knew exactly what Alex was thinking and she knew how that felt. When she had seen Alex with Agent Brackett she thought she would break in two. They had just made it over one hurdle and now here they were again. "Brian, please, where is she?"

"She's at her apartment now….but Cassidy…she's still working… I know her."

"Yeah… well, so do I…better than I should."

"What?"

"Brian…can you stay here…just for a bit…please?"

"Cassidy…"

"Where is Alex's apartment?" Cassidy was growing insistent.

"You can't go over there alone, Cassidy…let me go get her."

"You and I both know that will never work," Cassidy said flatly. She couldn't believe it but she started up the stairs.

"Where are you going?"

"To get Dylan. If I can't go by myself than you can take us both." Agent Fallon scratched his forehead. There was a determination in Cassidy's voice that told him there was no way he could win this argument. He couldn't let her go alone and she would never leave a stranger with her son. There was no other choice. And he hated to admit it, but he agreed.

Chapter Nine

Files were spread across Alex's coffee table and floor. She knew there was something more here and now she was more worried than before. She was certain that Cassidy had a stalker and she was convinced that someone was leveraging that to make an attempt on the congressman. The only questions still milling in her mind were if the stalker was real or just a diversion, who and most importantly, why? There was little doubt in her mind that someone in the press held the clue, or perhaps someone hiding in the press. She thumbed through profiles and backgrounds looking for any thread.

The agent sat on the old blue couch that sat in the center of her room and threw her head back in frustration. She closed her eyes in an effort to concentrate but all she could see was Cassidy in the congressman's room. The right thing for her to do was to step back, for so many reasons. She tried to gather herself. Her heart ached for the woman, in so many ways. She missed Cassidy now, and as she returned her attention to the files spread across the room she suddenly felt terrified. It didn't matter whether she stepped away or not; she loved Cassidy. There was simply no way to avoid that reality. The thought of anyone hurting Cassidy, even Alex herself, was unbearable to the agent. She resumed her task and looked some more, her frustration building. "Who are you?" she yelled at the pile before her. "Dammit!" She threw a file across the room as a knock came at the door. She released her breath in a frustrated huff and headed for the door.

***

Cassidy had managed to milk the whole truth from Agent Fallon in the car. She knew that Alex suspected that the letters came from two places and she knew that Alex was concerned about a lot more than just the case. Agent Fallon found Cassidy engaging. He could understand his partner's feelings and he did not want to hold back from the woman. He trusted her. He knew Agent Toles did as well. Cassidy grew quiet as the car slowed, approaching Alex's building. "Listen," Brian Fallon began, "I know it's not my place..."

Cassidy forced a smile. "Say what you're thinking, Agent."

He pulled in front of the building and looked at her. "I think she loves you."

Cassidy smiled. "Yeah? You think so?" He nodded. Cassidy smiled as she got out of the car. Fallon opened Dylan's door as Cassidy threw the backpack over her shoulder. She scooped Dylan up and onto her hip and reached for the handle of the booster seat.

"At least let me help you," Fallon offered.

The woman smiled and jostled her son upward slightly. "One set of stairs, right?"

"Yeah, first door on the left...210," he answered. She started to make her way up the front stairs and Fallon ran up behind her. "Code...here," he pressed the code for the front door and held it open for the fully loaded woman. "Do you want me to wait?"

She smiled sweetly realizing that he was as genuinely kind as Alex had described. "No," she said. "Just wish me luck."

***

The agent reached the door, irritated and expecting Agent Fallon to be behind it with some lecture. "You know...it's not," she began to scold him verbally as she opened the door.

"It's not easy carrying all this is what it's not," Cassidy said looking at the agent who was in complete shock. "Well?" Cassidy urged.

Alex grabbed the booster seat and closed the door behind Cassidy. "Cassidy, what are you doing…"

The teacher did not allow the agent to finish. "What am *I* doing? What are *you* doing?" she asked looking at the files spread across the room. Alex was suddenly far more nervous than irritated. She tried to avoid Cassidy's gaze but failed. "We need to talk, Alex."

The agent felt as though her insides had turned to gelatin. She could not believe that Cassidy was actually here. "Cassidy… how did you?"

"Agent Fallon brought me." She watched as Alex moved to the window to look for her partner's car. "Don't bother. I sent him home." The agent turned in disbelief to face the teacher.

"You sent him…"

Cassidy interrupted, gesturing to Dylan as she spoke. "Yeah. You're not running away from me again." Alex gently scooped the boy from his mother. Cassidy's words traveled straight through the agent's heart. It was true. She did it again, just like she did earlier. She ran. Maybe there was work to do, but it could've waited until morning. She carried the boy into the spare room and laid him down on the bed. When she didn't return immediately Cassidy made her way to the doorway. Alex was staring at the boy, her hand lovingly stroking his head. "He asked for you," Cassidy said. Alex felt her heart sink. Her feelings for this woman and for this child who was so much like his mother were not something she had ever anticipated she could feel. The sound of Cassidy's voice, the boy before her, the weight of Cassidy's stare behind her, all of it reminded her of how in love she was with this woman. Slowly the agent turned "Why did you leave?" Cassidy asked.

"I had to go, Cassidy." Alex said, armed with her own excuses. "You were…"

"I was what?"

"You were with the congressman. I didn't want to disturb you."

"Mmm....so that's why you didn't call?"

Alex pointed to the mess in the room. "Cassidy...I was ..."

The blonde woman slowly made her way to Alex. "You thought that I wanted to be with Chris."

"No...I just..." Cassidy raised her eyebrow at the agent. Alex took a deep breath. She couldn't lie to Cassidy even if she tried. "You were with your family. I don't want to come between..." The smaller woman moved so close to the agent that they were nearly touching. Alex started to ramble. "I know he loves you and it's not....he..."

"Yes." Cassidy agreed. Alex looked at the floor. "But I don't love him, not like that." The agent looked at the beautiful woman standing before her. "What did I tell you this afternoon?" Alex was puzzled and Cassidy knew the agent was rattled by her forthrightness. She pulled the agent's face toward her own, "I said...I said I didn't want you to let me go."

Alex swallowed hard. She remembered and she remembered her response. She recalled everything about those hours. "Cass..."

"You said, 'never'." Alex looked at the teacher with a tear in her eye. "Did you mean that?" Cassidy asked searching the eyes she had already become lost in.

Alex fought to breathe. She never imagined this conversation would occur with Cassidy at its helm. The confident voice of the agent faltered now. "Yes...I did."

"Mmm. Then don't," Cassidy said as Alex gave over and kissed the woman. This kiss was different. Alex felt herself being pulled under by Cassidy's presence. There was something wonderfully tender about the way they touched, the way this woman felt in her arms. The agent felt Cassidy's tongue dance with her own, the woman's hands now softly running along the agent's neck. Alex needed to feel Cassidy closer. She wasn't certain this was the right time but she couldn't help but allow her hands to begin to search the woman in her arms. Cassidy sighed and the words just fell from her. "I love you, Alex," she said. Alex pulled back slightly and brushed the hair from the woman's eyes. She needed to slow this down, for them both, and it was much harder than she imagined it could be. "What is it?" Cassidy asked searching the agent's expression. She was suddenly afraid that Alex was unsure. Alex immediately sensed her anxiety and kissed her tenderly. "What?" Cassidy asked again as Alex pulled back a little.

"I love you, Cassidy." Cassidy looked at her questioning, wondering if that was so, what was wrong. The agent smiled. "No...Cassidy...listen to me...I'm in love with you."

"I am in love with you," Cassidy admitted with confidence.

"Mmm. I know," Alex said playing with Cassidy's hair. She looked into the pools of green that seemed to hold the secrets to her own soul. "Not like this," Alex said. "Let me hold you. Just let me hold you." Cassidy would not have believed that she could love Alex more than when she walked into the apartment just a short while ago. It was ironic that she realized she was in love with Alex while she was standing in the congressman's room. As he spoke to her; she felt love for him, but she wished Alex was there to hold her. Now, as Alex stepped back from her own desire to 'love' Cassidy, Cassidy knew she had fallen instantly deeper into this woman's grasp. "Alex..."

The agent pressed a finger to Cassidy's lips and led her to the bedroom. Cassidy couldn't breathe. She felt a longing for the woman next to her that she had never experienced. Her breath could not seem to fill her lungs and her entire body seemed to tingle with energy. Alex smiled as she pulled Cassidy close to her. "Sleep now," she said.

Cassidy could not imagine how that would be possible. "How am I supposed to sleep?" The teacher asked the strong but gentle form holding her.

Alex chuckled with understanding but she knew this was not the time for them. No matter how badly she wanted to feel Cassidy now, they were both emotionally and physically exhausted. She played with the blonde hair that cascaded onto her chest and felt Cassidy begin to drift away in her embrace. "Never," the agent said.

"What?" Cassidy mumbled as she helplessly faded into sleep.

"I will never run away from you again," the agent whispered. "Never."

***

A light tug on her sleeve woke the sleeping agent. She struggled to open her eyes. "Alex," the small voice seemed to almost be asking if it was really her. Alex's heart skipped realizing Dylan was standing next to her bed, his mother wrapped in her arms and a wave of panic swept over her. She hadn't even thought about the possibility that Dylan might see them and she had no idea how he might react, much less his mother. Gently she tried to pull away from Cassidy but the woman beside her tightened her grip. "Hey, Speed Racer," was all she could manage as her voice trembled slightly.

She suddenly felt Cassidy move and a chin came to rest on her chest. "Dylan?" Cassidy called over to her son, making no move to release her grip on the agent. "Did you have a nightmare?" The agent couldn't move, couldn't think. A warm surge of emotion seemed to be rising through her, filling her senses in a way that no words could ever hope to describe. There was no question now in her mind, Cassidy O'Brien loved her. Right here in this simple moment Alex Toles felt more loved and more at home than ever before. Dylan moved closer to the agent and Alex propped herself up a bit. The boy's eyes were wide, but it was the fear solicited by a bad dream that drove his expression. As Alex moved to lift him onto her bed she realized that like his mother, he seemed to be completely unfazed by the two sleeping beside one another. He moved between them and Alex thought she might explode from the emotions that filled her as she watched Cassidy brush the hair from his small eyes.

"Just a dream, sweetie," the small woman beside her said lovingly, comforting the boy. Cassidy looked up to Alex who was sitting against the headboard. Instantly the teacher saw the agent's reaction. It touched her. She had always wished that her family could be this way. When she was pregnant with Dylan she would imagine that she and Chris would do these things together; that having a child would begin to settle him; but that never came to pass. She knew that he loved them both in his own way but the congressman was always preoccupied with other things and he lacked the ability to be still in any moment.

"It's all right, Speed Racer," Alex said. "Do you want to sleep here with your mom?" He nodded and Alex starting to pull herself off the bed when a small hand grabbed her shirt and pulled. Cassidy watched her son position himself firmly against the FBI agent and realized he had fallen in love with Alex as much as she had.

Cassidy watched the agent's expression as Alex laid down beside Dylan and accepted his small head onto her shoulder. She could tell that Alex was clearly overwhelmed by his gesture. The agent had worried about coming between Cassidy's family just hours ago. She smiled at the woman holding her son, her green eyes twinkling the message that she could not convey in words. 'This *is* my family,' she thought. If Cassidy had allowed herself even one moment to think, she would've asked herself how she could be so sure of something in such a short time; something completely different than she had ever expected. Dylan quelled all of her reasoning. Children often saw what adults failed to allow themselves to believe. Cassidy knew that. As she laid her head back down, placing her arm over the son she loved more than life, she gently grasped the agent's hand. "I love you," she said softly as all three drifted back to sleep.

***

Alex smiled at the sight before her as she maneuvered off the bed. She silently shook her head, wondering how in the world her life could've changed so much in less than a week. A small sigh escaped her as she forced herself to remove her stare from the sleeping pair. Somehow she knew this was not the last time she would look at the picture in front of her and that left her feeling incredibly grateful. Making her way to the small kitchen, she picked up the pot of cold coffee, poured it in a mug and threw it into the microwave, retrieving it before its signature beep blew through the apartment. She made her way back to the mess of files that still littered her living room. Plopping down on the couch that seemed to consume her when she sat on it, she sipped the coffee. She grimaced as it trickled down her throat. "Terrible," she muttered, accepting it to her lips for another sip. She picked up a random file and began scanning it. Then she had an idea. She pulled the photos from several files and lined them beside one another on the coffee table. They were surveillance photos of the press taken at the congressman's events over the last few months. She leaned over the table and concentrated on the faces. Her eyes were almost slits as she brought her face within inches of the photos. "That's Carl," a small voice said moving alongside the agent.

Alex jumped and coffee splashed on her face. Dylan giggled. "What?" the agent asked now, perplexed by his statement.

"Right there," he pointed to a face that appeared in one of the photos. "That's Carl!" He said in his typical 'don't you get it' manner.

Alex lifted the picture and studied it closely. The faces were small but she could clearly make out the face the boy had pointed to. "Dylan," she started cautiously, "Do you know this man?"

"Can I have juice?" was his response.

Alex pinched the bridge of her nose. "Yes," she said leading him to her refrigerator. She opened the carton of orange juice and sniffed. Her eyes watered at the strength of its smell alone. "Ummm...no juice...ummm...How about...well," she looked through her cabinets as a pair of small eyes followed her nervous pacing. "I have....Yeah... I have this orange drink...uh stuff?" She pulled down some packets of powder and held them up with some reservation for the boy's approval. Dylan shrugged his agreement. Alex set about stirring the packet into some water. "Dylan," she said as she handed him the glass, "who is Carl?"

He shrugged again. "I dunno...some guy." Alex wasn't sure where Dylan recognized the man from but she wasn't ready to write it off. "Does he know you?"

"Sure," Dylan said sipping his drink. "Can I watch cartoons?"

Alex took a deep breath and looked at the boy. The agent in her wanted to press harder but as she watched him explore the tiny sugar crystals that rose to the top of his glass with his finger, something else took over. She scratched her eyebrow and chuckled. "Sure...Come on." She led him to the television and flipped on a station with cartoons. She started back to her former task, but a glimpse of Cassidy sleeping in the other room made her stop momentarily. She smiled at the sight of the small blonde woman sprawled across the bed before making her way back to the couch. She started rummaging through the files until she found the one that she hoped was there, *Carl Edward Fisher.* "Who are you, Carl Edward Fisher?" she whispered to herself opening the file. "Twenty-nine. Huh," she grabbed a piece of paper and followed the words with her index finger. "Stanford.....Photographer....Christopher O'Brien for Congress." She stroked her chin in thought. "Dylan," she called to him. "Did Carl take pictures of your dad?"

"Yep."

Alex took a deep breath. It might not mean anything, but it might mean everything. She picked up her cell phone and headed into the spare room, closing the door slightly. "Fallon?"

"Hey, Toles," the voice on the other end answered cautiously. "Everything okay there?"

"Yeah…Listen…Fallon….can you run another background on someone. I have the preliminary but I think there is probably an FBI file already. Can you do it, quietly?"

"Yeah, why?"

"Just…"

"A feeling?" He chuckled.

"Not exactly…but yeah," she said.

"Okay." He said running to get a pen, "What's the name?"

"Carl Edward Fisher."

"Okay…you got it…I'm not there yet…."

"Good," the agent continued opening the door back up and taking note of Dylan fondling the sugar crystals in his fingers. "Then you can stop and get some milk and cereal on your way and stop here before the office."

"What?" Fallon asked.

"Yeah…and get some bagels and juice while you're at it."

"Toles…"

"Hey… you dropped them off here. Christ, Fallon, you let her carry all that crap by herself?"

Agent Fallon shook his head and Alex swore she could actually hear him grinning from ear to ear. "On my way," he groaned caving into her request.

***

"Here you go," Fallon said to his partner handing her the bag. She accepted it gratefully and headed to the kitchen. He followed her and took a seat at the small table in the corner watching as she started a fresh pot of coffee, filled a bowl with cereal and milk and poured a glass of juice. She walked past him into the other room and handed the boy the bowl and glass.

"Thanks," he said as Alex touched the top of his head.

"You're welcome, Speed Racer." She stopped and picked up a folder, flipping it onto the table in front of her partner. "Take a look," she said continuing to the counter to pour them each some coffee.

"What am I looking at?" he asked, accepting the cup with a smile.

Alex leaned against the counter and shook her head. "Dylan recognized him from the O'Brien campaign."

"That doesn't necessarily mean anything, Toles."

"Maybe it does and maybe it doesn't," she agreed, turning to start putting the cereal away and cleaning up the counter, "all I know is someone is watching Cassidy and the congressman is in ICU. As far as I'm concerned everything is something until we prove it otherwise."

Cassidy had rolled out of bed at the sound of voices in the other room. She shuffled past Fallon putting a hand on his shoulder and offering him a smile. "Morning," she greeted, coming up behind the agent.

"Morning," Alex responded letting the woman fall against her slightly. Agent Fallon dropped his face behind the file trying to hide his widening smile. "Go on," Alex prompted him as she poured Cassidy a cup of coffee.

"What?" her partner chimed, making his best attempt at playing dumb. Cassidy tried not to laugh and thanked the agent for her coffee with a peck on the cheek before smirking and heading for the living room. Alex watched her leave and looked back at her friend.

"Just say it," she instructed him.

Agent Fallon pondered the look on his partner's face. He knew she expected him to give her hell. "I'm happy for you, Alex," he said simply. "Cassidy's great." Alex looked at him as if he might have hit his head and then he continued. "So don't screw it up," he finished, returning his attention to the file. Alex just shook her head.

"Fallon...I know you think this is probably nothing, but I don't think that the congressman's accident was any accident."

Her partner took a deep breath. "Yeah, Alex...about that, I went back over the file last night....I don't think so either."

Alex looked at him and moved to the table, not wanting Cassidy or Dylan to overhear anything. "What do you mean?"

"I don't want to say too much...I have to pull some footage this morning to be sure....but there's footage from a security camera nearby. The light, I don't think it was red."

Alex set down her coffee and rubbed her eyes. "Fallon if that's true, it would mean whoever was driving the congressman ran into that car deliberately." He just looked at her silently acknowledging that her observation was his fear. "All right," she looked into the other room. "I'll meet you at the office in a while...Cassidy's mom is flying in." He nodded and headed for the door calling out his goodbyes. Alex opened the door and leaned into the hallway, "Fallon..."

"Yeah?"

"If there are two...if we're right, Cassidy and the congressman are both in danger."

"I know," he said.

Alex glanced over her shoulder at Dylan and Cassidy. "Do me a favor...keep the footage between us for now."

He gave her a crooked smile. "I was thinking the same thing."

Alex worried now that there could be someone within the FBI involved. "Fallon, be careful."

Agent Brian Fallon stopped halfway down the hall and turned back to the agent. "Toles..."

Alex spun on her heels to face him again. "Yeah?"

"She really is great."

Agent Alex Toles offered her partner a crooked smile, noting the sincerity in his voice and the affection on his face. "Yeah...I know.....don't screw it up," she winked. "I got it."

***

"Hey…Toles," Agent Fallon beckoned his partner to follow him.

"What's up?"

"I've got something I want you to see." Alex followed Fallon into a small room. He stopped behind her, locked the door and pulled the small shade in the window down.

"Is it the footage you told me about?"

He pulled a chair up to the computer and inserted a disc. "Just look." Alex stood over her partner's shoulder and leaned toward the computer screen as he slowed down the footage. "Just watch," he instructed. Both agents kept their eyes firmly set on the video as it rolled slowly. The congressman's car was approaching the intersection at what appeared to be an average speed. It slowed slightly and the left blinker began to signal. It was clear that the driver was preparing to make the left turn normally. The car gradually began its curve to the left when in an instant there was a crushing blow to the driver's side, sending it sailing at least fifteen feet sideways and across the street onto the curb.

Alex stood up. "Okay, but Fallon, that seems to jive with the report."

Agent Fallon shook his head. "Yeah… I know… but there's a couple of problems… watch." He typed in numbers on the keyboard cueing a different point in the video. "You have no idea what it took to get this footage," he said.

Alex moved around the side of her partner's chair, completely obstructing her partner's view. "Play it again," she ordered and he complied. "Where did you get this?"

"There's a little convenience store just about a block from the intersection. Just so happens they installed two outdoor cameras a few days ago after a break in. They record movement in both directions toward the store," he explained, rolling the video again.

Alex watched closely as the blue SUV drove down the street at a fast pace and continued straight through the green light. "He's not going eighty...speeding, but...Fallon....stop it right when they are about to hit." Agent Fallon backed the tape up and played it, pausing it just before the collision. "Again," Alex instructed. "Can we split screen this? Show both?" Fallon looked at his partner. "Fallon....if both lights were green..."

"I know...neither driver had a chance."

"Does that store keep recordings for more than the current day?" Alex asked.

"I don't know, why?"

Alex sighed and began to pace. "The lights didn't turn green on their own, Fallon....Aren't there traffic cams at that intersection?"

He frowned. "There are." Alex put her hands in the air questioning him silently. "That's where I got the tape of the congressman's car."

"Okay, so what about the tape of the SUV?" He cued another point on the video and set it in motion. Alex pinched the bridge of her nose hard.

"I know," her partner said.

Alex sighed. "So, that's where the eighty miles per hour scenario came from....somebody altered that footage."

"Yeah....and the log for the lights. It clearly shows that the Pennsylvania light turned red six seconds before the collision." Alex took a deep breath continuing to pace and rub her temples simultaneously. "So...what now?" Fallon asked. "Do you think Cassidy's off the hook?" Alex didn't answer. "Toles, if this is all about O'Brien...I mean... it makes sense that Cassidy... the letters were probably meant to scare him off...you know... I mean..."

"Yeah, I know.... But there's a problem with that scenario. I agree...the later letters probably were meant to throw him off....something....or to try and paint him in a negative light.... he didn't bite, didn't go public and we got put on the case....

BUT, Fallon.... The first letter, that was all about Cassidy, not politics...the fifth, the picture....somebody who knew about that first letter....somebody leveraged that...or tried to," Alex stopped her pacing and rubbed her eyes.

"What is it?" Fallon asked.

Alex looked at him now. "If the light was green...Where are all of the witnesses?" She shook her head. "The middle of the day...middle of the day, Fallon...What about the car behind the SUV? What about the pedestrians? No one saw this?"

"What are you saying?"

"I'm saying...this is a lot bigger than a car crash. Get those witness statements."

"What are you going to do?" he asked.

"I want you to run backgrounds."

"On the witnesses?" he asked with some reservation.

"Yeah...Fallon...on the witnesses."

"What about Tate? Don't you think..."

"I think this stays between us for now, Fallon. Tate made it clear to me this morning he was not pushing to open a review of the accident. I don't know if that's his decision or someone else's....BUT, knowing Tate, with what I did tell him, it wasn't his call. There's got to be more than one thing going on here." Alex paused and looked at the frozen image on the screen. "Whoever is behind this didn't count on our involvement."

"What about Cassidy?" he asked. "You still want that background for that photographer?"

Alex looked at him. She felt sick. This was much bigger than she anticipated. She still suspected there were two very different motivations behind the letters. That meant Cassidy was in far more danger than the agent had originally thought. "Yes. I'm not discounting anything. Someone goes to these lengths to deter a congressman....If he lives...."

Fallon nodded. He looked at his partner whose face was grim and he could feel the tension pouring from her in a way he never had before. "Toles?"

"Yeah?"

"Maybe…. Maybe this will…you know….take the heat OFF Cassidy, even if there are two." Alex swallowed hard and forced a fake smile. "Toles, really…"

"Fallon, just run the backgrounds…and no emails or calls… okay? I'll call you in a couple of hours and let you know where I am. Bring them hard copy…. And pick up some Chinese food on your way."

"What?" he asked.

"Look, Fallon…no one can know we suspect this…understand?" He nodded as she began to head out the door.

"Is Cassidy going back to the congressman's?"

"No. She doesn't want to stay there."

"She staying with you?"

"My place is not really….Well….No. I have a friend who has made arrangements for Cassidy and Rose to stay at a condo in Arlington his family owns."

"A friend?" Fallon shook his head. "You're talking about the president."

Alex gave the first hint of a real smile seeing that her partner was still annoyed by her failure to share her friendship with the president with him. "Fallon, we've always kept our friendship quiet. I'd prefer it stays that way, okay?" Fallon didn't really understand but he smiled and nodded his agreement. "I've got to go…stuff to do before we head over the bridge. I'll call you when I get there….Get those files."

Chapter Ten

Alex pulled up in front of the congressman's apartment building and stared up at it. She didn't know how she could keep all of her suspicions a secret from Cassidy, but she didn't want to cause the woman she loved anymore fear or stress than she already was dealing with. Still, the truth was that Cassidy could seem to read the agent like no one else. Alex suspected that she would have to tell her something. She took in a deep breath and let it out. Years of profiling killers, stalkers, terrorists, arms traders and criminals of every kind had taught the agent a great deal about people and their motivations. There was little doubt in her mind that Cassidy had a stalker. What frightened the agent was the reality that she might now be in danger from a political agenda as well.

Alex was tempted to call on her friend, the president. The truth was there were only three people she would trust right now and John Merrow was one of them. But, she feared that he too might become compromised. She'd learned many years ago during her military career that nothing was more dangerous than someone on the inside; someone you believed you could trust; someone that in truth wanted to do you harm. She'd survived that with her former commander. Now, here they were again. This time, however, the stakes were much higher for the agent. There was nothing that she wouldn't do to keep Cassidy O'Brien safe. The agent made her way to the apartment door and again paused to compose herself. She pressed the buzzer, stood in front of the camera and waited for the door to open. Heading down the long hallway she stopped and acknowledged the Secret Service agent that was positioned outside the door. He returned her nod and opened the door for her. Immediately, she heard Rose's voice and followed the sound to the kitchen. Rose and Cassidy were sitting at the table engaged in a conversation about how long Cassidy intended to stay in Washington. "I can't just stay here and wait. Thursday...Thursday either way, we're going home." Cassidy looked over and saw the agent approaching. She hadn't seen Alex since the agent had dropped her back at the apartment to go and pick her mother up at the airport that morning. The tension in her body seemed to evaporate as she captured Alex's stare. Rose watched the severity in her daughter's face transform gradually into the hint of a smile. "When did you get here?" the teacher asked looking at the agent.

"Just now."

"We were just..." Cassidy began.

"I heard," Alex raised her eyebrow. "The condo should be all set. I talked to Tate. The Secret Service is being pulled off once you move there. The FBI will have full jurisdiction. So, you'll have a little more privacy. Well, except for having to put up with me, of course."

Cassidy chuckled. "I think I'll manage," she said flirtatiously, soliciting a sideways smirk from her mother.

Rose tried to contain her laughter. "Well," Rose began, rising to her feet somewhat dramatically. "I think I will go get that boy together and give you and your 'protector' here a few minutes to discuss your, *plans*." The older woman stopped and faced Alex closing her left eye slightly and raising her right brow before heading off.

"Ummm...did you tell her?" the agent asked the teacher nervously.

"Tell her what?"

"You know....about...."

Cassidy laughed. "No.....But, Alex....my mother, well... Let's just say I don't usually have to tell her much." Alex sat down in the chair Rose had recently occupied, her face suddenly a pale gray. Cassidy looked at the agent and shook her head. "Alex...it's all right."

The agent forgot completely about everything she had been mulling over in her mind on the way to the apartment. "She must....Oh, she must think I'm..."

The small blonde woman reached across the table and placed her hand over the agent's. "Alex, if I love you, she'll love you." The agent looked up at the green eyes that sparkled across from her. There was happiness in Cassidy's eyes as she looked into the agent's now. Suddenly, the moment was all that mattered to the agent. She searched Cassidy's eyes as the woman finished her statement with a quiet, but decided admission, "and I do...love you." Alex struggled for a moment to speak. She was consumed by her emotions as the reality of what she had learned earlier began to swirl in her mind again. As she feared, the woman she loved immediately recognized the agent's subtle change in expression. "Alex, what's wrong?"

"Nothing," Alex clasped the hand over her own gently. "Nothing you need to worry about."

"You are a horrible liar, Alex Toles." Alex unconsciously pinched the bridge of her nose. "See," the teacher observed. "That's exactly what I am talking about."

"What?" Alex looked at her curiously. "I didn't say a thing."

Cassidy pursed her lips a bit, "you're worried."

"Of course I am worried....You're upset about being here.... and there's the letters..."

"No," Cassidy said, "It's not that." Alex's eyes darted sideways and she pressed on her temple with her thumb lightly. "See...right there...when you are worried you always do that."

Alex could not help but let out a chuckle. "What do I do?"

"Rub your temples, pinch the bridge of your nose... ummm...squint sideways."

"Is that right? Think you have me pegged, huh?"

"Stop trying to change the subject."

Alex sighed. "I am worried, Cass, I am. But, that's my job... you know?" She tried to change the tone of the conversation and Cassidy understood that whatever was driving Alex's concerns she either wasn't ready or she couldn't tell the teacher now.

"Okay," Cassidy conceded momentary defeat, which surprised the agent.

"Okay?" Alex asked curiously.

Cassidy moved to the agent, prompting her to pull out her chair. The smaller woman took the opportunity to sit on the agent's lap and wrap her arms around Alex's neck. "Yeah, okay." Alex scrunched her face into an expression of playful doubt. "You tell me when you're ready," Cassidy said plainly.

The agent relaxed and felt her heart swell. "I love you, Cassidy."

"I know," the blonde answered capturing the agent's lips. As she slowly broke their kiss she looked into Alex's eyes. "Whatever it is, Alex, just promise me...."

The agent stopped the teacher's words with the gentle pressure of a finger to the woman's lips. "You let me do the worrying right now." Cassidy smiled. "Go get your things," the agent said. "Let's get you someplace where we are all more comfortable." Cassidy kissed the agent on the cheek and began to make her way slowly out of the room. She knew there was something Alex wasn't telling her. It was in her nature to push, but she trusted Alex completely and with every moment that passed she seemed to gain a greater understanding of the woman she had fallen in love with. Whatever it was, Alex would tell her when the time was right.

"Alex," she called back.

"Yeah?"

"How big is the condo?"

Alex tried to hide her amusement. Their brief interlude had left the agent a bit breathless and she knew by Cassidy's question that the teacher had a similar response. "I don't know...big." The agent bit her lip.

"Hmmm," Cassidy mused as she continued out of the room.

"Oh boy, Toles," the agent whispered to herself. "You're in trouble."

"I heard that," a playful voice called back.

"How does she do that?" Alex laughed. She didn't know how she was going to handle this case, but right now handling the rest of the evening seemed both more important and more nerve-racking.

"That too," the voice called. Alex shook her head. Silently she thought to herself, 'I don't know how you do it, Cassidy O'Brien.'

***

The man took a deep breath as he watched her emerge from the building. Click. Click. Click. The tall, dark haired woman took the bags from her hand and placed them in the open trunk. The beautiful blonde was watching her closely. He grunted as the taller woman closed the trunk and made her way to open the door for the blonde. "Bitch," he groaned as his finger pressed the button again. Click, click, click. He shuddered at the sound. He looked at the seat next to him, his companion a dirty, red duffle bag. Again he pointed the lens. Click, click, click, click. A deep sigh escaped him as the black sedan pulled away. He tossed the camera aside, unzipped the bag and retrieved a small flask, raising it to his lips and gulping the fluid down as if quenching an insatiable thirst. He wiped his lips with a swift pass of the back of his hand, closed the flask and returned it to his companion on the seat.

A deafening screech pierced the silence of the automobile. He grasped the offender and looked at it with deep resentment. Placing it to his ear he spoke, "yeah." Again there was silence. His face contorted as he listened to the words echoing through the little black box. "Yeah. I got it. Yeah. Yeah she's there." He clawed at his own cheek leaving a red streak across it, "understood." He tossed the small black box onto the dash board and pulled at his hair. "Understood," he muttered to himself again as he turned the key in the ignition. "She'll understand," he groaned closing his eyes momentarily. "She'll understand."

***

The building was dark inside. A tall figure in a business suit stood at its center watching as the woman approached. "What did you find out?" he asked as her figure came into clearer view.

The woman smirked and pulled a chair out from the small table that was positioned in the otherwise vacant building. "She wasn't there long....other things to attend to, I suppose."

"Well, it's your job to find out what those other things ARE," the man's voice deepened.

The woman crossed her legs and leaned leisurely back in the chair. "I would imagine they have something to do with a cute little blonde right now," she mused, licking her lips.

The man moved closer, bending over her and placing his forehead squarely against hers. "I don't care about that...you find out what she knows, not who she screws." He removed the contact and stood erect.

"What are you worried about?" She tossed her hair with her hand. "The congressman's out of commission and his ex-wife is...well...she's preoccupied."

He walked slowly across the room toward the large rolling door that marked its entrance. "Don't underestimate Toles. That would be a mistake that you will regret." He completed his walk, a smaller man rolling the door open so that a beam of light momentarily struck the woman's red hair. He did not turn when he spoke. "Find out. Don't disappoint me." He was gone.

***

Alex shook her head as she placed Rose's bag in one of the large bedrooms. "Christ, what is it with these people?" she mused. The townhouse was immense, four bedrooms, a study, three full bathrooms and another half bath, an enormous kitchen, three fireplaces and a finished basement. "Who the hell needs all this?" She rolled her eyes.

"Alex!" Cassidy called up the stairs. "Brian is here!" The agent filled her cheeks with air and then released it making a whistling sound as it passed. She knew Fallon would have at least some of the files she asked him to get, and she knew Cassidy would suspect that her partner's visit had less to do with Chinese food than it did with work. She was relieved at the woman's earlier agreement to let her questions lie but she knew that would not last forever. That wasn't even the fact that troubled her the most now. Alex couldn't avoid the inevitable much longer and the she knew it. Her desire to be with Cassidy seemed to be growing by the second. It invaded her thoughts and the normally confident and suave agent was beyond nervous. Cassidy, in a short time, had become the most important person in the agent's world. She loved the teacher in a way that seemed to defy the logic she always relied on both in her work and in her life. Expressing that to the woman who had unexpectedly captured her heart was something Alex was unsure of. Alex hated to admit it, but she wasn't certain she had ever made love to anyone. Seduction was a skill she had mastered long ago and sex was its mistress, until now. Cassidy was different. She didn't want to seduce the teacher, she wanted to love her. That was more disconcerting to Alex Toles than any case had ever been.

Alex sat down on the edge of the large king size bed and put her face in her hands. Her anxiety was made worse by the presence of both Dylan and Rose. One thing she knew for certain after Cassidy's afternoon kiss, making the presence of family in the house a reason to postpone time alone with the blonde was not going to fly. Cassidy might be willing to give Alex space where the case was concerned, but when it came to their burgeoning relationship, Cassidy O'Brien was not going to be as patient and Alex knew it. "Alex!" Cassidy's voice called up the stairs again. "Did you hear me?"

The agent took another deep breath and called back, "yeah...I'm coming." She let out a nervous chuckle at the timeliness of her words amidst her current thoughts. "Shit." She put her face back in her hands, shaking her head.

"She's not gonna' wait forever," Rose joked from the hallway.

"What?" Alex jumped with a quiver in her voice that sounded as if she were a small child caught with her hand in the cookie jar.

Rose laughed. "She's called up here twice already." Alex let out an audible sigh of amusement and relief. Rose looked at the agent and offered her a motherly glance of understanding. "Alex..." The agent looked at the mother of the woman she loved and pressed her lips together tightly, wondering what Cassidy's mother might say. "You love Cassidy, don't you?"

Alex felt like someone had barreled her over, knocking the wind completely from her lungs. Cassidy's mom really did just 'know' things. "It's that obvious?" the agent asked a bit sheepishly.

"To me, yes." Rose McCollum smiled. "Come on, we'd better get down there before she comes up here and reads us the riot act." Alex pulled herself up and met the woman in the doorway. As they approached the stairs the agent felt a comforting touch on her back. "She loves you, Alex. I see it in her eyes every time she looks at you. Just be yourself...that's who she fell in love with."

Alex tried to breathe. She looked at the older woman as they reached the bottom of the stairs. Rose McCollum had the same eyes as her daughter. They were a vibrant green that occasionally changed offering a bluish hue that glistened in the most peculiar and intoxicating way. The agent had never worried much about other people's approval. She had never managed to garner the approval of her own parents and it taught her to be independently confident. But now, what Cassidy's family thought of her, it mattered. "Rose, I…"

Rose gently prodded the agent forward toward the kitchen. "Agent Toles," she said with a lighthearted sarcasm in her voice. "Cassie has never asked for my approval. She never had to. Neither do you."

"What took you two so long?" Cassidy asked with mock annoyance as Agent Fallon unpacked cartons of Chinese food on the table behind her.

"Well," her mother said, "perhaps if you traveled a bit lighter…"

Cassidy poked at her cheek with her tongue. "Very funny," she quipped at her mother. "I am watching you two," she pointed at them with a kidding sense of caution.

Alex laughed a bit and headed for the table. Dylan was opening the tops of the containers and peering into each curiously, one by one. "Chicken fingers!" He exclaimed.

"Good call," Alex said to her partner.

"Yeah…I do have three kids, Toles."

The group took their seats and enjoyed some lighthearted laughter over their dinner. As the cartons began to empty, Dylan looked at Alex. "Alex, can we go play pool?" The basement rec room had a large pool table in it and it was the most intriguing thing the boy had noticed on his exploration of the house.

Cassidy noted that Alex was searching for an answer. "Dylan, I think Alex and Mr. Fallon have some things to do." She glanced at Alex. Alex smiled, looking into Cassidy's eyes. She felt as though the world disappeared every time Cassidy looked at her. She really did need to talk to Fallon, but in this moment she made the decision that there was something more important at stake, at least tonight. Dylan had been through a great deal the last two days and so had his mother. She needed to keep them safe and she suddenly understood that meant more than just protecting them from physical harm. Rose caught the expression passing between her daughter and the agent and smiled. The agent turned to Dylan. "Actually, I do have to talk to Agent Fallon." Dylan looked down at his plate in disappointment. "BUT…Fallon here, he thinks he's quite the master at pool. I think we should prove him wrong." Dylan looked up at her with a hopeful glance. "So, why don't you help your mom and your grandma clean this up, get your pajamas on….and you and me, we'll teach Fallon here a few things before bed. What do you say?" He nodded with excitement.

Cassidy looked at Alex, stunned and moved by the gesture. There was no doubt in the teacher's mind that there had been a greater purpose than dinner to Fallon's visit; after all he had his own family waiting for him. She didn't even think as she looked into the agent's eyes and mouthed the words, "I love you." Alex forgot anyone was even there as a smile swept across her face; the exchange noticed by all.

"All right, Dylan," Rose grabbed her plate. "Let's get this mess cleaned up."

Alex snapped out of her haze and was surprised that the public affection she had just shared with Cassidy did not bother her. She touched Fallon on the arm and the pair headed for the study. "See you in a few, Speed Racer," she said. The boy nodded and picked up some napkins running for the garbage.

Cassidy met Rose at the sink. "Oh just say it," the younger woman looked at her mother. Rose just smiled. "I know you want to say *something*."

"No, Cassie, I just want you to be happy."

Cassidy turned to her mother with a tear in her eye. "I am."

Rose put her hand on her daughter's cheek. "Then hold onto her," she said before returning to the dishes.

"I will."

***

Alex took the stack of files and opened the top one. "Anything stick out at you?"

"Not immediately…but it is strange, Toles."

"What's that?" Alex said, peeling her eyes off the paper in front of her and looking upwards at the sound of Dylan's laughter upstairs. She couldn't help but shake her head with a smile. She loved the boy as much as she loved his mother.

Fallon sighed. "We can talk about it tomorrow."

"I'm sorry, Fallon," the agent said. "It's just…he was so upset last night. He climbed in bed with us." Fallon's eyes became as wide as saucers. Seeing his expression, Alex let out an animated guffaw. "I didn't *sleep* with her," the agent continued to laugh.

The sound of small footsteps trampling the floor caught the attention of both agents. "I think," Brian Fallon said to his friend, "that I should teach you who the senior agent is on the pool table. We can talk about this in the morning." Alex was grateful for his understanding and for his friendship. She nodded and the pair began the short trek to meet the rest of the group in the basement.

"Hold on," Alex put up a finger and scurried into the kitchen emerging with a small step stool she had noticed during dinner. "He's gotta' be able to reach," she said as the pair headed down the stairs. Brian Fallon shook his head. Alex Toles suddenly had a family. He never thought he'd see that. "All right, Speed Racer!" Alex put the stool down next to the pool table and Dylan hopped up from his position between his mother and grandmother on the large leather sofa a few feet away. Cassidy watched as Alex helped the boy pick out a cue stick, showed him how to use the chalk and stood behind him, instructing him on how to hold the stick that was just as tall as he was. Dylan listened intently to all of the agent's directions, nodding his understanding and concentrating as hard as his young mind would allow as they stepped to the table.

"You guys break," Agent Fallon offered.

"Okay...that's us, Speed Racer."

Dylan looked at the agent. "Will you help?" he whispered.

Alex smiled. Dylan melted her heart every bit as much as his mother did. She silently winked and picked him up to put him on the stool. Cassidy and Rose watched as the tall, commanding woman at the billiard table gently placed her hands over the boy's. She spoke softly to him as she helped him guide the stick back and forth. "Keep your eyes on that pack of balls, okay?" He nodded. "Now, feel the stick as it moves. Take your time." There was no question that it was Alex's strength behind the sound that erupted as the balls traveled across the table, leaving Dylan elated.

The game continued the same way. Fallon would deliberately set up an easy shot for the boy and Alex would help him sink the ball in the pocket. Then her partner would make a couple of shots before missing another deliberately. Rose watched Cassidy nearly as much as she did the game unfolding across the room. She had never seen such lightness about her daughter. There was no doubt in Rose McCollum's mind as she watched her grandson high five the beautiful dark haired woman he clearly adored, her daughter had finally found what she'd always been missing, a complete family. "Okay...time for BED!" Rose called over to Dylan.

Fallon shook the boy's hand and then winked at Toles. "I gotta' go...Kate's gonna' kill me!"

"I'll walk you out."

"Nah...you need to stay here and practice," he joked. "I expect a rematch."

The boy's mother moved to scoop up Dylan and Rose stopped her with her hand. "I've got him," she said. Cassidy looked at her mother. "I think maybe Dylan will stay in *my* room tonight." Rose raised an eyebrow at her daughter. Cassidy was used to her mother's way, but she felt a bit embarrassed, suddenly realizing her mother's agenda and her face flushed.

"Cassie," her mother whispered, "I wasn't born yesterday.....
say goodnight to your son and go spend some time with Alex."

Cassidy kissed Dylan goodnight. "Love you."

"Love you too, Mom," he kissed her back on the cheek.

His mother watched as he clung to the beautiful woman
that she could not keep her eyes off of. "Night, Speed Racer,"
Alex said. "Sleep well."

He looked up at her and pulled her down to him repeating
the affectionate gesture he had shown his mother. "Love you,
Alex," he said to her.

Alex felt a tear form in her eye. "Love you too, Speed Racer."
Rose followed the boy out of the room and turned back to the
two women behind her. She said nothing, just offered them a
loving smile.

***

Cassidy was suddenly very nervous. She had been thinking
about being alone with Alex all day. No one had ever made
her feel the way that Alex Toles did. She knew that Alex loved
her. She could feel it through her entire being. When they
kissed she felt as though the world fell away from them and
she longed to be closer to the woman, to feel Alex touch her
and know what it was like to be loved completely by her. At the
same time she was terrified. Alex was strong and confident. She
was also experienced in ways that the small blonde woman was
afraid to imagine. How on earth could she possibly measure
up? She would have been shocked had she known that across
the room, the woman she viewed as the picture of assuredness
was quivering inside.

Alex held her breath for a moment looking at the beautiful
woman just a few feet away. She had imagined over the last few
days that when all of this was over, she would take Cassidy away
somewhere, maybe by the ocean again, a room that looked out
over the water. She would open a bottle of wine and spend a

quiet evening with the woman who had unexpectedly captured her heart before gently taking her to a new place, someplace Alex longed to travel. That was not going to happen. About the only thing she could take from that scenario now was a good bottle of wine. The two stayed still, waiting for the other to move. Alex lightly rubbed her eyebrow. This was awkward. She did not expect their first time to be so soon and she did not want the first time she made love to Cassidy to be awkward. Everything else in their relationship seemed to flow so naturally. "How about a glass of wine?"

"Sounds good. How about you teach *me* to play pool?" Alex was behind the bar opening the wine fridge. She was surprised at the suggestion, but it would be a welcome diversion for a while.

"You don't play pool?" Alex asked as she opened a bottle of Chardonnay and poured two glasses.

"No." Cassidy took a seat on the other side of the bar and accepted the glass. "I always wanted to learn." She had tried a few times in college when she and Chris would go out but he liked to tease her and show off so she stopped being a participant and became a spectator.

Alex took a sip of her wine and moved around the bar. Cassidy took another large sip from her own glass and watched as Alex re-racked the pool balls on the table. The agent's hands began to tremble as she picked up a pool cue and the teacher made her way over, accepting it with a longing gaze into the agent's eyes. "First," Alex began, "you have to learn how to hold the cue." She stepped behind the smaller woman and positioned the long stick in her hands. Cassidy felt the agent's body press up against her. Alex leaned into the teacher and whispered her instructions. "Feel the weight of the stick," she placed her hands over Cassidy's and Cassidy closed her eyes at the sensation of Alex's breath on her neck. The agent gently guided the stick back and forth and Cassidy became unsteady by the overwhelming sensations their physical contact brought on. Alex instinctively dropped a hand to Cassidy's hip in an attempt to steady her, but the smaller woman took her by surprise, dropping the stick and turning in the agent's embrace. Cassidy looked up at Alex who was instantly entranced by the green eyes searching hers. The agent gently moved to touch the smaller woman's cheek and silently bent over for their lips to meet.

Alex felt Cassidy's fingers press into her side as their kiss deepened and the agent lost her senses. She moved her kiss to the woman's neck and heard Cassidy sigh her name aloud. It sent a jolt through her body unlike any she had ever felt and she moved to meet the blonde's lips again. Cassidy's breath was shallow and Alex was ready to lift her onto the pool table when their eyes met again. The agent closed her eyes and sighed. She was lost in the moment, and had this been any other woman she would have taken Cassidy right there. But, it *was* Cassidy. Cassidy caught her breath and looked deeply into Alex's eyes. It reminded the teacher a bit of the night before when Alex had insisted they stop and she was suddenly fearful. "Alex…"

"Cass…I just want this to be…"

Cassidy closed her eyes and inhaled. "Alex…"

"Please, just…let's just go upstairs…please." Alex stroked the woman's long blonde hair. "Just go up to your room…I will be right behind you. I promise."

"Alex…I'm so…"

Alex knew what the teacher wanted to say. She understood that this was not only their first time with one another, it was Cassidy's in many ways. That was all the more reason that she wanted to be certain the woman in her arms understood that this meant everything to Alex. It did. The agent knew that the stops and starts were difficult for them both. She also knew that within a short time everything would change between them. Feeling Cassidy as she did now, she had no doubt that making love to the woman would mean the complete surrender of her soul. "Cass… not here…just trust me."

"It doesn't have to be perfect, Alex." Cassidy felt the butter-flies in her stomach swarming. She was so self-conscious about the prospect of being intimate with the agent, and at the same time she desired Alex in a way that she had never experienced. She was afraid of disappointing the woman who held her now; afraid that in spite of the fact that Alex loved her; maybe she would not be enough.

"Cassidy, you are worth far more to me than a lustful spin on a pool table. Not here." She kissed the woman gently. "I will be right behind you. I want to be where I can wake up beside you."

The smaller woman reached up to the agent and caressed her cheek. Those were the words she needed to hear. "Don't take too long," she whispered tearing herself reluctantly from the agent's embrace and moving out of the room.

Alex sighed and closed her eyes as the woman walked out. "God help me, I love you," she said as she grabbed the bottle of wine and the glasses.

"I love you too," a voice called back. Alex smiled. It might be a long night.

Chapter Eleven

C assidy was thankful to have a few minutes to pull herself together both emotionally and physically. She had no way of knowing when she packed to leave for Washington that this would be happening here and now. She rummaged through her bag on the bathroom floor wishing she had something appropriate for the occasion. She looked in the mirror and laughed at her own silent admission; she felt like a teenager. She wanted to take the agent's breath away like no one ever had. She shook her head disbelieving that she was actually touching up her makeup and refreshing her perfume. This was an unfamiliar routine and not something she would have imagined in her wildest dreams a few days ago. She smiled and closed her eyes as the memory of Alex standing at her front door passed through her thoughts. Her nervousness was rivaled only by the incredible sense of how much she was in love with Alex Toles. She chuckled softly as the question entered her mind for the first time. "Oh my God; am I a lesbian?" She chuckled again and shrugged in amusement. The lipstick in her hand fluttered when she heard the bedroom door close. True to her word, the agent was close behind her. Her amusement at the situation changed suddenly to palpable anticipation. She continued her tasks wondering what the sounds outside the door were.

The bedroom was large and it was elegantly decorated. Alex stopped to place the bottle of wine and the two glasses on a bedside table. There was a large four poster bed adorned by a beautiful white and blue quilt. The agent smiled noticing that all of the artwork on the walls depicted the ocean. Perhaps this wasn't as far from what she had imagined as she initially feared. In the corner was a gas fireplace. The agent crossed the room and started the flame. She turned off the other lights, allowing the glow from the fire to create a soft light that filled the room. There was a large cabinet across from the bed. She opened it and found the flat screen television inside. She clicked the mute button while she searched for the music channels, finally finding one she thought was appropriate and increased the volume to a low but audible hum. The agent took a deep breath and looked at her clothes. She was wearing jeans and a white blouse; her signature attire when she was not at the office but expecting to be away from home. "Shit," she groaned, wondering how she must look and feeling the need somehow to impress Cassidy. She pulled the elastic from her hair and ran her hands through it, imagining what the woman behind the closed door was doing. She felt her body trembling, picturing the expression on Cassidy's face just moments ago as they looked into one another's eyes.

Cassidy heard the sound of soft music emanating from the other room. She had decided that she would at least attempt to entice the agent in some unexpected way. She feared that Alex might view her inexperience as unattractive somehow and she wanted the agent to desire her. She took in a nervous breath and tugged on the oversized denim shirt she had put on. After another moment of attempting to calm her increasing jitters, she looked in the mirror a final time hoping that her efforts would be appreciated by the woman outside. She closed her eyes, inhaled a breath for courage and opened the door. Alex Toles turned as the sound of the opening door carried through the small room. There she was, Cassidy O'Brien. The agent felt her heart jump inside her body but she could not move. The sight of Cassidy in the denim shirt that fell just to her mid-thigh and buttoned just below the line of her cleavage was the sexiest thing Alex had ever seen. If the teacher had worried that any woman might rival her in the agent's eyes, those fears had been vacant and unnecessary. The woman's blonde hair fell gently to the front of her right shoulder and slightly behind her left. The glow of the orange and yellow flames further softened her feminine features. Alex fought to swallow. The agent labored to take a full breath and stepped toward the woman who was slowly walking toward her. "You are beautiful," the agent said as her eyes traveled the full length of Cassidy's body.

Cassidy thought that her knees might give way as she moved closer to agent. Alex's hair fell softly on her shoulders, framing her face perfectly. She was the most incredible vision Cassidy had ever seen. Since they first met the teacher had found Alex attractive and marveled at her body and the blue eyes that at times seemed to dance. But now, here in the firelight, the way that Alex was looking at her, the light that was cast on her skin, Cassidy was certain she had never been so riveted by any person. She reached the agent who looked deeply into her eyes. They stood impossibly close and impossibly still for what seemed like many minutes until finally Cassidy reached out and touched the opening of Alex's blouse.

The agent felt the slight brush of the woman's hand connect with her skin and she trembled. Cassidy was completely enraptured by the way the fire highlighted the opening in the agent's shirt, barely revealing her skin. The smaller woman looked up to see that the blue eyes she searched for now had closed at the slightest touch from her. Alex took in a breath and opened her eyes to meet the shimmering green searching for hers. Her hand brushed Cassidy's blonde hair aside and she whispered softly to her as she moved her lips closer, "I am so in love with you."

The smaller woman reached up and pulled the agent closer. "Alex, I need you," she confessed. The agent felt her heart quicken and her hand continued to tremble as it reached slowly for the opening of the denim shirt. She let her hand softly travel along the opening, feeling just enough of the woman in front of her to send a pulse throughout her entire body. Finally, the agent pressed her lips to the other woman's. Slowly and gently their lips began to part and Alex lightly brushed Cassidy's tongue with her own. She felt the woman's desire as Cassidy began to deepen the kiss, still soft but her tongue searching with more urgency. Alex tried to breathe. She felt the teacher's soft caress travel the length of her back. Cassidy's touch was so gentle and so loving. The agent lowered her kiss to the woman's neck. She gently kissed every inch, longing with each soft kiss to continue her journey. "Alex..." the woman sighed, "I love you."

The agent smiled and inhaled the words into her soul. She took the smaller woman's hand silently and led her to the bed. Again she lowered herself to accept Cassidy's lips to her own. She had no words as she guided the beautiful woman she loved so deeply onto the bed, taking a position over her and returning her lips to the softest she had ever tasted. Again she moved to Cassidy's neck, soliciting a soft moan. Alex pulled away slightly looking down at the woman underneath her and marveling at her beauty. The agent's eyes began a loving dance as they whispered her desire silently to the woman she loved. Her hand carefully moved to the buttons on the denim shirt. Slowly she released them, returning her kiss to Cassidy's waiting lips and stopping only to allow her kiss to follow the trail her hands had left behind. She pushed the shirt gently open, revealing to her for the first time the full sight of the woman who held her heart. Alex drank in the sight, and Cassidy was overcome with emotion as she witnessed the expression in her lover's eyes. "You are the most beautiful woman I have ever seen," the agent said as she trembled from her own desire.

Cassidy reached for the buttons on the agent's blouse. Alex was surprised at the deliberate and confident way the woman addressed them. The small blonde's fears evaporated as her thoughts became consumed by her desire for the strong and sexy woman above her. She reached the last button and pulled the blouse open, instantly losing her breath at the sight of Alex's breasts. The agent smiled slightly with satisfaction feeling her lover's desire increase. She lowered herself again and kissed Cassidy. Her kiss was passionate and more demanding now but it remained incredibly gentle. Her lips trailed over Cassidy's body, discovering on their journey the places that seemed to solicit the desired response. The agent's hands made their way along the woman's curves as her kiss finally reached the soft breast that she so longed to taste. She looked to Cassidy for permission, but the teacher had closed her eyes feeling the agent's warm breath wash over her. "Alex...please," Cassidy asked her lover. It was the only permission the agent required to continue.

The sensation that traveled through Cassidy's entire body as she felt the agent's tongue dance across her, gently and firmly reminded her that Alex loved her. Alex felt Cassidy's body as it relaxed underneath her, their skin touching. She moved her other hand to Cassidy's lips, lovingly caressing them with her finger tip. Cassidy kissed the hand that touched her and the agent felt a warm rush run through her. Alex caught her breath as she witnessed the expression of ecstasy that swept across the beautiful face resting just slightly above her own. The music played softly in the background and Alex felt her own body begin to glide against the woman she loved in time to its slow and sensual beat. Her breathing became more rapid and she could see the pounding of Cassidy's heart as she covered the woman's chest with a trail of light kisses. Her hand very sensually caressed her lover's hip and worked its way intentionally lower, tenderly exploring the place she longed to travel. Cassidy gasped at Alex's touch and the strong agent pulled herself over the blonde woman again. She removed her touch and coaxed the woman's eyes open with a kiss on her forehead. Cassidy looked into her lover's eyes with a knowing smile, understanding completely what the agent wished to ask her now. "Alex..."

"You know…I've fallen in love with you, Cassidy," Alex said looking into her lover's eyes as a tear washed over her cheek. The agent had never experienced anything close to what coursed through her now. Every inch of her felt Cassidy running through it. Her desire to make love to the woman was soulful. As Cassidy looked at her and raised her hand to gently wipe away the agent's tear, Alex knew she was looking at the rest of her life before her. Right now she wanted to show Cassidy. She wanted the woman who held her soul to understand in the one way that no words or glances could ever completely convey that she would love her completely and forever.

"I know, Alex." Cassidy wiped another tear away from the Alex's cheek, now understanding that Alex Toles was truly and deeply in love with her. She captured the agent's lips and allowed her hand to begin to explore the form above her. Instinctively she moved her kiss over Alex's neck and pulled herself up to allow her tongue to lightly trail across the woman's chest. Alex closed her eyes and fought to catch her breath as she felt the Cassidy's soft kiss make its way to her breast.

"Cass…" Alex barely managed to speak. Cassidy was completely lost to her own desire now. As the agent responded to her touch, she was amazed at how naturally they moved together, as if perfectly in sync with the music, the flames, and the other person's needs. Alex lifted the woman's face back to her own and kissed her slowly. The agent's kiss left the teacher's lips and continued across every inch of her body; her neck, her shoulders, her chest, her stomach. She stopped and moved her hands to grasp Cassidy's as her exploration finally reached its intended destination. She heard Cassidy sigh and felt the smaller woman's body respond by rising to meet her touch.

Cassidy could swear that light suddenly filled the entire room as she let out a sigh filled with the sound of Alex's name. Her body was trembling so hard from Alex's tender exploration that she became dizzy from the loss of breath. She held onto Alex's hands tightly as she felt her body lose control. "Please…

Alex…" Alex's kisses and touch became more insistent as the words fell from her lover. Cassidy felt as if she were being gently pounded over and over by rising waves that increasingly began to carry her away. As it seemed to be with everything about Alex Toles, when Cassidy could no longer hold back and the sensations that coursed through her caused her body to shudder, her emotions followed suit, continuing to travel through every inch of her body until they took up residence in her soul. "Alex," she called through her release. Alex slowly and gently kissed every inch of her lover's body again. Releasing her grasp on the agent's hands, Cassidy tenderly touched the agent's back and slowly reached for the agent's face to guide it back to her own, needing to see Alex and look into her eyes.

"Cass, I love you…I love you," the agent repeated over and over, seeming to be as overwhelmed by the experience as the teacher was.

Tears fell now from Cassidy's eyes as she searched the blue ones above her, telling her everything she needed to know. "Don't let me go," Cassidy said to the woman who brushed the hair from her face and kissed her forehead.

"Never," Alex said as she laid down beside the woman she had just made love to and pulled her close.

Cassidy's head came to rest on the agent's chest and her finger very lightly danced across the agent's skin. The smaller woman remained quiet for a moment allowing her breath to slowly return before deliberately positioning herself above the beautiful woman that held her. Alex swallowed hard as Cassidy kissed her softly and then moved to whisper in her ear. "I will never let you go, Alex Toles," she said kissing the woman's neck and gently capturing her ear between her teeth for a moment.

Alex thought she might lose consciousness as Cassidy confidently took command and allowed her kisses to explore every inch of the agent's body. The woman above her was soft in every way. The feel of Cassidy's skin against hers, the way she kissed the agent so tenderly and the way her hands lightly caressed Alex's body; no one had ever made love to Alex before; not like this. Cassidy tenderly communicated in every touch the love that she held for the agent. When Alex felt Cassidy begin to move her kisses over her stomach she jumped, suddenly terrified by both her desire and a worry that her new lover might feel obligated. She sat nearly straight up and was astonished by the understanding smile on the blonde's face.

Cassidy gently pressed on the agent's shoulder and laid her back on the bed, hovering above her and looking into her eyes. "Cass…you don't have to…"

Cassidy raised her eyebrow and smiled again capturing the agent's lips in the most loving kiss Alex had ever known. "Let me love you," Cassidy said stroking the agent's cheek. Alex's breath was ragged as she closed her eyes signifying her permission to continue. Cassidy kissed her gently and whispered again, "I've fallen in love with you too, Alex." Slowly the agent relaxed as Cassidy took her time, again exploring every inch of Alex before finally beginning to take the agent as her own. Alex looked down at Cassidy and sighed. Cassidy was the gentlest soul she had ever known and that was evident in every touch, the way her tongue danced over Alex, the way her hands lovingly searched for the agent's. Alex released her breath as their fingers interlocked. She struggled to let go and Cassidy sensed her anxiety, knowing that Alex's concern was for her. She held Alex's hand tighter to reassure her and the agent finally gave over. Her body twitched uncontrollably and she felt every muscle pulse with desire. "Cass…." She gasped for air and her tears fell freely. She felt as if her body was being lifted by the energy running through it. Emotions and an incredibly gentle but overwhelming pounding seemed to crash over her until her body had no choice but to submit fully, her heart a willing partner. She sighed as her lover's grip softened. Cassidy pulled her hand away and slowly lifted herself to a position above the agent. Green eyes sparkled as they gazed at the agent now, in spite of cheeks that were stained by tears. Making love to Alex, feeling her let go completely had overpowered Cassidy with a surge of her own emotions. Alex caressed the woman's cheek and pulled her close. Neither could seem to speak as they lay silently caressing one another; a reminder that this was a sacred place to them both. After a long period of silence Alex spoke, gently stroking Cassidy's arm. "I never..." She stopped, feeling a growing lump in her throat at the admission she was about to make.

"What?" Cassidy asked quietly kissing the skin beneath her.

"Made love....and, Cass...I..."

Cassidy pulled herself up and looked at Alex, immediately understanding the agent's reluctance to allow Cassidy to make love to her. The smaller woman smiled and kissed her lover. "Alex, I never had anyone make love to me before either...not like this, and never...well..."

Alex smiled. Every experience with Cassidy was new. As Cassidy collapsed back into her position within the loving embrace of the agent, Alex sighed. "Cassidy?"

"Hum?"

"I think....I want to be with you forever," Alex choked a bit on her words.

Cassidy smiled. "I'll hold you to that."

***

Alex lay on her side silently watching the woman next to her sleep. The sun was just beginning to peek through the tiny slits in the blinds and the light caressed the beautiful face that Alex could not stop gazing at. She reached her hand out and brushed the hair from the woman's eyes. Slowly she bent over the woman's face and kissed her forehead, allowing her lips to linger there for a long moment. Cassidy shifted a bit and her short set of blinks turned to a sleepy squint. "Morning," the agent said softly.

Cassidy took a deep breath, closing her eyes and releasing it with contentment. She felt Alex next to her and sighed again. "You're here," she whispered.

"I told you I wanted to wake up beside you," the agent said as she continued gently caressing the woman that she loved. Finally, Cassidy opened her eyes. There was an expression in them that piqued the agent's curiosity. It was loving, not lustful, but there was something more this morning that they seemed to convey. The teacher closed her eyes and gently tugged on her bottom lip with her teeth. "What is it?" Alex asked gently.

Cassidy opened her eyes and touched the beautiful face before her. Alex repeated the question. Her new lover sighed and fought to summon words. "I just…"

"Cass…"

"Alex…I don't want to say something that will…"

"Will what?" Alex asked. Cassidy continued to caress the woman's cheek. "Cassidy, you can say anything to me."

The blonde woman smiled and her eyes began to twinkle as a hint of the sun struck them. "How can I know that …I just know…this is…"

Alex smiled, "I know…I don't want to explain it. It is, Cass… it just is." She kissed the woman and smiled.

"Forever's a long time, you know?" the teacher smirked.

"Might be for you," Alex joked, poking fun at herself.

"Oh…I think I'll manage," Cassidy quipped back. The mood was still full of emotion but noticeably lighter.

"Mmmm…I will remember you said that." The agent rolled over and began to toss the sheets aside when she felt an insistent grasp pulling her back.

Cassidy ran her hand over the woman's strong, lower back. "Alex, what is this?" she asked noticing the long scar that ran across the agent's lower back as she gracefully and tenderly stroked it.

"Just an old injury." She started to pull away again and Cassidy grasped her firmly. Seeing the raise of the eyebrow and the way her lover's gaze had narrowed, Alex knew her off handed explanation was not going to fly. "It's nothing."

"Oh…and I suppose it had nothing to do with that episode the other day either?"

Alex almost laughed. How Cassidy was able to put all the pieces together where Alex was concerned she didn't know. If she had entertained any doubts that somehow this woman simply understood her, last night had completely removed them. "It happened when I was overseas. An IED attack. I got hit with some large shrapnel." Cassidy's hand fell on the agent's leg and she gently ran her fingers over it as she listened intently, encouraging her to continue. Alex looked at her reassuringly. "I'm fine, Cass, it's a scar…it was a long time ago." The teacher's skepticism was well placed. The agent was not in any danger from her old injury but Cassidy's observation was correct, some of the damage had been permanent. Had it not been for her good friend, John Merrow, she would never have gotten the full waiver for the FBI. Alex smiled, "it tore through all of my muscles and damaged two vertebra…. and my spleen. It's okay, just acts up sometimes." She kissed Cassidy who knew there was more to the story and that the story would have to wait.

The teacher watched as the agent got up and grabbed her clothes. "Are you leaving?"

Alex was getting dressed. "I need to go shower and get to the office."

"Alex?"

"Yeah?"

"I am taking Dylan to see Chris today." Alex turned with concern. The congressman was still in an out of consciousness with heavy swelling in his brain. His room was a conglomeration of tubes and monitors, an unsettling sight for an adult, never mind a six year old boy. The teacher saw the very parental protectiveness in the agent's eyes. Alex was finishing buttoning her shirt and Cassidy patted the bed for her to sit.

Alex's expression showed concern mixed with a hint of fear as she sat down.

"Cass…Are you sure you, I mean Dylan might…"

Cassidy put her hand over Alex's. "Do you have any idea how much I love you?"

"What?"

Cassidy smiled. "Alex, if anything…if Chris doesn't make it; Dylan needs to see his father." Alex sighed. It was true and the fact was that the congressman was still Cassidy and Dylan's family.

"You're right. I just know he might get scared."

"Yeah…Alex…"

"Yeah?"

"Can you take us? I know you have to work, but later? It won't be along visit." Alex looked at Cassidy with genuine surprise. She would have expected that one of the Secret Service agents assigned to the congressman would pick them up. "Dylan loves you, you know?" Cassidy said. Alex loved Dylan, but she wasn't certain it was her place. "I need you there, Alex…just to know you're there and so does Dylan."

Alex Toles swallowed hard. "I don't know about all of that, but of course I will take you. I just don't want to…"

Cassidy sat up, the sheets falling from her and Alex lost her breath. The teacher raised her brow. "You listen to me, Agent Alex Toles….You said you'd never let me go and I intend to hold you to that. You are not an intrusion in my life." She stopped, wondering if she should continue. Looking at Alex, she couldn't help but allow the words to pass, "you are my life."

Alex was absolutely blown over by the woman's honest and plain admission. She kissed Cassidy on the forehead. "I'll pick you up around three." The teacher smiled, knowing by Alex's unflinching reaction that she felt an equal gravity in their connection. Alex looked at her now with a slight gleam in her eye, the sheets at Cassidy's waist as she sat. "You are beautiful," the agent sighed receiving an appreciative grin in return. Alex put her hand on the door and turned back, "I love you, Cass."

Cassidy pulled the sheets back up and laid back down. "I love you too, Alfred."

***

Agent Brian Fallon was at his desk sipping a cup of coffee when his partner entered. "You drinking that sludge we get here?" Alex asked jokingly.

"It works."

"Yeah. What do you say that you and I got get some REAL coffee?"

Fallon closed the file on his desk. They could not speak freely in the office, not about everything. The pair headed down the street to a small coffee shop and Alex ordered them two coffees while her partner grabbed a corner table. "So, you started to tell me something last night?" Alex asked.

"Yeah...how was *your* night?" Fallon poked, noticing the bounce in his partner's step.

"My night was fine, Fallon; yours?"

"Mhmmm."

"So..." Alex implored, changing the subject.

"Okay...look...there's no FBI file on that photographer, Fisher?"

"That's impossible. It's standard procedure to complete a work up on congressional staff," Alex replied in disbelief.

"Yeah...well, standard or not...it ain't there." Alex rubbed her temples. "You think he's the stalker?"

"I don't know...I didn't really think anything until right now," she paused in deep thought. "Fallon? What if there WAS a file...I mean at one time. How hard would it be to find that out?"

Fallon groaned. "Depends, I guess.....You mean like, if someone destroyed the file?" Alex raised an eyebrow. "Why would anyone do that?"

"Why would anyone send fake letters to the congressman? Why would someone change street lights, edit traffic cam footage? Christ, Fallon, that's the question right? I mean if we find out why, maybe we find the 'who'....If we find the 'who', maybe we find out why." Fallon rolled his eyes. "It's call investigation, Fallon, it's what we get paid to do," Alex said sarcastically.

"Oh you're a regular comedian today, aren't you?"

Alex started to speak when she felt a hand on her shoulder and noticed Fallon looking deeply into his coffee. "Agent Toles....nice to see you back in Washington."

Alex turned. "Brackett," she acknowledged coolly.

"Oh, come on...you're not still mad at me are you?"

"Actually, no...just disgusted," Alex replied.

"Toles...come on...let's kiss and make up," the redheaded agent half kidded and half flirted.

Alex flashed a fake smile onto her expression of obvious disdain. "What do you want, Brackett?"

The tall redhead pulled up a chair. "Just to say I'm sorry."

"Okay. You said it," Alex replied as Fallon sipped his coffee silently.

"Geez...she always this touchy, Fallon? Look, Toles...how was I supposed to know you were diddling the congressman's wife? I mean not that we were exclusive...but why would I think that?"

Alex's jaw visibly tightened. *Diddling?* Fallon pulled at his eyebrow fearing his partner might literally throttle the rookie. "Brackett...the point is that there is a certain decorum we use when we are on a case."

"MMM....like sleeping with the victim?" Alex shot her another look of repulsion. "Oh come on, I'm just kidding...ease up already....no hard feelings...How *is* Mrs. O'Brien? Any leads?"

Alex's gaze narrowed. "She's fine, and we're actively working a few possibilities. Thank you for your concern."

"Well....my only concern is to be certain that you accept my apology. If I can help at all, you let me know. It would be awful if anything happened to the poor woman now…with the congressman and all…and that adorable…"

Agent Alex Toles had reached her limit, "nothing is going to happen to Cassidy or Dylan, Agent Brackett. Agent Fallon and I have things under control." Alex pushed out her chair and motioned to her partner.

"Well, just the same," Brackett remained in her seat.

"Have a nice day, Agent," Alex said dryly heading out the door.

"What the hell was THAT?" Fallon asked. "What the hell did you do with Brackett to get her that pissed?" Alex was silently rubbing her temple as they walked. "Toles?" Alex continued forward with no response. "ALEX!"

"What do you know about Agent Brackett?"

"No more than you…in fact I would have to say I know a whole LOT less than you," Fallon tried to make a joke.

"Funny. I don't know anything. Except that her first name is Claire and she's overanxious in bed. That's it; since you seem so curious," Alex's tone was sharp.

"Toles, she's just jealous."

"Yeah…why is she so curious about the case?"

"God, you are starting to be paranoid," Fallon said as he tossed his cup in a trash can.

"No…not starting…I am. See what you can find out about Fisher. I have someone I need to talk to."

***

The rookie stayed in her chair watching the pair walk away through the large window. She sipped on her latte with satisfaction. A large yellow envelope dropped over her shoulder and landed on the table. She unclasped it and pulled out the stack of photos. The man that slowly crouched to take a seat across the table smelled of booze and cigarettes. "What the hell is this?" she asked. He glared at her. "So, she's opening a trunk…

holding a door…who gives a shit? That was not the assignment." His scowl only increased. "You get me what I asked for…get closer…and do it soon." She pushed the envelope back at him.

He put the pictures carefully back into the envelope, stopping to notice his favorite. He held it for a long moment, staring at the blonde beauty in the photo. "Closer," he muttered.

***

Cassidy emerged from her shower feeling refreshed but already missing her new lover. It was a welcome feeling. She dried her hair with the towel and pulled the black sweater over her head. Voices were coming from the large kitchen and she entered to find Dylan coloring with a glass of juice next to him and her mother perusing the morning paper with her coffee. Cassidy smiled again, feeling the bounce in her step and grabbed herself a cup of coffee. "Gooood morning," Rose called from behind the paper.

"Morning," Cassidy answered making her way to the table.

"Sleep well?" Rose chided.

Cassidy smirked, "actually, Mom, I did. Thank you for asking."

"Yeah exercise does that," Rose joked, causing Cassidy to spit her coffee across the table and splatter Dylan's page.

"MOM!" Dylan yelled.

Cassidy stared blankly at her son. "Dylan," Rose said fighting off a fit of laughter. "Why don't you go put some cartoons on in the other room? You remember how?"

"Sure," he said picking up a Matchbox car from the end of the table and heading off, leaving his coffee stained picture behind.

"So?" Rose asked.

"I cannot believe you said that," Cassidy shook her head.

"Well, dear, you weren't exactly silent last night."

Cassidy choked again. "What?"

Rose laughed out loud. "Oh don't pay any attention to me. I'm just jealous."

"Mom! You didn't really hear us." Cassidy got up to get a towel. Rose looked into the paper smirking away. "No...you're just....Oh my God," the teacher continued to muse to herself as she wiped the coffee from the table.

"Oh Cassie, I'm just teasing you, but thank you for the confirmation," she winked.

"That was mean."

Rose smiled. "You look very happy, Cassie."

"Mom?"

"Mmmm?"

"I love her," Cassidy admitted.

"I know, dear."

"No, I mean I really..."

"Cassidy, I know," her mother cut her off.

"Do you think that's weird?" Cassidy asked.

"Why would I think it's weird?"

"Well, because...."

"Does it feel weird to you?"

"No." Cassidy answered definitively. "But you might think it is."

Rose tried not to giggle. "Cassidy, Alex is a beautiful, intelligent woman who loves you and your son. Why on earth would I think it was strange for you to love her? Because she's a woman?"

"Well...."

Rose rolled her eyes. "Well, Cassie, I can't speak for the rest of the world but I adore Alex. I certainly can understand what you see in her. So, no...not in the least."

"Mom?"

"What?"

"I love you."

"I know you do," Rose smiled.

"Thanks."

165

"Cassie, don't thank me too soon. You're on your own with Dylan tonight. He's a kicker." Cassidy laughed. It would be another long day but Alex would be part of it and so would Dylan and her mom. It was her family, strange as that seemed. It simply was.

Chapter Twelve

A lex walked down the long hallway and stood in front of the camera positioned over the door at the far end of the corridor. She held up her identification and waited for the click to turn the handle. Entering the room she was greeted immediately by a somewhat rotund man with a moustache and a receding hairline. "Captain Toles," he smiled.

"Michael...It's good to see you," she said. The man led her past several desks to a small office at the back of the long and narrow room. She entered and he closed the door behind them.

"I have to say, I was surprised to get your message. I would've expected you to call on the colonel."

Alex sighed. John Merrow would have been her first choice were it not for the political nature of the situation. Michael Taylor was her only other resource. She did not relish the idea of turning back to her NSA roots but Taylor and Merrow were about the only people she trusted implicitly. They had earned that very unique place many years earlier and the three had an unspoken understanding and bond that Alex Toles was grateful for. "I don't think it's wise to involve the president."

The man stroked his chin. "All right. You wouldn't be here without a good reason, Alex. What's going on?"

"I need a favor, Taylor."

"Okay..."

"I need two backgrounds...and I need it strictly between us," the agent explained.

"Name it."

"Claire Brackett, FBI and Carl Edward Fisher–preliminary says he is a Stanford grad, twenty-nine, from Santa Monica and working as a photographer."

The man looked at her curiously. "Not exactly what I would expect," he inquired. "Can I ask what this is about….I mean other than the O'Brien case?"

Alex took a deep breath. "Taylor," she paused. "I don't want to say much yet. It's a feeling…about Brackett anyway, and about this case. I'm sure there is more than one thing going on here."

"You haven't told me much about it, Toles," he reminded her. "That tells me almost everything I need to know."

Alex pinched the bridge of her nose. "Taylor…is there an open case on Congressman O'Brien?"

"Not that I'm aware of. Why?" Alex shook her head. Michael Taylor studied her expression. "Look, Toles," he continued. "Say no more."

Toles, Taylor and Merrow had all served in Iraq together; Merrow the colonel, Taylor her captain and Toles, at the time a lieutenant. They worked in and around Baghdad determining possible terrorist threats aimed at targeting both the troops and the states. Alex spoke seven languages; an ability attributed largely to her eidetic memory; a trait few realized she possessed. She was fluent in Arabic, Farsi and Kurdish as well as Spanish, French, Italian and Russian. The agent's ability to remember fine details and large bodies of information with ease often meant she saw pieces in a puzzle that others missed. That ability saved the lives of the three friends many years ago. It formed an unbreakable bond of trust that continued over the years. When Taylor took a leadership role at the NSA, Alex followed. Her decision to leave the NSA and take a job at the FBI was one Taylor initially resisted. But, in the last three years their respective positions had often become an asset to the other. Cooperation between investigative agencies was often more competitive than it was collegial. The ability to tap one another's knowledge and resources proved highly beneficial on more than one occasion.

"Toles?" Taylor began. "These letters, I looked at the files you sent me." Alex nodded, seeing immediately that her friend identified the same issues she had. "I'm curious, I can understand the photographer….Why the agent?"

Alex's jaw line became taught. "More than one thing. Cocky, too cocky for one. Rookies aren't that cocky." Her friend leaned back in his chair knowing it was more than that. "All right…a couple of weeks ago I noticed an envelope on her coffee table. The handwriting looked just like the ones that came to the congressman's office. I didn't get a close look."

"You think she's a spook?" Alex shrugged. "All right. I'll see what I can find." Alex rose to head to the door. "Toles… whatever you're into here…just be careful."

The agent stopped. "Taylor…nothing to John for now; okay?" He nodded his agreement.

"Alex," he said. "I don't want to pry, but her coffee table?" He smirked.

Alex laughed. Taylor was well aware of his friend's conquests. "It wasn't anything, believe me," her eyes sparkled a bit as the congressman's ex-wife entered her mind momentarily.

"Really?"

Alex shook her head knowing her friend could read her fairly well after so many years. "Conversation for another time, Taylor."

The man smiled, "I'll look forward to THAT."

"I'm sure you will, Taylor. Thanks," Agent Toles said earnestly.

"Anytime, Captain. Sorry, but Agent just doesn't sound right to me," he winked. "I'll be in touch."

***

"Thanks, Fallon...Do me a favor, let me know when you finish talking to those witnesses.....yeah.....I have to go...I will..... no....pick me up at the townhouse in the morning....yeah that works. Thanks." Alex hung up with her partner and looked at the front door of the large townhouse. She put her face in her hands and tried to rub out the realities from her day. The case was preoccupying her thoughts now. There were a lot of puzzle pieces on the table and she was certain they all fit together somehow. If she could just get the frame done, then maybe she could see the whole picture. She was still worried about Cassidy but she felt a sense of relief having Taylor in the loop. Fallon was a terrific agent, better than she often gave him credit for, but Taylor was a literal genius and he knew how to maneuver red tape like no one Alex had ever met, not even the president.

Alex's NSA background was classified, and for good reason. It was not something that either her partner or A.D. Tate had any knowledge of. As she took a deep breath and tried to quiet her thoughts she found herself wondering when she would declassify her life to the woman that waited for her inside. It was strange. There was no question of *if*, it was only a matter of when. That was one way she knew that she wanted to hold on to Cassidy O'Brien. Alex exhaled her thoughts as she transitioned her mind to the people awaiting her inside; people she had grown to love more than her heart could fathom in such a short time.

Cassidy was on her cell phone when Alex walked into the spacious living room. "Yeah...no...I'll be back on Monday....I appreciate that but it isn't necessary....No.....I'm sure. I emailed the lesson plan...Just please ask that the sub hands it out....yes...thanks." Alex leaned up against the doorway and listened. The conversation she overheard was just one more reason that she loved Cassidy. The blonde woman turned to catch the agent observing her with obvious admiration. "How long have you been there?" she asked. Alex just smiled. "What?" Cassidy asked, puzzled by the agent's continuing silent gaze.

"I guess I just missed you," she said in a warm, soft whisper. Cassidy seemed to transform the commanding presence of the FBI agent immediately into that of a gushing teenager.

"Is that right?" The teacher raised an eyebrow. "Well, I guess it's a good thing you are home then, isn't it?" Alex felt a sense of lightness overtake her body. It was an innocent statement from the woman but it held something within it that resonated for the agent in an immeasurable way, *home.* Cassidy walked to the agent and kissed her on the cheek. "I missed you too," she whispered.

Alex planted a light kiss on the woman's lips and smiled, looking into her eyes. "Aahheeem," a voice interrupted, flushing the agent's cheeks into at least fifty shades of crimson.

"Yes, Mom," Cassidy answered giving an encouraging caress of her thumb to the agent's blushing cheek.

"Your son does not want to leave that pool table. He's down there lining balls up over and over again and he refuses to get his shoes on," Rose said to her daughter before turning to the agent with a deliberate smirk. "Oh. Hello, Alex." The agent smiled sheepishly and Cassidy chuckled knowing her mother was deriving great pleasure in the agent's embarrassment.

"You have created a monster," Cassidy joked to the agent.

"What?" Alex asked innocently.

"He's been down there all afternoon going on and on about how Alex said where to look at the ball and Alex said hold the stick this way....and Alex..."

Alex sighed, "I'll get him."

"Good luck with that, Agent," Rose laughed. Alex nodded and made her way to the stairs.

"You enjoyed that, didn't you?" Cassidy shook her head at her mother.

"I have no idea what you are talking about, Cassie." Rose began to walk back into the hallway. "I'm going to walk down to that small market and get some pasta for dinner." Her daughter laughed. One of the things Cassidy was the most grateful for in her life was her mother. Rose McCollum was smart, attractive and good natured, attributes she had passed on to her daughter. The two shared a friendship that transcended mother and daughter and Cassidy understood how rare that was.

Small legs were dangling and kicking in mild protest through uncontrollable giggling as the agent entered the room. "Come on, Alex!" He cried out his objections through his own laughter.

"Sorry...no can do, Speed Racer... Sneakers or you can forget another lesson. That's the deal."

"Awww," he groaned as Alex sat him on the large chair.

His mother picked up the shoes and squatted in front of him. "Dylan," she gently cautioned him, soliciting yet another warmhearted grin from the agent.

"I'll get the car," Alex said giving the young man a narrowed gaze.

"When we get home?" he called after her.

"We'll see," Alex called back in an effort to hide her amusement.

***

Alex paced the hallway for a few moments wondering how the visit was going. She already knew that Dylan was a sensitive child and she was worried. If the flashes of cameras had unsettled his young mind, she worried that the beeping of monitors and the sight of his father in a hospital bed attached to tubing might truly frighten him. There was something she wanted to do. She hesitantly walked to the door and peeked in the window. Dylan was sitting in the chair with Cassidy standing beside him. Gently she rapped the window. Her lover nodded, touched the boy's shoulder and came to the door. "Everything okay?" Cassidy asked Alex.

"Yeah," Alex looked over the woman's shoulder at the small boy. "Are you going to stay a little while longer?"

"I was going to…but if you…"

"No, no, no," Alex returned her eyes to the woman. "I need to run out for about twenty minutes…I just wanted to know if I had time."

Cassidy looked at the agent pondering what she was thinking. It was only a short time ago that Alex had worried about coming between the congressman and his family. Cassidy wanted to be certain Alex felt secure. "Sure. Take whatever time you need. But, Alex, seriously are you sure you are…"

"I'm fine Cass…I just forgot about something. Shouldn't take me more than half an hour at most."

"Okay, if we're done I'll wait for you in the lounge."

"Okay."

When Alex returned about half an hour later Dylan's eyes were red. Cassidy had his hand in a firm grip and she looked at Alex with an unmistakable expression of regret. It was a necessary visit but the agent's instincts were right, Dylan was rattled. The agent's heart sank, both for the boy and his mother. If anyone understood the anxiety hospitals could produce it was Alex Toles. "All right you two," Alex lifted her voice. "Let's blow this clambake; as they say." Cassidy looked at her as though she were pleading forgiveness for doing something she had to do. Dylan kept his small eyes on his feet. Alex knelt down to him. "Get on." He looked at her questioning. "Well, come on, piggy back out of this place. We have a lesson to get to and I can't play on an empty stomach so let's get a move on." The boy was still quiet but he offered her the faintest hint of a smile and grabbed onto her neck so she could piggy back him to the car. Cassidy was silent and remained so for the forty minute drive home. Alex unbuckled Dylan and he ran up the front stairs, happy to be anywhere but where he had come from. The agent looked at her lover. "Cass…"

"I should have listened to you."

"No, you were right…It'll be okay. Go in. I'm sure your mom has dinner ready."

"What about you?"

"I brought some things from home. I just want to go put them away. I'll be right behind you, I promise." Cassidy gave an unconvincing smile and headed into the townhouse. Alex waited until she was through the door and opened the trunk. She retrieved two bags and quietly headed through the door. She set one down at the edge of the stairs to the second floor and the other she set inside the door to the lower level before making her way into the kitchen. "What do I smell?" she called out lightheartedly.

Rose turned to her with a smile. "Pasta. In fact, I was assured it was THE best pasta and meatballs this side of the Potomac."

"Oh? Did you get that at Rossi's?" Alex asked.

"I did," Rose declared bringing a piping hot dish to the table where Cassidy was pouring drinks and Dylan was sitting resting the weight of his face on his elbows.

"Well, then you have discovered one of the great truths of the area. They make their pasta fresh every morning," Alex supported the woman's statement. As they sat at the table Alex watched Cassidy twirl the pasta repeatedly without bringing any to her mouth and Dylan pick endlessly at the plate beneath him. Given the fact that both mother and son could polish off twice as much as Alex in a given sitting, it was another indication of the tension left by their hospital visit. Alex looked at Rose who tilted her head sideways in a bit of a helpless shrug. "Okay," Alex pulled out her chair. "I'm going to go get those pool balls racked." Dylan looked up at her but Cassidy remained quiet. "You need to eat that meatball, Speed Racer, before I get back…okay?" He nodded. Alex looked helplessly at the woman she loved and then to her mother who gave her an encouraging wink.

The agent was only gone a short time when she reappeared in the doorway. "Okay you three, let's go," she said with some excitement in her voice.

"You guys go. I'll clean up," Cassidy said.

"NOPE," Alex said. With a wide grin she grabbed Cassidy's hand. "Leave it. Let's go. You too, Rose. This is gonna' be a match for the ages!" Dylan and Rose headed down the stairs where the pool table was already racked and three glasses of wine and a wine glass filled with ginger ale were laid out on the coffee table. Alex led Cassidy to the couch to sit beside her mother. She leaned in and whispered to her. "He needs to see you are all right and then he will be. By the way, I love you." Rose heard every word in spite of the agent's soft voice and smiled. Cassidy took a deep breath allowing the words to penetrate her and gave the first smile she had in more than an hour.

"Okay, Dylan. Now, we're gonna' play a REAL game, since I know you've been practicing." She walked to the small chalk board that hung over the bar and wrote out the words as she announced them, "SPEED RACER versus THE CAP." Cassidy wondered what that was all about and smiled earnestly as she watched Alex bounce about, knowing it was all in an attempt to cheer mother and son up. Dylan made his way to the wall and started thumbing across the pool cues, considering seriously which one to take. Alex disappeared from view momentarily behind the bar. Her excited voice pulled both Rose and Cassidy's attention to the blank space her face had just occupied, "NO...no...not those."

She emerged carrying a small elongated box by its handle and handed it to Dylan. He looked at her asking silently what to do. "Open it," Alex said with a huge smile on her face. He sat down on the floor and unclasped the two clasps that lay at either end. "You can't play a real game unless you have a REAL cue, one that's your size," she said. Dylan jumped up and ran to her, throwing his arms around her waist. "Awww... you're welcome...But hugs or not The Cap is still gonna' beat ya'," she affirmed returning his squeeze. Cassidy suddenly felt twenty pounds lighter and the weight continued to lift as Dylan's laughter filled the room over the next hour. Cassidy and Rose clapped and gave ooo's and aww's dramatically as the pair made and missed shots; Alex sneaking in behind the boy and helping him set up his shots and egging him on when she would sink a ball with the cue behind her back.

"I hope you know," Rose leaned into her daughter's ear, "how lucky you are."

The words traveled through every part of Cassidy and lodged in her heart as she watched Dylan sink the eight ball and 'The Cap' hang her head in a playful show of defeat. The teacher laughed. It was an honest and spirited laugh at Alex's display. "I do know," she said watching the agent's antics continue. "I do."

***

"So?" the man asked in an abrasive tone.

"She's hiding something," the female agent responded.

"You shouldn't have slept with her."

Brackett scoffed at the assertion. "Really? I think that has worked out perfectly. She just thinks I am a jealous rookie."

"Does she suspect anything about the accident or not?"

"I don't know...she seems far more focused on the blonde, if I didn't know her reputation I'd almost think she was 'in love'. That might come in handy though, if he survives."

"Perhaps....That vote cannot go through."

"Relax," she said, running her hands along his chest. "You worry too much. He's unconscious, no one's talking to him." She began to seductively nuzzle the neck before her. "Come on..."

He pushed her away and retrieved a glass from the table. "I told you, Claire, be careful with Toles. She's got a reputation for more than her conquests of women."

"Mmmm...did she steal your heart?" She batted her eyelashes.

"Just keep digging and do it quietly. What about Fallon?"

"He's an oaf," she asserted.

The man looked at her severely. "Brian Fallon is many things, Claire, he is not the 'oaf' he appears. Watch your back."

"Oh...stop worrying...I've got it covered anyway," Brackett assured the man.

"Mmm....we'll see," he said kissing her fully.

***

"Maybe we should take him into..." Cassidy began, looking at her son sleeping in the bed.

"Cass," Alex said with some caution. "If he needs you he will come into the room. He was fine when he went to sleep."

"I know, but the nightmares."

Alex put her arms around the woman as she kept watch over her son. "Cassidy, stop. He's all right. I'll bet you he sleeps through the night."

"How can you be so sure and I'm such a mess?"

"Look," Alex turned the woman around, "because I'm not the one beating myself up so much I can't see straight."

"Yeah, well, he stayed with Mom last night."

"Yes, and if he needs one of us he knows exactly where to go. What do you want to bet me?" Cassidy was unconvinced. "Come on. What do you want to bet I am right and we wake up before he does?" The truth was, Alex had some experience with nightmares. She could see the look in the boy's eyes before he drifted off. He was thinking about becoming a billiard champion. She suspected he would be dreaming about that, at least for tonight. The nightmares would probably come, but that would likely take a few days and they would have to deal with it then. For now, he needed to rest and Alex was fairly certain he would.

"Why *The Cap*?" Cassidy asked.

Alex closed one eye and pursed her lips. "If I tell you, will you promise to come to bed and stop beating up on yourself?" Cassidy sighed. "Come on. No bets. You come with me. I'll tell

177

you the story behind *The Cap*. And, *if* I'm wrong and he wakes up I will promise to do all the cooking for a week."

Cassidy shook her head. "Yeah, I'll come with you and you can tell me…keep the cooking to yourself, Agent Toles."

Alex smiled at Cassidy's playful response. Slowly the woman was relaxing. "I thought that was a GREAT deal!"

"You would."

"Come on," Alex said stretching out her hand. The woman followed the agent from the room, albeit a bit reluctantly.

Alex pulled on her sweats and climbed into the large bed next to Cassidy who was lying on her side propped up on one elbow. "So…spill it agent," the teacher directed.

"Yeah, yeah," Alex said mirroring her lover's pose. "Have I told you that you are gorgeous?"

"Uh huh, twice… spill."

Alex couldn't help but laugh. It was strange that she found herself so amused because she was certain that a superficial explanation of, 'It was just my rank', would not satisfy the curious and quite perceptive blonde. "Well, I was a Captain. That was my last rank before I went to the FBI."

"In the Army?" Cassidy asked.

"Yes."

"So they called you 'The Cap'?"

"Yeah, but not until I got moved to the Pentagon."

"You worked at the Pentagon?"

"Yep…for five years, actually," Alex explained.

"I suppose you can't tell me what you did. Right?" Cassidy raised her eyebrow awaiting the agent's denial to give more details.

Alex took a deep breath. "Actually, Cass, there isn't anything I wouldn't tell you." The agent moved to her back and looked to the ceiling. "But you might want to get comfortable."

Cassidy was shocked. "Alex…you don't owe me any…"

Alex smiled and pulled the woman into her arms. "Well, you might be wrong there. I just hope you won't…well…"

"Alex, there is nothing you could tell me that would change us. Not a thing." Cassidy was as decisive in her statement as the agent had ever heard anyone be. She knew that the teacher's profession was true. That was part of the reason she wasn't going to wait for something to force her hand to tell the woman about her past. For tonight it would only be part of one chapter.

"Well, when I got out of the hospital and John decided to run for senate, I got a call from someone else that had served with us in Iraq, a good friend. Actually, he had been *my* captain. He was taking a position at the NSA. He asked me to accept a position under him." Cassidy remained silent, her fingers drawing slow circles on Alex's chest. "They needed someone who could both profile and who was multi-lingual. Russian and Arabic were crucial."

"Alex?"

"Yeah?" Alex asked.

"You speak Arabic *and* Russian?"

"Yeah."

"Anything else?" the teacher inquired.

"Uhhh...actually yes." Cassidy tipped her head on the agent's chest waiting for clarification. Alex sighed. She always felt like divulging her language skills sounded like she was bragging. It had been easy for her to learn and she didn't like to feel as though she were showing off. "I can speak and write seven fluently, five others well, if you don't count English."

Cassidy pulled herself up. The English teacher was completely astounded. "You speak SEVEN languages?"

"It's not a big deal," Alex shrugged with embarrassment.

"Uh....Alex...I struggle to teach English to most people and they already know HOW to speak it."

"Well...it's a bit unfair really. I have eidetic memory. It came easy for me," the agent shrugged. Cassidy let out a laugh at Alex's nonchalant explanation. "What?" Alex asked feeling uncomfortable about her ability.

"Nothing," the teacher smiled. "I'm sorry." She resumed her position and her gentle exploration of the woman next to her. "Go on."

"Well, I spent most of my time investigating possible terrorist groups and also some possible leaks within the government. Knowing human behavior and being able to translate actively made uncovering information much faster."

"So...Why 'The Cap'?"

"Well, my position was technically still military. My clearance was based largely on my rank. I had to deal with a lot of different people as contacts and many didn't speak English, so I went by 'The Cap'. It stuck with my co-workers. That's pretty much all anybody called me, Cap, The Cap or Captain until I went to the FBI."

"Wow."

"Yeah...Listen Cass," Alex lowered herself to look at her lover. "Fallon doesn't know. Actually, no one at the FBI knows, about my background at the NSA. They just know that I worked at the Pentagon in Intelligence for the Army." Cassidy was silent. "Cass?"

The teacher looked at the woman lying beside her and considered her response. She kissed Alex on the cheek. "Thank you."

"For?"

"For being honest with me about something you probably aren't supposed to tell me."

The strong agent melted into putty again. "Cassidy, I don't think there is much point in my trying to keep things from you."

"Really? Why is that?"

"You'd figure it out anyway," Alex chuckled receiving another peck on the cheek. "And anyway...I want to tell you."

"Alex?"

"Hmm?" Alex mumbled.

"When you left the hospital today, you went to get that pool cue, didn't you?" The agent shrugged. Things like this still made her feel embarrassed. She wasn't used to being affectionate so openly. Cassidy brought that out in the agent and so did Dylan. She wasn't quite used to that yet, allowing herself to be so vulnerable. "That's what I thought." The smaller woman moved over the tall figure beside her. "You," she kissed the agent's forehead. "Are full," she kissed the agent's cheek. "Of surprises," she brought her lips to Alex's and kissed her passionately.

"What was that for?" Alex said biting her lip and fighting to slow her heartbeat.

"I might have a few surprises of my own," Cassidy flirted before beginning to plant kisses the entire length of the agent's body.

"Uhhh…Cass?"

"MMM?" The small blonde woman stopped momentarily and raised her eyebrow at the agent who met her gaze with a slight blush. "Quiet down, 'Cap'," she smiled.

"Is that an order?" Alex asked somewhat hopefully.

"It is now."

Chapter Thirteen

Alex reached for her phone, Cassidy still wrapped around her. "What the hell time is it?" She groaned as she answered it. "Yeah, Toles. Taylor? What?" The agent hopped to her feet without thinking, waking her sleeping lover. "Are you sure? Taylor...He what?....Doing?... Christ." Alex was pressing on both sides of her temples with her fingers forcefully. "What about Brackett?" Alex was facing the wall with her back to the bed. She was so engrossed in her conversation she forgot where she was, that she was stark naked and that Cassidy was in the bed behind her. At the mention of the redhead's name Cassidy sat up like a shot. "He's a spook? A spook? I don't know Taylor...But why? Why Cassidy? Yeah...yeah...Okay. Thanks." Alex hung up the phone and closed her eyes tightly. Some of the puzzle pieces were showing their colors now.

"Why Cassidy, what?" the woman called from behind her.

Alex sighed and rubbed her face. "Shit," she mumbled.

"I'll say...what the hell was that? Who's Taylor?" Cassidy's fear was building. She heard the tone in Alex's voice. The agent took a deep breath and slowly made her way back to the bed. She put the phone down, climbed in next to the woman and nodded in preparation of the truth. "Alex?"

Alex kissed Cassidy's forehead gently. "I love you, you know that?"

"Of course I know it...Alex, what is going on?"

The agent hadn't intended to tell her lover what her suspicions were about the congressman's accident, at least not yet, but she had to make a choice now. She could either lie or tell Cassidy what she knew and what she thought it meant. There was no way she was going to lie to the woman she loved. "The guy that's been stalking you, I think anyway….he's Intelligence."

"You know who it is?"

"Yeah…I think so."

"Who is it? Alex…."

"Cass, you have to promise me you are not going to freak out, okay? You have to trust me if I am going to tell you this. I mean it…..Believe me when I tell you I will not let anything happen to any of you."

"Dammit Alex, just tell me what is going on."

"Okay, I don't think the congressman's….. I don't think it was an accident," Alex said cautiously.

Cassidy nearly gasped. "What are you saying?"

"I'm saying someone wanted him out of commission, if not dead."

Cassidy felt sick. She dropped her face to her hands in disbelief and frustration. She exhaled and looked back at Alex. "Okay, what does that have to do with me?" Alex bit her lip hard. "Alex…"

"Well…I'm not totally sure. At first I thought the letters were from two people, someone leveraging the letters about you to scare him off of something….but this Fisher guy…"

"Carl Fisher?" the teacher interrupted.

"Yeah."

"Oh Jesus, Alex…"

"What?" Cassidy's face went completely white. "Cassidy? What is it?"

The blonde woman got out of the bed and put on her robe. "Carl Fisher, he worked on Chris's campaign."

"I know that."

"I made Chris get rid of him."

"Why?" the agent asked. Cassidy sat down in the chair and dropped her face again. Alex suddenly felt her stomach turning violently. She suspected the reason. "Cass...." Alex got up and moved to her, throwing her shirt on while she moved.

"I caught him watching me, you know..."

Alex felt an anger she had never experienced. The thought of anyone violating Cassidy in any way propelled her anger to a frightening level. "What did Chris do?"

Cassidy began to cry. "He refused...to fire him...said I was imagining things...I backed off at first...but..."

"Cass?" Alex gently urged her lover to continue.

"I was getting Dylan into the tub and I saw him outside... I mean he did work for Chris, but I just....It wasn't right. I could feel it. I just thought it was a tabloid thing, you know? I just ...I told Chris if he didn't get rid of him I wouldn't do any more campaigning. He was furious...refused to talk to me for a week, but I didn't see Carl again. That was over two years ago."

Alex put her hands on Cassidy's. "Cassidy, Carl Fisher is CIA." Cassidy looked at the agent in shock. "Yeah, I know. Look...that's enough for tonight. What you told me, it helps."

"Alex, why were you talking about her?"

"I don't trust Brackett, Cassidy. I just don't trust her. I need to spend another day here in D.C. I know you planned on leaving Friday morning but I'd like to get you back to New York tomorrow night."

"Why?"

"Cass...Please just trust me. Please."

"I do trust you, Alex."

"Then let me do what I do. Taylor, he'll...well...he'll come through...he always has."

"He's the one...isn't he? Your Cap?"

"Yes, Cass, he is....and he thinks New York is safer for you right now. You trust me. I trust him."

Cassidy nodded, her tears beginning to flow as the gravity of the situation suddenly hit her full force. "Alex, what am I going to do?"

"Nothing. You're going to let me take care of you and fig-ure this out. That's it, just that." Alex held the woman tightly. "I love you, Cass. I promise...I will keep you and Dylan safe, no matter what."

***

"What's going on?" Fallon asked as Alex let him into her apartment.

"Did you have any luck on Fisher?"

"Toles...I told you..."

"What would you say if I told you he was a spook?" Alex asked.

"What? How could you know that?"

Alex picked up a file from her coffee table. "Trust me...it's true."

"Why the hell would the CIA be watching Cassidy?"

"Good question. I'm not sure they are."

"I don't follow," Fallon said taking a seat on the couch.

"Cassidy caught him watching her, when he was working for the congressman. She made him fire Fisher, apparently that didn't go over too well with our friend O'Brien."

"Shit. Toles, do you think the congressman set up Cassidy?"

"No. I don't, but I am curious why a CIA operative would be masquerading in a congressional campaign." Fallon's left eye started to twitch. "What are you thinking?" Alex asked noticing her partner's physical response to the information.

"Well, Toles...years back I investigated this money launder-ing thing...when I was still P.D. Thing is, it looked like there was money going through this campaign, a couple actually. Thought it was drug money but after some digging," Fallon paused and shook his head.

"What? Fallon...after some digging what?"

He looked at his partner. "It looked like arms sales, and I don't mean guns, Toles." Unfortunately for Alex her partner's revelation did not surprise her. She had worked several cases like that at the NSA. "They took the case. FBI, ATF… never heard anything more. Never set right with me either. One of the guys, Ciarcia, who was setting up the funds? I swear to you he was CIA."

"He was."

Fallon's body jerked. "What?"

"He was CIA. Congressman Jeffries, right? Oklahoma, but all the transactions went through the D.C. office," she said.

"How do you know that?" Fallon asked.

"Look, Fallon, all you need to know is I saw a lot when I was at the Pentagon…a lot. You think this guy was funneling through the O'Brien campaign?"

"I don't know, just feels familiar. Christ, I sound like you."

Alex laughed. "Well, I think you might be right, but I don't think that's why he's watching Cassidy."

"You actually think he's stalking her?"

Alex felt her anger rise again. "Yes. I do."

"So you think it's just coincidence? The congressman and the letters?" he asked her.

"I didn't say THAT," Alex said. "The doctors told Cassidy this morning that the swelling in his brain seemed to be going down. Maybe he can shed some light on Fisher when he wakes up."

"Are you going to talk to him?" Fallon asked.

"No. You are."

"I thought you'd…"

"I'm taking Cassidy back home on an eight o'clock flight tonight. I'm pretty sure Fisher is here, in D.C."

"I'm not going to ask how you would know that," Fallon said.

"What about the witnesses?" Alex asked.

Fallon sighed, "two are dead ten years plus, and the other is wheelchair bound in a nursing home in Minnesota."

Alex stretched and let out a powerful sigh, "figured."

"Toles, this is deep...maybe we need Tate."

"No. No Tate. What about Brackett?"

"So far everything seems normal," he said. "I think she's just a bitch, Toles."

"She is, but I still want you to keep an eye on her." Alex got up and started for the door. "You have the key with you?" Fallon nodded. "Good. I'm going to meet one of my Pentagon contacts before I pick up Cassidy. Watch yourself, Fallon."

***

Alex picked up her phone, "Toles." She was surprised to hear the voice at the other end.

"Alex."

"Colonel?"

"Listen...we need to talk."

"What's going on?" Alex asked. When John Merrow called Alex Toles it was always as a friend but there was always, without question, something he wanted.

"Can you come here?" he asked.

"To the White House?"

"Yes, I don't want to talk on the phone."

"John, I have an eight o'clock flight..."

"I know that," he said bluntly.

"Of course you do. How silly of me," Alex answered a bit annoyed.

"Alex, I will get you to the flight and I will get Cassidy there. We need to talk."

"Fine. I'm on my way." Alex knew whatever was going on, she was moving in the right direction. If Taylor hadn't called Merrow then the president was keeping a closer eye on things than she realized. The three had always kept the closeness of their relationship somewhat quiet. Generally, that was an asset in situations like the current one. Knowing the president's overly cautious nature that meant something was wrong and

188

that worried the agent. She picked up her phone and dialed Taylor who confirmed he had not spoken to their friend; her captain taking the opportunity to give her another cautionary advisement.

***

Alex entered the president's private study to find him poised on the corner of his desk waiting. "Alex," he smiled. "I'm sorry about this. I just thought it best we speak here."

"It's fine. What is it?"

"Sit," he said offering a seat and moving to a blue arm chair. "Carl Fisher."

"What about him?"

"You suspect him," the president said.

"I do. I wonder why the CIA would be involved in a congressional campaign," she said flatly.

"It is interesting," he agreed. "More interesting though, Alex, he's not CIA anymore."

"What do you mean? I have the file from…"

"Yes, well, even Taylor doesn't bat a thousand." He stood and headed for the small liquor cabinet. "You want a drink?" Alex shook her head. "Seems his firing from the congressman's campaign caused him some issues. He's been working freelance ever since, kind of a drunkard from what I understand."

"Why the interest?"

He returned with his scotch in hand. "Because, Alex, I have suspected for a while that Christopher O'Brien is not the ally he appears to be."

Alex felt her jaw stiffen. "How so?"

"Oh, some financial things started it. Hence the CIA at the campaign," he lifted his glass. "But recently some meetings to his office. Fisher being one of them, and Jonathan Krause. I'm sure you remember that name." Alex certainly did know that name. Jonathan Krause was widely considered to be one of the most pivotal brokers of large arms sales to foreign nations. He had a storied Naval Career and was well connected, had worked overseas with the CIA and was credited with foiling several large scale attacks on financial markets. But, many insiders suspected that he had his own interests. He was elitist, highly intelligent and a true charmer; everything a great spook needed to be and everything that made them so dangerous if they went astray.

"Why didn't you tell me this before?" Alex asked.

"Because, I wasn't sure, and frankly, I hoped I was wrong. The accident changed that." Alex remained stoic. "Oh come on, Alex. I know you already suspect that was no accident. Doesn't add up, does it?"

Alex shook her head. She was curious about the congressman and his dealings for a number of reasons. Right now, Cassidy was her concern. Her friend studied her as closely as she observed him. "Alex?" She looked to him. "I know about Cassidy…and you."

"I assumed."

He nodded and let out a strong sigh. "Fisher, I don't know his agenda. I do know he is dangerous." Alex suspected that already.

"You think O'Brien's behind this, with Cassidy?" Alex asked.

The president shrugged. "I don't know what I think, Alex. I just know that Congressman O'Brien is in ICU after he's been meeting with an arms broker that no one can seem to pin. What role Fisher plays, well…only the congressman knows that."

"So what do you want from me, John?"

"Well, I'd like you to look into the congressman's dealings with Krause. But…I would also like you to keep Cassidy and Dylan safe. Cassidy has been a good friend to my administration."

"You needn't worry about Cassidy or Dylan," Alex assured him.

"Never thought I'd see that."

"What's that?"

"You, in love," he said.

"Jealous?" She smiled now.

He nodded. "Alex, O'Brien is still central to a lot of things for this administration. I can't...It has to remain an accident in the public view."

"I understand. It stays here." Alex hated this part of her job. It was the president before her now making this statement, her Commander in Chief, not simply her friend.

"Not even to Cassidy," he said. Alex's gaze narrowed. "Toles?"

"I wouldn't tell Cassidy anything about the congressman unless I was sure, John." He nodded and walked her to the door.

"Be careful, Alex. Fisher's a loose cannon and we don't know who has their hand on the wick." She gave him an acknowledging smile. "Tell Cassidy I said hello. I have to say, she has always been charming. More so than even I would have imagined," he smiled.

Alex shook her head. "I'll be in touch."

***

Click. Click and a sigh. He looked out the window as the car pulled up and the man opened the door for his passengers. She was talking to the older woman. Click. Click. The dark haired agent was noticeably absent. Click. Click. Click. Click. Another sigh as he watched her bring the phone to her ear. More clicking and ticking, driving him to distraction. She got in the car. Fumbling about, he picked up the back box. "She's not with them....Yeah I'm sure.....Fine." He pulled the silver container from his passenger seat companion and opened it, taking a large gulp followed by a low groan. Back to the bag it went. Again the black box pressed to his ear.

"Fisher...Awake? I see... Understood....Closer....by Friday." He smiled and tossed the black box onto his companion.

"Change is coming." He lit a cigarette and took a long breath, relishing the sensation of the hot smoke traveling through his lungs. He grabbed the notepad and the black marker and began to write. *Well Cassidy finally. We will see. You and I. She'll be gone. Will be soon. We will dance. You will die.* He stopped and took another long drag of satisfaction.

***

The agent was unusually quiet during the trip home. She was relieved to be with Cassidy and Dylan but something about the way things continued to unfold in the case bothered her. Based on her profile of Christopher O'Brien she would not be surprised if he engaged in some shady funding practices, but she saw him with Cassidy and Dylan. She found it very hard to believe that he would put them in danger knowingly. She wondered why O'Brien had been upset about firing Fisher if what the president told her was true. If it was, O'Brien should not have known Fisher was CIA. Then she wondered if Fisher had been playing both sides of the fence and Cassidy was just an unforeseen bonus for the sadistic son of a bitch. She knew his type too. They either became assassins or serial killers, same difference in the agent's view. He had been the former now she feared Cassidy might be the first game piece in his quest to become the latter. This case was so much like what she had confronted all those years ago in Iraq. It was like peeling an onion that has endless layers, a puzzle that was missing just enough pieces that you couldn't seem to link anything. That just made Agent Alex Toles more determined. Only now she feared that Cassidy might be hurt in more ways than one. Alex brought in the last bags just as Cassidy was coming back down the stairs from putting Dylan in his bed. The petite blonde stopped on the bottom stair, falling nearly eye to eye with the taller agent. "So...you want to tell me what's wrong?" Cassidy asked.

"Nothing's wrong," Alex tried to sound convincing.

Cassidy put her arms around the agent's neck. "Terrible liar."

"I am, huh?"

"Yeah."

"Mmm...maybe I just missed you today," Alex flirted.

"No. You're worried. You rubbed your temples for the entire ride home."

"I am worried about you. I hated leaving you this morning when you were so upset." Alex knew this would be believable because it was true.

"Well, I'm okay. I don't want to talk about any of that tonight, okay? Maybe not tomorrow either. You do what you need to. I just want to enjoy a couple of days at home, not think about it. If that's okay?"

Alex felt a weight lift from her. Cassidy needed space from the case and Alex needed to keep Cassidy out of it as much as possible. The teacher's request meant that the agent did not have to feel she was being secretive or worse, that she was lying. "I think," Alex said looking into the woman's eyes, "that sounds perfect. In fact, I have some things to do in the morning at the field office, but after that I am free. I was thinking...A Batman marathon and tacos?"

"You were, were you?"

"Well, yes. I was."

"Mmhmm. I don't suppose a little Speed Racer put you up to that?" Cassidy raised an eyebrow.

"No, actually. I like Batman and I like tacos."

Cassidy smiled. "Yes, I remember that, Alfred." Alex laughed at the pet name.

"Ummm...children?" Rose called from the kitchen. "I made tea."

"Oh, look at that," Cassidy said. "My mother must have known we had an English butler stopping by." She kissed the agent gently and stepped off the stair. Alex stood still, breathless as this woman always seemed to leave her, watching as Cassidy walked down the hall.

"Hum," the agent raised an eyebrow. "I wonder if the lady will require the butler's service," she laughed.

"She might," Cassidy called from the kitchen doorway. "There will be dishes to do."

***

"Goodnight, Alex," Rose said heading to one of the spare bedrooms for the night.

"Night, Rose." Alex walked into the bedroom to see Cassidy already under the covers.

"Tired?" the agent asked.

"Yeah, I am," Cassidy said fighting a yawn.

Alex went to the side of the bed and sat on the edge. "Cass?"

"Hmmm?" The woman's eyes were already closing.

"Never mind," Alex started to get up and Cassidy quickly pulled her back down.

"No you don't. I'm not asleep. What is it?"

"It's nothing. Go to sleep, sweetheart." A wide smile crept onto Cassidy's face and her grip tightened on the agent's arm. "What's that about?" Alex asked.

"What?" Cassidy asked.

"That," Alex traced the smile on the woman's lips with her finger.

"You called me 'sweetheart'."

"I guess I did." Alex ran her hand through the woman's hair.

"What were you going to ask me?" Cassidy opened her eyes.

"Nothing. Really. Go to sleep," Alex kissed Cassidy's forehead. This time the agent made it to her feet and to the bathroom. She washed up, brushed her teeth, put on her oversized, gray ARMY T-shirt and climbed in behind the sleeping woman. She kissed the soft blonde head next to her. "I love you so much, Cass. I wish you knew." The agent rolled onto her back and put her hands behind her head, staring at the ceiling as though it were a starry night sky.

Cassidy rolled over and put her arm over the agent's middle. "I do know," she said softly.

"I thought you were asleep."

Cassidy let out a sleepy groan. "Alex, what's bothering you?"

"I told you," she kissed the woman's head again, "nothing. I just…"

"Alex…"

"Cass…I just don't want disappoint you."

Those words woke Cassidy completely and she propped herself up to look into the face of the woman she loved. "Where is that coming from?" Alex shrugged. "Uh-uh…you promised."

"What?" Alex asked.

"No running, spill."

Alex took a deep breath. "What if I screw up, Cassidy?"

"What do you mean by 'screw up'? Like cheat?"

"What? No! God. That would NEVER happen."

"Okay? Lie?" Cassidy asked.

"No."

"Alex…I'm at a loss here."

"What if I screw up with Dylan?"

"What? You're great with Dylan." Cassidy took a deep breath. She thought for a minute and she suddenly wondered something. Things were moving fast for the pair. Maybe it was too much for Alex, a six year old always around. "Alex, if you need to slow this down…"

Now Alex shot up from her position to face Cassidy fully. "What?"

"Well, I guess I didn't really think…I mean…Dylan is here 24/7. That's a lot, for anyone."

Alex laughed. "Cassidy, that's not at all what I meant." Cassidy took a deep breath and searched the agent's eyes for her meaning. "I just don't want to overstep my bounds…like last night."

"Alex, if it wasn't for you last night would have been a disaster for both me and Dylan."

"It's not my place, Cass, to tell you where he should sleep… stuff like that." Cassidy kissed Alex. "What was that for?" the agent asked.

"I had to check if you were real," Cassidy traced Alex's lips with her finger.

"What; am I trading in Alfred for Pinocchio now?"

"Maybe," Cassidy smiled. "Dylan loves you. My mother loves you. I love you….and it is your place." The woman let out a nervous chuckle.

"What?" Alex asked.

"I forget sometimes that we really have all just met," Cassidy admitted.

"I know. Me too."

"I need to tell you something," the teacher began tentatively. "And I don't want you to get scared off."

"Cass…seriously?" Alex chuckled.

"I am serious."

"I'm sorry. Tell me," Alex pulled Cassidy into her arms. "It's all right, whatever it is."

Cassidy let out a long breath. "All the things I imagined when I married Chris," she hesitated.

"Yes…" the agent encouraged her lover to continue.

"They never happened, not really. I thought when Dylan came…but…and then he wanted to have another baby…conveniently, when he decided to run for office."

"You didn't?" Alex was surprised. Cassidy was a wonderful mother and Alex knew already how much she loved children.

"I did, but not like…not with Chris. I guess that's when I really knew it was over."

"Cass? Why would that scare me off?"

Cassidy swallowed hard. "Because I don't feel that way with you. When I see you with Dylan…"

Alex chuckled. "You think because you want to have more children one day the big goofy agent is gonna' turn tail and run." Cassidy shrugged. "Cassidy, look… if you had asked me a few weeks ago if I would EVER settle down, fall in love, I would have said no. That's the truth." Alex felt a tear through her shirt and lifted the smaller woman in her embrace so that she could look in her eyes. "I love you, Cass, and right now I want to get through all of this mess, but there isn't anything you could ever ask of me that would make me walk away from you, or Dylan for that matter….and truthfully? It scares the hell out of me sometimes, but it doesn't scare me half as much as the thought of losing you."

"I'm sorry," Cassidy said.

"For what?" Alex laughed a bit.

"I just, well…it's a crazy thing to say to someone you've known a week."

"No…it's not. No crazier than the fact that we're together," the agent said. "Actually, it makes me feel a little better."

"It does?" Cassidy asked with surprise.

"Yeah. It does."

"I love you, Alex."

"I know…go to sleep, Cass." Cassidy let out a happy, audible sigh. "I love you too. More than you could ever know," Alex said as she silently thanked the stars she couldn't actually see for being happier than she ever thought possible.

Chapter Fourteen

Christopher O'Brien sat up slightly in his hospital bed and took his first sip of water. His throat felt as if it were burning in the desert with no moisture to sooth it, making his voice raspy. "I don't understand." He swallowed more water and strained to finish his thought, "why Cassie isn't here."

"Congressman," Agent Fallon began, "it is safer for both Mrs. O'Brien and your son in New York right now. Agent Toles is there." Brian Fallon had spoken at length with his partner that morning. He was now aware that the congressman had met with Fisher and who Fisher was and was not. She had also filled him in on the fact that his original feeling regarding money laundering and arms might not only be a reality, but that the congressman might be both privy to it, and worse still, involved in something of that nature. Fallon liked and respected Cassidy, and although he sometimes resented Alex for not sharing much of her past, he both trusted and loved his partner. His once amicable feelings toward the politician in the bed were less than charitable this morning.

"Danger? The Letters?" The congressman forced the words from his lips.

Fallon tried to calm his inner anger. "What do you know about Carl Fisher?"

The congressman avoided the agent's eyes, "photographer."

"I see. On your campaign?" Fallon went along. The congressman nodded. "You released him?" The congressman nodded again. "Why?"

"Cassie…" the congressman wheezed, "asked me…"

"I see. Why was that?" The congressman shook his head as if not really knowing.

"Hmm…Were you aware that Mr. Fisher worked for the government when you hired him?" The congressman did not answer. "I see. Were you aware that Mr. Fisher was an intelligence agent when you released him?" The congressman threw the agent a visual dagger. Fallon was unimpressed and unfazed. "You met with Mr. Fisher recently." The congressman stared. "Well, Mr. O'Brien," the agent deliberately stripped the man of his respectful title. "It appears that your friend, Mr. Fisher, has a thing for your ex-wife. That is why she is not here." Fallon hoped his firm questioning and deliberate assessment would at the very least give the congressman some things to 'chew' on. "You need your rest," Agent Fallon tipped his head. "I'll be in touch when you are feeling more talkative."

***

Agent Claire Brackett picked up her phone. "He's awake. I'm not certain when they arrived, but the wife said she was returning to New York on Friday. I need to know what Toles is doing. Who she's seeing…No, I can't go to New York…she already is suspicious of me…..I have to go." The tall redheaded agent walked to the water cooler, grabbed a cup and sat back down at her desk.

"Brackett," Assistant Director Tate called from the door. "My office."

"Sir," the young agent opened the door.

"Sit down, Brackett."

"Yes, Sir."

"Brackett, this was on my desk this morning." He passed her an envelope. She opened it and pulled out the photo. "Why were you outside Congressman O'Brien's room yesterday?"

"Sir, I was just checking on Agent Toles." Tate folded his arms. "As you know, Agent Toles and I..."

"What I know, Agent Brackett, is that the O'Brien case belongs to Agent Toles and Agent Fallon. They were assigned by me; you were not. Now...I have not spoken to Agent Toles since early this morning and I imagine you would prefer she did not know you were watching Mrs. O'Brien and her son."

"Assistant Director, I understand...Agent Toles and I had a disagreement...I simply..."

"Brackett, here's a piece of advice, Toles is Toles. Work is work. Your cases are your cases and her cases are her cases. Are we clear?"

"Yes, Sir."

"Good. Now go deal with your case."

Agent Fallon peered in the door as Agent Brackett left. "Sir? A word?'

"What is it, Agent Fallon?"

"I'd like to request some undercover protection for Mrs. O'Brien," Fallon explained.

"Well, you could do that Agent Fallon but Agent Toles already took care of that this morning. Is that all?"

"Yes."

"Fine." Fallon turned to leave. "Next time you want to know what my conversation with another agent is regarding," Tate said shuffling papers on his desk, "ask me."

"Sir..." Agent Fallon left the office to apprise his partner of all he'd learned in Washington.

***

"Fallon.....What do you mean she was *watching* Cassidy?" Alex was burning. "When yesterday? What did she say to him?... Tate said what?...Great.....No, I'm in the car. Fallon.... I don't know yet.....What did O'Brien say?......Really? He played dumb?...He definitely met with Fisher....P.D. might be better on this than the bureau. Fisher's gotta' have someplace close by here. You have any New York contacts?...Okay....Trust him?...Okay....Yeah, set it up...I'll meet him tomorrow.... Yeah...you too," she hung up the phone. "Shit." Alex Toles pulled over and opened the glove box. She pulled out a small black flip phone. "Taylor?"

"Toles?"

"Yeah."

"What's going on?" Michael Taylor asked.

"You find anything on Brackett yet?" Alex's voice gave away her concern.

"No. You want me to keep digging, don't you?"

Alex took a deep breath. "She's not FBI."

"Are you sure?"

"Pretty sure, yeah," she answered.

"A feeling?"

"No, remember that bookstore on Mutanabbi Street? The shopkeeper?"

"Of course," he answered.

"Remember that conversation, on our weekly sweep?"

"I do."

Alex pressed her thumb into her temple. "Just happened with the Assistant Director."

"Toles..."

"Taylor...I speak seven languages and this smells like shit in all of them."

"Understood," he said. "Toles...just be careful. I found out what Fisher did in the Marines."

"Yeah?" Alex Toles asked nervously.

"Let's just say I wouldn't want to cross paths with him."

"How bad?" Alex asked.

"Toles, he makes that bookshop look like a birthday party. He's a sociopath with an IQ of 189." Alex closed her eyes and tried to breathe. This situation felt too familiar. Two of the most dangerous scenarios just became reality; someone on the inside was working against them and they had to deal with a genius who was a psychopath.

"Taylor, Cassidy, can you…" the agent began to ask for her friend's assistance in protecting the woman she loved.

"Already done," he said plainly.

"How do you know what I was going to say?"

"Captain Toles, when you almost die next to someone… Well, I can hear it. You love her. I get it. I'll have Brady sweep the house tomorrow."

"Thanks."

"Don't mention it….. Really, don't," he laughed.

Alex appreciated the needed levity. "Understood, Cap, understood."

***

Alex Toles drove down Cherry Circle remembering the first time she had arrived here. It was impossible for her to believe that it had only been a week ago. It felt like an eternity; an eternity that she had loved Cassidy O'Brien and an eternity that she had been struggling with this case. Her life was completely different now. The things that suddenly mattered most to her had changed in ways that the agent found incomprehensible in certain moments. They were moments like this. She pulled into the driveway and turned off the car feeling glad to be *home*. But, it wasn't really *her* home. Alex wondered what would happen when the case ended and there was no reason for her to be here with Cassidy. Reality was beginning to press in on Alex Toles. She looked through the windshield at the house in front of her and unconsciously pressed her thumb to her temple. After her conversation with her friend, Michael Taylor, she knew that her fears about a stalker were valid. Maybe Carl Fisher was a piece of a bigger puzzle but there was no doubt in Alex's mind he had other plans for Cassidy. That should have been her greatest worry as she opened her car door, but something else had risen to the surface. It wasn't about money laundering or even psychopathic stalkers. Where, Alex wondered, would she fit into the puzzle that was Cassidy's everyday life? She grabbed her case off the passenger seat and headed for the front door. Cassidy was exactly where Alex knew she'd be. She was in the kitchen chopping up vegetables and sipping a glass of iced tea. Alex stopped in the doorway to silently observe. "Are you going to hold up that wall all afternoon?" Cassidy asked remaining focused on her chore.

"I was just doing a little investigating," Alex flirted.

"I see. Don't you usually have to get closer to things to investigate them?" Alex smiled and moved behind the smaller woman at the counter, wrapping her arms around the woman's waist. Cassidy's breath seemed to catch momentarily in her chest. The agent's touch both calmed and excited the teacher at the same time. She shivered slightly in Alex's arms. "Discover anything?" Cassidy asked as she tried to concentrate on the pepper in front of her.

Alex felt a grin creep across her face at Cassidy's physical reaction to her presence. "I have to get closer to see clearly," she whispered heavily in the blonde's ear, reaching for a piece of the pepper on the cutting board and being quickly rewarded with a playful smack of her hand. Alex giggled and stepped back, chewing on the strip of pepper and pouting her innocence to the woman that had turned to face her.

The agent's expression prompted a motherly shake of the teacher's head followed by a howl of laughter that seemed to light Cassidy from within. The pepper fell limp in the agent's mouth as she became completely beguiled by the face before her. Cassidy's laugh softened to a snicker as she reached the agent and pulled the pepper from her lips, replacing it with a kiss. "I am glad you are home," the smaller woman softly murmured, straining to reach the taller agent's ear. Alex's response took both of them by surprise. She pulled Cassidy closer to her and kissed her passionately. As the kiss broke the blonde woman in her arms found it difficult to speak or even open her eyes.

"I think," Alex kissed the woman's neck, "I might be onto something." Cassidy's breath escaped in a quiver and Alex kissed her again gently. "I'll have to undress the facts later," she whispered in the woman's ear.

"Alex…"

Alex gloated devilishly as Cassidy's eyes opened to meet hers. There was something about this moment that made Alex feel as though she had fallen in love with Cassidy all over again. Green eyes danced with blue as they met silently. It was such a simple moment and yet it held within it everything that had meaning for Alex. She pulled Cassidy close, her heart bursting. The words fell from her lips, "*Tu es l'amour de ma vie.* (You are the love of my life)."

Without missing a beat the teacher responded, "*Je veux être avec toi pour toujours.* (I want to be with you forever)."

Alex took the face before her in her hands. "You will be," she promised with a tender kiss.

***

Cassidy was drifting off on the couch when Dylan jumped in between his mother and the agent. Three hours of Batman had worn out Dylan's mom and it was only seven o'clock. Dylan, however, was wide awake but growing tired of the caped crusader a bit himself. "Alex?" He bounced partially into her lap. The agent raised a brow at him. "How come you have a gun?" Cassidy listened closely.

Alex let out a quick but strong sigh. She had tried the last few days to keep the sidearm concealed around Dylan. Alex hated guns. She hated everything about them. She also understood their necessity in her work and she wanted to be certain that Dylan knew that her pistol was neither a toy nor was it something she enjoyed carrying. "Well, Dylan," she said pulling him onto her knee. "You know, what I do when I go to work is like a policeman in a lot of ways. Sometimes there are people; people who want to hurt other people....And it's my job to keep people safe. That's why I have the gun."

He considered her statement. "Can I have a gun?" Cassidy watched the agent's jaw line stiffen. "Why would you want a gun, Dylan?"

"I can be like you."

Alex nodded. "Dylan, I wish I didn't have a gun."

"Why?"

"Because my job is to help people, and guns...guns can hurt people. It's just something I have to do and it took me a long time, Dylan, to learn how to use it without hurting anyone."

Dylan was curious. "Did you shoot anyone?"

Alex swallowed hard. "Yes, Dylan. I have."

"Did they die?"

Cassidy sat up ready to intervene and Alex shook her head. "Dylan, one time...quite a long time ago, there was a man who did some very bad things. He hurt a lot of people. He even tried to hurt me. I had to stop him." Alex smiled at him gently. "And that was a day I wish never happened, for him or for me. You listen to me, if you want to be a good guy, you be like your mom." He looked at her quizzically. "Real heroes don't carry guns, Dylan. They don't even wear capes, or drive fast cars or even catch bad guys."

"But you're a hero," he said proudly.

Alex laughed uncomfortably. "Well, your mom's *my* hero."

"She is?"

Cassidy felt her eyes begin to water as she watched and listened to her lover address her son compassionately and cautiously. "Yes, she really is and do you know why?" He shook his head. "Because she doesn't need a gun to protect people. She just loves them and teaches them how to be better people and people like your mom; they are the people that someday will make it so nobody has to have a gun or a cape." She whispered in his ear, "but maybe we'll keep the cool cars." Dylan smiled and nodded. He looked at his mother and hugged her hard.

"What was that for?" Cassidy beamed.

Dylan shrugged. "I'm glad you're my mom." He hopped down. "Wanna' watch *Cars*?" He headed heading for his stack of movies.

"Sure," Alex called back.

Cassidy turned and put her head in the agent's lap. Alex played gently with her hair, watching the woman's eyes slowly close in contentment. "I love you, Agent Toles," Cassidy said quite plainly as she drifted off. Alex inhaled and leaned back comfortably as Dylan crawled back onto the couch beside his mother; Cassidy resting on the agent and the boy resting against her.

"Alex?" he said in a whisper.

"What is it Speed Racer?"

"You're still my hero too."

"Right back at ya' little man."

***

Cassidy felt the bed start to move and she turned to see Alex jerking slightly in a dream. "Down.....down....Cap..." Alex seemed to groan some more unintelligible words before she spoke clearly again. "Where is he? Cap....not right...no... it's.....CAP!"

Cassidy gently took hold of the agent's shoulder shaking her lightly, "Alex...wake up....Alex."

"CAP!...NO!" The agent's knees were suddenly drawn into her chest.

"Alex, please wake up...it's a dream."

"Ma hatha! Arba'aïu 'arkān!" Alex sat straight up; her eyes darting and her body shaking violently.

"Alex," Cassidy whispered as she put her arm slowly around the agent who was hyperventilating. "Alex, it's okay." Suddenly realizing where she was the agent helplessly collapsed into Cassidy's arms. "Shhh...it's okay," Cassidy whispered as Alex sobbed uncontrollably. "It's okay. Oh Alex....I'm sorry." Alex had woken this way many times over the years. The nightmares were far less frequent now and she was never certain what brought them on. She had always been alone; never with the comfort of anyone beside her. Feeling Cassidy's arms surround her seemed to break the dam that she had built and her emotions poured through now like a raging river. She tried to speak but her words were lost in her tears. "Don't," Cassidy said to quell any speech. "Just let me hold you. Slow down....I'm here....I'm here, Alex."

It took almost twenty minutes for Alex to regain any composure and even as her tears began to subside; she felt her grip on Cassidy remain firm. It was foreign to the agent. She was used to being the protector. What she had said to Dylan was true. Cassidy was her hero and with the teacher, Alex was as vulnerable as she had ever been. She had never trusted anyone so completely. "Cass?" the agent whispered.

"What, love?" Cassidy asked, continuing to softly rock the strong woman in her arms.

"I need you," Alex felt her tears surge again.

"I'm right here."

"I'm sorry...I haven't had that dream..."

"Shhh," Cassidy kissed the woman's head.

"I was there, you know? It feels like I'm there.....Taylor fell...and..."

Cassidy pulled Alex to her. "Alex."

"I should have seen it." Cassidy stroked her long dark hair and wiped the tears from Alex's cheeks. "How could I not see it...the trap...it was all..."

"Alex, stop this. Whatever happened there, I know it wasn't your fault. Stop."

"No. It was. I should have known it was a trap....four corners...I missed it." Alex sighed and looked up to Cassidy as her body began to relax more. "Cass?" The teacher looked at her lover with tears in her own eyes. "I can't lose you."

"You're not going to lose me. *Je veux être avec toi pour toujours*, remember?" Alex forced a smile. No one had ever seen the agent like this. She was grateful for Cassidy's arms and terrified realizing how much she needed them. Cassidy smiled and kissed her lover, "*Je t'aime.* (I love you)."

"French," Alex said.

"I too have some talents, my love," Cassidy said as she kissed the agent softly.

"Je t'aime," Alex whispered.

"Forever," Cassidy answered. "Sleep, love," she said holding the agent lovingly. "*Je t'adore.* (I adore you)."

Chapter Fifteen

Fallon entered the room to find Congressman Christopher O'Brien far more alert and mobile than he expected. The ability to eat and to sit for long periods of time was helping to increase the congressman's speech and concentration. "I see you are feeling better," the agent greeted the man.

"Agent Fallon, what brings you here?"

Fallon pulled a chair alongside the hospital bed. "Well, Congressman, I had hoped you could shed some light on Mr. Fisher."

"Carl Fisher was a photographer on my campaign."

"Yes, I know, and Mrs. O'Brien asked you to dismiss him," Fallon said.

"And I did."

"For what reason?"

"I assume you know that, Mr. Fallon. Why don't you get to your point?" the congressman said abruptly.

Fallon nodded. "Fine. What made you employ a CIA agent as a photographer?"

"I have no idea what you are talking about, Mr. Fallon. Mr. Fisher was recommended to me by a fraternity brother, Jon Krause."

"I see. So, when Mrs. O'Brien first told you she had concerns about Mr. Fisher...you refused to let him go."

"Look, Agent...not that it is any of your business..."

"Congressman, anything that might endanger Mrs. O'Brien, you or your son IS my business," Brian Fallon asserted.

The congressman narrowed his gaze. "Not that it is your business, but Mrs. O'Brien was quite emotional then."

"How so?" Fallon asked.

The congressman gave the agent a look of disgust, "we were trying to conceive and it was not going well. She was very distraught."

"So you thought her distress over this inability to get pregnant made her hysterical?"

"Not hysterical, emotional," Congressman O'Brien answered.

"But you finally let him go?"

"Yes. I did. Though I never thought he was a threat."

"Well, we believe he IS a threat," the agent offered.

"You also believe he is CIA," the congressman rolled his eyes.

Agent Fallon nodded. He had spent many years as a detective interrogating suspects and he knew how to play nearly every game a suspect or witness wanted to engage in. Congressman O'Brien knew *something*. What it was, Fallon was not certain. Whatever Christopher O'Brien was hiding, he was willing to risk Cassidy's safety to keep it a secret. "Congressman," Agent Fallon rose to his feet and turned his back to the man in the bed, "I don't, as you put it, *believe* that Carl Fisher was a CIA agent; I *KNOW* that he was…when he worked on your campaign."

"Why would the CIA be interested in my campaign, Agent?"

"If I knew that Sir, I would not be here asking you."

"Perhaps you should ask Cassie," the congressman shot back.

"Why would Mrs. O'Brien have information about that?"

The congressman smirked as his girlfriend entered the room. "Jon Krause. He and Cassie were good friends when we were together."

"Your fraternity brother?"

"That's right. Cassidy studied in France for six months her senior year. Jon was working there at the time. They became close. That's how Fisher got the job." The congressman turned to his girlfriend. "Is that all, Agent?"

Agent Fallon offered a fake smile. "For now."

***

Alex put her mug in the sink and kissed Cassidy on the head. "Gotta' go," she said. "Cass?"

"Yeah?"

"Thanks."

"For what?" the teacher inquired.

"For everything," Alex smiled at her lover receiving a knowing smile in return. "See ya' Speed Racer!" She called into the living room.

"BYE ALEX!" He yelled.

Alex opened the front door and stopped. "What the hell?" The agent slowly closed the door and headed back in the house to the kitchen, her hand gently resting on her sidearm.

"Forget something?" Cassidy called lightheartedly before looking up from her coffee to see Alex's expression.

"Cass, go into the study with Dylan and lock the door until I come for you. Do you understand?"

"Alex, what's…"

"Cassidy…just do it. Please." Cassidy's felt her heart drop and her stomach rise as she nodded and headed to retrieve her son.

"Mom!"

"Dylan," Cassidy cautioned.

Alex walked to the doorway and looked directly at the boy. "Dylan, do as your mother says." The boy saw the intensity in his hero's eyes and obeyed. Cassidy looked at Alex in fear as she moved down the short hallway. "Cass, just go…I'll be back." The agent withdrew her side arm and began to sweep through the house. It was empty. She headed back to the door and opened it slowly. She pulled the phone from her pocket. "Fallon?"

"Toles? What's wrong?"

"Fallon, he was here."

Brian Fallon felt his heart begin to pound. "Fisher? How do you know?"

"There's a letter on the door. It's him, it's definitely him. I need you to call that contact of yours at the P.D."

"Toles...I'll get Tate..."

Alex cut her partner off, "no....no Tate."

"Why?" Fallon asked.

"NO TATE," Alex answered forcefully, "just....Fallon.... shit....."

"What? What is it?" Agent Toles remained silent. "Alex..... what the hell is going on?"

"Well Cassidy finally...we will see...you and I...she'll be gone....Will be soon...we will dance...you will die," Alex read the words aloud.

"Is that the letter?"

"Yeah." Alex felt sick. "I need to get this bagged and I need to get to Cassidy."

"Where is she?"

"She's here."

"Look Toles, maybe this isn't the time but...."

Alex was running low on patience. "What is it, Fallon?"

"Well, O'Brien...he told me he hired Fisher on a recommendation from some fraternity brother...said the guy was friends with Cassidy when she lived in France. Jon Krause."

Alex went numb. "What was his name?"

"Krause. Why? Do you know him?"

"Not exactly. He knows Cassidy?" Alex pinched the bridge of her nose.

"According to O'Brien."

"Shit. How does he? Never mind. Fallon, call that detective....and check on Brackett, see what case she's working."

Fallon was confused. "Why? What does Brackett's…"

"Just do it, Fallon. I'll call you later." Alex took a deep breath. She made her way to the trunk of her car and retrieved her case. Slowly, she peeled the letter from the door, placed it in a bag and deposited it in her case. She took a deep breath, closed the door and headed for Cassidy and Dylan. "It's me."

Cassidy opened the door and looked at the agent. "Alex?" There was a distance in the agent's eyes that scared Cassidy more than what had just happened. "Alex…what…"

"Call your mother," Alex said. "See if she can come get Dylan."

"Why?"

Alex looked at her lover with a vacancy in her stare. "We need to talk. I'll be back in a few a minutes. Please call her." Alex walked away through the front door and put her face in her hands. Why would Cassidy be involved with Jon Krause? What hadn't Cassidy O'Brien told her? She sat on the stoop and tried to calm her anger and her doubt as a million questions collided with endless emotions. She walked to the car and sat in the passenger's seat, opening the glove box and retrieving the small black flip phone she kept there. Why would Cassidy lie to her about anything? What was going on?

"Toles?" the voice came over the phone.

"Taylor, is Brady coming here?"

"Yeah, why?"

"Can you process something for me, here in New York if I give it to him?"

"Of course."

"Can you put someone outside this afternoon?" Alex asked.

"Yeah. Toles…what the hell is going on?"

"What do you know about Jonathan Krause?" Alex asked her friend.

The phone was quiet for a few beats. "Smart, CIA…maybe more, connected. Why?"

"He knows Cassidy."

"How?" Taylor asked.

"I don't know, something about France," Alex explained.

"She told you that?" he asked.

"No. She didn't."

"Toles...I'm sure it's just..."

"There are no coincidences, Taylor. Wherever four corners meet...they meet for a reason."

"Toles...."

"I gotta' go," Alex said dryly.

***

Rose scooted Dylan out the front door and Cassidy made her way to the living room. She sat down on the large sofa with her hands in her lap and looked at Alex. The agent seemed almost cold and Cassidy felt as if her heart were breaking in two. "Alex, please....Tell me what is going on."

"Jon Krause." Alex said. Cassidy looked at her as if to ask why that name was important. The agent turned her back momentarily before facing the teacher again. "You know him."

"Of course I know him," Cassidy said as a pure matter of fact.

"How?" Alex asked pointedly.

"What does Jon Krause have to do..."

Alex interrupted her lover. "How, Cassidy?"

"He's one of Chris's fraternity brothers."

"And?" Alex asked.

"And what?"

"Why were you in France with him?"

"What?" Cassidy asked, beginning to move from worried to angry.

"Well?" Alex pressed.

"I wasn't in France with him."

"That's not what your husband says."

"My *husband?*" Alex stared blankly at the blonde woman. Cassidy let out a sarcastic chuckle. "Well, my *ex-husband* might have told you that Jon and I lived in France at the same time. We did not live together."

Alex's temple twitched. "Why were you in France?"

Cassidy had reached her limit. "Why were you in the Army?"

"This isn't about me, Cassidy."

"Really? You sure about that, Agent Toles?"

"Why?" Alex asked again.

Cassidy nodded in disgust. "I studied French abroad for six months my senior year. It happened to be my minor."

"And Krause?" Alex asked trying to suppress her emotion.

"He worked there for some contractor. He was a friend; an American friend in a foreign country."

"That's all?" Alex asked, the skepticism evident in her voice.

"Should there be more?"

"You tell me." Another sarcastic chuckle erupted from the small blonde whose anger was now reaching the boiling point. "Why wouldn't you tell me that?"

"Tell you WHAT? That I know Jon Krause or that I studied in France?" The agent did not answer. "I don't know, it didn't come up in the last WEEK."

Alex took a deep breath. "Yeah. So what do you know about Krause?"

Cassidy was done with the questioning and disgusted by Alex's apparent mistrust of her. "Well, okay....He lived in France. He likes cappuccinos, but only with skim milk, old movies, he went to Stanford and he tried to put the moves on me once, unsuccessfully, I might add. What else do you want to know?"

"It's not funny Cassidy. I'm trying to protect you."

"No. You're interrogating me like I have something to hide from you." Cassidy rose to her feet and met the agent eye to eye. Pain and anger burned within her. "You know what, Alex? I don't know what the hell this is about and I really don't care. If you don't love me enough to trust me then we have nowhere to go. I have no idea where this is coming from but I will be dammed if I will sit here after everything I have said to you, given you, and have you treat me like a common criminal. Whatever it is, Agent Toles," she looked directly in the agent's eyes, "figure it out. You know where I am." Cassidy left the room. Alex stood silent as she heard the bedroom door slam, suddenly aware of what she had done.

Alex sat down on the chair in the corner of the living room and put her face in her hands as her phone rang. "Toles," she answered as she fought to get any words to escape her lips.

"Alex?" Brian Fallon heard something strange in his partner's voice.

"What is it, Fallon?"

"Are you okay?" he asked with concern.

"Fallon, what is it?"

Brian Fallon sat in the front seat of his car holding a file folder and thumbing through the various papers it held. "Toles, Brackett....it doesn't make sense."

"What doesn't make sense?" Alex asked as she picked up a picture of Cassidy and Dylan that sat on the table beside her.

"Her case...I mean...it's a case that had no reason to be reopened, near as I can tell."

"And?" Alex found herself completely preoccupied with the faces in the photo; her finger lightly tracing the outline of Cassidy's smile.

"Well, Toles...I shouldn't have, but I checked her computer log."

"You what?" Alex was shocked.

"Just listen. She's pulled files on all your past cases, on O'Brien, but she...she hasn't pulled one file for her own case... and...well...Alex," he paused and took a breath. "She pulled the traffic logs from the day of the accident."

Alex took a deep breath and pinched the bridge of her nose hard. She released her own grasp and looked again at the picture. "Fallon?"

"Yeah?" he answered anticipating his partner to react to all he had discovered.

"What *exactly* did O'Brien say about Cassidy and Krause?"

"What?" he asked. "Did you hear what I told you?"

"Yeah, I heard you. What did he say about Cassidy?" Alex repeated.

"He played it off, said she was *emotional* back then...about Fisher... and that Krause recommended Fisher to him."

"Emotional?"

"Yeah, you know, he said they were trying to get pregnant and she was upset when she couldn't. He thought she was just over reacting to Fisher."

Alex let out a disgusted sigh. "Yeah, sure he did." Now Alex truly felt sick. Cassidy had already confided in her that she never wanted another child with the congressman. O'Brien was playing Fallon. "What about Krause?"

"What's with this Krause guy?" Fallon asked. "I thought you didn't know him."

"I don't. Fallon, what did he say...EXACTLY?"

Agent Fallon sighed. "He said she was studying in France and they became friends."

"That's all?" Alex asked.

"Yeah."

"Listen, Fallon, I want you to do something for me."

"Okay..."

"Follow Brackett this afternoon; see where she goes."

"Why? You think she's involved?"

Alex had a decision to make and she made it quickly. "I think she's NSA."

"What are you talking about?" Fallon said almost laughing.

"You heard me. She's NSA."

Fallon was beginning to think his partner's personal involvement in the case was impacting her reasoning. "Toles...I think this case is..."

"Fallon, look...I know the signs. Pulling my old files, the old case assigned, she's NSA."

"You're watching too many X-Files reruns," he laughed.

Alex looked at the picture in her hands again and shook her head. "Fallon, I know because I was NSA."

"What the hell are you talking about?"

"I'll explain when you get here," she said.

"When I get *there*? Toles, why would I come to New York?"

Alex stood and rubbed her right temple with her thumb. "Just get on a flight for tomorrow. I'll explain when you get here. I have to go. I have something I have to do."

"What about the letter?" he asked.

"Call your P.D. contact and see if he can meet us tomorrow. I have the letter covered." She hung up before he could answer, leaving Agent Brian Fallon looking at his phone in disbelief and confusion. Alex reached in her left pocket and pulled out the small black phone Michael Taylor had given her. She took a deep breath and opened it. She popped open the back and searched for any signs of any recording mechanism. She fastened it back up, hit the number 2 and # and waited.

"Toles?"

"Here," she said quietly.

"Brady there yet?" Taylor asked.

"No. Today's not good," Alex replied.

"Why?"

"Cap," she said, "the woman is at the center."

Michael Taylor froze. This phrase had only one meaning. It was the code they had used for many years. Someone was listening and someone was watching, someone on the inside. He cleared his throat slightly. "Well...that *is* unexpected."

"Yes," she agreed trying to keep their conversation as natural as possible.

"Do you want me to have Brady reschedule?"

"No...I think we're okay. I'll finish, but tell Brady I appreciate his help." Alex kept rubbing her temple as she approached the stairway.

"Very well," Taylor answered. "I'll be in touch."

"Thanks, Taylor." She hung up the phone and looked up the stairs. Her mind was racing. Brackett was almost certainly NSA; she was sure. O'Brien was hiding something and Krause was almost certainly involved. Tomorrow she would need to face Fallon with the truth and worse than any of that, she had to face Cassidy now, knowing that she had treated the woman she loved unfairly. Cassidy had held her while she cried, rocked her back to sleep, loved her, accepted her and still she somehow doubted the woman. Maybe it was the dream. Maybe it was just her fear that when this was over she would lose Cassidy. Or maybe, she allowed herself to think for a moment; maybe she was just rattled by Cassidy being in harm's way. She took a deep breath. It was everything, all of it, and none of that mattered.

***

Alex went into the room Cassidy had given her a week earlier to change and gather her thoughts. She heard Cassidy's door open and the woman's footsteps travel down the stairs. The agent reached for her jogging pants. She wanted to run. She heard the front door close and her heart stopped. Alex ran down the stairs so fast that she nearly fell. She opened the door to find Cassidy's right hand about to grab the outside handle and the mail in her left. "Cassidy!" The agent's voice echoed both panic and relief.

"What?" The teacher looked at the agent a bit startled.

Alex felt her heart sway in her chest. She could see the anger and the hurt that lingered in her lover's eyes. All she wanted to do was erase the morning, take it back and take the woman into her arms. "I thought you left...I..."

Cassidy nodded her head in understanding and pressed her lips together. "No, Alex, I don't run away. That's not who I am." She walked deliberately past the agent and headed for the kitchen. Alex stood in the doorway and closed her eyes. Cassidy O'Brien knew her and knew her well. She had just been ready to do exactly that, run, again. The agent fought to inhale and held the little breath she managed to take in. The only thing she knew, beyond any reason or doubt, was that she was in love with Cassidy and she was not going to lose her; not to anyone or anything; not even her own stupidity. She exhaled with deliberate force and made her way to the kitchen.

Alex walked through the doorway to find Cassidy sitting at the table opening the mail piece by piece. She stopped at the kitchen island and stood impossibly still. The smart and strong agent felt like a small child awaiting her punishment. An incredible sense of guilt and sadness flowed through her at the realization of how much she had hurt the beautiful woman sitting nearby. "Alex, the counter can stand on its own," Cassidy said, never removing her eyes from the piece of mail she was opening.

The agent sighed and started toward the table. Slowly she pulled out a chair across from the teacher. "Cass," the agent swallowed hard and raised her right thumb to her temple. "I…I'm sorry, Cassidy."

Cassidy took a deep breath and released it in a sigh. "I know you are, Alex. I just don't understand why."

"Cassidy…I…you have to understand…I just….I don't know why, I…it's just…it's Krause and Brackett and this Fisher….and then Fallon said you knew Krause."

"Alex, you're rambling. Look, I have no idea what Jon has to do with any of this. We were friends a long time ago, that's all. I just don't understand why you couldn't ask me…just ask me…anything. I would tell you."

"I know that," the agent said.

"You do?"

Alex suddenly felt defensive. She just wanted to say she was sorry and move on. That might work with her casual lovers, but not with this woman. Cassidy expected more. "Yes, I do. I just fell into the job…"

"No, Alex…."

"No?" the agent asked.

"That's not what happened."

"Yes it is," Alex said definitively.

"No. It's not. You suspected me of something, not telling you some secret…something."

"I didn't suspect you." Cassidy finally looked up and raised an eyebrow at the agent. "I just didn't understand. I needed to know."

"Well, now you know. Is that all?" The teacher was determined to stand her ground.

"Cassidy, I said I was sorry."

"And I accept your apology, but you are not being honest with me."

"I love you," the agent said.

"I know that. I love you. That's not the issue."

"Why does there have to be an issue?" Alex asked.

"Because, Alex, I trust you with my life….with everything, my son, my heart….I can't be with someone who doesn't trust me, no matter how much I love you. I just can't. I can take anything and I would, but trust….I just can't compromise that, Alex. I can't." The teacher started to stand and Alex grabbed her arm.

"Cassidy, please….I just…."

Cassidy stopped and looked at her lover. "What, Alex?"

"Dammit." Alex put her hands over her face. "I'm scared Cassidy…I just got scared and I took it out on you…I'm sorry."

The teacher squatted in front of the agent. "What are you afraid of, Alex?" The woman knew the agent's fear was not about the case. Alex was an adept agent, experienced and intelligent. She'd seen war. Cassidy also knew they could not move forward unless Alex was honest; not only with the teacher but with herself. "Alex?"

"I wanted you to lie to me," Alex admitted. "I did....and I knew you wouldn't."

"Alex, why? Tell me why." The small blonde woman took the agent's hands, suspecting she might already know the answer.

Alex looked at their hands as they joined. "What happens when this is over, Cassidy? You won't need me here."

Cassidy rose and sat in the agent's lap, lifting Alex's chin gently with her hand. "Alex, of course I will need you here."

"How? Where do I fit, Cass?" The agent was beginning to do battle with mounting tears.

Cassidy looked at Alex and smiled sweetly. "Alex Toles, what are you talking about?"

"Cass...this is...I'm in D.C....you are here....I'm a......and you're..."

"You're a what?" Cassidy started laughing and then turned serious. "Alex, you hurt me. I understand but you need to talk to me. So, we'll figure it out. Somehow we'll figure it out. You can't push me away anymore and you can't run away. I can't handle that. I need to trust you too. I've dealt with dishonesty. I've lived with loneliness. I can't do that with you. I love you too much."

Alex looked at Cassidy and saw the tear fall across the woman's cheek. "I love you so much, Cass...I just don't know how to do that."

"Yes. You do," Cassidy said.

"I want to."

"You already are, Alex. Promise me you will talk to me... please."

Alex nodded. She was still shaking. "I am supposed to be protecting you, Cassidy, and here you are again...protecting me."

"Alex, you can protect me from the bad guys all you want and I welcome it, but you can't protect me from everything.

You are not Batman. Even Bruce Wayne had pain, needed comfort," she chuckled. "He had Alfred. You don't always have to be the caped crusader. I love you just as much as an English butler," Cassidy smiled.

"I feel like it's always been this way and I know it hasn't. I can't stand the thought of losing you," Alex admitted.

"Then don't," Cassidy answered as their lips met.

"Cass...."

"Come on, Alfred. I think we have some making up to do," the teacher winked.

***

For some reason Alex felt very nervous as they reached Cassidy's room and her lover sensed the stress. "What is it?" Cassidy asked. Alex gave a shy grin. "Are you nervous?" Cassidy smiled broadly. "You are," Cassidy beamed.

The agent looked at the beautiful woman standing in her arms. She kissed her gently. "Cassidy, I want to make love to you." Sparkling green eyes searched the agent's deep blue. There was something in Alex's voice that told Cassidy that Alex needed to say something more. She stroked the long dark hair that framed the agent's exquisite features, studying every line, every slight crease and every curve in Alex's lip. Alex slowly leaned over and kissed the lips she desired. She tenderly caressed the smaller woman's face and her body began to quiver when Cassidy's lips parted slightly, inviting her to explore them. She sighed through their kiss and felt Cassidy's hands begin to wander. Alex gently grabbed Cassidy's hands, breaking their kiss momentarily. "No," she said firmly but softly.

"No?" Cassidy asked with a smirk.

"No. I want you to know how much I love you." Alex's voice was low and sensual. It resonated with so much emotion that it took Cassidy's breath away more than any kiss ever could.

"I already know," Cassidy whispered.

"Cass," Alex kissed the woman's neck and moved behind her ear. She whispered, "You are the first woman I ever made love to and you will be the only, the last." Cassidy lost her breath completely as the agent confidently undressed her; seeking nothing from Cassidy except her trust and her love.

"Alex…" Cassidy struggled to speak her lover's name. "I…"

"Shhh…" Alex hushed the woman as she delicately moved her hands and her lips over the body that now submitted fully to her touch. "Let me show you," Alex said as she lovingly kissed across Cassidy's breasts and recaptured the soft lips that seemed to somehow call to her. "*Je t'aimerai toujours* (I will always love you). Cass…always…" Alex lowered her kiss slowly; stopping only every so often to look back at the radiant face she had come to cherish. She felt Cassidy reach for her, pulling her closer. Alex held the woman tighter, pulling the small, soft body as close as she could to her own. She closed her eyes at the feel of Cassidy's skin against hers, reveling in feeling her warmth. Alex could think of nothing that compared to the sensation of Cassidy O'Brien in her arms.

"Alex…please…" Cassidy was overcome by the sensations Alex's touch seemed to produce within her. Her mind went silent. The feelings that traveled through every inch of her body consumed any thought or reason. She could only feel. It felt as if Alex were becoming part of her. She could not tell where she began and where Alex ended. It was beyond anything Cassidy had ever experienced; even when they had made love before. The more they were with one another; the more their bodies seemed to merge with their souls. As much as she hungered for Alex to send the final waves of ecstasy though her, a part of her longed for this to last forever and she thought she might willingly allow the woman loving her to consume her completely.

The agent gradually entered her lover and returned her kiss to her lips, moving in a slow, melodic rhythm that left the smaller woman beneath her gasping for air. Cassidy accepted her lover's kiss and met it with passion as she felt Alex move gently inside her, sending her tenderly but forcefully over the edge of sanity. "Oh my God, Alex...." Cassidy held the agent's head and looked into her eyes as the ripples of pleasure turned to pounding waves that pulled her under. Her eyes searched the agent's, finding all the love and the comfort she could ever imagine amidst a passionate sea of desire. "Don't let me go," she pleaded as her body began to tremble.

Alex pulled her closer, holding her tightly with her right arm and quieting her quivering with her kiss. She pulled back slightly as Cassidy's body slowly relaxed. "I will never let you go, Cass...I am so sorry."

Cassidy curled into the agent's embrace as her tears fell. "Don't, Alex, I know...I know you are...just hold me, please."

The agent inhaled all of her own emotions. Cassidy's presence in her life and in her arms seemed to fill an emptiness she had failed to recognize. She pulled the teacher's face upward to look at her. "I don't think I ever lived before you," Alex admitted as her tears begin to fall. Cassidy stroked her cheek and collapsed back into her.

The teacher was shaken by her own need. As she lay in Alex's arms the truth escaped her lips, "I have never loved anyone except you." She held on to the woman she loved and drifted off into sleep knowing that she was lying in the arms of the person she was meant to spend her life with. Alex closed her eyes promising she would never again run from the woman beside her; she would never let Cassidy O'Brien go.

Chapter Sixteen

"Where are you going?" Cassidy pulled the agent to her as Alex pulled herself up.

The agent stopped and bent over, kissing Cassidy gently. "I have some things I need to take care of."

"Now?"

"Cass...don't make this any harder." Cassidy sighed playfully. "I will be back in a couple of hours. Fallon will be here tomorrow and I need to go check on something before he gets here."

"Brian is coming to New York? Why?" Alex rubbed her temple. "Alex?"

"It's nothing to worry about." Cassidy raised her eyebrow as she gently caressed the agent's arm. "Don't worry," the agent touched her lover's cheek.

"You are," Cassidy observed.

Alex bit her lip to suppress a chuckle. "How do you do that?"

"What?" Cassidy asked. Alex looked at her, searching her eyes. The teacher smiled. "Well, Agent, you are not as hard to read as you think."

"Is that right?" Alex asked.

"It is."

"What am I thinking right now?"

Cassidy's face was overtaken by a mischievous grin. "That you'd rather be climbing back in this bed."

"That's what you think?" Alex tried to be serious but when Cassidy looked at her she started to laugh. "I give up," Alex kissed the woman. "I do love you, Cassidy O'Brien," she said as she made her way to her feet.

"Alex?" Cassidy called to the agent.

"Yeah?"

"You would tell me, right? I mean if I needed to be worried."

Alex made her way back to the woman in the bed, buttoning her shirt along the way. "Cass, you let me worry about this case, okay? I will not let anything happen to you, believe me," she stroked the teacher's cheek and Cassidy closed her eyes.

"I know," Cassidy sighed.

Alex finished getting dressed as Cassidy continued watching the agent's every move. "Do you want me to get Dylan on my way back?" Cassidy was silent for a long moment. Her heart filled at the simple gesture the agent offered. Alex looked at her and saw the love spilling from her. "What?"

"You," Cassidy smiled.

Alex shook her head. "Call your mother. I'll get him."

"Just take my car, Alex," the teacher suggested.

"What?"

"Then you won't have to take Mom's seat. Just take the SUV."

"Cass…" Cassidy smiled and pulled the covers up. Alex was surprised. All of these little things, they meant more to her than she could ever express to this woman. "Okay, how about pizza? Maybe George's?"

Cassidy smiled as the agent's hand opened the door. "I love you, Alex."

"Yeah? Well, that's good because I love you. I'll see you," Alex called back.

Cassidy pulled the pillow to her and breathed in the scent of Alex as the agent passed through the door. She'd never felt so complete, so loved, and strangely, so safe in all her life. They were feelings that she didn't know could exist as they did now. The teacher could tell the agent was concerned about something. That worried her, but in some strange way she was thankful for the current chaos. It brought her Alex. She closed her eyes trying to recall what life had been like just over a week ago. She remembered it but she couldn't feel it. The agent had changed her life in a way she had only dreamed possible. Now, she just waited; waited for Alex to walk back through the door.

*****

Alex made her way up the narrow staircase. A tall, broad shouldered man met her at the top. He was in his thirties, handsome with sandy colored, short hair and deep blue eyes. The agent smiled when he offered her a hug. "Brady," she greeted him.

"Toles...what the hell is going on?" the man asked as he broke their embrace.

"Ahhh. I'm not sure Steven...this Brackett..."

"Yeah, I did some digging," he reached in his jacket and handed her a manila envelope.

Alex opened it and slid out several sheets of paper. "What the hell?" Steven Brady nodded his own surprise. "I figured the NSA. She's DCIS? At the Pentagon?"

"Appears so," Brady confirmed.

"Does Taylor know?"

"Yeah, he found it. You know him; he can uncover any needle in any haystack."

"All right...so why is the DOD looking into my old case files? Shit, Steven...I *was* DOD."

Steven Brady and Alex Toles had worked many cases together at the NSA before he moved to the New York office. He had been a Navy Seal, had served overseas for several years as well, and had lost several of his men in an unexpected IED attack in Afghanistan. The two had a great deal in common and were able to read each other well. "Alex, I don't know," he confessed. "What's the deal with O'Brien? I saw the traffic cam."

"I don't know...but Krause is involved somehow...and now DCIS..."

Brady's surprise was evident. "Jonathan Krause? You think O'Brien's involved in arms sales?"

"Maybe. Campaigns cost money and he sure does live high on the hog."

Brady spoke carefully. "What about his wife?"

Alex ran her tongue along the inside of her bottom lip. "She doesn't know anything. She does know Krause."

"Maybe she knows something that she doesn't realize is important," Brady suggested. That thought had crossed Alex's mind but she knew she needed to be careful how she approached her dialogue with Cassidy. "Look at the last picture," Brady instructed Alex.

Alex's face fell. She reached for the bridge of her nose and held onto it for a long moment, grasping it so hard she left an imprint. "Brady…"

"Yeah…apparently they go way back…"

Alex swallowed hard and looked back down. "Fisher? Christ, Brady….They knew they were going to assign me to this. They knew it." Brady nodded his agreement. "But why?"

"I don't know."

Alex let out a sarcastic laugh. "They didn't count on Cassidy…wild card," she muttered.

"What do you mean?" Brady asked. Alex sighed and looked at him, offering a slight tilt of her head. "Ooohhh," he said, gaining a new understanding. "Haven't lost your touch, I see," he smiled.

"It's not like that," Alex said seriously.

"Don't tell me the congressman's ex actually tamed the beast," he lightened the mood. Alex shrugged a bit. "She must really be something, Toles."

"She is. Brady, if the letters…if they started as a way to divert attention… make a play at O'Brien…"

"What do you mean started?" Brady asked. Alex reached in her jacket and handed him the most recent letter. As the man studied it his gaze narrowed and his jaw twitched. "This guy's the real deal." Alex nodded. "Looks like there's more than one wild card, Toles. What do you need me to do?"

"Process that. See if you can get anything at all from it, anything. And see if you can find out who set her up in the FBI. Tate knows she's undercover. I am certain of that. This has deeper roots, someone in the Pentagon, CIA, something. It's not just Krause, not given all this....And Fisher? He has to have some place local. That's got to be my priority."

"You want me to work that here?"

"No. Fallon will be here tomorrow. Think I'll try a different angle on that front."

"P.D.?" Alex nodded. "What about Brackett?"

"I told Fallon to trail her today. We'll see if she shows her hand. She's brash...cocky."

Brady looked at his friend. "You think Tate is in on all this?"

"I think Tate knows she has another agenda...whether he's a player or he's being played; I don't know."

"I'll work that one a bit," Brady smiled eagerly. Alex knew he enjoyed these challenges. The agent turned to start her way back to the stairs when Brady grabbed her sleeve. "Toles..."

"Yeah?"

"Be careful," he cautioned.

Alex nodded. "Just see what you can find. You work Brackett. I'll work Fisher. I don't want him anywhere near Cassidy."

"She feel the same?" Brady asked. Alex just smiled. "Shit, Toles... From what I know...O'Brien's gonna' pop when he finds out," her friend could not help but smirk a bit.

Alex took a deep breath. "Yeah, well Congressman O'Brien and I have different priorities where Cassidy is concerned." Brady was surprised at his friend's forthrightness. Alex was not joking about Cassidy at all. He had never seen his friend this determined nor had he ever seen the concern he saw in her eyes now. "See what you can get," Alex said as her foot hit the stairs.

"Toles? I hope it all works out....For you, I mean." Alex turned back and smiled.

***

"What the hell?" Agent Brian Fallon said to himself as he pulled his black sedan over. "What is she doing?"

Agent Claire Brackett accepted an affectionate hug from the tall blonde woman in front of the coffee shop. "How's he doing?" Brackett asked as the two headed for the entrance.

"He's ornery. Keeps going on and on about the wife, you know," the blonde answered.

Brackett laughed. "I think he can forget that."

"What do you mean?"

"I think the congressman's ex is otherwise engaged," Brackett gloated her knowledge.

"With who?" the woman asked.

Brackett licked her lips and shrugged. "Let's just say under-cover has a new meaning at the O'Brien house."

The woman was stunned. "Cassidy and..." Brackett shrugged with delight.

Fallon picked up his phone. "Toles?"

"Fallon? What's going on? I thought you were going to tail Brackett."

"I am. Toles....She just met the congressman's girlfriend for coffee."

"WHAT?"

"Yeah, tell me. I can't get close. I have no reason to be on this side of town," he explained.

"Can you see if she has anything?"

"Yeah, coffee," Fallon said smartly.

"Funny, Fallon."

"What the hell is it with these people?" Fallon asked.

Alex had a sinking feeling. It made sense that Brackett would find a way to penetrate the congressman's personal life and the agent could guess what her former lover's agenda might be. "Fallon, just stay on her. See if you can get a view...if she passes the girlfriend anything."

"You think his girlfriend's involved in the accident?"

"No...I think this is about something else," Alex sighed.

Fallon was puzzled. "What?"

"Me," Alex said flatly.

"You? Why would? Oh Christ....Alex, you think Brackett's telling her? I mean...."

"That's exactly what I think. Get here as early as you can tomorrow, Fallon. We have a lot to talk about. I have a feeling the shit is about to hit the fan."

"What are you going to do?"

Alex took a deep breath. She knew now what was coming. No one expected her involvement in this case to go any deeper than finding a stalker. No one expected her to fall for Cassidy and certainly no one expected the congressman's ex-wife to fall in love with her. Now, Alex knew more than she was ever supposed to. She had dug in and she needed to be put at bay. Cassidy was about to be outed, at least to her ex-husband. Alex needed to prepare the woman she loved for the inevitable fall-out. It was yet another wrinkle she would need to press out. "I'm on my way to get Dylan. Just get here. I have other things to deal with tonight, Fallon."

"Alex, if he reports..."

"I know. Cassidy's safety is the priority now, Fallon. Make sure your P.D. contact knows that. Focus on Fisher and Brackett. I'll explain the rest when I see you tomorrow."

"Toles, are you okay?" Fallon asked with genuine concern. Alex smiled. She was confident that she and Cassidy would weather this. It was inevitable that their relationship would be exposed. She knew that since the beginning. The agent had simply hoped it would happen after the case was put to rest. Nothing about this case was simple. Nothing. And no one planned to make it easy. "Toles?" He repeated.

"I'm fine, Fallon, really. I'll see you in the morning." Alex hung up the phone and took a deep breath. She was determined now more than ever to get to the root of the case. Congressman Christopher O'Brien did not know Alexis Toles. She was an adversary unlike any he had faced in an election and her love for the teacher made her even more formidable. Whatever came to pass, Alex intended to prevail.

***

"You did what?" The man bellowed at the woman sitting in the chair. "What were you thinking?"

"I don't know why you're so upset," Claire Brackett answered him. "You were worried about how close she was getting; problem solved."

The man laughed. "I told you to be careful with Agent Toles. You are too confident when it comes to Alex."

"Alex?" Brackett mocked as she crossed her legs casually. "That's informal."

He glared at her. "Listen to me, Claire, and listen carefully...Alex Toles is a genius... and she's tenacious. You have no idea what you are playing with."

"Relax. What can she do? The congressman will..."

"The congressman will ask that she be pulled from this case and that will just make her more determined."

Claire Brackett rose from her chair and stepped in front of the man, running her finger down his chest, "she can't do anything when she can't access anything."

He moved her hands away abruptly. "I am telling you. Back off Toles. You are feeding the fire. Maybe this is about more than just your assignment."

Brackett rolled her eyes. The truth was that Claire Brackett was not used to rejection and she did not care for it at all. "Don't be ridiculous."

A door behind the pair opened slowly. "I'm sorry..."

"What is it?" the man answered abruptly.

"You're needed downstairs, Mr. President."

John Merrow nodded and turned back to the tall redhead. "Alex is the smartest woman I know. She figured you out in the first five minutes. You overestimate yourself as much as you underestimate her. Watch yourself, Claire."

***

"Mom!" Dylan burst through the house in search of his mother.

"Slow down, Speed Racer," Alex called ahead.

"Are we going to George's?" he asked excitedly.

Cassidy looked over the boy standing in front of her to captures the agent's glance. "That's what I hear," she smiled at Alex who returned her affectionate gaze. "Go put your backpack away." Alex leaned against the counter and offered the woman a crooked smile. Her thumb instinctively reached her temple and began massaging it. "Okay...out with it," Cassidy said as Alex fidgeted a bit. "Alex..."

"You're right. We need to talk about some things, but not now, Cass."

"Alex, we agreed..."

"Yes, we did, but I think after today...what happened earlier, we should just go have a pizza with Dylan and talk when we get back." Cassidy looked at the agent, studying her carefully. "Cassidy, look, you and I both know sooner or later people are going to find out about us."

"Is that what this is about?"

Alex shook her head. "It is. Partly...only partly."

"Alex, I'm not worried about..."

"I know that, but there are things we have to talk about Cass. I am technically on the job. Let's just talk about it after dinner. I will tell you everything I can then," the agent promised as Cassidy walked into her arms.

"You're worried about Chris, aren't you?"

Alex brushed the woman's hair aside lovingly. "I'm worried about you."

"I'm a big girl, Alex."

"Mmm…I know," Alex said as Cassidy smiled and kissed the agent.

"Mom!" Dylan yelled. Finding his mother kissing the agent, he cringed. "Gross."

Alex became shaky and her face flushed at the realization Dylan was there. Cassidy laughed and put her head against Alex's chest. "Not as gross as those fruit rollup things you love," his mother said.

He shook his small head. "Are we going for pizza?"

"I don't know, are we?" She looked at the agent.

Alex took a deep breath. It still surprised her how comfortable Cassidy was with their relationship. She wondered how that would fare when the congressman found out. "We are," she said decisively. Dylan pulled on the agent's hand lightly. "Yeah, okay. We're coming," Alex laughed. He ran out of the kitchen and down the hallway hoping his mother and the agent would follow quickly.

"You all right, there?" Cassidy asked the agent who responded with a forced smile. The teacher gave the agent a kiss on the cheek. "Alex, if you're going to be here, he's going to see us."

"I know. Let's go get that pizza," the agent said, thankful for a diversion if only for a while.

***

"Alex…Come on," Dylan pulled on the agent.

Cassidy tried to hide her amusement. "Only if your mother agrees to challenge us," she encouraged Cassidy.

"A little confident?" Cassidy quipped. Alex lifted her hands as if to say 'Bring it on'. "Okay," the teacher whispered in Alex's ear. "I'll bet you back rubs for a week *I* win."

Alex was surprised at Cassidy's competitiveness. "You are on," the agent winked. The teacher laughed as she climbed into the seat of the truck cab. Alex leaned over into the teacher's ear and teased, "I hope you're not a sore loser."

Cassidy tilted her head back and softly gave her reply. "You're not a very good gambler, Alex. Either way I win." She turned back to the game leaving Alex with a lump in her throat and a tingle down her spine. Cassidy surprised Alex at every turn and the agent loved it. The small blonde woman jostled herself into position and concentrated on the screen, or rather the road, in front of her. She turned and weaved through obstacles, over hills, along steep curves, slowing down here and there and then speeding up her virtual car again.

Dylan looked at the agent in amazement and then back at the screen. "MOM!" Cassidy swerved and avoided a collision. "You're at level 38! Alex!" Dylan was almost as wide eyed as the agent. "She's gonna' beat us, Alex."

"Nah... just wait. Here comes the tough level," Alex assured him.

Three more levels passed before Cassidy finally wiped out over a virtual guard rail. The small blonde woman got up and shrugged. "Level 41!" Dylan said excitedly, quite proud of his mother, who greeted his enthusiasm with a wide grin and a hug.

"All right," Alex lifted Dylan to the front of the cab and onto her lap. "Your mom's been holding out on me," she whispered.

"I heard that," Cassidy cracked back.

"Figures," Alex tried to whisper softly.

"And that," Cassidy said.

Alex Toles was naturally competitive and she did not want to lose this bet, although she had to admit the idea of owing Cassidy back rubs for a week was not a punishment by any measure. She bit her lip and her heart quickened at the reality of the wager the woman she loved had levied. Another reason to love Cassidy; she was smart. There was no loser in this bet except the agent's pride if she somehow lost to the teacher. "Okay, Dylan," Alex put her feet on the pedals and her hands over the small ones gripping the wheel. "Let's show your mom who is king of the road!"

Cassidy watched the agent and her son, caring very little about who won any bet. The sight of her son in Alex's lap, the sound of his laughter and Alex's enthusiastic but gentle encouragement made her heart soar. She wasn't sure she'd ever seen Dylan so happy. She thought to herself, 'Can this be real?' Her daydreaming was abruptly ended by the buzzing of her phone. "Hello," she put a finger in her opposite ear trying to hear over the sounds of the game accompanied by the agent and Dylan's exclamations as they dodged cars and rocks and turned and skidded across pretend pavement. "No...I'm at George's with Dylan...What? Hold on," Cassidy stepped out of the cab and into the restaurant. Engrossed in the game and the small boy bouncing on her lap, Alex didn't realize immediately that the teacher was gone.

"What?" Cassidy asked.

"What the hell is going on there?" the voice on the other end boomed.

"What are you talking about?" Cassidy asked pointedly.

"When did you start sleeping with women?" Cassidy cocked her jaw in disgust but did not respond. Now she understood what Alex had been worried about. "Well? When did you start sleeping with her?"

"My life is none of your business, Christopher. You gave up the right to ask questions a long time ago."

"You divorced me," he shot back at his ex-wife.

"Well, thanks for reminding me why," the teacher responded in kind, now walking out the front door of the restaurant for some privacy.

"What do you want to ruin me or something? What about Dylan? Is she there now?"

Cassidy let out a sarcastic chuckle. "You can ruin yourself all by yourself, Chris. You don't need my help. As for Dylan, he is happier than I have ever seen him. And as for my relationship with Alex? I don't ask you about your girlfriends; in fact I never did; so you can extend me that same courtesy."

"Relationship?" he yelled. "Do you know anything about this woman, Cassidy, at all?" Cassidy pursed her lips as her anger burned hotter by the moment. "If you think I am going to let you…"

"Let me? Let me, what, Chris? This isn't about me and it's not about Dylan; it's about you, your image. Let me say this so you understand. That is not my problem."

"Cassidy, I am warning you…"

"You know, that may work with your little minions in Washington, not with me. This conversation is over," Cassidy hung up the phone as the congressman attempted to continue his admonishment of her. She exhaled audibly and tried to steady her nerves, the fury within her powerful.

"Hah! Level 39! Cass, you're…" Alex glanced to the side but she did not see Cassidy. Through the side window she caught sight of the small blonde woman walking back through the front door. Cassidy smiled and shook the hand of an older woman before continuing back through the restaurant. Alex could tell she was angry. She'd seen that look earlier in the day.

"ALEX!" Dylan exclaimed. Alex's momentary distraction had caused a virtual collision with an oncoming truck. "AWWW!" Dylan sighed as Cassidy walked back through the opening to the truck cab. "You won Mom!" He said with more pride than disappointment.

"Did I?" Cassidy smiled at her son. Alex lifted Dylan off her lap and looked at the teacher with concern in her eyes. Cassidy tightened her lips, acknowledging in her glance that, yes, she was upset about something. The teacher had no intention of spoiling her son's night. She looked at him and smiled genuinely. "Well, as the queen of the road, I say we get some ice cream to celebrate." She turned and looked at the agent for support.

"Okay. You are the queen of the road, after all." Alex looked at Dylan, "ice cream it is." She caught Cassidy as they made their way back to the table. "Are you okay?"

The teacher clasped the agent's hand. "Later," she said.

Alex's heart dropped. She had a strong feeling she knew what had happened. "Cass?"

Cassidy turned back and saw the fear in the agent's eyes. She grasped Alex's hand again and smiled. "You're not getting out of those back rubs that easy, Alfred." Alex smiled. She was not looking forward to this conversation. One thing was clear, Cassidy loved her and Alex was certain that the only person who could ruin that was Alex.

***

Cassidy came out of the bathroom wearing a pair of jogging pants and a tank top. Alex wished this evening could have a different agenda. The more she was around Cassidy, the more intoxicating she found her. Cassidy was a beautiful woman to be sure. The simple moments, watching Cassidy cook, watching her brush her hair, when she put Dylan's jacket on, when she walked out of the bathroom still brushing her teeth, Alex thought those were the moments that she loved the woman the most. And, there was scarcely a moment she did not long to be closer to her, even just to feel Cassidy sleeping in her arms. Right now they needed to talk. The teacher sat down on the end of the bed and looked at the agent who was sitting on the arm of a large chair across the room, nervously waiting. "So, Chris called while we were at George's," Cassidy offered. Alex sighed and rubbed her face. "He knows." Alex nodded again. "I don't know how he knows."

"I do," Alex said. Cassidy looked up to the agent. "Brackett."

"Agent Brackett?" Cassidy asked with surprise, "Why...."

Alex took a deep breath and released it. She walked to the bed and sat beside Cassidy. "Brackett is a DCIS agent." Cassidy looked at the agent with confusion. "Department of Defense, she works for the DOD."

"She's an FBI agent," Cassidy questioned.

Alex sighed again. "No, but she's working in the FBI. I thought she was NSA; that's where I went this afternoon."

"Why would Brackett tell Chris about us?"

Alex stood and began pacing. "Me...Look Cass, they're going to pull me back to D.C. and off the case. He'll make sure of that; that's why."

"They can't do that."

"Yes, they can and they will. I violated my duty and I compromised this case."

"Because of me?" Cassidy said with both hurt and guilt in her voice.

"Cass, listen to me, that's what is going to happen. I need you to just trust me. This case is bigger, Krause..."

"What is it about Jon, Alex?" The agent continued pacing. She was trying to choose all of her words carefully. She was worried about Cassidy and what might happen when she got pulled off the case. Fisher was a loose cannon which worried the agent. Alex also wasn't certain what she would do when she was called to pay the piper and she knew Cassidy would not want her to quit the bureau.

"Alex?" Cassidy called, "you are making me dizzy."

The agent couldn't help but chuckle. Cassidy was tougher that she gave the teacher credit for. She made her way back to the bed and sat beside her lover. "Krause is CIA.'"

Cassidy closed her eyes tightly and rubbed them with both hands. "What?"

"There's more. Cass, look, there's good reason to think Jon Krause is involved in international arms sales."

"You mean like guns?"

Alex pressed her tongue to her cheek and placed her right thumb on her temple. "No. I mean like missiles." Cassidy stared blankly at the agent as Alex continued. The agent

couldn't control her need to move and began milling about
the room again as she spoke. "Look, Cassidy, for quite a few
years the NSA has been watching Krause and a few others.
They have a high level of access to information... and," the
agent hesitated.

"What, Alex?"

"There've been instances of money filtered through political campaigns, PAC money specifically, rerouted to foreign
banks. There's been some evidence of trades, hard to track...
Croatia, Ecuador, even Iraq. We were never able to determine if
it was actual parts or only the technology, fringe groups or governments or both, but the campaign piece, that was certain."

Cassidy sat with her face in her hands. "Alex, Jon worked
for Technologie Appliquée in France. I just remembered that
this afternoon." Alex knelt in front of the teacher. "What does
any of this have to do with me, with Carl Fisher?" Cassidy asked,
the anxiety evident in her expression.

Alex took Cassidy's hands. "It wasn't supposed to have anything to do with you, I don't think. The letters were a diversion to try to press the congressman off of something, or into
something. They set a good precedent in case they needed to
act. They provided a cover. Fisher was a bad call. Now you're
stuck in it."

Cassidy searched the agent's eyes. "Alex, did they really try
to kill Chris?"

"I think so, yes."

"And me?"

"Krause is no threat to you. I am the threat to whatever is
going on. That's why Brackett played the card she did. Fallon
and Taylor, they'll handle Fisher. You'll be safe, Cass, I promise
you."

"Are you going to get fired?"

"It doesn't matter."

Cassidy was beginning to tremble. "Alex..."

"He's a congressman Cassidy; that's how the game is played. I have friends too. Best case scenario they suspend me." Cassidy covered her face and then looked to the ceiling. A few hours ago they were laughing and now she felt as though she were in the middle of a spy novel. "Cass, look at me, please?" Cassidy shook her head still looking at the ceiling and trying to determine what she felt. "Please?" Alex implored her lover.

Green eyes that were beginning to overflow looked at the agent. "I'm sorry, Alex."

"What are you talking about?" Alex said softly.

"My crazy life. Now you are in the middle of it...and..."

Alex smiled and took a deep breath releasing it slowly. "You," the agent hesitated briefly, realizing the gravity in what she was about to say. She took another breath. It was hard to fathom, but Cassidy needed to know how Alex felt and Alex needed to say it. "You *are* my life, Cassidy. It doesn't matter, as long as you are safe and Dylan is safe."

Cassidy stroked the agent's cheek, "Alex, I can't believe that he'd..."

"I know," Alex said. "Cass, we don't know what your ex-husband is really into."

"Why did they put you here if..." Cassidy began to muse.

"I imagine to track Fisher, get rid of their problem for them. Three things they didn't count on." Cassidy looked at the agent inquisitively. "Brackett knows Fisher intimately, Fisher's a screwball," Alex paused to search her lover's eyes.

"And?" Cassidy urged her to continue.

"And I fell in love with you."

The smaller woman took the agent's face in her hands. "Make it four. I fell in love with you," she said searching the blue eyes before her.

Alex smiled and kissed the woman. She climbed onto the bed and pulled Cassidy into her arms. "It will be okay, Cass."

"I know it will," Cassidy answered running her hand over the strong woman who held her close. "I don't want you to go, Alex."

Alex inhaled her lover's words. "Let's just see what tomorrow brings."

"Alex?"

"What?"

"Promise me you will be back," Cassidy said with some fear.

"Cassidy, there is nothing that could keep me from you, nothing." The smaller woman held onto the agent tightly. Cassidy knew that was true, but she wanted Alex close now. They lay in silence for a long time, awake but needing to process all of their emotions. After a while, Alex looked down and kissed Cassidy's head. "Cass?"

"Hum?"

"Where did you learn to drive like that?"

Cassidy giggled. Even in the middle of all this uncertainty and unimaginable drama, Alex was thinking about that video game. "I was sick for a full month when I was pregnant with Dylan. I couldn't move from the couch most days. Play Station was my companion, well…that and a bucket."

Alex laughed. "I see."

"Not as interesting as you thought, huh?" Cassidy chuckled.

"Actually, I think it's the most interesting fact I discovered all night." Alex's endearing comment might have seemed patronizing were it not the truth.

"Well, I'm no spy," Cassidy said.

"Cass, you could disarm James Bond. Don't sell yourself short." Cassidy closed her eyes and sighed into her lover's chest. "*Je ne pourrai jamais te laisser partir.* (I will never let you go)." The agent said with a light kiss to her lover's head.

Cassidy's reply filled Alex's heart. She could scarcely believe the depth of the love she felt for the woman in her arms. "That's good," Cassidy began, "you owe me some back rubs."

Chapter Seventeen

Alex watched as Cassidy moved to the stove and started breakfast. The agent was anxious for Brian Fallon's arrival. At the same time she was trying to prepare herself for the inevitable call that the congressman's new found information was certain to bring. She had no idea when it would come, only that it would. The agent loved watching Cassidy when she was doing these types of things. She felt a sense of home that she couldn't explain in words. In a short time the pair had become quite comfortable in the everyday activities of life together. They just fit. She moved behind the small woman who was mixing ingredients in a bowl and kissed her on the cheek. "What's that for?" Cassidy asked.

Right now Alex was wishing there was no case, no congressman and no FBI. She knew they would have to part, at least for a while, and the thought of being away from the woman she loved, particularly now, distressed her. "I just love you," Alex said sweetly.

Cassidy looked at her, twisting her face. "Are you all right?" she joked. Alex set down her cup and pulled the woman closer. Her heart was sinking for some reason. She just wanted to hold on. "Alex?" Alex bent over and kissed Cassidy softly. The teacher fought to regain her breath as Alex pulled away. "Good morning," Cassidy sighed. The sound of the doorbell interrupted the moment. "That's probably Brian," Cassidy said, suggesting with her voice that Alex should answer.

"Probably," Alex said continuing to search the green eyes before her and making no motion to leave the moment.

"Alex?"

"Hmmm?"

"The door?" Cassidy raised an eyebrow.

"He'll wait," the agent kissed the teacher again. The small blonde woman in the agent's arms opened her eyes to the sound of the doorbell again. She looked at Alex and smiled. "I just wanted you to know," the agent said as her phone began to buzz.

"I do," Cassidy touched her lover's cheek.

Alex took a deep breath and picked up the phone. "Yeah, I'm coming already." Cassidy shook her head and laughed. She knew what was to come and she didn't want to think about it. She'd spent most of the night thinking about reality. She couldn't remember when Alex hadn't been in her life. It all seemed like a dream; her past. Waking up and feeling Alex next to her, watching as the agent dressed in the morning, the way Dylan looked for Alex as soon as he woke up; there were so many moments now that she wished she could freeze and exist in forever. She hated the idea of Alex being away. She'd just found her, after all.

"What took you so long?" Fallon asked. Alex just smiled. "Oh."

Alex led her partner toward the kitchen. "Hi, Mr. Fallon," a small voice called from in front of the television.

"Hey, Dylan."

"Alex? Are you coming?" Dylan asked hopefully.

"Maybe in a little bit," she answered. He looked at her sadly and she winked at him. Brian Fallon regarded the interaction between the boy and his partner and smiled. "What?" Alex asked as they reached the kitchen. She set her gaze back upon the woman who was now cooking pancakes and sighed.

"Brian, how are you?" Cassidy turned.

"I'm well, Cassidy," he smiled.

"Well, sit down you two. We might as well all START the day right," the teacher said with a note of apprehension in her voice. Alex looked at her and the two exchanged a glance of understanding.

"What's going on?" Fallon asked as Alex put a cup of coffee in front of him and pulled up a chair.

Cassidy brought over a plate of pancakes and set them on the table and the agent looked up at her. "How about I go take Dylan his?" the agent offered.

"I think that would be great. God knows he's been waiting for you all morning," the teacher agreed.

Fallon watched the two women closely as Alex put a plate together and rose from the table. "I'll be right back," she said, still focused on Cassidy who was now grabbing her own coffee.

Brian Fallon was not certain what to make of the situation. He knew Alex was eager to talk to him and yet here she was leaving him alone with the congressman's ex-wife. Cassidy saw his confusion and smiled at him as she took her seat at the table. "Eat," she said. He nodded. She looked out of the room toward the agent's intended destination and closed her eyes before returning her attention the man seated nearby. "She's just struggling this morning, Brian," Cassidy explained. Fallon looked at her over a forkful of pancakes, questioning her comment with his eyes. She let out a strong sigh, glancing away again and then back at him. "Chris called me last night." The male agent nearly choked on his mouthful. Cassidy nodded and pursed her lips. "Yeah...He knows." Fallon blew air from his mouth and rubbed his forehead. "There's more. She told me a lot, but I'll leave all that to Alex."

"Cassidy?" he began his inquiry.

"Yeah?"

"What do you think he'll do?"

Cassidy rolled her eyes and shook her head. "Exactly what she expects."

The sadness in the woman's voice cut through Brian Fallon. He'd never see his partner in a relationship but he knew Alex. When Alex Toles committed to something she was unshakeable. "I know it's not my place, but Alex, I told you...I can tell..."

The teacher smiled. "I know," she said reaching for his hand. "I love her too." Fallon nodded as Alex reentered the room.

The agent walked to the table and sat down, retrieving her coffee and watching as Cassidy put breakfast on a plate for her. She looked at her lover and then to her partner, "So the news is out."

Fallon felt horrible and his empathy for his friend was obvious, "Alex...I..."

"Don't. It was inevitable, Fallon." She took a bite of her pancakes but had to admit she was not feeling very hungry. "Listen, we need your P.D. contact to work Fisher. We can't go through the FBI."

"Why not?" Fallon asked as Cassidy got up to get more coffee for everyone.

"Because, Fallon, we're compromised there."

"What are you talking about? Alex, seriously where is all this coming from?"

Alex looked up and into her lover's eyes as the woman poured coffee into each of their cups, placed the pot on the table and sat down across from the agent. The agent took a deep breath. "Fallon, Brackett is DCIS."

He shook his head. "How could you know that? And why would..."

"It's not that uncommon," Alex stated as fact. "Look, I never told you because that was part of the deal when I went to the FBI...But, I was NSA for a number of years, Fallon...Before I went to the FBI. That's how I know."

Her partner ran his hand over the top of his head gathering his thoughts. "That's how you know the president?"

"No. I served under him in Iraq. But yes, I did work with the White House briefly on some things."

"All right. Why then? And what does Fisher have to do with any of this?" he asked.

Alex looked to Cassidy for encouragement and her partner's eyes followed, surprised to realize that Alex had obviously shared a great deal with the teacher. Seeing the loving expression from the woman across from her, Alex sipped her coffee, set down her mug and sighed. She immediately saw the surprise in her friend's eyes. "Fallon, Cassidy knows everything I know, pretty much anyway…So you can speak freely," she smiled at her lover and Cassidy's gaze retreated into her coffee cup as Alex continued. "When I was with the NSA I worked with DCIS on several cases." She paused and took another sip of her coffee in an effort to gather her thoughts. "Notably, cases that dealt with potential sales of missiles, technology and other military armaments; sales that were laundered, embedded and hidden though PAC donations to certain congressional campaigns." Agent Brian Fallon set his mug down slowly. "Yeah," Alex Toles continued. "Sound familiar? Look, I don't know WHAT the deal is here, Fallon. I suspect your hunch was right. Money was filtered through the O'Brien campaign." Alex stopped briefly noting the sharp intake of breath from her lover. "Whether O'Brien knew, or what he knew, I don't know. He knows something. Whether Brackett was assigned this to investigate O'Brien or whether she's involved, I don't know that either. Near as I can figure Fisher is just an unfortunate consequence for us all, probably assigned in the campaign to gather intel. At least that's what one of my sources indicated. His dismissal did not play well and now he's freelancing. And guess who he knows well?" Fallon shrugged slightly. "Claire Brackett."

"Toles?" Fallon looked momentarily at the teacher. "What's Fisher's deal then?"

"Loose cannon," she sighed, the worry in her voice unmistakable. "And obsessed with Cassidy."

251

"They're gonna' pull you. Maybe pull *us* when they find out I've known."

Alex nodded. Cassidy looked at the table and the agent noticed the tear escaping her eye. The agent slowly reached across the table and took the teacher's hand, softly caressing it. "I expect that. That's why you need to work with your P.D. contact. I have my NSA resources. If I have to," she paused, "I'll call in the big guns."

"You mean the president," he noted, prompting Cassidy to raise her head and look at Alex nervously.

"I do."

"What about Brackett?" Fallon asked.

Alex raised a thumb to her temple and pressed hard. This time it was the teacher to squeeze the agent's hand for reassurance. Alex nodded. "Cassidy's safety is the priority. Fisher first, Fallon. I have someone working the other angle. But Fallon, you should know, Tate knows who Brackett is."

"What are you saying?" Fallon asked.

"Only that A.D. Tate knows she is DCIS."

"Alex…"

"Look, Fallon, like it or not this is bigger than we thought. That means players, people on the inside, and believe me when I tell you…Well, let's just say I've seen it go up the chain of command higher than you'd like to imagine."

"Toles?" Fallon swallowed hard.

"Yeah?"

"What exactly did you do before this?"

Agent Alex Toles looked across to her lover. She had only given Cassidy the cursory explanation. "I investigated covert operations, off the books operations; things not legal but sanctioned."

Cassidy closed her eyes, understanding what Alex meant. Fallon reacted. "What do you mean *sanctioned?*"

"I mean sanctioned by people in command at very high levels. That's what I mean; actions that agents and others became complicit in without a full understanding of what was happening. That is what I mean."

Brian Fallon covered his mouth in disbelief. "And you think that is what is happening here?"

Alex's temple began to twitch. "Yes." She looked squarely at her partner. "They never counted on Fisher being crazy enough to stalk Cassidy. They never counted on Brackett knowing Fisher *intimately*. Fallon, they assigned us to get rid of the Fisher problem for them. That played to their diversion scenario. Putting me here, that also got me away from Brackett in the office. So whatever she was really looking for in my files...well," she shook her head thinking better of continuing her current statement. "But then they got thrown a wildcard they never could have seen coming." Fallon looked at his partner. She deadpanned her answer, "Cassidy and I, well, they would never have imagined that." A small smile crinkled onto her face.

"So what do we do?"

"We meet with your P.D. contact first. I have a meeting later this morning with a friend from the NSA."

"Alex?" Fallon began cautiously. Alex raised an eyebrow at him. "How serious is it that you told me all of this?" Alex just forced a crooked smile. "That's what I thought."

***

Carl Fisher inhaled the drag from his cigarette fully and savored it. He gently shifted the glass in his hand, swirling the yellow liquid from side to side before bringing it to his nose and then sipping it with satisfaction. He looked at the picture on the table of the beautiful blonde woman and licked his lips as his breath began to quicken. He slammed the glass down when the buzzing of a black box on the table interrupted his thoughts. "Fisher," he answered.

"She'll be gone shortly," the voice on the other end offered.

"Hummm," he exhaled.

"Do you have a plan?"

Fisher took another long drag from his cigarette. "It's set."

"Good. Just so we're clear, I don't like this," the voice came across the phone.

"No, you wouldn't," Fisher smirked picking up his glass and tracing the photo again with his hand.

"What do you need?"

"Confirmation," was the only word Fisher spoke.

"Where?"

"Here," Fisher replied.

"Understood."

***

Detective Pete Ferro entered the café casting his glance about for his old friend. The detective had worked in the city for over twenty years and could still not imagine retiring, if only because the work was in his blood. A third generation police officer, he bled blue and he loved his work. He had worked everything from a street beat to homicide and there wasn't one assignment he regretted. He had weathered the years and the strain of his job well and had been approached by all the major federal investigative services but preferred the city role. A large man, nearly 6'4 with black hair that had just started to show a hint of gray in the side burns; Pete Ferro was both hand-some and an intimidating presence. He noticed his friend with the attractive woman in the corner and smiled. "Pete," Brian Fallon greeted with a strong handshake.

"Well, Agent, federal life is treating you well I see, particu-larly if this is your partner," Ferro complimented.

Alex smiled which surprised her. Generally she did not like professional compliments that alluded to her gender. Detective Ferro was charming and his manner was not chau-vinistic, but seemed genuine. Fallon stumbled a bit, worried what his partner's reaction might be. "Uhh, yeah, this is my partner, Alex Toles."

"Detective," Alex smiled. "Thank you for meeting us."

"No...Happy to help a friend. So, what is it you feds need from this beat boy?" He kidded, looking directly at Alex. That told the agent what she needed to know. He had that sixth sense; the ability to read people and he knew Alex held the information. Alex pushed a file toward him across the table. He opened it and studied it, taking a brief moment to thumb through each page. Occasionally he sighed and rubbed his chin, his eyes remaining intense through every glance. After a short while he closed the folder and looked at the pair across from him. "Psycho." Alex nodded and raised her eyebrows in agreement of his assessment. "So...what do you need?"

Alex pulled out an envelope and handed it to him. He looked at her probing her thoughts with his eyes. She gestured to him to open it. He pulled out several letters and photos. "Originals?" She nodded.

"He's got to have some place nearby," she said. "Detective, Carl Fisher is a former CIA agent. He's the real deal, crazy, incredibly intelligent and beyond sophisticated when it comes to training."

The detective nodded his understanding. "You want me to see what we can gather locally? See if we can find where he might be? I can do that, but New Rochelle is not my town, Agent."

Alex poked at her cheek with her tongue and looked at Brian Fallon. There was one thing she had not told any of them yet. "Harlem," she said. Agent Fallon looked at her with great curiosity and the detective stared forward eyeing her carefully. "The first pictures, they were outside the school. He's near Cassidy's school," she gestured to one of the letters.

The detective held it over his head to the light and snickered at her discovery. Most people would never have seen what

Alex did. It was so faint he barely saw it. "They didn't find this in the lab, did they?" He laughed. She shook her head.

"Find what?" Fallon demanded.

"Your partner here should be a beat cop," Ferro mused. "She knows the old fashioned ways, been in the field at some point I'd say." Alex acknowledged his appraisal of her. Fallon still did not follow. "Well, Fallon, there is just a tiny impression on the far left corner… 'lem'…that's it…just 'lem', but it might tell the story," Detective Ferro smiled.

"How the hell?" Fallon said.

Alex shook her head. "Something I picked up in the field. You just learn all the technology in the world isn't always as good as a bright light and a strong pair of eyes, Fallon. You'd be surprised what analysts and forensics miss with their case loads." The detective nodded his respect. Alex had gone over every letter a least a thousand times in the last couple of weeks. She never dismissed anything. And, she had learned that sometimes, many times, local law enforcement was more tenacious than her federal compatriots. They didn't sit at computers. She respected that.

"Okay," Pete Ferro said. "I'll get on it."

The female agent smiled. "Detective?" He looked at her as he was rising to leave. She scrawled out a number on a napkin. "Use this number, it's…" The detective understood. Former CIA was all he needed to know; whatever his friend and his partner were into they needed to be off the grid. Pete Ferro started to leave and Alex stopped him again. "Last thing. It may or may not come to pass," he looked at her curiously. "You may hear some things about me." Alex was anticipating a press leak on Cassidy. She hadn't told her lover her fear, but it made sense. In some ways Christopher O'Brien would do himself the most harm by going to the press, if keeping their relationship quiet was his goal, but he was imprudent and reactionary and Alex fully expected a leak to come from him.

"What is it, Agent?"

"The congressman's ex-wife," she began.

Pete Ferro smiled. Cassidy was a popular figure around the city, far more popular than her ex-husband. Alex had witnessed that firsthand when people would approach her at the grocery store or at George's, just wanting to talk to the pretty and affable school teacher. "She's quite the lady," he offered.

Alex couldn't help but get a twinkle in her eye. "I agree," she said with a tilt of her head.

The detective chuckled. "Can't say as I saw that coming," he winked. "But, you're a lucky woman, Agent. You'll break an awful lot of hearts with that one." Alex chuckled at his good natured response. "Don't worry about it. We'll find him. I know how to reach you." Alex felt much better. Pete Ferro clearly could read all of her signals and in between the lines.

"Fallon?" Alex called across to her partner.

"Yeah?"

"Promise me...whatever happens...well...just keep her safe."

"Whatever it takes," was his simple answer.

***

"Cassie, what's wrong?" the woman's mother asked. The school teacher sighed as she took a seat on the couch, folding her legs beneath her. Rose McCollum was certain her daughter was on the verge of tears. "Did something happen with you and Alex?"

Cassidy couldn't help but let out a small laugh as she felt tears begin to sting her eyes. "Not like you are thinking, no. Chris...He called. He found out."

Rose took a deep breath and nodded. "Are you worried about Alex?"

"She's probably going to be reprimanded and removed from the case."

"You don't know that for certain, Cass...."

The small blonde woman looked across to her mother with assuredness. "I do know. I know him."

Cassidy's mother moved to her daughter's side. "Cassie, Alex loves you."

The teacher's emotions were in overdrive. "I know…but…"

"But what?"

"This could ruin her career, Mom, and it's my fault." The small blonde woman couldn't hold back any longer and her tears broke forth.

"Cassie…" Rose rubbed her daughter's back.

"The worst part, Mom? I almost don't care about her career. What if she doesn't come back? What if she leaves and she ends up hating me for it? God. How selfish can I be? I should just let her go; who needs all this?"

The older woman bit her lip to contain the smile that seemed determined to make its presence known. She had seen her daughter and the agent, the way that they looked at one another. She was as certain as she had ever been about anything that no job and no person would keep Alex Toles from her daughter for long. But, she could feel her daughter's fear and pain. "Listen to me, Cassidy, Alex loves you. I don't think anything will change that, not from what I have seen." Cassidy's tears were turning to sobs as she collapsed into her mother. She couldn't speak. The thought of losing Alex was far more frightening than Carl Fisher had ever been. She didn't want the agent to know how insecure she was feeling or how guilty. Cassidy was not accustomed to breaking down, but at the moment all she wanted was to cry and as she did she began to think that it might never stop.

***

Carl Fisher dragged the large man to the corner of the room. The resemblance was uncanny. Fisher stood over his prey, admiring him. He stroked his own face and his eyes took on a slight glow. He lifted the weight into the chair and considered the form before him again as his eyes began to grow a shade darker. He made his way into the bedroom and retrieved the shotgun, carrying it at his side to the other room. There were a few more last details he needed to complete. He placed a picture carefully in the lap that sat before him, but not before examining it closely. He inspected the neatly polished finger tips of the man, admiring his handiwork. Three steps back, perhaps too far, he thought. He stepped eye to eye with his victim. Carefully he moved back, just a quarter of a pace. He put the man's hands around the barrel and.....

***

"No, I understand...Thanks, Brady....yeah...I got it....what about that French company? Ever heard of them?...You think the congressman knows?......No, right now I'm more worried about Fisher....I agree...Brackett might be more involved..... No, he knows.....No, I'm sure....Just waiting really....I appreciate that...I don't want to call Taylor....better if you and I stay in contact. Okay. I'll let you know when it goes down." Alex hung up the small flip phone and took a deep breath.

"What was that about?" Agent Fallon asked.

"That was my contact at the NSA. No meeting today; he's been digging into Krause and Tate and Brackett. Apparently, Brackett's father was at the Pentagon for years. He was a Rear Admiral. Not sure what he did but he was very connected until his formal retirement two years ago, AND he was connected to Jon Krause. Brady will keep digging. There are still bigger fish to fry here. Everything he's found on Fisher seems to match what we already know. We need to find him, sooner than later."

"Toles," Fallon began, "maybe the letter thing is over and the...Well, maybe the spook is spooked."

"Spooks don't get spooked, Fallon. That's why they are called spooks."

"But he's not CIA anymore."

"No and that's what scares me. He has all that training and no structure.... And he's obsessed. It's like starting a fire with gasoline."

Fallon looked at his partner. "It's more than that. I can see it on your face."

Alex wasn't certain how to answer so she did so bluntly. "I said no structure. I never said there was no one else involved. Our involvement is a liability. Now people, people who are connected to whatever is going on here, know about Cassidy and me. I'm just worried who is going to light the match."

"Toles...you think he's gonna' make a move?"

"Let's just say I hope your friend Ferro finds something fast. That, or someone views Fisher as the greater liability." Alex paused and looked at the agent seated across from her. "Fallon, whatever happens, if you need to walk away from this; I will understand."

"What are you talking about?"

Years of training and the ability to distance her emotions kicked in. She had lost friends before and understood the risks. She would never let that happen to the woman that she loved. Alex was determined to get to the bottom of things eventually, but nothing mattered more than the teacher's welfare. "I mean that I will do anything to keep Cass safe. Anything."

Chapter Eighteen

Alex dropped her partner at his hotel and headed back for Cassidy's. The expected call still had not come and it was Friday afternoon. She pulled onto Cherry Circle and smiled. It wasn't very long ago that the destination at the end of the street was something she anticipated with antipathy. Now, the drive was comforting. She was looking forward to seeing Cassidy and Dylan. Pulling into the driveway the agent looked up at the large colonial and felt a deep sense of satisfaction knowing who would be awaiting her return, and that someone was waiting for her to return. She had just turned the key off in the ignition when the phone rang, 4:35 p.m., she noted the time and answered. "Agent Alex Toles," she identified herself. Her face fell, back to reality. "I understand.....yes.....I will be....yes, Sir." That was it. The agent took a deep breath and readied herself to face the occupants of 1215 Cherry Circle.

Cassidy was in the kitchen which did not surprise the agent. She could hear the clanking of pans and was certain that her lover was in the process of making dinner. She peeked in the living room and saw Dylan sitting at the coffee table with two of his action figures. The agent stopped and watched him act out a battle between Batman and some figure she could not identify. Dylan was adorable. He had his mother's charm and a little bit of a mischievous streak. The agent could feel her eyes getting misty. She looked forward to seeing him in the morning and watching Cassidy tuck him in each evening. A hand on her back startled her slightly. "Oh... Rose," Alex choked back a tear. "I was just..."

Rose's expression conveyed immediately to the agent that Cassidy had spoken with her. The older woman's eyes were full of both compassion and reassurance. Before Rose could speak a small body thumped into the agent. "Alex! You're home!"

"Looks that way, huh?"

He grabbed her hand and pulled her into the large room. Alex looked back and Rose gave her a wink. "LOOK!" On the floor the boy had built some structure from Legos. "It's the Batcave, Alex!"

"That is quite the building, Speed Racer, look at that." The agent felt him cling slightly to her neck and she smiled. Rose McCollum kept a watchful eye on the duo for a few moments before making her way out the front door. Alex had already taken a seat on the floor and was smiling broadly and studying with great interest every detail Rose's grandson pointed out to her. Cassidy's mother felt a wave of happiness take her over. Cassidy needn't worry. She could see it as plain as day. There might be things to fear; losing the tall agent was not one of them. "Hey...I've got to go see your mom for a while, okay?"

"Okay," the small voice answered. "Will you help me build a car after?" Dylan asked excitedly.

"You got it, Speed Racer," Alex said pulling herself up and taking in a large breath as she headed to the kitchen.

Cassidy was in front of the counter with a large pan in front of her. Alex walked up quietly and put her hands on the woman's waist. Cassidy turned slowly to face the agent and knew in an instant that the call had come. Alex's eyes were a dead giveaway. "When?" Cassidy asked.

"Monday morning," the answer came. The smaller woman tried to still her emotions. Alex could tell she had been crying by the puffiness in her eyes. The agent pulled the teacher closer and Cassidy's tears began to flow again. "Don't cry, Cass." Cassidy buried her face in Alex's chest trying to speak but unable to form words. She had promised herself that she would not let Alex see her this way. The more time she had to think about things after Alex had left that morning; the more afraid, guilty and lonely she felt. Alex just pulled her close. "It's not forever, Cassidy, come on," the agent lifted the woman's face with her hands. "Stop. We have two days before I have to leave. Let's try not to dwell...come on," Alex kissed Cassidy's forehead. The teacher had seemed much calmer earlier that day and Alex wondered what had changed between the time she had left and now.

Cassidy took another minute to slow her breathing and put her hands on Alex's chest, looking straight forward, afraid that eye contact would only erupt another wave of emotion. "Let me finish the lasagna."

"Cass..."

"Alex, I can't...not now...I don't want to upset Dylan."

Alex took a deep breath and kissed the top of the woman's head. "Okay." The agent thought for a moment before releasing the teacher to her task. "I love you, Cass," she whispered, "I hope you know that."

"I do."

***

Dinner had been fairly quiet. Alex wandered off with Dylan and gave Cassidy a little space to clean up. The agent suggested a movie and by nine o'clock a small form had fallen asleep between two larger ones on the couch; two hands joined softly on his back. "I'll get him," Alex said as she scooped Dylan up and headed to his room. They hadn't told him anything yet. In fact, they hadn't spoken about Alex's departure since their brief exchange before dinner.

Cassidy watched as the agent tucked the small boy in and stood over him, fiddling with the blanket. There was no doubt that Alex loved Dylan at least as much as he had fallen in love with the agent. "He'll be there in the morning," Cassidy said, feeling a sudden sense of calm as she witnessed Alex's affection for her son.

"I know," Alex said.

The teacher put her hand on Alex's back, "Come on...I need you." Alex turned and looked at the most beautiful woman she had ever seen. She understood this was a roadblock for them. She had spent endless hours mulling over what she could have done. She should be more focused on Fisher. She should have kept a professional distance; she should, she should. It was hopeless. Alex loved Cassidy and right now that was all that was on her mind or in her heart. The agent complied with the teacher's request and followed her to the bedroom.

Cassidy didn't want to talk, not yet. She needed to feel Alex. She reached up and gently ran the back of her hand down the side of the agent's cheek, looking deeply into the clear blue eyes that seemed just a tiny bit darker tonight. Alex opened her mouth to speak but any words were quickly quelled by the pressing of two fingers to her lips and the smaller woman in her arms pulling her into a soft kiss. No words. Cassidy undressed the agent slowly. Her touch was so tender that Alex could not keep her eyes open. She could barely let a sigh escape as she looked briefly into the brilliant green eyes that remained slightly red from the many tears that had fallen earlier. Still, they were the most magnificent eyes Alex had ever seen. The feel of the smaller woman in her arms, completely taking the agent over was mind numbing for Alex. She breathed Cassidy in as she felt the woman's hands and lips slowly discover every inch of her. "Cass," she whispered as a tear fell down her cheek. She never wanted to leave, never. Alex could hardly form a coherent thought. The only clear thought passing through her mind left her wondering how she could feel so wonderful and so heartbroken at the same moment. She let herself go and held Cassidy's hands as her body released all of her emotions physically. Struggling to fill her lungs she whispered her words, "always... Cass."

The pair stayed wrapped in each other's warmth in total silence for what seemed like hours. Cassidy resumed her normal unconscious habit of tracing small circles with her fingers across the agent's skin. "What will they do?" the teacher finally asked.

"I don't know. I imagine it will be a suspension pending an investigation."

"Alex, how long?"

Alex swallowed hard. "I won't be gone long, Cassidy."

"But if you're...."

Alex tried to gather her thoughts. "Please, just trust me...I won't be gone long, no matter what they say."

"What are you saying?" Cassidy propped herself up. Alex just stared at her. "Alex you can't quit; that's not what you're saying... Alex?"

The agent wasn't certain how to answer. "Let's just see what happens Monday."

Cassidy collapsed back onto the agent. "Alex, I don't want to ruin..."

The strong agent tightened her grip on the woman in her arms. "Don't say it. Don't think it. I know you were crying before I got home today, Cassidy. I'm not leaving you, not ever. Not for good, and the only thing you ruined was my habit of eating macaroni and cheese nightly. Well, that and constant back pain from running so much." Cassidy giggled. "Go to sleep. I love you," Alex encouraged, stroking the soft blonde hair that cascaded over her.

"I'm sorry I am such a..."

Alex stopped the thought with a soft kiss. "You are perfect."

"I love you, Alex."

"I know. Sleep. It will look better tomorrow."

***

The morning was progressing as Alex had hoped. She was not looking forward to telling Dylan that she would be away for a while. She and Cassidy had not spoken about Alex's departure again and the agent knew that there were things that still needed to be said. Right now, Alex thought that perhaps an afternoon away would be good for all three. She was hoping she might hear something from Pete Ferro or Steven Brady, but she didn't anticipate they would need to see her. The agent still wasn't certain what had gotten her lover so upset the day before; though she suspected it was a mixture of all of the changes and realities pressing down on them both. She wanted Cassidy to be assured that she and Dylan would be safe and moreover that Alex would be back. "Are you going to tell me what you are planning?" Cassidy asked sipping her coffee as Alex entered from the deck, hanging up her cell phone.

"You'll see."

"Umm hum...."

"I just think getting away from here for a bit might be a good idea," Alex smiled. "Just get Dylan ready and we'll leave by ten, okay?" The teacher shook her head and shrugged stretching up on her toes to peck Alex on the cheek before turning to corral her son. The agent kissed her lover's head and inhaled. She had no intention of talking about the case with Cassidy, the FBI, or her departure until evening. She turned her nose slightly at the feel of her phone buzzing in her pocket. "Agent Toles," she answered.

"Alex..."

"John?" Alex was surprised to hear President John Merrow's voice on the other end.

"How are you doing?" the president asked.

"I'm all right. I assume there is a reason for your call, though."

"I'm sorry, Alex." Alex took a deep breath and sighed. "It's out of my hands," he continued.

"I know that," the agent replied.

"How are Cassidy and Dylan?" He asked and Alex noted the concern in his voice.

The agent listened to the voices in the other room as Cassidy attempted to wrangle up Dylan and pry him from his new Batcave to get dressed. The sound of his laughter lifted her spirits and she couldn't help but smile to herself. "We're fine, John."

"Good. Listen, Alex," he paused. "I received some more information. I thought you should know that there is a DOD presence involved."

"I know."

John Merrow sat down at the large desk in his private office and took a sip from the glass of scotch he had placed there earlier that morning. "Why does that not surprise me?" he mused. "Taylor?"

"I didn't want to involve you," Alex explained.

"I appreciate that."

"Why is the DOD in my old case files?"

"Can't answer that. Perhaps just because you were assigned the O'Brien case," he offered. "Yeah...well," Alex paused listening as Cassidy followed Dylan up the stairs before continuing. "That 'presence' as you call it....Brackett, she's met with Fisher."

"Carl Fisher?" The president nearly choked on his scotch. "Are you sure?"

"Yeah, I am," Alex said.

John Merrow stood and began to pace. "Why would DCIS be involved with Fisher?" he inquired.

"They have a history, common roots, I guess. That's all I know," Alex said. The president's jaw became taut and his eyes narrowed to nearly slits. "John, I have to leave Monday morning...."

"I heard."

"I figured," Alex chuckled. "I don't want Fallon..."

"I'll see what I can do," the president offered. "Any leads on the accident?"

"Not really, but right now I am more concerned about Fisher."

"I understand. I wish I could do more," he said plainly.

The agent hung her head slightly. "It's better if you keep a distance. I'm working it."

The president nodded at his desk. This he already knew. Alex was not going to give him many details. It wasn't a lack of trust preventing her from being forthcoming and he knew that. She was protecting her Commander in Chief and her friend. "I'll see what I can…" he began.

"I appreciate that. I'll be fine."

"Alex?"

"Yes?"

"I am sorry," he said sincerely. "For all of you."

Alex took a deep breath. "I know you are," she said hanging up the phone and placing it back in its normal home.

John Merrow sat down on the corner of the desk and took another sip of scotch. He slowly sat it down and picked the receiver back up. "Get Claire Brackett here…now."

***

Dylan ran into the kitchen and stopped in front of the agent. "Are we going to George's?"

Alex laughed. "No."

"Are we going to the movies?"

"No."

"Where are we going?"

Cassidy leaned in the doorway and watched her son interrogating her lover. "Well, if I tell you it won't be a surprise. Get your pool cue. That's your only hint." His eyes grew as big as saucers and he flew out of the room and back up the stairs.

"Just what are you up to?" the small blonde woman in the door asked.

Alex moved slowly to the woman with a flirtatious smile. "Think of this as YOUR case to solve," Alex raised her eyebrow and whispered into the teacher's ear before continuing on into the hallway. Dylan was barreling down the stairs already. "Come on Agent O'Brien," Alex called back with amusement. Cassidy chuckled to herself. Alex was enjoying this plot she had created and Cassidy was thankful for the agent's tactics.

***

Congressman Christopher O'Brien was happy to be home. He was still weak but his anger over the discovery of his ex-wife's apparent 'relationship', as she had called it, was fueling a new found energy. He was taken aback when his girlfriend entered the room with the large, blonde man. "What are you doing here?" O'Brien asked.

"Just checking on a friend," the man answered as the woman left the room.

"People are asking questions about you," the congressman said in frustration.

"Are they?" The flip reply came.

"What do you want, Jon?"

"Now, Chris, I told you...I came to check on a friend."

The congressman gave a sarcastic reply, "yeah, well *friend*... I am fine."

Jon Krause leaned back on the large leather sofa in the middle of the room and stretched his arms casually along its back. "What did you tell the nice agent about me?"

The congressman twitched slightly at the coolness in the other man's voice. "Nothing. Just that we were fraternity brothers."

"That's not all, though," Jonathan Krause led the congressman to continue.

"What do you mean?" O'Brien asked defensively.

"You told them about Cassidy?"

"I told them you were friends."

"And…"

"And what?" the congressman asked.

"What else did you tell them, Congressman?" Christopher O'Brien's mind was still hazy on many points. "You told them about France."

"I suppose."

Jon Krause was controlled and deliberate in all of his actions. It was impossible to tell from his even tempered nature what he was driving at. That was the mark of the perfect 'spook'. He was intelligent and charming, disarming, handsome and above all he was controlled. "Chris…Chris, why did you report that pretty agent?"

The congressman wasn't certain whether to be angry or afraid. "She's sleeping with my wife."

"Really?"

"Yes, really."

"Your *wife?*" Krause raised his eyebrow.

"Yes."

"And here I thought that was your girlfriend that just showed me in." The congressman felt his hand ball into a fist. "You're making a lot of sloppy mistakes, Congressman."

Christopher O'Brien began to stumble on his words, "I…"

Krause shook his head again and walked behind the desk in the corner of the room, looking out the large picture window. "I suggest, if you want what is best for Cassidy," he paused, "and your son….Let this go."

"It's too late," the congressman said with a surprising amount of resolve in his voice. He was furious with Cassidy and he did not like to be questioned. "I can't change it now," he said flatly.

"Well," Krause began, "we all make mistakes."

The congressman watched as the larger man circled the desk and then sat on its surface. "I would think you would be happy to have her out of the way," the congressman asserted.

"Would you?" Jon Krause laughed. "I was speaking to a friend this morning," he said. "Alex Toles is not the average agent, Congressman. Not at all. You just took a bloodhound and turned it into a pit bull."

"She can't do anything. She'll be lucky if she has a job.... and Cassidy...whatever this..."

Krause shrugged and laughed a bit as he considered his own time with Cassidy O'Brien. "You don't really know your ex-wife very well, do you?"

"What the hell does that mean?"

Jon Krause offered the politician a sly smile, changing the subject. "I suggest you *rest* as best you can....you need time to.....*Recover.*"

"I'm fine," the congressman said with disdain.

The blonde man considered the politician before him. He walked deliberately and calmly to the congressman in the chair, "terrible about your accident." The congressman looked up at him as he continued. "I think Cassidy is capable of her own decisions, don't you?" The congressman felt his heart begin to quicken its pace as the man in front of him stared coldly into his eyes. Krause stood erect again and tipped his head to the side. "Some things are out of our control, Congressman O'Brien. Some things....some things are not. I suggest you learn the difference." The man began to exit the room and stopped. "I'm glad to see you are feeling better. When you do speak with Cassidy, extend my best wishes. I hear Agent Toles is quite the catch."

The congressman sat stunned but also keenly aware of the veiled warning. The accident, perhaps it was no accident. He placed his face in his hands wondering what he should do and feeling out of control. Why was Krause so concerned about the agent? Did Krause just threaten his family? He took a deep breath. His mind was still fuzzy on so many points. He needed to clear his thoughts and make a decision. Who could he reach out to now? Was there anyone?

***

"When the hell did you meet with Carl Fisher?" he yelled.

"What's the problem? Fisher knows what he's doing, even if he is a drunk," Brackett snickered.

"This is not a game, Claire."

"Really?" She smirked arrogantly.

The president's anger was mounting. "Where is Fisher now?"

"No idea," she answered. "He got what I asked for. He took care of the letters. That's it."

"What did you ask for?"

Brackett leaned back in her chair leisurely and smiled with satisfaction. "Proof."

"I see." He sat down across from the redhead. "You have no idea what you have just put into motion with all of this, Claire…no idea."

She shrugged. "What? Toles will be suspended and out of the way. You'll be able to persuade the congressman, I am sure to stop that bill…he'll be terrified of his *reputation*… And, the goods will be moved where they need to go. The congressman will never say a word. He'll be too preoccupied with damage control. Everyone gets what they need…problems…SOLVED."

"For a woman with an IQ over 140, you certainly are stupid."

"Excuse me?" Brackett seethed.

John Merrow shook his head. "You think this is about one deal? One move? One operation? You think congressmen have *accidents* over some small trade of information or a few missiles or some basic money laundering? Jesus Christ, Brackett…Find Fisher."

"He's probably long gone."

"Yeah. Claire, find him, and do it quickly before this blows into something that can't be contained."

"You're overreacting," the woman shook her head.

"Congressmen aren't the only ones who have *accidents*, Claire." He moved his face within inches of hers. Calmly he finished, "find him."

Chapter Nineteen

"Is it taken care of?" the tall blonde man asked picking up his cell phone.

"It's done," a hoarse voice answered on the other end.

"Where are you?" There was no response. "Fisher? Where are you?"

"Waiting…"

"Where?" The voice became impatient. "Don't do anything yet." Fisher's breath became ragged with anticipation. "I don't like this," Krause offered.

A deep sigh preceded the answer. "We both get what we want."

The voice on the other end of the phone cracked slightly. "Don't be so sure. Just wait." He hung up.

Reaching across the seat of the car Fisher sighed and his lips curled into the hint of a smile. He watched as the car turned the corner. "Soon…."

***

"You're enjoying this, aren't you?" Cassidy smiled at the agent as she got into the car. Alex tried to hide her amusement but couldn't help but smirk. "That's what I thought," the teacher shook her head as the agent kissed her on the cheek and gently shut her door.

"Alex?" a voice called.

"What's up, Speed Racer?"

"Will you teach me how to do that trick?"

"What trick is that?" the agent asked curiously as she turned the corner off of Cherry Circle.

"You know, when you make shots behind your back?"

"Hmmm…Well, actually, there might be someone more qualified to teach you that where we are going." Cassidy looked at the agent inquisitively. "I told you; this is your case Agent O'Brien," Alex smiled. "Look for the clues." Cassidy just shook her head and put her hand on Alex's knee. There was no doubt that this was the agent's way of taking the teacher's mind off of everything. It reminded her of their first drive, their first dinner alone. The teacher closed her eyes and let out a soft sigh of contentment remembering Alex smiling at her in the firelight as the ocean lapped the shore behind them. Alex caught her lover's expression. "What are you thinking about?"

"Falling in love," Cassidy answered, never opening her eyes.

Alex felt her heartbeat quicken. "You know, you're gonna' miss all the clues if you stay like that."

Cassidy was unflinching. "*Je ne m'inquiète pas*," (I don't care). Alex laughed. Cassidy could be adorable and this was one of those moments. The woman beside her was clearly lost to some memory and Alex was delighted at the knowledge that she was the heart of it; whatever it was. They drove for a while with Dylan chattering in the back asking Alex all kinds of questions about playing pool. The agent taught Dylan the license plate game and the two sought to spy plates from different states along the highway. Dylan couldn't read all the states but he would find one and Alex would tell him where it was from and then try to explain the markings. She explained the cactus and the desert on the Arizona plate and where Arizona was. She told him about Tombstone and the OK Corral. She explained the waves on a Rhode Island plate. When a car passed them with a Massachusetts plate that had a Red Sox symbol, the agent cheered and told Dylan the Yankees were Stankees. He laughed so hard that small tears fell from his eyes.

Cassidy sat quietly, eyes closed, listening and smiling. It was impossible to think about anything but the moment and she didn't care if they just drove all day. Listening to Dylan's laughter and Alex's obvious delight at his interest in everything she said, Cassidy thought it was the most beautiful sound she had ever heard. She thought about how lucky she was to have the two people she loved more than anything, love each other. They had been driving for quite some time when Cassidy opened her eyes. "Alex?"

"Hmmm?"

"Are we going to Nick's" The teacher asked, noticing that they were in Connecticut.

"Well..."

"To the restaurant?" Cassidy continued her thought.

"Not exactly," Alex smiled.

"Who's Nick?" Dylan chimed in.

"Nick is my brother." The teacher studied the agent's face. Alex caught her stare. "You might make a decent agent, O'Brien."

"So," Cassidy led the agent to answer.

"About fifteen minutes and you'll see," Alex grasped the hand on her knee.

***

"How are you feeling?" the president asked.

Christopher O'Brien thought silently for a moment as he held the phone to his ear. His mouth had gone dry but his hands were sweating, "still a bit fuzzy...and tired of this chair."

"I can imagine. That was quite a hit you took, I hear." John Merrow responded.

"That's what they tell me.....Listen..."

"What is it Congressman?"

"Jon Krause was here," the congressman said.

"Is that right?" the president feigned his surprise at the congressman's point.

"Mr. President," the congressman stopped and considered his words carefully. "I am worried...about Cassidy."

"Oh?"

"Well...I just....do you know about...."

"About Agent Toles and Cassidy? Or that you reported Agent Toles to her superiors?" There was silence at the other end of the phone. "So? Congressman?"

"You sound surprised," the congressman interjected.

The president laughed. "Chris, I am not surprised by either...but I think your actions were foolish." Again there was silence. "You know that. You don't know Toles; I do," the president said flatly.

"What about Krause?" the congressman asked.

John Merrow decided to be blunt. "Krause does not answer to me. Even if I'd like to think it, Congressman. We all have roles to play. I do not pull his strings." The president continued his assessment. "You have a lot to learn, Chris. I hope it's not too late for you to heed the lessons. I would have thought your time being married to a teacher might have taught you something about discipline and commitment." Merrow chuckled slightly, "well, at least discipline."

The congressman continued nervously. "If Agent Toles..."

"Agent Toles will be placed on suspension Monday. She will be in D.C. You threw out the pitch, now we have to wait for it to cross the plate. I can't do anything about Agent Toles, not now. I suggest you get some rest."

"Cassidy doesn't know any...."

"What Cassidy knows or doesn't...Well, Agent Toles is good. Cassidy might have information that seems innocuous to her. Alex will find it with time."

"I would think my report would have been helpful then," the congressman interjected.

"Do you?" The president pushed down his anger. "You think a suspension will stop Toles?" He laughed. "You can't control Toles anymore than you can Cassidy. You've just increased her resolve, and Alex is not someone you want as an adversary; trust me."

"So...what am I supposed to do?"

"Pay more attention," the president answered.

***

Alex pulled down a winding New England road. There was a long stonewall that seemed to travel along with them out the passenger side window. Trees lined the street on both sides. "Alex?" Cassidy began an inquiry just as the agent pulled into a narrow driveway.

"We're here," the agent announced.

"Uh...where is here?" Cassidy asked looking behind her as Dylan released himself from the grips of his seat excitedly.

"Hey!" A voice yelled as Alex opened her door. Stepping off the front porch of the green Cape Cod style home was a tall man who looked very much like the agent.

"Who's that?" Dylan asked as Alex let him out of the car.

"That's Nicky," the agent answered, her smile broadening as the figure approached. Dylan held onto Alex's jacket when he noticed another figure appear on the wide porch that ran the entire length of the home.

Nick reached his sister who was now standing beside the teacher with Dylan between them. "You still letting this lackey hang around," he kissed Cassidy on the cheek.

"Hi Nick," she greeted him affectionately.

"All right," Alex shook her head. "Lackey?" She felt a slight tug on her jacket and looked down at the small boy who was pointing to the porch. She laughed. "Oh...That....That, Dylan is Christian, my nephew." Large eyes that almost took on his mother's color when he was excited peered up at the agent and then to his mother as Christian bounced his way to the group.

"So, Dylan this is my brother, Nick."

"Nice to meet you, Dylan. I hear you are quite the little shark," Nick winked.

Again Dylan looked at the agent. "It means you are a good pool player," she explained. He brightened. "And this is Christian. You can call him Cat. We all do."

"Hi," Christian said.

"Hi," Dylan answered.

"Are you all going to stand out there or what?" An attractive woman was now standing on the porch calling to the group.

"That's Barb," Nick smiled. "I'm her lackey."

"I'll say," Alex laughed.

"Watch it," he playfully cautioned. "Let's go in. Cat, why don't you take Dylan and you can show him the rec room?"

Dylan looked back at Cassidy who smiled assuredly. "Go ahead."

Cassidy was surprised when she felt Alex's hand slip around her own as they made their way toward the house and the agent caught her expression. The agent squeezed a little harder and winked. She leaned into the teacher's ear, "Dylan will have a blast and I want you to know this is where you belong." The teacher felt her heart stop for a moment. She wasn't quite sure what to expect from the day. What was clear to her was the agent's intended statement. It was about family. It was meant as an assurance. Cassidy pulled the agent down to whisper in her ear. "What is it?" Alex asked as they reached the porch.

"Thank you," the teacher answered.

***

The day was progressing nicely and Alex was thrilled to see that Cassidy felt at ease with Nick and his wife. It was hard for her to fathom that she and Cassidy's relationship was so new. They hadn't had a chance to talk about so many things yet; one of those things being family. The agent had more than one purpose to the visit today. Alex wanted Cassidy to understand and to believe that the she was committed to their young relationship. She also wanted Cassidy to know that the teacher had a place to go while the agent was away. Alex had a nagging sensation of worry about leaving now. She didn't like the way things were going with the case. Detective Ferro had called earlier and told her he was working a couple of potential leads, but Fisher was still out there. On top of it the agent was certain that the congressman's accident had been arranged. She feared for the teacher and any absence, even a short one, filled her with a sense of dread. Her fear was something she could not make visible to the woman that sat beside her now. Whatever started this entire case was much larger than she had ever imagined. It reminded her of her time in Iraq and that bookshop. Unconsciously, she raised her thumb to her temple as a myriad of thoughts passed through her mind. Cassidy noticed the change in the agent's expression and the telltale indicator of stress for Alex; her habit of rubbing her temples. "What is it?" Cassidy whispered into the agent's ear.

Alex smiled across the room to her brother and leaned into Cassidy, "just a little headache." The teacher decided it was best to accept the agent's answer given where they were.

Nick had also caught the shift in his sister's demeanor. Sensing that his sister and her new partner might need a moment alone he gestured to his wife. "What do you say you help me get that dinner started?"

"What can we do to help?" Cassidy asked genuinely.

"Oh no… I think there will be plenty of time for that," Nick laughed. "Accept guest status while you can," he winked.

"He's not kidding," Barb joked as the two headed off to the kitchen.

"Alex?" Cassidy looked at the agent with some concern.

"I'm fine."

"How many times do I have to tell you? You are a terrible liar," Cassidy raised an eyebrow.

The agent sighed and kissed Cassidy on the cheek. "Cass, I just wish I could…"

The teacher could've guessed the end to that sentence. Alex wished she could change her departure and she wished that the case was solved. "I know you do," Cassidy smiled. The day had been wonderful so far. Dylan was off with Christian and every so often the adults would chuckle at the sound of playful laughter rising through the house. Nick and Alex had traded jabs and stories about growing up and the trouble that Alex seemed to always coax her brother into; things like stealing apples from a neighbor's orchard at night. The two siblings had gotten into a fit of laughter when Alex explained how they got chased by a dog one night after stealing apples and ran frantically to escape home safely; only to find that the dog was their own, Barney. Barb was charming and easy going and Cassidy immediately felt welcome with the pair. Whatever was to come could wait. She put her hand on Alex's cheek. "Let's not think about it today," she suggested, soliciting an appreciative grin from the agent.

"Sounds like a great idea," Alex agreed.

But, as life would have it their brief moment and their plan for the day was abruptly changed when a small boy came crashing into the agent's lap with tears in his eyes. Barb followed with Christian in tow looking sheepishly on. "You're leaving me too," Dylan cried. Alex lost her breath and looked at Cassidy, neither sure what had brought this on.

"Dylan," Cassidy said gently reaching over to her son who was sobbing into the agent's shoulder, "why would you say that?

"Cat told me. You came to see him before you leave," Dylan pulled back and looked at Alex.

Alex inhaled deeply and let her breath escape slowly. "Dylan, I am leaving Monday…"

"See!" He said somewhere between devastation and anger. Barb looked down at her son and pointed to the kitchen sternly. She lingered for just a moment watching Alex and Cassidy with the small child before them and smiled softly. She wasn't certain what all the facts were but in a few short hours one thing had become clear to Alex's sister-in-law; the sometimes hardheaded agent was very much in love with both Cassidy and her son.

Cassidy brushed a tear from Dylan's cheek and she and Alex looked intently at one another. The teacher offered a crooked smile of understanding as Alex put her hands on both the young boy's arms. "Dylan...I want you to listen to me, okay?" Alex began. The boy looked down and did not answer, leaving the agent to turn to his mother for support. Cassidy smiled again and gave the agent a gentle nod. "I have to go back to my house just for a little bit, Speed Racer. Remember when you were there?" He nodded. "I have a couple of things I need to take care of, but Dylan," he slowly began to look up into her blue eyes. "I am not leaving you or your mom, not for very long." Cassidy heard the conviction in her lover's voice and she felt her own tears begin to surface.

"When will you be back?" he asked. Alex sighed. She really wasn't certain exactly when.

Cassidy took over. "Dylan, Alex and I...We have a lot of things we need to talk about...Grown up things."

"Like you and Dad," he mumbled.

Cassidy nodded, "some, but not because Alex is leaving... Alex is not Daddy." He looked at his mother.

"I don't want you to leave," he said trying not to cry again.

Alex felt her heart breaking for him. She looked at Cassidy and smiled. Then she turned to the small form on her lap. "I love you Dylan," the agent said assuredly. The words took Cassidy off guard as Alex seamlessly continued. "And, I love your mom. I would never leave you...unless you wanted me to." He threw himself back into the agent and Cassidy saw the tears roll down her lover's cheek.

"Promise?" he asked seeking reassurance.

"I promise," Alex answered hugging him and looking at Cassidy. "Why do you think I brought you and your mom here?" He sat back and shrugged. "Because this is my family."

"You're lucky to have a brother," he said.

"MMM….Yes. I am," Alex said. "And now you will have an uncle to teach you pool tricks while I am away, and a cool cousin to play with." Cassidy felt her eyes widen. "While I am away, you and your mom can always call me and whenever I have to be away; you can always come here." Cassidy could not contain her tears as Alex looked into her eyes. "You are my family too now," Alex said.

Nick had reached the doorway after hearing his son's explanation of the events that had led to Dylan's upset. He listened carefully to his sister's discussion with the boy and understood fully what he was witnessing. Cassidy was engaging, beautiful and compassionate and Dylan was a cute and lovable little boy. His sister had finally found something solid and he could see in Alex's eyes how much these two people meant to her. Alex was not one to share her emotions unless she really felt them deeply, and Nick knew this was the real thing for his sister. He'd seen it that night in the restaurant. The last thing he wanted to do was intrude, but Alex's last statement seemed like the perfect opportunity to enter the emotional conversation gracefully. "Ahhhemm," he cleared his throat. "You know, Dylan… two things about this family…" The small boy looked at the handsome man approaching. "Everyone learns how to help in the kitchen and everyone is expected to eat more than they can handle," he winked. Cassidy snickered. "And, any nephew of mine needs to know his way around a pool table. So whatya' say?" Dylan let out a slight smile as Nick offered one hand to the boy and pointed to Alex with the other. "We've tried getting her in the kitchen," he shook his head. "She does the AFTER parts, otherwise no one would be able to eat more than they can handle. She can't cook," he leaned over and whispered into the boy's ear just loud enough that his sister could hear.

Dylan grinned but offered the agent an innocent six year old defense. "Alex makes the best cereal."

Nick and Cassidy both laughed. "You tell him, Dylan," Alex folded her arms in mock disapproval of her brother's criticisms.

"Geez, holdin' out on me, eh, sis? Come on Dylan. Come help your Uncle Nick with a couple of things. Then you and I will teach Alex and Cat a thing or two about billiards."

Dylan started to follow and then stopped. He turned back and kissed his mother on the cheek and then looked at the agent for a moment. "Go on with Uncle Nick," Alex said.

Dylan whispered to her. "Can I really call him Uncle Nick?"

"That's what the man said," Alex smiled. Dylan hugged the agent. "I love you, Alex," he said with some exuberance and trotted back off to take the hand of the man waiting.

Cassidy watched the pair leave the room and marveled at the lightness in her son's steps. She turned to the agent and looked at her lovingly. "We have a lot to talk about, don't we?" Alex nodded. "Alex, I hope you know…"

"Cassidy…I meant everything I said and so did Nick. Let's stick to the plan. We can talk tomorrow. After you sit through a dinner with us you might want to reconsider all of this anyway," Alex winked.

"Hummm," Cassidy pretended to be considering something.

"What?" Alex asked.

"Just wondering."

"What?"

"How an English butler managed to get by without any culinary skills," the teacher shrugged.

"Funny."

"I know."

"I love you, Cass."

"I love you too Alfred," Cassidy laughed.

***

Detective Pete Ferro entered the apartment building and lifted the line of yellow tape that cordoned off the second floor hallway. He slowed his pace to don a pair of latex gloves as he entered the small room. "What do we have?"

"Looks like a suicide," a young officer answered.

The seasoned detective approached the body that lay slumped in the chair. He stood about two feet from the man and took his time surveying the scene at a slight distance. Carefully, he studied the blood stain on the carpet and the patterns that were evident on the man, the wall and the floor. Slowly, he circled the scene keeping the same distance. Then he moved a step closer and repeated the action; each time searching the fine details of what lay in front of him until finally he reached the feet of the man in the chair. With his forefinger he gently probed the side of the man's head. Without moving anything he looked at the shotgun, where it fell, how it fell. He picked up the man's hand and studied the very smooth finger tips. About six feet behind the chair a large wall was lined with newspaper clippings and photographs. The detective walked deliberately toward the shrine, gradually making his way inch by inch past the collection. He took a deep breath and shook his head. "There's no I.D.," a younger man directed his statement to the senior officer.

"No, I don't imagine there is," Ferro answered.

"What does that mean? This guy…"

Ferro ran his finger across several of the photos. "It means this guy doesn't really exist." He twisted his mouth and considered the scene a final time. "I need to make a call."

***

Nick had Dylan sitting on the side of the pool table with Cat on a tall stool. He demonstrated the finer points of trick shots with great animation as the rest of the family looked on. Alex's brother was a character. He made faces and spun his cue in all kinds of patterns. He set the balls up on the table in what seemed to be impossible patterns and then one by one sunk the balls into different pockets. "That's awesome!" Dylan practically squealed.

"Show off," Alex muttered. Cassidy laughed at the agent who actually appeared to be moderately pouting.

"Get used to it," Barb whispered to the teacher. "Wait 'til summer when we open the pool. Then it will be Mr. Peacock over there sulking in a lounge chair," she nodded toward her husband. Cassidy looked at the woman curiously. "Oh yeah," Barb explained. "Alex is quite the master of the diving board, even with her back. Those two are impossible," she laughed.

Alex was shaking her head on and off as her brother continued with his antics to the boys' delight. Cassidy found the agent's reactions endearing. "Oh honey, I'm sure you'll get him back," the teacher kissed her lover on the cheek.

"Yeah, I will," Alex said just as she felt her pocket vibrate. She looked at the number displayed on the phone and stood. "I'm sorry. I need to take this," she said returning a kiss to Cassidy's cheek and excusing herself from the room.

Barb took the agent's absence as an opportunity to start a private conversation. "Dylan is so sweet," she complimented.

"He is," Cassidy beamed. "I've really never seen him happier." The teacher stopped and sighed. "He has taken to Alex. It's so funny, really. He seems to know where she is at every moment."

Barb watched Cassidy's expressions as she spoke. She was struck by the effortless nature of the school teacher. Conversation flowed easily with the woman. And, she could understand exactly what Alex saw in the pretty blonde. Not only was Cassidy attractive; she was down to earth, friendly and clearly head over heels for Alex. "Well, I am happy for Alex,"

Barb said. "Nick came home after she brought you to the restaurant and said 'I think Alex is in love'." She smiled.

"Really?"

"Mmhmm. Yeah, he did. Those two can read each other
like a book. It's always been that way." The woman turned to
the teacher. "And…as usual he was right."

"It's crazy in a way."

"Why is that?"

"Oh," Cassidy laughed as she watched Dylan attempt to put
his pool cue behind his back. "We have so much still that we
need to talk about. It just…well…It's just happened so fast."

Barb nodded. "Well, I don't know, I still remember the first
time I saw Nicky. He walked into my dorm. I think I knew the
moment I saw him. He wasn't doing anything special. I just
knew."

Cassidy smiled. "I guess if I were to admit it…I felt something when I answered the door that day….but it's so…"

"What?" Cassidy looked at the woman next to her. Barb
smiled. "I understand," the woman said patting the teacher's
knee.

"I just don't want her to leave, not even for a day," Cassidy
admitted. "Pathetic, huh?"

"No. I have a feeling she feels the same way," Barb observed.

***

"What's going on Detective?" Alex asked.

"Agent Toles…I think we found your man?"

"Fisher? Really? Where?"

"In Harlem just as you suggested he would be," the detective answered.

"Did you take him into custody?" Alex asked sensing that
this was not simply a call to give her a location.

"In a manner of speaking, yes," he said.

"What manner is that?" the agent inquired.

"Well...Agent...he's dead."

"He's dead?"

"Yep. Dead. Looks like he blew his head off with a sawed off shot gun; really ain't much left."

Alex pinched the bridge of her nose. "Why do you think it's him?"

"Uh... You know the usual 'spooky' things, lack of prints... and uh, well...some other things."

"What other things?" Alex pushed.

"Son of a bitch has a shrine in that apartment...you know.... To the pretty lady I suspect is with you."

Alex blew out her breath with some force. "Are you sure it's him?"

"Well, look...you and me. We both know this might notta' been a suicide, but it has spook all over it. Pretty sure."

"All right...Well, let me know if you get a positive I.D."

"Agent Toles?"

"Yes, detective?"

"I'll run everything I can...If the spooks show, we'll know. I think you can rest a little easier though, really."

"How long to process the scene? I'm over an hour and a half away."

"Nothing you can do here, Agent. Come down and check out the scene tomorrow. M.E. is already removing the body."

"Ferro?"

"Yeah?

"Thanks."

"Anytime, Agent. Take care of the lady," he said affectionately. "She's a keeper."

Alex smiled. She still had her reservations about the detective's news. But, even if Fisher hadn't killed himself it was possible that he had become a greater liability to someone else. At least that is what the agent hoped. It was in her nature to cross every possible 'T' and dot every 'I', but she also felt a slight sense of relief. And, she was flattered by the detective's words.

Cassidy melted a lot of hearts and if anyone could understand why, it was the agent. "She is," Alex acknowledged. "No worries, Detective, though I think she might be the caretaker," the agent admitted, soliciting a chuckle on the other end of the phone.

"I'll talk to you tomorrow, Agent."

"That you will. Good night, Detective."

***

Alex seemed just a bit lighter as she said her goodbyes to her family. Cassidy was curious if that was the result of the visit with Nick and Barb, having gotten a weight off of her after telling Dylan about the separation, or if it might have something to do with the phone call. As Alex moved to hug her nephew, Nick pulled the school teacher aside. "Listen, Cassidy," he paused as he led her slowly toward the car. "I want you to know that you and Dylan, you are always welcome here, anytime."

"That's very sweet, Nick."

"No...Look, I know Alex is worried about something. She's tight lipped about work. Actually she's tight lipped about a lot," he mused. "But not about you. She's just....Can I be blunt?" Cassidy nodded. "I've never seen my sister...well, she really loves you, Cassidy."

Cassidy looked at the man that had spent much of the evening playing the role of class clown. She was certain she could see just the hint of an affectionate tear in his eye. Barb had told her at one point during an episode of play that he and Alex called the Duel of Champions Billiard Bonanza; for the boys' sake of course; that Nick had always worshipped his sister. Alex had never shared much about her parents and Barb filled in some of the reasons for Cassidy why that might be. She said that while Alex's parents were always kind to her; they were always hard on their children. Alex got the worst of it and Nick had called her his protector when they were small. Now, the teacher could see the great love the man had for his sister. Gently, she grasped Nick's arm, "I love her too, Nick."

"I know," he said quietly. "Just please promise me, if you need anything, you or Dylan…I am a phone call or a car ride away. Barb too." He took the teacher into a bear hug. "Thank you," he said.

"Thank me?" Cassidy was perplexed.

"Yeah." He confirmed the sentiment.

Cassidy patted his arm. "Thank you, Nick," she smiled as Alex came to the door and opened it for her.

"Hey! Teach him how to do that, will ya'?" Barb mocked as she led her son back toward the house.

"What?" Nick feigned his innocence.

"Yeah, yeah," she called to him. "Tell him Alex…chivalry is NOT dead."

Alex laughed and playfully slapped her brother on the back. "Still learnin' huh?"

"Yeah, you talk to me in thirteen years, see if you're still holding the door," he quipped.

Alex glanced in the window to see Cassidy trying to gently calm Dylan's over excitement. "Umm, you don't want to make that wager, bro."

Nick shook his head as he walked with his sister toward the back of the car. "You got it BAD," he teased.

Alex just shrugged as she opened her car door. "Nick?"

"Yeah," he turned back to his sister.

"If I need a place…"

"Anytime," he smiled with understanding, receiving her nod of appreciation.

***

It wasn't very long before both Dylan and his mother were sound asleep in the car, Cassidy's hand resting on the agent's thigh. Alex was running possible scenarios through her mind about

Carl Fisher. Suicide didn't make sense, but she had to confess the idea that someone wanted him out of the picture seemed a viable possibility. The agent could tell Ferro had seen similar things in the past and he seemed fairly certain that Fisher was dead. That was the ultimate relief for the agent. If that was true, then she could start working on the congressman's accident and his relationship to Krause. After everything that had happened, Alex Toles had no intention of walking away from her investigation into the congressman and his dealings. She could have let go the entire fact that he reported her relationship with Cassidy, but she could not let go the reality that his actions in so many instances hurt the woman she loved and Dylan; not to mention put them in harm's way. "Selfish," she whispered as she made the turn into the driveway. "Hey," she gently took the hand from her thigh and kissed it. "Cass, we're home."

"Hmmmm?" the teacher mumbled. "Sorry…"

"Come on," Alex coaxed. "I'll get the champ back there," she smiled.

Dylan stretched and grabbed onto Alex's neck. The agent carried him to his room and laid him down on his bed while his mother retrieved his pajamas. "Why don't you go and relax. I'll get him set," Cassidy smiled.

"Feel like a glass of wine?" Alex asked.

"Love one," the teacher answered.

"Okay…I'll meet you downstairs in ten." Alex made her way down the stairs and poured two glasses of white wine before taking a seat on the large couch and stretching her legs out onto the coffee table. She closed her eyes and tipped her head back. Two small but strong hands began to tenderly massage her shoulders and she sighed, "Mmm."

"You sore?" Cassidy whispered. She had noticed that Alex was walking a little slower than normal as she left Dylan's room.

"A little," the agent sighed, feeling the tender touch of her lover as it relieved the last remaining bits of tension from her drive.

"Your back?"

"Mmm…"

"You should have let me drive," Cassidy said with some concern.

Alex chuckled. "Come here."

Cassidy slowly made her way around the couch and Alex pulled the woman onto her lap. Tenderly, the agent tucked the woman's long blonde hair behind her ears. "Do you know," Alex stopped and kissed the woman's nose, "how happy you make me?"

"Ummm? Tell me."

Alex smiled and looked into Cassidy's eyes deeply. "I never felt like this, Cass. Not with anyone."

"Really?" Cassidy said a bit playfully.

"Really."

"What's gotten into you, Agent?" Cassidy kissed her lover's forehead.

"You."

"No, no, Alex Toles…It's something else, though I appreciate the compliment."

Alex considered the woman's assessment. "All right, I don't know for sure yet but I think we may not have to worry about Carl Fisher anymore."

Cassidy's body jerked almost in disbelief. "Why?"

"Well, looks like maybe someone took care of that problem for us. I'll know more tomorrow, but for tonight I am going with the belief that there is one less worry." She placed a soft kiss on Cassidy's lips and felt the smaller woman's body relax dramatically. Cassidy repositioned herself and laid back placing her head on the agent's lap and looking up at her. "Don't you want your wine?" the agent asked.

"Not right now. I just want to be here." Alex gently stroked her lover's hair with one hand and sat her glass down on the table beside her. "Alex?"

"Hum?"

"When you said that we….That we're your family," Cassidy faltered.

"Yeah…."

"Well, I want you to know that I feel the same way about you."

"I know that," Alex answered.

"I don't want you to go," Cassidy confessed taking hold of the hand that was slightly entwined in her hair.

"I don't want to go, either, Cass…but it won't be for long."

"Yeah, but Alex…That's where your life is."

"No, it isn't."

"Alex…I…"

"No, Cass…That's where my life was."

"What are you saying?" Cassidy asked searching the eyes above her.

Alex sighed. "Look, I don't know what's going to happen. I'm betting a suspension…and I've been thinking….I talked to Taylor…"

"Alex…." Cassidy was worried about the agent's intentions and did not want to completely uproot Alex's life.

"Listen, Taylor's wanted me back at the NSA since before I left. Maybe it's the right time…there's a great office here…"

Cassidy sat up and came eye to eye with the agent. "Alex. Look, I want to be with you. I know that, but wouldn't it make more sense…I mean with Chris in D.C. so much…if Dylan and I were to…"

The agent smiled and caressed her lover's cheek. "No."

"You didn't even hear what I…"

"Mhmm…I know what you were thinking and the answer is no. Cass, your mom is here…Christ, my family is here. No….I'm coming back. I'll find someplace that's…"

Cassidy put her finger on Alex's lips. "If you are coming back, then it will be here…until we find someplace else." Alex shook her head trying to suppress her chuckle. "What's so funny?" Cassidy asked almost offended.

"No...no. It's a joke....about lesbians....you know, and U-Hauls." Cassidy shook her head not understanding. Alex laughed. "Look it up," the agent smiled.

"I guess I'm pretty clueless," Cassidy said.

"No, you are refreshing....and you are beautiful," Alex kissed her lover.

"Are you sure about this? I mean, Alex..."

Alex kissed the woman again and felt the breath leave her body. She pulled back slowly and looked in Cassidy's eyes. "Cass, I have never been more certain about anything in my life." Alex sighed and closed her eyes as Cassidy laid back down in her lap.

"Alex....What is it?" Cassidy asked softly, noting the tear that had escaped Alex's eye and was rolling down her cheek. She lifted her hand and brushed it away.

"When Dylan ran into the room tonight," Alex struggled to continue.

"Yeah?"

"I just wanted to call and quit....Seeing him that upset...I just..."

Cassidy closed her eyes. "I love you so much, Alex."

"Where did that come from?"

"I don't think you could know, what it means to me...Seeing you with Dylan, how much he loves you. Just...I can't explain it to you. I wish I could...How that makes me feel....like I have a family; like HE has a family."

"I think I understand, Cass...Seeing you with him, every time I do....I fall in love with you all over."

"Alex?'

"Yeah?"

"Can we just stay like this....for a while? I don't want to lose this moment."

The agent took her lover's hand and inhaled deeply. Tenderly her fingers caressed the smaller hand and she smiled in contentment. "I think that sounds perfect," she answered.

Cassidy nestled her head against the agent's stomach, placing a gentle kiss there. "*Merci de m'aimer,* (Thank you for loving me)."

"*Vous êtes mon monde. Merci d'avoir été ma famille.* (You are my world. Thank you for being my family)," the agent replied softly.

"Always, my love," Cassidy sighed. "Always."

Chapter Twenty

"**M**r. President…"

"Yes, Congressman. What is it I can do for you?"

"I heard from Krause this morning," the congressman began.

"I thought you might," John Merrow answered.

"Is it true? Carl Fisher…is he dead?"

There was a measurable pause in the conversation. The president cleared his throat softly and gave his answer. "That is what I have been given to understand; yes."

Another long pause ensued as Christopher O'Brien considered his options. "Sir…Are you certain?"

"Well, Congressman, if you are asking if I ordered a hit on the man the answer is 'no'. If you are asking me if Fisher was a liability to Krause and to our operations, the answer is 'yes'. As far as I know the man is dead."

Christopher O'Brien maneuvered the wheelchair out from behind his desk and shifted his cell phone to the opposite ear. "Then…The FBI will no longer be at Cassidy's?"

"That is my understanding. I already told you, Agent Toles is due in the Washington Bureau Office at nine in the morning tomorrow. She will be placed on an indefinite suspension pending a review of her actions. And yes, as soon as we have confirmation of Fisher's…well…of his demise, the FBI will consider the case closed," the president explained.

"I see," the congressman said quietly.

"I should think you would be thrilled, Congressman. After all, you reported Alex."

"I am," the congressman mustered a confident tone.

"Well then, was that all your call was regarding?" Merrow inquired.

"I have a teleconference tomorrow at noon with the chairman of Ways and Means," the congressman said.

"Yes, I heard," President Merrow replied.

"The trade agreement with the EU and the limits on certain kinds of metal and the tariffs that France is pushing for," the congressman continued.

"Yes?"

"What would you like me to advocate?" Christopher O'Brien asked pointedly.

"I think you know, Chris. I am less concerned with the tariffs than the limitations in the agreement, but you know that. What about HR 1929?"

"There is a great amount of support for increasing trade opportunities, but also increasing controls."

John Merrow retrieved a glass and began filling it with his favorite scotch. "Yes, I am aware…I agree, but not at the risk of compromising our relationship with our French and Russian partners; that is a concern."

"The bill enjoys…" the congressman began.

"The bill has issues, Congressman…find them. Our friends in France will appreciate your efforts."

Christopher O'Brien took a deep breath, "I understand, Mr. President."

"I'm sure you do, Congressman. Cassidy speaks French, doesn't she?" the president asked.

"Yes, fluently…why?"

"Hmm…pity you are on such poor terms…she could be an asset."

"Sir?"

"Well, Congressman, I'm sure you'll have no issue explaining things to our friends if need be, though I think your ex-wife has cornered the market on charm. They would have loved her."

"I will take care of it," the congressman assured.

"I'm certain. Have a good afternoon, Congressman," John Merrow replied as he hung up his phone.

***

Alex walked through the small apartment slowly, determined to maintain a calm and professional exterior. These were all things she had seen before, the blood spatters, the mural of photographs and clippings. Alex Toles was no rookie. She lingered around the chair and looked at the patterns on the fabric. Deliberately she headed for the far wall. Her stomach sank and then rose into her throat nearly choking her. The agent struggled to take a full breath as her eyes passed across the myriad of photos of her lover. Cassidy and the congressman, Cassidy and the agent, Cassidy at campaign stops, Cassidy in the newspaper, Cassidy walking into school, in the grocery store, with her mother, Cassidy, Cassidy, Cassidy. The agent's exploration stopped abruptly toward the right hand side of the display. There it was. Cassidy was looking down at a small boy who was looking up at her curiously. The teacher's face was bright; a smile that only her son could command. The agent ran a gloved finger over it and swallowed hard, attempting to relieve the lump that had embedded itself in her throat and was suffocating her. Detective Pete Ferro leaned in the doorway. "It's disgusting."

Alex inhaled as much air as she could and released it, still looking at the photo in front of her. "How sure are you?" she asked.

"Pretty sure. M.E. says dental agrees. Well, what dental they were able to get, not much. Some back teeth. Found his mother; they are claiming the body," the detective answered.

Alex pivoted slowly on her heels to face the detective. "Where did they get the dental?"

"His mother. I took the leap and put out Fisher's name. Apparently, she had the records; some work he had done before leaving for service." Alex rubbed her temple as the detective continued. "He was only twenty-nine. How'd he do all that do you think? Stanford. Marines. Spook?" the detective asked.

Alex rubbed harder. "I'm sure he was older than twenty-nine...and not so sure about Stanford."

"What do you mean? There's a record..."

Alex pursed her lips. "Yeah, well, Detective...we both know records are only as good as whoever writes them." She turned back to face the wall.

"You still don't buy it?"

"I don't know. You're sure about the mother?" Alex inquired.

"Yeah, sure as I can be. I've known Collins for twenty years, he's a great M.E. He's convinced; I'm sold," Ferro answered.

Alex nodded taking one last look at everything; memorizing the details of the room, the placement of the photos on the wall, the headlines on the clippings that Fisher chose for his mecca. She stopped at a small table just inside the door and looked at a partially used roll of stamps and a small stack of manila envelopes. She picked up the envelopes and started thumbing through them. "They're empties," the detective said.

"Yeah," Alex placed them back on the table.

"Guess he didn't get to use 'em all," Ferro asserted to another nodded response from the FBI agent. "You ready?"

The agent stopped again in the doorway to make one final pass with her eyes. Her view again was drawn to the wall in the distance. "You're lucky I didn't find you," she whispered as she closed the door behind her.

***

"MOM!"

Cassidy was busy cutting up vegetables for tacos when she heard her son's call and he crashed into her, forcing the knife she was holding to slip and cut her left hand. "Dylan! Where's the fire?" Cassidy grasped her left hand with her right and walked to the sink to run it under some water.

"Sorry, Mom," the boy said sincerely. He looked up at his mother and saw the small trickle of red water falling into the sink. "Are you okay?"

"What happened?" A voice called from the doorway.

"It's nothing," Cassidy said continuing to allow the water to run over her cut. "I'm glad you're home."

Alex walked up behind the teacher with Dylan looking at her timidly. The agent touched his shoulder gently and smiled before reaching for his mother's hand and pulling it toward her. "Let me see it."

"It's nothing," Cassidy resisted.

"Yeah? Good, then you don't mind if I look at it," Alex raised an eyebrow and contemplated the hand before her. A steady trickle of red ran down the side of the small hand. "Dylan, go upstairs and get my black bag off your mom's bed." He nodded and ran out of the room.

"Alex...it's fine," Cassidy insisted. Alex stared at the teacher's hand. Her thoughts turning to the display she had just seen; spatters of blood that adorned the beautiful face she loved spanning feet at time. "Alex? Hey..."

Dylan nearly tripped himself running back into the room. Alex accepted the bag and set it on the counter. She gently guided Cassidy's hand back under the water and then placed a towel over it. "Hold this on it," she directed as she reached into the bag. "I have some butterfly strips in here somewhere."

Cassidy watched the agent's expression as Alex focused her energy and attention on her exploration of her bag, one hand still holding Cassidy's two. "Dylan," the teacher said, "why don't you go pick out a movie for all of us, okay? I'll be in to see what you find in a minute." She gestured with a tip of her head toward the other room. He nodded and headed off. "Alex…"

"They're in here…."

Cassidy pulled her hand away and placed her right hand under the agent's chin. "Alex…"

"Cass…I need to get…"

"Look at me," the teacher said. "Alex…what is going on?" The agent lifted her gaze and the teacher immediately saw the pain and worry in her lover's eyes. "Honey, it's just a cut."

Alex shook her head and took the smaller hand. "I don't ever want to see you hurt."

"What happened today, Alex?" The agent just shook her head.

Cassidy sighed. "That bad?"

Alex shook her head again. "He's gone, Cassidy."

"Then why are you so upset?"

Alex forced a smile as she slowly began to realize where she was. She looked again into the bag and finally pulled out a small box. "Let me do this," she said softly. As she applied the small bandages she concentrated on the present; the woman she loved standing in front of her.

The teacher complied with the agent's request and watched silently as the Alex tended to her long, shallow cut. "Maybe you should have been a doctor," Cassidy complimented. Alex tenderly stroked the back of her lover's hand. "You have a wonderful bedside manner," Cassidy flirted, still concerned about the agent's behavior but sensing a lightened mood was in order.

Alex looked up and smiled. "Do I?"

"Yes, you do," Cassidy replied. "Are you all right, Alex?"

The agent closed her eyes and wiped the memories from the hours that had since passed away. She opened them again and stroked Cassidy's cheek. "I'm just glad to be home, with you and Dylan," Alex said. Her expression changed again and Cassidy looked at her curiously. Catching the teacher's response the agent leaned into her ear, ".....and looking forward to showing you how good my bedside manner really is."

"Mmm...Well then this teacher had better finish her homework, also known as tacos," Cassidy quipped. Alex leaned in and kissed Cassidy's neck seductively, leaving the teacher momentarily breathless, "Alex...if you..."

The agent gently trailed kisses further up her lover's neck until she reached her ear and whispered to her, "If I what?"

The small blonde woman bit her lip and let out a soft moan, "I can't finish if you..."

"Mmm? If I?"

"Alex...."

Alex slowly pulled back and looked at the woman in front of her. She cleared all conscious thought and questions and looked into green eyes that had darkened slightly from desire. The agent smiled. "Be careful with your homework. I have plans to show you a different component of my 'beside' manner later," Alex winked.

Cassidy caught her breath as Alex smirked and began heading out of the room. "Where are you going?"

"See what Dylan picked," Alex shrugged. Cassidy shook her head. She was concerned about Alex's obvious mood swing. But, it seemed that at least for the moment, the agent was in a good place. The agent had her plans for their evening, and so did Cassidy. She would find out the truth later with her own bedside manner.

***

Cassidy leaned against the wall just outside her son's bedroom and listened.

"Alex?"

"Yeah, Speed Racer?"

"Are you really coming back?"

"Yes." She answered.

"Will you miss us?"

Alex sighed. She was already missing Cassidy and Dylan and she hadn't even left yet. On the drive back from Fisher's apartment she had seriously considered just quitting the bureau again; walking into the New York field office, putting her badge, I.D. and sidearm on a desk and walking away. But there was still the congressman to consider and she knew if she quit Cassidy would be furious. Still, leaving Dylan and the thought of being apart from her lover was tearing the agent to shreds. "Dylan," Alex sat down on the edge of the boy's bed. "I'll miss you like Alfred misses Batman when he's away."

"Alfred is like Batman's dad."

"He sort of is, isn't he?" The agent agreed.

"My dad doesn't miss me."

Alex took a deep breath. She had little use for the congressman, but she knew that was not true. "That's not true, Speed Racer."

"But he's why you are leaving."

"What are you talking about?" The agent was genuinely concerned for the small boy.

"I heard Mom…talking to Grandma."

Alex nodded and licked her lips. "Well, your dad just wants what's best for you and your mom."

The boy considered the statement. "If Alfred is like Batman's dad…then you can be my Alfred."

The agent chuckled. "I would be honored. Does that mean I have to cook dinners when I get home, though?"

"No…just my cereal," he said plainly. "Batman didn't have Mom."

"Oh…well then, how come your mom doesn't get cereal duty?"

"Don't tell her…."

"Tell her what?"

"Too much milk," he crinkled his nose.

The agent tried not to laugh. In the hallway, Cassidy wiped a tear from her cheek. The innocence of her son and the tenderness of her lover overwhelmed her. "I see," Alex answered.

"Alex?"

"Yeah, bud?"

"Will you be back for my party?"

"What party is that?"

"My birthday."

It suddenly dawned on the agent that there was so much she still needed to learn about this family she somehow had become a part of. She thought for a moment recalling the dates in the files she had studied so many times. She smiled picturing the date and the picture on the front of Dylan's small bio. Today was March 30th. Dylan would be seven in just a week. That determined everything. "I wouldn't miss it, Speed Racer, not even if the president himself asked me to."

"Really?"

"Really." She bent over and kissed the small head. He wrapped his arms around her tightly. "Get some sleep, Speed Racer...back to school tomorrow." The agent stood and started for the door.

"Alex?" She stopped and turned to face the small boy. "Chocolate or vanilla?"

"What?" The agent was confused by his question.

"Mom always asks me what kind of cake....chocolate or vanilla." The agent cocked her head not understanding the six year old sentiment. "What's your favorite?"

Alex thought her heart might burst. This little boy who had been through so much wanted her to pick his birthday cake. "Alfred likes everything," she smiled. "And he always wants Batman to be happy. I love both. Get some sleep."

"Okay. Night, Alex."

"Good night, Speed Racer."

***

Alex backed out of the room, closing Dylan's door partially and as she turned she saw Cassidy leaning against the wall smiling and gazing at her. "So...chocolate or vanilla?"

Alex shrugged and walked toward her lover. "If you make it, it won't matter."

"Alex, Dylan's birthday is..."

"I know, next Saturday."

Cassidy looked at the agent curiously. "How are you going to..."

"Mmm...heard all of it, didn't you?" The agent leaned in and kissed her lover's forehead. "Well, I guess you'll be seeing me pretty soon."

"Not soon enough," Cassidy said with a hint of sadness.

"Hummmm..."

"What?" Cassidy asked.

Alex reached for her hand and led her toward their bedroom. "Sound like you're in need of some doctoring, some TLC," the agent suggested. As they turned into the doorway Cassidy stopped and kissed Alex passionately. The agent's knees weakened and as Cassidy broke their kiss Alex stood completely in awe. "You keep doing that I'll be taking short vacations frequently."

"Oh...no," the teacher cautioned. "That was just a preview. You don't get the show until you tell me what had you so upset earlier."

Alex had hoped to avoid this topic but she knew Cassidy's persistence and she also knew that she could not fool her lover even when she tried. It was amazing to Alex the way Cassidy could read her emotions and thoughts. She had expected that her lover would want some explanation. She sighed and led Cassidy to sit on the edge of the bed. "Cass...I don't want to talk about it...not really." The agent stopped and looked at the floor for a moment before turning her attention back to the woman she loved. "All you need to know is...I see a lot of things, Cassidy. Things I never want you or Dylan to see. The one thing I could never be prepared to see is either of you hurt...or in danger...or afraid...used..."

Cassidy gave a solemn smile. She could guess what might have triggered Alex's earlier episode and she didn't want to know the details. The bottom line was that Alex loved her and Dylan. Whatever the agent saw or discovered; it didn't matter now. Still, she did want the agent to believe that she would always listen. "Alex...you do know that you can talk to me... even if it's..."

Alex Toles shook her head. "My protector."

"What?"

"You....always protecting me," Alex smiled.

"I love you," Cassidy gave her reason.

"MMMM....well....I'm glad....I love you too...even if you do put too much milk in the cereal."

"Hey!"

Alex laughed and then gradually moved to tenderly kiss her lover. Slowly their lips began to part and Alex softly allowed her tongue to brush against Cassidy's. The agent's gentle and loving exploration moved effortlessly down Cassidy's neck and across the top of her chest. She deliberately dropped her hands to the buttons on her lover's blouse and began to release them one at a time with precision. Her kisses lightly trailed up the other side of the smaller woman's neck until the agent pulled slightly back to look at the face of the woman she had fallen in love with. "You are so beautiful, Cass."

"Alex...I..."

"Shh..." Alex kissed her lover again as a soft moan escaped Cassidy's lips. The agent's hands very gently caressed Cassidy's breast and the teacher completely lost all conscious thought. Deliberately the agent's kisses followed; every touch worshipping the small, delicate form in her arms. "I want you to remember how you make me feel when I am gone," the agent whispered as she turned her attention to her lover's firm stomach before journeying to the place she most longed to travel.

"Oh God… Alex….I…"

Alex smiled as she felt her lover begin to succumb to the waves of pleasure traveling through both their bodies and their hearts. She felt the smaller woman's hips rise to meet her and sighed as her emotions seemed every bit as overloaded as her body. The sound of Cassidy's breathing as she barely managed to whisper "I love you," through her release pushed the agent over the edge and sent her body into a series of shudders that she could not fathom. Making love to Cassidy was unlike anything she had ever experienced, every time. It was like air and water and fire all conspiring together to lift her body and soul to heights she had never dreamed. Sensations of hot and cold; rushing air that fanned the flames of her own desire, burning so hot that Alex could not breathe until the flames were replaced by a quivering rush of chills that traveled over her body like a winter breeze. Finally, small hands would reach out and take hold of the agent's firmly, pulling her back to the safety of the earth and grounding her in a peaceful calm that existed in the safety of Cassidy's arms. "Cass…"

"You are amazing, Alex."

"Cass?" The agent collapsed her head onto the teacher's chest, feeling Cassidy lovingly run her fingers through the agent's long, thick hair.

"Hmm?" Cassidy mumbled closing her eyes in contentment.

"I can't wait to come home."

"You are home," Cassidy said softly.

"I know….I miss you already," Alex admitted.

"Chocolate or vanilla?" the teacher asked.

"What?" Alex was confused.

"Cake…chocolate or vanilla….and what kind of frosting?"

"You're serious right now, aren't you?" Alex asked amused.

"Yeah…When you come home, I want it to be right. I'd hate to use too much frosting or something," Cassidy joked.

Alex kissed her lover's chest. "I like everything you make…. just be careful with knives while I am gone," the agent jested.

"Yes, doctor," Cassidy kissed Alex's head.

"Cass?"

"What?"

"Dylan...I mean, I hope he knows that I...."

"He knows," Cassidy assured.

"I'll be back for Saturday."

Cassidy smiled and held the agent closer. "I know you will....
Alex?"

"Yeah?"

"Never mind," Cassidy sighed.

Alex propped herself up and looked at her lover. "What
is it?"

"Someday...Well....Maybe we'll have....I mean maybe we
will be..." the teacher grew quieter as her insecurity mounted.

Alex gave the teacher wide smile. "Vanilla."

"What?" Cassidy asked.

"Next week make chocolate cake. That's Dylan's favorite. I
heard him tell Nicky that."

"I'm confused," the teacher said.

"Ummm...you like vanilla," Alex said. "Ice cream, cook-
ies...so I'm guessing cake too."

"Alex...what are you...."

"Me too...I like vanilla."

Cassidy looked at her lover and squinted. "I'm not
following..."

Alex chuckled and kissed Cassidy's cheek. "Someday we'll
have vanilla...a big one," Alex smiled.

"I don't...."

Alex laughed. "Yeah...well...not next week, but someday."
The agent laid back and pulled Cassidy over to her.

The agent's train of thought suddenly hit Cassidy like an anvil.
"Alex, you know...I wasn't trying to make you feel like you..."

Alex laughed. "Like what? Like vanilla cake?"

"You know what I mean," Cassidy said. "I don't want you to
think that I am pushing..."

"Cass...Relax...but I am serious about the vanilla."

Cassidy shook her head and grasped the agent's side tighter. "All right, I got it...vanilla."

"And...Cass?"

"Hum?"

"You do use too much milk."

"I never knew you were such a cereal connoisseur," Cassidy quipped.

"*Oh oui...majordomes ont affiné goût,* (Oh yes, butlers have refined taste)."

"Go to sleep, Alfred," Cassidy giggled.

Alex chuckled, "I love you Cass."

"*Je t'aime aussi, rentre bientôt.* (I love you too, come home soon)."

"You won't even know I'm gone."

"Yes. I will."

***

The agent couldn't sleep no matter what she tried. She had spent most of the night softly stroking her lover's hair and placing small kisses on Cassidy's head. The faintest hint of daylight was just beginning to become evident in the sky and Alex's nervousness was palpable. She carefully pulled herself from the bed and headed for the shower, stopping in the doorway to the bathroom to look back at the woman sleeping soundly a few feet away. Cassidy was beautiful in every moment to Alex. The agent stood silently watching and tried to calm the anxiety she felt. Another deep sigh and the agent made her way into the shower. The water flowed over her freely and Alex lifted her face to greet it. She hoped that it would somehow wash away the sadness and stress that she was feeling. It was an unfamiliar sensation. As the agent ran her hands over her face to clear the water from her eyes she found herself speaking aloud. "I should just quit...just forget it all." Alex turned off the shower and continued to ready herself for the coming day. As she reentered the bedroom she found herself again entranced by the small blonde woman sprawled across half of the king sized bed. The agent finished closing the last buttons on her shirt and closed her eyes.

She quietly exited the room and crossed the hallway. Peering around the door a blonde head began to come into focus. The agent tiptoed to the side of the bed and gently ran her fingers through his hair. "I'll be back, Speed Racer," she whispered. He shifted slightly without ever opening his eyes and the agent smiled. "I told your mom, chocolate cake...I know you told Uncle Nick you love that. I love you." Alex bent down and kissed his head. She stood back up and took in a large breath, shaking her head. It was unbelievable to her. She'd seen war. She'd seen atrocities, violence and experienced the apprehension of it all. Nothing, not one thing in her life, had been this difficult. She'd never been in love. Sometimes she had wondered if that could even exist amidst all the chaos in the world. She had her answer now. Love existed here with these two souls and somehow life seemed to conspire to pull her from them.

Alex kissed the small head one last time and made her way out of the room. She looked at the bags that leaned against the front door; right where she had placed them the night before and shook her head. It should be the day she was going home and instead she felt as though she were leaving home. It unsettled her. The agent walked into the kitchen and started the task of brewing coffee. She wished she could talk to Dylan before she left, but she didn't want to wake him. The coffee had just started to drip when she felt two arms encircle her waist. The agent closed her eyes and clasped both the small hands that held her. "Good morning," she said softly. There was no response, just a tightening of the grip that held her close. The agent shifted and turned to look into the watery green eyes behind her. "I know," she said. "I'll be back before you know I was gone...I promise."

Cassidy looked into the agent's crystal blue eyes and summoned a smile. "I know when you are gone for five minutes," she confessed.

Alex smiled. She had no doubt that was true. No matter how interesting or challenging any situation the agent was engaged in was, since she met Cassidy, it was inevitable that at some point her thoughts would turn to the woman and the time they shared together. Sometimes she struggled to banish her emotions so that she could focus on her work. They hadn't truly been apart more than a few hours since they met. Although Alex knew it had been a very short time, it often felt as if they had always been this way. "Come on...let me get you some coffee," the agent suggested. The pair silently sipped their morning coffee; both understanding that this separation would be short and neither able to fully comprehend why it was so painful for both of them. Alex took a final sip and placed her mug in the sink. She offered a crooked smile to her lover and Cassidy sighed.

The agent extended her hand and the teacher accepted, following the dark haired woman she loved to the door without any words. Alex took hold of Cassidy's face and searched her eyes. She leaned in and gently kissed the woman, struggling to pull back and release her. There was a sensation building within the agent that she could not describe. For some reason she felt an overpowering urge to stay. It was almost a physical reaction. The teacher sensed her partner's apprehension and swallowed her own sadness to offer some reassurance. Cassidy kissed Alex's cheek. "Go...call me when you are out of your meeting."

"You'll be in class," the agent said.

The teacher smiled. "Then leave a message. I will call you when Dylan gets home from school," Cassidy said. Alex stroked her lover's cheek and the teacher offered a knowing smile.

The agent grabbed the handle of her bag and started through the door. She stopped abruptly and kissed Cassidy again. "Cass..."

"I love you, Agent Toles."

Alex returned the teacher's affectionate smile. "I love you too, Cassidy. I'll see you in a week." Cassidy watched as the agent lifted her bag into the trunk and then moved to her seat in the car. She gently grabbed her lower lip with her teeth as she heard the ignition start and forced a smile to accompany her wave. The car pulled out of the driveway and paused one last time before making its way out of sight. "I miss you, Alex," the teacher closed her eyes, "already."

***

The man fidgeted with the bag on the passenger seat of the blue sedan. He squirmed in his seat to get comfortable. Fingering the items in the bag he sighed. Some rope. Some tape. Ahh, there it was, the envelope. He pulled it out and removed a stack of photos, his favorite subject. She was beautiful and he smiled. She thought she could deny him. He answered to no one now; no one. She would answer to him. What she could tell him mattered very little from his point of view. He didn't care if she spoke at all. He would ask the questions and play the game he had been taught before he indulged in his own recreation. He'd earned it. Then he would be free of all of them. He would search out another; no ties to hold him anywhere; no one caring who he was. He was dead now.

A few more hours was all he needed. He pulled a silver flask from the glove box and lifted it to his lips with satisfaction. She was turning down the street now. The clock had begun to tick. No more clicking cameras. No more annoying distractions. Another large swig of the powerful liquid and his hand reached for the cigarettes. Now he would move where he longed to be. His patience would be rewarded. The small black box suddenly interrupted his thought. He looked at it with disdain. The strength in his hands grew as his anticipation swelled. He threw it with force against the dashboard and its deafening cries waned to a squeaky whisper. No more conversation. "My turn," he whispered.

***

"Did you find him?"

"He's not answering," Claire Brackett replied. "I've tried."

"Idiot," John Merrow mumbled. He picked up the cell phone on his desk and lifted it to his ear. "We have a problem," he said.

The voice on the other end seemed to be expecting the call. "Fisher," it replied.

"Yes....Do you know where he is?"

"Yes," the man answered. "He's in New York."

The president glared at the redheaded woman across from him. "Unacceptable."

"Understood," the man answered. "However, it could be advantageous...with the agent gone."

The president shook his head and attempted to quell his anger. "If you want to create a crisis...Toles will not rest....not ever."

Brackett shifted in her seat unsure what this conversation was regarding. The president continued. "O'Brien called me yesterday."

"Yes.....did you convince him?" the other man asked.

"I believe so."

"Good," the man responded. The president kept an unflinching glare on Brackett as the voice continued. "I will take care of the situation," the voice concluded.

"I'll expect your call," John Merrow hung up the phone. "You realize what you have created?" The president moved toward the woman.

"I did as you instructed," Brackett said.

"No. You did as you pleased," he placed his forehead against hers menacingly. "Get to the field office and play nice. Let me know when Toles leaves."

"Why? She'll be on suspension," Brackett answered.

"Mmm...just do it, Claire. Toles is a lot smarter than you are."

"You want me to follow her?"

"No," he pulled back. "I want you at the office. I don't want her having any trail to me...or to anyone else you've met with...understood? Don't increase her suspicions. We have enough problems already thanks to your carelessness. You'd better hope that phone call I made works out." Brackett was not easily intimidated but the tone in John Merrow's voice told her if ever there was a time to comply, it was now. "I can't protect you, Claire. This is not my game...I am only a player....just like you. If he fails...well...."

"You're the president," she said definitively.

"How do you think one achieves that, Claire? Through campaigns?" He laughed. "You have no idea. You are just a girl....a baby in this world. The way to the White House is paved with a lot of things, money, promises, betrayals, blood. And those who will shed the blood of their friends...they are the most dangerous beasts in the world. Watch yourself, Claire. No one is indispensable. Not even me."

***

Alex walked to her desk and sat in the large chair. She rolled it back and forth and traced the top of it with her fingertips. She closed her eyes for a moment as her hand instinctively dropped to the I.D. badge on her hip. She pictured Cassidy in her mind. Cassidy was standing at the counter making breakfast. There was a small dusting of flour on her face, and just a hint had lifted through the air and rested in her hair. Alex sighed. "I miss you, Cass," she whispered and then chuckled at the thought that if she were home, Cassidy would have heard her faint whisper nearly a full room away.

"You okay?" Brian Fallon asked as he placed a hand on his partner's shoulder.

Alex swiveled her chair and smiled. "Must be that time, huh?" He nodded with sadness evident in his eyes. "Hey," Alex smiled. "It's all right, Fallon. Some things are worth it." She patted his shoulder as she stood and began the short trek down the hallway to a small conference room.

"At least Fisher is out of the way," her partner offered.

"Yeah," Alex nodded, "give me some time to pack." He looked at Alex inquisitively. "Like I said, Fallon....some things are worth it," with that she was gone.

"Agent," Assistant Director Tate greeted Alex as she entered the room.

"Assistant Director," she returned the greeting.

"Please...sit," he said as she complied. "Let's just get this over with," he said plainly.

Chapter Twenty-One

Claire Brackett felt the heat of his stare and looked up from her desk. "Can I help you with something?" Brackett asked smugly.

Brian Fallon was considered one the most even tempered agents in the bureau. Often people mistook his good nature and his sense of humor as a sign that he was somehow less capable or less commanding. There was another side to the agent that few ever saw. He seldom felt the inclination to let out his anger. Experience taught him that anger and competitiveness were counterproductive to his work. Very few things brought out the harsher side of Brian Fallon. Right now one of them was sitting in front of him. Slowly he leaned his body over the desk and locked eyes with the young redhead. "I don't know what your game is…Miss Brackett."

"That's agent," she began.

"Oh….I think we both know better than that; don't we?" He smirked but kept his voice steady. "Let me give you a little piece of advice. Tread lightly in your time here."

"Or what?" She smirked.

Fallon moved even closer. The severity in his voice dripped with animosity. "Don't test me, Brackett. Anything happens to Toles or Cassidy…I promise you; you will see a side to me you'll wish you'd never witnessed." Brackett swallowed hard. Alex was just making her way back down the hallway when she caught sight of Fallon in Brackett's face. The agent covered her mouth to hide the smile that had instantly appeared. She had only seen Fallon get angry a couple of times. She sometimes forgot how intelligent and determined her partner was. One thing she always understood was the level of his loyalty to her and their partnership. She felt sorry for anyone who was foolish enough to disregard Brian Fallon as anything less than a stellar investigator. She trusted the man with her life and that was a rarity for Alex.

"Hey now," Alex called from slightly behind her partner, whose nose was just about touching the younger agent's. "You can get suspended for that, you know?" Alex said making a joke at her own expense.

Fallon pulled back slowly but kept his eye on the agent at the desk. "We were just chatting," he said as he moved his focus to his partner.

"Ahh…I see," Alex nodded. "Well, it appears I have some vacation time to take," the dark haired agent smiled. Brackett looked at her former lover with contempt. "I guess you can report that to DCIS," Alex gloated.

"You're awfully cheerful for someone losing their career," Brackett responded, ignoring the agent's assertions.

"Hum? Don't get too excited, Claire….You did want me to call you Claire, as I recall?" Alex shrugged and continued. "There's always a chance I'll go home."

"I thought you'd be going back to that cute congressman's wife…"

"Oh…yes, Cassidy…I wasn't referring to my family. I meant my career, Claire. There's always the Pentagon," Alex winked and walked away with Fallon following behind.

The agent retrieved a few items from her desk and Fallon studied her closely. "Well?" Fallon asked.

"What?"

"How long?"

"Indefinite," Alex answered and saw her partner's stress rise. "Fallon, listen…walk me out." She handed him a small box and they continued out the door.

"You're not really thinking about the Pentagon…Are you?"

Alex sighed as they reached the car. "Fallon, you know there isn't anyone I'd rather work with…but things," she opened the trunk and put a box in before closing it again. "I'm driving back to New York in the morning."

"Alex…do you think that's wise? I mean…"

Alex smiled. "They can fire me. I already told Tate if I am reinstated I have my own conditions."

"What?" Fallon asked.

"Transfer," Alex explained.

Fallon felt as if the wind had been knocked from his chest momentarily. He looked at Alex in disbelief and then saw the gleam in her eyes. His partner had just been suspended and she looked happier than he had ever seen her. "New York, I assume." She nodded. He shook his head. "Well, Toles…It won't be the same here…What if they….uh…."

Alex shrugged. "I have other options."

"You really driving back tomorrow?"

"Yeah…Cassidy doesn't know," Alex smiled.

Fallon shook his head again. "Need anything?"

Alex put her hand on his shoulder. "You'll be the first to know. I'll call you."

Brian Fallon watched as his partner pulled away. Two weeks had changed both their lives. He couldn't imagine his life without Alex in it. She was part of his family. His wife and his children loved his partner. He shook his head wondering what would be next for him. "Good luck, Alex," he whispered.

***

Cassidy sat at her desk waiting for her next class. She pulled the phone from her drawer and saw the message on the screen, 'Voicemail'. She pressed the button and waited.

Well…I told you, you wouldn't even know I was gone. The teacher smiled as she listened to the agent's voice. *So….it's official…I'm taking some forced vacation time....I was thinking, you know; about that birthday cake?* Cassidy snickered. *Maybe you could make both chocolate and vanilla. I'll bet Batman would like that kind.* Cassidy shook her head and muttered, "Sure...it's all about Batman." The voice message continued. *Call me when you get home....I gotta' do some shopping.... I was thinking....Do you think we could invite Nick and Barb and have them bring Cat to Speed Racer's party? I mean...you don't have to but....* "You're rambling again, Alex," Cassidy mused to herself, "and that's already done...talked to Barb this morning." The teacher shook her head again as she listened to the agent's long winded message. Cassidy thought it was funny how Alex was prattling on. It was obvious the agent missed Cassidy in her voice and it had only been hours since they parted. She loved hearing her lover's voice as she went on and on about so many trivial things; things that now seemed to matter more than anything else to them both. With no one threatening Cassidy, Alex had shifted her priorities to other things like birthday cakes and presents. "God, I love you," the teacher said aloud as the message finished. *Anyway...Fallon got in Brackett's face...I wish you could've seen it...it was priceless. I miss you, Cass. Crazy. Call me, okay? I love you.* Cassidy put the phone back in the drawer as her next batch of students entered. Alex's voice was still lingering in her head. She was anxious now to get home and call the agent. 'Two more classes,' she thought silently. 'Just a few hours.' The teacher was beginning to think of some unique ways to welcome the agent back. She shook off her train of thought when a young, tall student walked to the front of her desk.

"Hey, Mrs. O...we missed you," he said.

"I missed you all too, James," Cassidy smiled.

"Did you read that story? The one I gave you?" the boy asked hopefully.

Cassidy had read it just as she promised she would. It was a heartfelt essay about the boy's two moms. The teacher had read it over a week ago before everything spun out of control. She thought back to some of the words he had written. Cassidy smiled at the new and unique understanding that she now had. She looked at the teenager before her and thought about Dylan. "Of course I read it, James. It was very beautiful."

He smiled broadly. "You didn't think it was...you know... like..."

"Weird?" Cassidy chuckled thinking back to a conversation she had with her mother about Alex. The boy nodded. "No, James. I think you're lucky...and so are your moms." The relief on his face told Cassidy everything she needed to know about his essay and his reason for writing it. "I'm proud of you," she said. As he took his seat Cassidy smiled. She was ready to write her own new story with Alex at its center and for the first time since she was a child she felt like maybe, just maybe she was really going *home.*

***

Alex walked into the small kitchen area of her apartment and started a pot of coffee. She looked at the clock on the stove that read 1:15 p.m. The agent looked out over the apartment and considered what she should take with her. The truth was that Alex spent very little time here. When she was at home she was either working or sleeping. She lifted her bag onto the couch and opened it. There was something wrapped on top of her clothes with an envelope attached. Her heart stopped for a moment as she recalled the recent envelopes she had opened. Closing her eyes, she shook off those memories and looked at it again, pondering what might be inside. The agent lifted the envelope and read the name: *Alfred.* Alex laughed and shook her head. Cassidy was impossibly silly sometimes. She pulled out the small notecard which had a picture of the ocean cascading over some rocks on its front. Slowly she lifted the cover to reveal the message:

Alex,

I don't know how it happened. It's strange. One moment I could predict the end of every day and then you arrived at my door and life became this crazy adventure. Every moment that I am with you is an adventure. It's like the ocean in so many ways; waves that are almost violent at moments and then in an instant turn to a peaceful and soothing caress, gently carrying me along. It's fitting that you brought me there; to the ocean that day. I was thinking about that night and your eyes in the firelight. I realize now that I loved you from the first moment we met. I think I knew that when we were sitting on that patio with the waves behind us.

As I am writing this you are upstairs with Dylan. I can hear him laughing. I can hear your voice playfully encouraging his stories. I love you more with every moment that passes. Sometimes I can't seem to recall when you weren't here with us. I am so angry with Chris for hurting you...but then I think to myself that without him I may never have found you. I may never have known what it feels like to fall in love. It's ironic. His actions, all of them, and your reaction to him, only remind me even more why I am so in love with you.

I can't wait for you to come home. Come home to me and to Dylan. I know you won't stay away long, but even just a day will find us both missing you. So, take this, I've seen you look at it many times in the last few days. This way we will be with you, or at least it can remind you that we are waiting for you. Sometimes it is hard for me to tell you what I feel. I am better on paper; perhaps that is the English teacher in me. All I know is that I want to spend my life with you, all of it.

Je t'adore, my love.

Cassidy

Alex took a deep breath and wiped a tear from her eye. "Je t'aime, Cass," she said as she put down the card and opened the small package that was wrapped in purple tissue paper. As she peeled away the purple layers two faces came into view, two magnificent smiles, the two people she loved now more than her own life. She inhaled deeply and savored the emotions coursing through her. Cassidy had Dylan on her lap in the picture that sat in a thin silver frame. They were both laughing. Cassidy was right. Alex looked at that picture every day. It was her favorite in the entire house. Mother and son almost seemed to glow with happiness in the photo. The love between them seemed to emanate from behind the glass. The agent ran her fingers over the faces and smiled. A knock at the door snapped the agent from her private thoughts. She set the photo down in the middle of the coffee table and looked at it again. Another knock sounded. "I'm coming," she called with some exasperation. She looked down one last time and smiled. "You'll be surprised Cassidy, when I am home tomorrow," the agent gleamed with anticipation. The knock repeated. "Christ, Fallon...give me a minute...I just left you for God's...." she stopped mid thought as she opened the door.

***

Cassidy nearly bounced her way off the train and to her car. She was anxious to get home and to wait for her mother and Dylan to arrive so that she could call Alex. The teacher was curious if her lover had opened her luggage yet and found the note and picture she had enclosed. Cassidy smiled as she turned on the car radio and a familiar tune began to play; one she had heard the agent singing to on their way home from Connecticut. She loved it when Alex would sing to the radio, but then she seemed to love almost everything about the agent. The teacher laughed at that thought. Even when Alex frustrated her there was no way for Cassidy to deny that she was head over heels in love with Alex Toles. This would be the first night since Cassidy said 'I love you' to the agent that she would sleep alone. Funny, she thought to herself now. For nearly the entire last year of her marriage she slept alone every night. She'd grown used to that and even comfortable with it. Now, the thought of not feeling Alex beside her was almost unimaginable. Turning onto Cherry Circle the teacher sighed.

She thought perhaps she would ask her mother to spend the night. They hadn't talked much in days and Cassidy was ready for some time with Rose. There was so much she wanted to share and so much she just wanted to say out loud. Alex had actually alluded to them getting married one day. The teacher was almost embarrassed to admit she found herself thinking about cakes and dresses a couple of times during the day. It was insane if she stopped to think about it. Cassidy had decided days ago that thinking was pointless when it came to her feelings for Alex. She could daydream and she did, often. There were two things that the teacher was certain of as she pulled into her driveway; she wanted to spend the rest of her life with Alexis Toles and she was going to.

Cassidy turned off the car and reached for her bag. She smiled and closed the car door and headed for the house. She opened the front door and got the faint hint of coffee wafting in the air. Could it really be, she wondered? Did Alex come right home? She would be the only person to make coffee in the afternoon. The teacher's heart skipped as she made her way toward the kitchen, her smile growing by the second. "What are you doing home," she started to say as she walked through the door. Her bag fell from her hand as she turned. "Oh my God..." she barely whispered.

***

"Christ, Fallon...give me a minute...I just left you for God's...." Alex stopped mid thought as she opened the door.

"Agent Toles," the man greeted her.

Alex's jaw tightened. "What the hell do you want?" she asked the man standing before her on two crutches.

"I'd like to talk to you," Congressman Christopher O'Brien answered.

"I'm not interested."

"It's about Cassidy," he said.

"Like I said…"

"Agent…please…it's about Carl Fisher and Cassidy," he implored.

"News slow down here or what?" Alex asked. "Fisher is dead."

"I'm not so sure," he said. The agent froze. Alex Toles made her life at reading people and the congressman's expression was transparent. He was afraid. Alex nodded and he gingerly made his way through the door. She led the congressman to a chair and gestured for him to sit. "Thank you," he said cordially.

Alex nodded. "Why would you think Fisher is alive? I saw the apartment."

Christopher O'Brien placed his crutches at the side of his chair. "Do you have some water or…"

The agent sighed heavily. "You want coffee?" She took a moment to remind herself that this was Dylan's dad.

"Sure…just black."

The agent made her way to the kitchen and called back to him. "So.…"

The congressman looked around a bit and began, "Krause is worried…about what Cassidy might have told you…what she might know…without," he paused as he noticed the picture on the table and swallowed hard. It was true. He shook his head and continued. "About what she might say without realizing it mattered."

Alex entered the room again and saw the congressman's stare was focused on the picture. He looked at the agent and she could see that there was genuine pain and worry in his eyes. She poked her cheek with her tongue and handed him his coffee. "What could Cassidy possibly say that would matter to Jonathan Krause?"

"I don't know," he answered.

"That still doesn't explain Fisher," Alex said. She studied the man before her, her skepticism evident.

"Agent Toles…Look, I hated coming here as much as you hate me being here….There is no one else I can trust."

Alex raised her eyebrows. "You trust me?"

"I think you care about my wife and I think she is in danger."

The agent had been ready to pounce on the congressman for referring to Cassidy as his 'wife' but the last part of his statement stopped her in her tracks. "What do you mean she's in danger?"

"Look, Agent Toles," he looked briefly at the picture again. "I don't know as much as you think I do. I do know Jonathan Krause and I know a threat when I hear it….If they think she might know anything…Well, let's just say they'll find a way to…"

Alex felt her stomach burning. Fisher's suicide never set right with her. She stared at the congressman for a moment and then picked up her cell phone. She looked at the time. Cassidy would be home now. She dialed the number and waited.

***

"Welcome home," a hoarse voice greeted the teacher.

"How the hell did you…"

"Get in here? Oh… that was easy…Know you like coffee… sit down," he said.

"Carl…what do you want?" Cassidy asked fighting to keep her composure and hide the fear that was racking every inch of her.

He poured a cup of coffee and retrieved the milk from the refrigerator. "I know…just milk," he smiled. Cassidy watched him carefully. "You're pretty calm for seeing a ghost," he said. He leaned into her ear, "BOO!" The teacher's body shuddered. "Mmmm…." He sniffed her hair. "Oh, thought we could talk for a few minutes…Now that the bitch is gone…and that idiot politician."

"Talk about what?" the teacher asked, determined to remain in control.

"Well...We could talk about why you never liked me, or we could talk about why you did like my friend Johnny so much."

"What?"

"Oh....Cassidy....Krause and I go WAY back....you liked him....or was it just France that made him interesting?" Cassidy closed her eyes as he moved within inches of her lips. His breath reeked of whiskey and she felt a powerful wave of nausea begin to overtake her. "Mmm." He moaned again beginning to get excited about his time alone with the blonde. "So....Johnny or France?"

Cassidy felt her breath growing shallower. She tried to picture Alex; tried to hear the agent's voice in her mind. "Neither," she managed.

"Really? Poor Johnny...don't like him either.... Mmm guess we're not really your TYPE." He licked his lips and then ran his nose up Cassidy's neck before sitting next to her. Her bag was buzzing on the floor and her eyes moved to it, desperately wanting to answer. Rose would be home soon with Dylan. How would she warn them? "Leave it," he commanded. She jumped and his hands grabbed hold of both of her arms tightly. "My turn," he whispered to her.

***

"She's not answering," Alex said. She looked at the time again. "Call Rose," she said to the congressman.

"What?" O'Brien asked.

"Call her and tell her to take Dylan home with her until I call...Just do it." The congressman pulled out his cell phone and followed the agent's direction. Alex was already making another call. "Ferro?"

"Agent Toles?"

"I need you to do something," she said.

"What?"

"Find out the dentist on those records for Fisher."

327

"Agent…"

"Detective, please…I don't have time…Call me back… It's Cassidy," she hung up without giving him a chance to answer and took a deep breath. "God, I hope you are wrong," she looked at the congressman. She dialed another number. "Fallon?"

"Alex?"

"Is Brackett still there?"

Brian Fallon walked a short distance down the hallway and glanced to his right. "Yeah…why?"

"I think Fisher is alive."

"Toles…"

"I think he might be at the house."

"Why? Wait don't tell me, a feeling. What do you want me to do?" Fallon asked.

"Get her out of the building…Find out what she knows about Fisher. If he's alive….I swear to God, if anything…"

"Toles… I got it…I'll call you."

Alex pinched the bridge of her nose and looked at the congressman. "What the hell are you into O'Brien?" She shook her head and looked at the picture on the table. She exhaled with force and dialed another number.

***

Carl Fisher circled Cassidy breathing in the scent of her hair and smiling. "You should have given me a chance," he nearly cooed. The teacher bit her bottom lip attempting to quell her increasing fear. What if Dylan came home? Her heart was racing and she was struggling to keep hold of any rational thought. "You're afraid," he whispered. "Hummm….I can smell it." Fisher moved into the blonde's face and placed a kiss on her lips. He was ready to continue when the sound of the house phone blared from behind him. "Fuck! Answer it," he ordered.

Cassidy stood and reached for the phone across the counter when the man grabbed her wrist with great force. "I'm listening...so be careful." She started to lift it and he whispered, "And I speak French."

Cassidy's body shook as she pressed the button and held the phone to her ear. "Hello?"

"Cass?" Alex's tone was nearly frantic and Cassidy knew immediately that her lover suspected something.

"Yeah...how was your trip?" Cassidy tried to stay calm as she felt the heat of Carl Fisher's stare on her.

"Cass...is Speed Racer there?" Alex knew the answer but wanted to give Cassidy some time to think if Fisher was there. She wanted to gauge the teacher's reactions. It was obvious something was wrong. Now the agent wanted to assess how much time she might have to put a plan in place.

"No. He's not home yet." Cassidy tried to listen to Alex's voice to steady her emotions. She needed to let Alex know Fisher was there, that something was wrong. "Did you get my present?"

"Yes, I'm looking at it right now and missing you." Christopher O'Brien noted the tension and emotion in the agent's voice as she spoke to Cassidy.

"Did you read my card?" Cassidy asked. She wanted Alex to know that she loved the agent and whatever might happen; that would always be true. The teacher fought her tears. "I meant it."

"I know," Alex sighed. "Cass..."

"Did you like the picture of the sunset over the mountain on the front?" That was it. Any doubts Alex had were gone. She picked up the card with the picture of the ocean on the rocks and a crystal blue sky. Fisher was there.

"Mmm...I did. I would rather watch the sunset with you, though," the agent said feeling a tear well in her eye. "When I get back."

"When are you coming home?" Cassidy's voice began to falter and Fisher grabbed her arm to caution her. The teacher closed her eyes and listened.

"I'll be home before you even know I was gone. You just wait for me....Cass..."

"Je t'adore, Alex."

Alex pressed on her temple with her thumb lightly and a tear escaped her eyes. "Chocolate and vanilla....okay?"

Cassidy managed a slight chuckle as a tear fell down her cheek. "I prefer Vanilla."

"I know you do. Cassidy, I love you more than anything... we'll have that vanilla cake, I promise."

"I love you too, Alex. Get home soon," Fisher took the phone from the woman's hand and put it on the receiver as Cassidy's tears flowed freely.

"Touching," he said. "My turn."

***

"What the hell is your problem?" Brackett pulled away from Agent Fallon's grasp.

"I don't have time for this, Brackett. Fisher...is he alive or not."

"What are you talking about?" The redheaded agent glared defiantly.

"One chance, Brackett...Don't test me." Fallon grabbed the woman's arm and pulled her to him. "If anything happens to Cassidy I will make it my mission to destroy your career. Do you understand me? And I can promise you that will be nothing compared to what Toles will do."

"Why would I know?"

Brian Fallon tightened his grip on the woman's arm. His eyes were narrowing to slits and his voice became a haunting echo as he spoke in her ear. "Yes or no."

Claire Brackett's body shivered. John Merrow had warned her about Toles and Fallon, to be careful. Now she realized his caution was warranted. There was more to Fallon than she thought and the tingle of fear running over her caught her attention. "Yes," she whispered.

Fallon let go and stood watching her with a fierce stare. He could not speak to her as he pulled out his phone. He pressed the necessary button and managed only three words, "you'd better pray."

***

Congressman Christopher O'Brien watched the tall FBI agent as she lowered her phone and rubbed her face forcefully. "Is he there?" the congressman cautiously asked. Alex felt her body shaking. Her anger and her fear were overwhelming her thoughts and she needed to put both aside if she hoped to help Cassidy. "Agent Toles?" he called to her.

Alex let out a sigh and looked at the congressman. "I don't care what you want to do to me, O'Brien...I don't care what you think of me, but I swear," she stopped and controlled her words. She shook her head, "yeah...he's there."

"What are you," before the congressman could finish his question Alex was on the phone.

"Brady here."

"I need your help."

"Toles?"

"I need you to get to Cassidy O'Brien's....quickly but quietly." Alex was rummaging through the top of a closet in her hallway.

"Toles...where are you?"

"D.C., Fisher is there with her."

"What?" Steven Brady asked in disbelief. "Taylor said he was..."

"He's not.... Listen, O'Brien is here with me."

Steven Brady was already walking out the door of his office. "How much time?"

"I don't know...he'll want to play," Alex's voice dropped an octave as she confronted the likelihood of what Carl Fisher was planning for her lover. "Depends on what you mean for time."

"Understood....any idea where they are?"

"Kitchen or bedroom, that's where the phones are...betting kitchen...he'll stay on the lower level...just in case he needs an exit," Alex said.

"I'm thirty minutes out, best case scenario. Windows?"

Alex swallowed hard. Thirty minutes was a long time. A lot could happen in thirty minutes; a lot more than the agent wanted to imagine. "Back yard... sliding glass doors to the deck off the kitchen...small window over the sink...good vantage point is a tree house just to the right...But he's smart, Brady... if you can get there—then maybe..."

"Try and spook the spook," he said.

"Maybe."

"I'm on my way."

"Brady...." Alex need to convey to her friend the urgency of the situation. Fisher would likely view Cassidy as a recreational activity. That could mean almost anything and the thoughts running through Alex's brain were making her ill.

"I know," he answered.

Alex hung up the phone and loaded the pistol she had pulled from the top of her closet. She attached her holster and put her sidearm in it when the phone buzzed again. "He's alive," the voice said.

"I know. Fallon, he has Cass."

"What now?" Fallon asked.

"Big guns....I gotta' go.... Call Ferro...Fill him in..." Alex looked at the congressman. "Where is Krause?"

"I don't know," he said flatly. "Agent Toles, I had no way of knowing..."

Alex let out a disgusted chuckle. "You play with fire Congressman, you get burned. Those are the odds."

"It's not what you…"

She turned on her heels and looked at him. "I don't care what it is. I don't care why it is. Now, I have to find a way to get Fisher out of that house before he hurts Cassidy."

"Maybe if there's nothing to…"

"Fisher doesn't care about what Cassidy knows, O'Brien. He's obsessed. He doesn't give a shit about you or Krause. Your jealousy and your selfishness created the perfect opportunity for him. I don't have time for this. You found your way here; you can find your way out." The agent grabbed her keys and her wallet, checked her sidearm and walked out the door leaving the congressman alone in her apartment to ponder the picture on the table in front of him.

***

"So….you are just full of surprises," Carl Fisher hissed in the school teacher's ear. Cassidy closed her eyes and kept picturing Alex. She knew Alex would do everything she could to protect her, but Alex was so far away. Cassidy couldn't imagine how Alex could do anything. How did she even know that Fisher might be there? "Do I make you….nervous?" Fisher whispered and ran a hand along Cassidy's leg. She shuddered at the sensation and fought her tears.

"Yes," she answered.

"Oh," he smiled with satisfaction. "But you like excitement, don't you? I mean politicians, FBI agents….mmmmm." His touch became more insistent.

"Not really," Cassidy replied growing as angry as she was afraid.

"Oh….I don't believe you….Agent Toles has quite a reputation you know."

"No, I'm afraid I don't know," the teacher said pointedly.

"Surely," he breathed in her ear, "you don't think you are her first? I mean," he stopped and licked behind her ear before whispering again, "you think she would give it all up for you? Hmmm? Like me..."

Cassidy swallowed hard and turned to face him with disgust. "Yes, actually I do." Maybe there was no way out but the teacher was not going to play the willing victim to this sadistic son of a bitch. There was no way if she was going to die here that she would betray who she was and what she felt for Alex.

Fisher stepped back a pace and ran his fingers over the top of his head in frustration. He turned and grabbed his red duffel bag off the kitchen table. Cassidy took the brief opportunity to survey her familiar surroundings, wondering if she could out run him, but that seemed unlikely. He let out a maniacal laugh as he came face to face with the teacher again and grabbed her. "You think you're brave?" He laughed harder and pulled her across the room, throwing her into a chair. "We'll see." He grabbed the rope from his bag and tied her hands behind the chair, pulling the rope so tightly that Cassidy winced at the burning sensation. "Now what were you saying...about that agent? You think she loves you?" he mocked the woman.

The teacher looked her assailant squarely in the eyes, a single tear rolling down her cheek. "No." He smiled with satisfaction at her response and then she continued, "I know she loves me."

Fisher became enraged. "ENOUGH talk!" He retrieved a roll of duct tape from his bag and ripped off a large piece. He slapped it over Cassidy's mouth, pulling her face to look at him as she attempted to turn away. "NOW...I will speak and you will listen...MY TURN."

***

Alex started her car as she waited for a voice to answer her call. "Alex?"

"John, I need your help," there was a distinct panic in the agent's voice that John Merrow had never heard.

"What is it?" the president asked.

"Fisher is at Cassidy's."

"Alex, that's…"

"John…please…"

The president sighed and swallowed hard. His fears were being realized. Fisher posed an exposure risk. He needed to be removed. If anything happened to Cassidy it would galvanize Agent Toles beyond the resolve he was certain she already had to get to the bottom of the congressman's dealings. He'd warned Brackett and he had hoped that his call the prior day would have prevented this. It appeared his efforts were too little, too late. Now, he would need to play the game very carefully. "What do you need?" President Merrow asked.

"I don't have my badge and I don't have time, John. I need to get there and quickly…and I need to be able to coordinate on the way."

"All right. Andrews. I will make the call."

"John…I …"

"Alex…keep your head in the game. Is anyone else there? Dylan? I will call Taylor."

"Dylan's with Cassidy's mom…Brady's on his way," she informed him.

"Well, we may have closer assets. How long?" the president asked.

"I spoke to him ten minutes ago…another twenty at least."

"Let me go, Captain…I'll take care of what I can. Expect Captain Abel at Andrews. I'll make the request…Have Agent Fallon meet you. You will be cleared."

Alex tried to concentrate on the road. "Thank you."

***

"Dammit!" The president yelled into the phone. "I thought this was taken care of."

"Where is he?" the voice asked.

"He's at the house....and NSA is on the way."

"Does he have her?" The man's voice seemed to tremble slightly.

"Yes."

"How far out is NSA?" the voice inquired.

"Probably twenty."

"I am almost there now...I will be there in ten."

"Too little, too late," the president said.

"Maybe not," the man answered.

"Take him out," Merrow said definitively.

"My pleasure."

The president grabbed the back of his neck and stretched. "I need him silent. I want her safe...Toles will dig..."

"I have it," the man answered.

***

The drive to Andrews Air Force Base took less than fifteen minutes but it seemed like an eternity. Fallon was on his way. The agent had enlisted all the assets she could trust. Now she would have to rely on them to communicate with her. She called Nick and asked him to bring Rose and Dylan to his house until she could get back and knew exactly what was going on. She didn't suspect that they were in danger, but she wasn't willing to take any chances. Alex knew that Nick and Barb could help keep Dylan occupied and Rose calm. As she walked toward the plane she pinched the bridge of her nose and spoke to Cassidy in her mind:

Please, Cass... just sit tight...don't try to fight him too much. I know you...it'll just make him want to hurt you more...just wait... hang in there....Brady, he'll get there. He will. I'm sorry. I should have seen it. Maybe I just didn't want to. I should never have left. I felt it, something was off. I thought it was just leaving...God, Cassidy....I love you...Please just hang in there.

"Captain Toles," Captain Abel greeted, "been too long."

Alex forced a smile, "Captain...I assume..."

"I know what I need to know, Cap. Your friend is already on board. You'll have full access. If all goes well you'll be on the ground in just over an hour."

"Thank you, Captain." Alex shook her friend's hand and boarded the Boeing 757.

"Toles," Fallon stood to greet his partner.

"Fallon," Alex forced a smile but Fallon could see the stress in his partner's eyes.

"She'll be all right, Alex."

Alex nodded and bit her lip. The agent knew Carl Fisher's type. He was psychotic, sadistic, and worse, he was smart. Her hope was that he was equally cocky and emboldened by what he perceived as her absence. "She has to be," Alex said. The agent took a deep breath and looked at her phone. Now she had to make the call she dreaded most.

"Alex?" Fallon inquired.

Alex looked up, closed her eyes for a moment and sighed. She hit the contact number and put the phone to her ear.

"Alex?" Rose McCollum was in a state of panic.

"Rose, calm down, okay?"

"What is going on? Chris called and..."

"I know. I asked him to," Alex explained.

Rose was now as confused as she was worried. "He said to wait for you... is he there? Alex what is..."

"Listen to me, Rose...okay? He was with me. I'm on my way back with Agent Fallon. You need keep Dylan there; wait there. I'm going to have my brother pick you both up and take you to his house, all right?"

"Alex...why? What is going on?"

The agent leaned her forehead on her hand and tried to breathe. Fallon watched his partner closely. The tension was pouring off of Alex unlike any time he had ever seen. He could feel her fear and her pain as he watched her struggle to maintain her composure. "Rose, Cassidy is in some trouble right now. She's not alone at the house; do you understand?" The only response was an audible gasp and what Alex was certain were tears. "I need you to try and stay calm, okay? We don't want Dylan to get scared."

"Alex…is she…"

Alex swallowed hard. "Rose, I don't know much. I did talk to Cassidy, just for a minute. She was all right, just worried, but she was calm and in control."

"But you're not here…Alex…"

"I have people on the way. They know how to handle this. Just try and stay calm. I promise I am doing everything I can."

"Grandma?" Alex heard Dylan's voice in the background. She could tell he was becoming afraid at the sight of his grandmother's emotions.

"Rose…let me talk to Dylan, all right? Nicky will be there in less than an hour now." The silence was almost deafening. "Rose…put Dylan on and try to calm down."

Rose took a deep breath and smiled down at her grandson. "Alex wants to talk to you," she handed him the phone.

"Alex!"

"Hey, Speed Racer…"

"When are you coming home?" he asked looking at his grandmother with concern.

"I'm on my way home now," she told him.

"You are?"

"Yeah…I am," Alex said quietly.

"Grandma says I have to stay here. Where's Mom?"

Alex rubbed her temple and tried to steady her speech. "Your mom had some things to do this afternoon…You know, big party coming, I hear."

"Yeah, my birthday," he said.

"I know. Listen, Speed…Uncle Nick's going to come and take you and Grandma to his house tonight for dinner, okay?"

"Why?"

"Well, because your mom and I have to do some things and I thought maybe you'd have fun with Cat. Maybe you can even spend the night….I know you wanted to do that," Alex offered.

"But, I have school."

Alex took a deep breath, "Yeah. Well, we'll see what time Mom and I get done, okay?"

"Alex?"

"Yeah?"

"Grandma is crying."

"She is, huh? Well, sometimes she worries about all of us, you know? It's okay."

"Alex?"

"Yeah?"

"Is Mom okay?"

Alex covered her mouth and shook her head. Dylan was a perceptive young man and she was certain that between his grandmother's tears, all the changes and the tension she knew she could not hide in her own voice; he wondered what was wrong. "Yes. She's okay, Dylan. I promise." Alex shook her head in anger. How could she promise him that? She wasn't even convinced of that and she certainly couldn't guarantee it. Hearing his voice the agent was determined that somehow she had to insure Cassidy was safe. She was never one to pray, but she thought maybe today was a good day to start.

"Alex…are you there?"

"I'm here, Speed. I'll be home before you know it, okay? I'll see you at Uncle Nick's with Mom."

"Promise?"

Alex nodded. "I promise."

"I love you, Alex."

"I love you, Dylan. Go take care of Grandma, okay? She needs a laugh."

"Okay.....Bye, Alex."

"See you in while," Alex hung up the phone and covered her face with her hands. Fallon put his hand on her back. "Fallon, she has to be okay. I can't tell them...I ..."

"She will be," Fallon said as they felt the plane lift into the air.

'I'm coming Cass,' Alex thought silently. 'Hang in there.'

Chapter Twenty-Two

Jonathan Krause pulled the Energy Plus van onto Orchard Drive and turned off the ignition. He retrieved the long, black bag as he slowly closed the door to study his surroundings. Straight ahead was a large blue colonial home. Just beyond it he could make out the side of an equally large white colonial. He cracked his neck and started forward deliberately. He made his way past the blue home and through the side yard with confidence, never removing his attention from the yard just beyond. At the far corner of the yard he stopped and moved behind a line of bushes. He pulled out a small pair of binoculars and looked ahead. A man in a black T-shirt was kneeling. He adjusted the view. Someone was in front him. The man in the T-shirt stood abruptly and kicked a chair. "Cassidy," Krause whispered as Fisher moved to the right. Jonathan Krause felt his muscles tense. He felt a pulling sensation in his chest and he fought to inhale deeply. "Son of a bitch. I told you to wait." Krause looked around the yard. He saw the tree house and grabbed the bag. Then he stopped. Another figure was approaching. He pulled out the binoculars again. The man was carefully making his way toward the oak tree that held the platform. "Dammit...NSA is faster than I thought." He looked around again and back toward the kitchen. "Careless," he muttered, noting that Fisher was providing a clear line of sight and a clear shot. Cassidy could be a complication. Krause sighed. "God dammit, Cassie...Why did you marry him?" Krause unzipped the bag and started assembling the rifle and scope.

He took another deep breath and searched for a new vantage point. Quickly he put the phone to his ear and hit the number. "I'm here...NSA too....yeah....I got him...she's okay....my pleasure."

***

Alex picked up the phone that sat on the desk beside her. "Toles?" the voice asked for confirmation.

"Brady?"

"I'm here...I can see him."

"Cassidy...." Alex began to ask.

"I can't see from here...he's pacing," Brady answered.

"Do you have a shot?"

"No, not clear...I need him to move a little...Need to try and see where she is," he said.

Alex grabbed either side of her forehead with her left hand, pressing her temples firmly with her fingers. "Brady, can he see you?"

"No. Well, he hasn't turned....Just pacing....Toles, I think he's losing it. I mean he was a spook right? A marksman?"

"Yeah," she confirmed.

"He doesn't even care that he's in front of glass."

"Yeah. He thinks he's clear...doesn't care....He also has her close to him. He'll use her if he senses anything. Stay out of sight; no shot unless you know."

"Toles, I can try another way. He doesn't appear to be armed."

"He is. Trust me. It will take less than a second for him to reach his sidearm. He might be crazy and he might be careless right now but he's not stupid, Brady. You don't get where he was by being stupid. Don't confuse the two. Crazy is much more dangerous when they're brilliant, careless or not." Alex thought she heard something in the background and stopped to listen.

"You're the profiler," he said.

"*Smotret', kuda on dvigayetsya* (Watch where he moves)," Alex said in Russian.

"*Kto-to proslushivaniya* (Is someone listening)?" he asked.

"*Nikogda ne slishkom ostorozhnykh* (Never too cautious). *Dayte mne znat', kogda vyvidite yeye* (Let me know when you see her)," Alex answered.

***

Christopher O'Brien sat dazed in the chair Alex Toles had given him. The apartment door was still partially open and he put his face in his hands. He took a deep breath and edged forward looking at the card the agent had dropped on the table during her conversation with his ex-wife. He studied the picture that stood just behind it and wondered where it all had gone so wrong. He'd seen the photo. He didn't know when it was taken. The congressman closed his eyes. He knew he shouldn't. He had no right. He couldn't resist the temptation; not after what he had heard; the tall, attractive agent professing her love for the mother of his son. He hesitated momentarily but then he stretched and took the card into his hands. He opened it and he read. The words were eloquent, clearly Cassidy's. He had forgotten how she once wrote poetry, many years ago. She had never written him anything close to what these words reflected:

I can't wait for you to come home. Come home to me and to Dylan. I know you won't stay away long, but even just a day will find us both missing you. So, take this, I've seen you look at it many times in the last days. This way we will be with you, or at least it can remind you that we are waiting for you. Sometimes it is hard for me to tell you what I feel. I am better on paper; perhaps that is the English teacher in me. All I know is that I want to spend my life with you, all of it...

Je t'adore, my love.

Cassidy

The congressman set the card down softly and closed his eyes. This was far from over. If they knew; if they found out he went to Toles. They would find out. What choice did he have? His phone buzzed and he lifted it. "Christopher O'Brien."

"You missed our call, Congressman," the voice said.

"Chairman...I apologize," the congressman inhaled and steadied himself. It was show time again. "I seem to still be a bit...well, hazy."

"Understandable, Chris. How are you feeling?"

Christopher O'Brien looked back at the photo and nodded silently. He grabbed his crutches and put them in front of him. "Stronger each day. How would four o'clock work? I will be in my home office by then," the congressman explained.

"That's should be fine, Chris...as long as you are up to it."

"Well, I may be moving slower, Congressman...but I am still in the game," O'Brien offered.

"Very well...four it is," the chairman agreed.

The congressman hung up his phone, placed it in his pocket and braced himself on his crutches. He glanced back at the photo and his lips curled into a small smile. "Still in the game," he muttered.

***

Rose's phone rang and she answered it without looking. "Alex?"

"No, Rose."

"Chris. What do you want?"

"I'd like to speak to my son," the congressman said.

"He's upstairs right now getting some things together from his room here."

"Rose..."

"I don't think it's a good idea, Chris."

"He's my son, Rose."

"Yes...well, I suppose he is that," Rose agreed.

"Is he all right? Where are you?" the congressman inquired. "What does he know?"

Rose McCollum licked her lips and attempted to quiet the anger that was festering within her. "He's fine. Alex spoke with him a while ago," the woman said with some satisfaction.

"I see. Alex spoke with him," his disgust was apparent.

"That's what I said."

"Well, I would like to speak with him now."

Rose took a deep breath and called her grandson. Dylan ran down the stairs. "Is it Mom?" Rose looked at him and shook her head slightly. "Is it Alex?"

"No, honey, it's your father."

Dylan frowned. He was very angry with his father. They had only spoken twice since the congressman came home from the hospital and both times the congressman had cut the conversation short when Cheryl had called to him. Then, Dylan heard his mother telling his grandmother about Alex leaving. Now, Alex was gone and Dylan knew with all these calls something was wrong. He reluctantly took the phone and put it to his ear. "Hey buddy," the congressman said gently. Dylan said nothing. "What's wrong, buddy?"

"Where's Mom?" Dylan asked.

The congressman cleared his throat. "I'm not sure, Dylan... I think she had some..."

"You know," Dylan said plainly.

"Dylan...I don't know," his father said.

"Are you coming to my party?" The boy changed the subject abruptly.

"What?"

"My birthday party?"

"Dylan, I have a lot of calls this week. I have to catch up. I will call you on...."

The doorbell rang in the distance and Dylan turned to see his grandmother opening the door for Nick. "It's okay. I know you're busy. Alex is on her way home," Dylan said to his father.

"Listen, Dylan, you and I will do something…"

Dylan interrupted his father's thought. "I have to go. Uncle Nick is here," he handed the phone to his grandmother. As soon as she accepted it he ran and collapsed into Nick. At six, all of the adults' stress was overloading him and as soon as he saw the strong man that looked so much like his hero he started crying.

Rose took the phone. "Who is Uncle Nick?" the congressman asked sharply.

Rose walked quietly into her kitchen, away from small ears and took a deep breath. "Chris, I always thought you loved Cassie, even when things were bad, even when you were screwing half your aides; I still thought you loved her."

"Wait a minute," he began to mount his defense.

"No. You wait a minute, Congressman. I have no idea what you have to do with what is happening to Cassidy but I know you have everything to do with why Dylan is crying and the fact that Alex is not here to take care of them both."

"Rose, Cassidy is my…"

Rose McCollum could see right through the congressman now and she had every intention of making that known. "Cassidy is your *ex*-wife. That was your own doing and you know it. Now, Alex's brother is here and Dylan and I are leaving."

"You're leaving with the agent's brother?"

"No, I am leaving with Cassidy's lover's brother, Chris. Cassidy's family, Dylan's family…. MY family. Don't call again. Dylan is upset enough. And, Chris? If you wanted to be here, you'd find a way."

"Dylan and Cassidy are my family," he said with his own frustration mounting, "not some FBI agent that…"

"No? You could learn a few things from Alex. Funny, you may have gotten her suspended, even fired…Yet, she's still on her way here to help Cassie; how I can't even imagine. And, I doubt the entire Army could stop her from being here for Dylan's party. Don't call. I'm sure Alex will call you when she knows something. You are Dylan's father after all." She hung up the phone.

***

Nick accepted the small boy into his arms and led him to the living room. He put Dylan in a chair and squatted in front of him. "Why are you crying, Dylan?"

"No one will tell me," Dylan said through his tears.

"Tell you what?"

"Where my mom is." The boy knew something was wrong and the only person that hadn't called was his mother. Even for a six year old, it was not a difficult puzzle to solve. At the end of the day, Cassidy was Dylan's life. He loved his mother every bit as much as she loved him and he was terrified.

Nick sighed. He didn't know all the details. He only knew that Cassidy was in some trouble and that Alex was on her way. He did know his sister. He had seen Cassidy's intelligence and was keenly aware that anyone who could capture his sister's heart had to be resilient and assertive as well as smart. "Dylan," he said softly, "did you talk to Alex?" Dylan nodded. "What did she say?"

"She said she'd see me at your house...with Mom."

"You know, if Alex told you that, then Alex will see you there with your mom."

"She promised but Mom hasn't called..."

The man stood and picked up the small boy, placing him on his lap. Rose reached the hallway and watched. His mannerisms were so much like his sister's, but he had an even greater softness about him. Nick could tell that the small boy had already added two plus two and gotten four. Dylan may not have known details, but he was astute enough to know something was not right and all the denials were making it worse for him. "You know," Nick began, wiping a tear from Dylan's cheek. "When I was your age, do you know what I called Alex?"

Dylan shook his head. "I called her my protector." Nick smiled as he remembered their youth. "Alex always protected me. She never let anything bad happen to me, Dylan. That's Alex. She loved me and she kept me safe."

"Did someone try to hurt you?" Dylan asked.

"Well, sometimes but Alex never let them. And, there was one time this boy who was much bigger than me managed to hit me at school," Dylan's eyes grew wide as he looked at the man he now called 'Uncle'. "Alex waited for him after school…"

"Did she beat him up?" Dylan's eyes grew wide.

Nick laughed. "No, but she made him apologize and then she made him walk through the playground in his underwear." Dylan giggled. "Listen, Dylan…Whatever is going on with your mom and with Alex, if Alex promised you she'd be at my house with your mom; she will be. She loves you both very much and she always keeps her promises."

"I know," he fought his tears. "I wish she was here."

Nick felt he might cry himself. He'd seen Dylan with his sister and Cassidy just a few days ago. He knew how much the boy loved them both. He also was certain his sister would move heaven and earth to keep Cassidy safe. "It'll be okay, Dylan. You know, we'd better go and get some practice in. Alex still thinks she and Cat can beat us at eight ball." Dylan let out a small smile and hopped off Nick's lap. "Plus, I hear we need to talk about birthday party games."

Dylan's eyes flew open. "Are you coming?"

"Of course! Your mom talked to Aunt Barb earlier. We wouldn't miss our favorite nephew's seventh birthday." Dylan hugged Nick's waist. "All right," the man said looking over to Rose. "We'd better get moving, if Alex beats us there, she'll have my head!"

"No, she's our protector," Dylan reminded his uncle.

Nick chuckled, "that she is, Dylan. That she is."

***

Carl Fisher paced back and forth in front of Cassidy. He was ranting and rambling. Every so often he would drink from a large silver flask and wipe his mouth with the back of his hand. There was a knife in his red bag that Cassidy noticed he would fondle every now and again. The teacher watched him closely trying to discern what he might do next. Her hands were bound tightly and it hurt to move them, but she kept shifting them as much as she could, hoping that her repetitive action would loosen the knots. He crouched in front of her and put his hands on her thighs. "Congressman, Agent....ohhh Johnny. My turn," he sighed. "You see them....I see you." Cassidy felt a chill run up her spine at his words. It reminded her of the letters. "MMM...I know you....yes I do." The small blonde woman was deceptively strong. She kept her legs still as much as she could. Gradually she shifted them forward into a position that she knew would allow her kick him forcefully if she needed to. She wondered if she did, what she could possibly do next. The thought of him touching her was making her ill. She kept trying to recall Alex's voice, Alex's face, Dylan's face. She was a teacher not a fighter. But, she was determined he would not have his way; not with her.

"You like it....the strong ones...tell me that....he was weak....not like me...Ummm..." Fisher ran his left hand along the inside of Cassidy's thigh and then to her stomach. She flinched and he grabbed her. "What is that? Listen to me. It's MY TURN. You are mine." He leaned in and bit her ear. A painful yelp escaped from behind the tape and Cassidy struggled not to throw up. He smiled and pulled back and then he looked at her. His eyes traveled the length of her body. He took another sip from his flask and set it down with force. His hands reached in the bag and she sighed at the instrument now in his hand. He grinned and licked his lips in anticipation. "It's MY TURN."

***

Krause pushed some brush aside that rested along the line of shrubbery separating the yards. He took stock one last time of the man not very far away who was lying on the platform in the tree. This could either be an asset or a complication. There was no doubt in Krause's mind that he had a better shot than the NSA agent. If they didn't look too closely, they would assume the NSA agent had taken out Fisher. That would be one less tie to any of the players. He maneuvered the barrel carefully through the brush and squirmed through the scratchy greenery so that he could see clearly through his scope. Now he would wait.

Fisher was reaching for something. Krause squinted to bring it into focus as the crazed man moved just enough to the left that Krause could see Cassidy. Through the scope he could see the expression in her eyes. She was afraid, but she was also angry. He couldn't help but smile. "*Tu étais toujours aussi têtu que vous étiez belle.* (You were always as stubborn as you were beautiful)." Krause concentrated. He had barely seen Cassidy these last few years. He remembered their time in France fondly and often. Cassidy had always kept their relationship platonic. The normally aloof Jonathan Krause fell for the good natured blonde almost immediately. He saw so much depth in her young eyes. She was always thinking, always exploring. He was not surprised that she had grown into a remarkable woman; just as he knew she would. His affection for the congressman's wife had remained throughout the years. He never could understand what she saw in Christopher O'Brien. She was far more intelligent than the congressman. She was quick witted, able to read people and an adept communicator. "You should have been the politician," he mused aloud. He had been making his way here deliberately when the president called and he had his own reasons. He felt an unusual flutter and a rare knot in his stomach as Fisher leaned toward Cassidy now. This motion was different. There was something in his hand. No more waiting. Krause felt his anger burning hot as his finger steadily applied the necessary pressure. "Now," he whispered with conviction.

***

Alex hung up her call with Steven Brady on the promise that he would call as soon as it was done. He needed to gain a good position. Fallon hung up the phone on the large desk at the rear of the plane simultaneously and turned to his friend. "Ferro will move in on your call."

"Good," Alex said. The agent felt the fatigue and worry of the day building in her back. She massaged her temples and a slight smile crept onto her face as she recalled Cassidy rubbing her shoulders gently. She shook her head and turned back to her partner. "Can't compromise Brady."

Fallon nodded his understanding. "Alex, if he kills Fisher your link to…"

"He'll kill Fisher. Even if he didn't, Fisher would be dead in hours, if not by his own hand then by someone else's." Alex exhaled with force and stood to stretch her back. She looked at her watch. "Less than a half hour now," she paced. The president wasn't joking about helping her. This was a plane normally used for the Secretary of State. He'd pulled more than rank. He'd called in favors and if ever Alex Toles was grateful for their friendship, it was now. The agent turned back to her partner, "Fisher's not the only link, Fallon."

"Yeah. What *was* O'Brien doing at your apartment?"

"Warning me…about Cass." Fallon's mouth flew open. "Yeah, tell me," she said with sarcasm.

"You think he's just, you know… Caught in something?"

Alex sighed. That thought had entered her mind but it disappeared just as quickly. She scratched her eyebrow and pursed her lips. She wished he was just caught in the middle of something he never intended to be involved in. He was Dylan's father and Alex never wanted to see either Cassidy or Dylan hurt. But, no, she was certain whatever he was in the middle of he had willingly put himself there. The fact that he suspected Fisher was alive meant he was embedded in something deeply. The agent considered a measured response but then looked at her partner and answered directly. "No. Whatever he's in, he knows more about it than he claims. And, he's scared; not just for Cassidy, either," she asserted.

Fallon shook his head. "Alex, do you think he knew? I mean that this…"

"I don't know. God knows I don't like the man. When he first showed, I thought, for a minute he was really worried about Cassidy and Dylan."

"And now you don't?"

Alex shrugged. "I do, as much as any narcissist can be concerned about someone else. But I saw him, that expression, looking at the picture of Cassidy on my table. I saw his possessiveness. Leopards don't change their spots, Fallon." Alex felt her phone buzz and looked at the number with concern. "Nick? What's wrong? Is Dylan okay?"

Nick Toles was taken aback by the audible panic in his sister's voice. "Alex, relax he's fine. He's in the car. I know you can't talk, but call him when you can, okay?"

"What happened?" Alex asked her brother.

"His father called."

Alex expected the congressman might do that. "Did he tell Dylan?"

"No, but Alex…he knows something is wrong. He's scared…. and I just…"

Alex took a deep breath. "Nicky, I'm almost back. Just try and keep his mind off things, okay? Tell him I will be there as soon as I can."

"Alex, what about…"

"Nick…please…"

Nick sighed. "All right."

"What's wrong?" Fallon asked.

Alex let out a nervous chuckle filled with disgust. "I'm going to figure out who is responsible for all of this, Fallon, if it is the last thing I do…I swear to you." Her phone buzzed again.

***

John Merrow looked at the man across from him and shook his head. "This has gotten too far out of control."

"I agree," the man answered. "Krause was closer than Brady?"

"Yeah, he was on his way there. Fisher just beat him to the punch."

The man scratched his head. "Mr. President, if Agent Toles is reinstated…"

The president laughed. "She will be reinstated and her conditions met; whatever they are."

Assistant Director Tate shook his head. "Do you really think that is advisable? Although, I suppose New York will be beneficial to you."

Merrow circled his desk. "Assistant Director, how well do you know Alex Toles?"

"Well, I think."

"Hum. You don't know Toles at all. You know how long she was at the NSA? What she did?"

"No, only what you've told me recently."

"Well, let's just say that Alex doesn't forget anything she sees, not ever, and she's tight lipped about that skill. I am talking FINE details; the shit that most trained agents and investigators miss after looking at something thousands of times. Alex will remember it in vivid detail ten years from now. She says she speaks seven languages, really it's more like thirteen and she understands even more than that. *You* think Toles is strong and assertive, BOLD." Merrow stopped and sat on the corner of the large desk. "She is, but she is also intelligent, compassionate, modest and full of integrity; more than anyone that ever served under me, ever."

Tate contemplated the president's complimentary assessment of the agent. "So then why not tell her?"

John Merrow let out a sigh and shook his head. "Did you hear what I said? Alex Toles has more integrity in her pinky finger than half the agents in your bureau combined. No, she would never agree," he sighed again.

"Mr. President, I have no idea what is really going on, only what I need to know but maybe you should think about it..."

"No," Merrow said firmly.

"You can't fight Toles and keep protecting her."

The president nodded. "Ever been in a war?"

"No," the Assistant Director answered.

"Ever come close to death?"

"No," Tate replied.

"Well, I have. Both, in fact, and the only reason I am sitting here right now is Alexis Toles. So, I will keep her as safe as I can, even if she has to be my adversary. That's all you need to know. Grant the requests. If it wasn't for Agent Toles, Mrs. O'Brien would likely be facing a different outcome." The president moved to look into the Assistant Director's eyes, "and, Tate, if you had kept Brackett where she was supposed to be....We would not be having this conversation. I may not have Alex's propensity for remembering everything, but my memory is still long, very long. Watch Claire Brackett like a hawk."

Tate swallowed hard. The message was understood. He was to follow whatever John Merrow said. And, he'd better deliver.

***

Steven Brady crept forward and rested the barrel of the gun gently on the plywood wall of the small tree fort. He watched carefully as Carl Fisher moved from side to side, noting the man's growing agitation. He still couldn't see Cassidy and he wanted confirmation that she was clear of any shot he might have. That wasn't just standard procedure; he knew what the woman inside meant to his friend. Brady had known Alex Toles for nearly eight years and he knew more about her than she suspected. Early on in their work together Alex had become very distant and Brady approached Michael Taylor about his concerns. They had been investigating the smuggling and exchange of ingredients for nerve gas. It had been sold to a radical Somalian group; a group that supposedly was seeking to root out Al Qaeda. It was a deal that was largely brokered by several high ranking Army officers as well as civilian employees within the Department of Defense and Homeland Security. Unfortunately, the true motives of the group were quite different from what they had claimed and the result was the loss of nearly a hundred innocent people, many children, as the group experimented with the weapon.

Taylor told Brady a story that day. It explained a bit about Alex Toles and the distance she often seemed to keep. It happened in 2004 in Iraq, he explained. He and Lieutenant Toles had made their daily rounds of the streets of Baghdad. Toles, he shared with the young agent, had a warm relationship with the locals. Her ability to speak the language and her easy manner were an asset and she had developed a deep trust with many of the families and local merchants. The young lieutenant spent her free hours teaching the young girls and boys in the area English and even instructed many of their parents privately. She was particularly close to one family. Aban Awad owned a small bookstore just off the corner of Mutanabbi Street. He was a trusted contact and his daughter Sabeen had become a good friend of Alex's. She was intelligent and beautiful, Taylor said. And while he knew that nothing was going on between the lieutenant and the woman; Taylor was sure that the young Toles was taken with Sabeen.

That day, as the sun was just beginning to set, a group of Americans were making their way to the bookstore for a dinner.

It was supposed to be a thank you from the locals for the assistance that the group had given the area merchants. Taylor, Toles, their colonel, and three other officers were just turning the corner when Alex stopped. Taylor didn't see it, but Toles did. She saw everything. She just saw it too late. Awad pushed Sabeen through the front door of the shop. The young Iraqi woman had a look of terror on her face. The next thing Taylor remembered Toles was pushing him and their colonel down, screaming. Then it went black. He recalled Alex crawling, or trying to, and screaming for Sabeen. When Taylor managed to open his eyes he saw the carnage. Three of their friends were dead. The colonel was bleeding from his head and had something deeply embedded in his left leg. Toles was moving, but barely. He could see that her shirt was soaked in blood as she turned, and Taylor could not feel his lower extremities at all. All told seventeen Iraqi civilians and three American servicemen died that day. Alex blamed herself. She'd missed the signs on the pass through. She'd misjudged Awad as a friend. She never understood that her quick thinking saved countless lives. That didn't matter to Alex Toles. The story stayed with Steven Brady. Alex didn't want to leave Iraq, Taylor told the young agent. She didn't want the children to think she had abandoned them, but her injuries were serious and she was sent to a German hospital before returning to the states to undergo surgery.

Over the years, Brady seldom heard Alex Toles talk about family or relationships. Alex was an extremely attractive woman and there were many men and women lined up to try and capture the agent. She was poised, had the body of an athlete and the face of a movie star. Yet, Alex Toles was not in the least bit conceited. She was confident and in command of her actions. She was intelligent and witty, but she was also quiet and humble. She was unique. Occasionally, she spoke of her brother and his family but that seemed to be where her personal attachments ended. That is until she showed up in New York. Brady looked through the scope and finally caught sight of Cassidy. Even with the tape on her mouth and the stress of the situation, the small blonde's eyes seemed to dance like flames. It was no wonder Alex had fallen for the woman. Brady admired Alex. He'd watched how she constantly put everyone else first and now he thought she deserved a chance; a chance to have something more than cases to solve and a never ending supply of Diet Coke in her refrigerator. Cassidy was that chance. Steven Brady was determined this time Alex would get a happy ending.

He watched as Fisher reached in the bag. The man paced back toward Cassidy. His hand was raised slightly and Brady strained to see what he was holding. One of Fisher's hands started reaching forward. Brady saw it now from his angle. He was ripping Cassidy's shirt and in his hand...Brady lined his shot up. "Not today you son of a bitch," he said as he felt the metal squeeze between his fingers.

***

"Now...It's my turn... Cassidy O'Brien... my turn," his breath became uneven as his excitement mounted. Cassidy bit the inside of her lip and tried to maintain her composure. She couldn't scream against the tape. Even if she could, no one would hear her. She felt his breath on her neck again and then felt him step back slightly to regard her as his prey. Fisher ran the knife along Cassidy's leg and moaned. "I have waited... you don't know...a long time... I watched you...with that agent....did you know?" He smiled. "I saw you...ummm...but now Cassidy...it's my turn," he pressed the knife a bit harder against her leg and Cassidy could feel the blade through her jeans. "She's not coming...no one is coming...you know why?" Cassidy looked at him as stoically as she could manage. "I'll tell you... No one can...no one knows...It's MY turn." He leaned over and breathed heavily on her and she felt the sting on the blade as it grazed her skin through her pants.

Cassidy saw his hand begin to rise slightly and his eyes become fixed on her chest. She closed her eyes but she could sense what was coming. She would fight him, but she knew he would overpower her. The bindings were still tight. She wouldn't be able to run. *Alex*, she said in her private thoughts, *I want to be with you. I am sorry. I don't know how to fight him. I love you so much. God. Please....it's crazy, I know it is, but please take care of Dylan....He loves you as much as I do....you know that...I'd give anything for you to tease me about my cereal....make me laugh...hold me. Tu es monmonde, mon amour* (You are my world, my love). *Je t'adore, Alex.*

Cassidy felt the material tear way from her. Her eyes were closed. Suddenly the feel of the knife on her leg stopped. She felt a weight replace it briefly. It was heavy. What was he doing? She couldn't open her eyes. There was a crash. She tried to force her eyes to open. They would not obey her commands. "Alex," she tried to speak as her tears began to choke her behind the tape. "Alex...."

Chapter Twenty-Three

Slowly Cassidy opened her eyes and lowered them. There was a small splatter of blood on her shirt, but it was not her own. Carl Fisher was in a heap on the floor. She looked about and heard the sound of the front door opening with force. "Down...Left," is all she heard. She could see out into the back yard. Something or someone was moving behind the oak tree. She nudged Fisher with her foot. He did not move and she felt hot tears stream down her cheeks. She tried to swallow against the dryness in her throat. *Alex*, she thought as she closed her eyes again, *not even here and protecting me.* There was no doubt in the teacher's mind that the agent had somehow figured out a way to save her. "Mrs. O'Brien.....Mrs. O'Brien," Detective Pete Ferro tried to coax the woman tied in the chair to open her eyes again. "This might sting," the voice said as the detective swiftly removed the duct tape from the teacher's mouth. She flinched slightly and felt her eyes continue to water. Reluctantly, Cassidy steadily allowed her eyes to flutter open. She saw strong but compassionate blue eyes looking at her. "It's all right, Mrs. O'Brien. Agent Toles is on her way." At the sound of Alex's name Cassidy released the breath she hadn't realized she'd been holding. "Cut this off!" He demanded and she felt the ropes loosen on her hands. She brought them around to her lap and rubbed her wrists. They were a deep red and just the slightest touch made them throb even more.

"We need to get you checked out," Pete Ferro said. "Can you stand?" Cassidy nodded and Ferro wrapped a blanket around her to cover her. She was surprised at how unsteady she was as she attempted to maintain her balance. He escorted her to the couch just as the paramedics were walking in. She couldn't speak, not yet. "Did he hurt you?" Ferro asked. Cassidy shook her head 'no'. He saw the blood on her jeans and sighed as he moved aside for the young paramedic.

The young man looked at Cassidy and smiled timidly. "Hello, Mrs. O'Brien," he said softly. Cassidy forced a smile. "I just want to take a look, okay? Then we'll get you to the E.R... just to be..."

"No," Cassidy said.

"Mrs. O'Brien," the young man urged.

"Not until Alex gets here."

Detective Ferro nodded at the young man and stepped back in for a moment. "I can have Agent Toles meet you there." Cassidy shook her head. She had no intention of moving until Alex arrived. The detective sighed. "All right," he nodded to the paramedic.

The young man looked at her wrists and grimaced at the sight. Cassidy again forced a smile noticing his concern. "I need to look at your leg," he explained, ready to cut her jeans. The teacher nodded her understanding and looked forward. It felt to Cassidy as though she were in a tunnel, all these sounds swirling around her. She could hear voices in the kitchen, the clicking of cameras and footsteps thundering up and down the hallway.

She couldn't make out any of the words. They seemed foreign somehow. She closed her eyes and put her face in her hands. "Mrs. O'Brien," the detective called her softly. Cassidy swallowed her tears and opened her eyes. She slowly took the phone from his hands.

***

"It's done."

"Are you certain?" Merrow asked.

Krause looked into the kitchen and saw Cassidy's foot kick Fisher. "He's dead."

"Get out of there." Krause was frozen. He watched her and shook his head. "Krause!"

"Yeah, I need to wait... NSA is on the move."

"Did he shoot?" the president asked.

"I think so."

"Jon, that means..."

Jon Krause sighed his understanding. "I know, two shots... P.D. is entering. Toles must've had that in place. Shit, she's good."

Merrow chuckled. "You didn't believe me?"

"No, I know she's good. You need to control the investigation," Krause said.

"We're talking about Toles here. She is one loyal woman. Don't count on control, Krause. We need cover stories. She's going to want to know every detail even with Cassidy safe."

Krause disassembled his rifle and put it in the bag. "Well, I did my part. You're the politician, that's up to you."

The president paused. "Are you certain that Cassidy was not hurt?"

"She'll be all right," Krause looked on as Ferro reached the woman. "She's pretty tough."

"Is that admiration I hear?"

"I have my job. I never said Cassidy wasn't a friend, John."

The president nodded to himself. Merrow had to admit it was easy to be won over by the teacher. Krause, Toles, they were hard sells. He was relieved and not just because of the risks the situation posed. This was the worst part of John Merrow's reality. People got hurt. Sometimes people he cared about. That didn't change what he had to do. "I'll start on my end. I need you to deal with something else, though."

"What's that?" Krause asked.

"Claire Brackett."

Krause put his bag on his shoulder, "fine," he answered. "I will see her when I get back to D.C., but that won't be for a few days."

"What?"

"I have meeting in Paris." The president sighed as Krause continued. "I hope you persuaded the congressman."

"So do I," Merrow answered.

***

"You're sure?" Alex asked nervously.

"Yeah," Brady answered.

Alex nodded to Fallon who promptly picked up the phone on the large desk just as a young Airman walked into their compartment. "Final descent. Captain Abel wanted you to know. You should strap in. We'll be on the ground in ten minutes." Both agents nodded their understanding.

Alex crossed to the seats on the right hand side of the plane and took a seat. "Brady?"

"Yeah?" Steven Brady answered stowing his rifle.

"I just...."

"Forget it Toles," he said. "Listen we'll figure it out, who's behind him."

Alex closed her eyes. She didn't even want to think about what still needed to happen. Fisher had to have had help faking his own death. This was deep. Right now all the agent could think about was Cassidy. "They're moving now," Fallon said.

***

"Cass?" Cassidy could not speak. The sound of Alex's voice washed over her and she felt her body tremble. She struggled to keep hold of the phone in her hand. Alex could hear her lover's labored breathing. "I'm almost there. On the ground. Twenty minutes, okay?"

"How?" Was all the teacher could manage to ask.

"Never mind. Go with the paramedics. I'll meet you...."

"No. Alex, I'm all right...just come home. Please," the need in Cassidy's voice rattled Alex.

The agent closed her eyes. "Ferro says you have some..."

"Alex..." the agent listened as Cassidy's plea became more insistent.

"Okay, let me talk to the detective. I love you, Cassidy." Cassidy wanted to answer but she did not want to break down. She handed the phone to the detective with a sad smile.

"Ferro?" Pete Ferro stepped away; glancing first at the cut on the woman's leg and shaking his head. "Ferro? Is she?"

"She's just shaken, Agent. None of the injuries are severe. Nothing that needs real attention...just the..."

Alex let out a shaky sigh, "just the trauma."

"Yeah," he said sadly.

"I'll be there in twenty," Alex said as she exited the aircraft.

"How are you going to make it here in..."

"I have friends. I'll be there." Alex hung up and looked at her partner. Fallon immediately noted the worry on his partner's face. "God, this is all my fault, Fallon."

"She was quiet," Fallon guessed. Alex nodded. "It's not you, Alex. You know that. Let's just get there, and it's not your fault." Alex rubbed her temples. She stepped into the waiting State Police car with a respectful tip of her head and picked up the phone again.

"Nicky?"

"Alex...where are you?" her brother asked.

"I'm ummm....On my way to Cassidy's.....Where are you?"

"Almost home," he answered.

"Can I talk to Dylan?" Alex asked.

"Of course, is..."

"She's okay." Alex waited as the phone passed to the small boy. As Dylan's voice began to break through she heard Nick faintly say "it's okay," to Rose.

"Alex?"

"Hey, Speed Racer."

"Are you coming to Uncle Nick's?"

The agent fought her emotions. "I am. I have to go get your mom first. Okay? So it will be a while."

"When?" Dylan asked.

"I'm not sure, you might be in bed."

"But you are coming?" he asked again, still feeling insecure.

"I promised, didn't I?"

Dylan finally smiled. "Alex?"

"Yeah, Speed?"

"Why are you sad?" The small boy immediately noted the cracking of the agent's voice.

Alex let out a slight chuckle. The boy was his mother's son. "I'm not sad."

Dylan could still hear the sadness in his hero's voice and there was only one thing his six your old mind knew to do. "I'll have the Batcave ready, Alfred," he said assuredly.

Alex laughed. "Okay, Batman." His words brought her a genuine sense of happiness and possibility. "I'll see you at the Batcave." Fallon looked at his partner curiously. "It's a thing," was all she said.

***

Detective Ferro paced the kitchen slowly and looked at the body. He pushed away a photographer and looked closely at the area. He glanced at the edge of the counter near the sliding glass door and then looked out into the backyard. Ferro slid open the door and started walking off the deck and then down in a straight line into the yard. "What the hell is he doing?" a younger detective asked.

Detective Jeff Scott laughed. "He's looking for something. Where the shot came from, I would guess."

Ferro looked left and looked right and repeated the movement several more times. He slowly pivoted on his heels. Gradually he made his way back toward the house, occasionally looking to his left or right as though he were following something with his eyes. "Oh shit," he mumbled. "Toles is not gonna' like this."

***

"Congressman, I hope you are feeling well enough for this chat," Congressman James Stiller greeted. Stiller was a senior congressman from Illinois. For the last four years he had served as the chairman of the House Ways and Means Committee, and was widely considered a favorite for the Governorship of the state if he should choose to run. He was a vibrant, intelligent man who had captured the imagination of many of his constituents and was on a short list of names often tossed about as a viable future White House contender. He was also a huge proponent of HR1929; a Trade Bill that would impact the taxable amounts of steel, certain chemicals and other materials that were exported to the European Union. It would limit the amount that the United States would agree to import. It would also tighten security in shipping ports owned or controlled by U.S. interests. Stiller had co-authored the legislation. He would be a tough sell. Convincing the chairman that the proposal set too many dangerous restrictions; restrictions that might harm important alliances strategically would not be easy. O'Brien's best asset was that he had the president's ear and that he sat on the House Committee on Foreign Affairs. O'Brien had been a key player in several pieces of legislation on the Subcommittee on Europe, Eurasia, and Emerging Threats.

"I am feeling much better, Jim, thank you. I do apologize about earlier. It's been a hell of a couple of weeks."

"I understand. We are hoping to vote next week," the chairman said.

"I know....but I have to give some caution. These restrictions..."

"Congressman, you and I both know we are importing far more than we are exporting....and you of all people know that what ports are utilized and how much we export must be carefully controlled. The threat of..."

Congressman O'Brien did understand. This resolution would put a stronger emphasis on exports. That was good. The port restrictions and the restrictions on the exports of certain chemicals such as organophosphorus compounds and steel, in favor of increased exports of such substances as liquefied natural gas, however, was a major concern. Combined with measures being taken in France and Great Britain that called for tightening on port security, this resolution severely threatened long standing initiatives to equip underdeveloped governments with certain resources. Resources that had already been committed by the Merrow Administration. "Jim, you know I agree, but these measures, combined with the initiative of some of our European partners...Well, the president is concerned. It could seriously compromise our strategic initiatives. And, some of our very important technological relationships."

Chairman Stiller remained quiet for a moment. "Are you saying you will not support the resolution?"

"As it stands? I would recommend revisions, Jim, so no...I cannot."

"Hmmm. I thought you were committed to tightening controls?" Stiller questioned.

O'Brien tapped a pencil on his desk. "I am, but not at the expense of long held alliances. I am not suggesting a defeat... just a revamp."

"Specifically?"

"Why don't I have Carol send you a draft? Senator Donaldson and I have discussed it. Congressman Treat has already begun a proposal. I can have Carol forward that along."

"I'm sorry, Chris...could you hold on one moment?" Christopher O'Brien waited. "Chris," the chairman's voice had softened. "Have you been contacted yet by the FBI?"

"No, why?"

"Ummm...I just had my chief of staff turn on the news. There's been some kind of situation at your home, at Cassidy's...."

Now O'Brien had to think. The congressman did know and if the chairman had any inkling of that fact; he would surely wonder why O'Brien had agreed to this call. "Uhh...I need to go," O'Brien said. His nervousness was genuine. Suddenly he wondered what had happened.

"Of course. I'll have Dennis contact Carol. If you need anything, Chris..."

"Thank you," the congressman said hanging up the call. "Shit," he ran his hands through his short hair. "Dammit, Cassie." He reached for his phone.

***

The car pulled in front of the large white house. Cherry Circle was inundated with police vehicles and emergency personnel. It was also becoming a media circus. Alex opened the car door and had no control over her body. Fallon tried to keep up, flashing his credentials as his partner's speed increased with each step. Alex reached the open front door and was met with a pair of sturdy hands blocking her entry. "Badge?"

"What?" Alex said. Fallon was trying desperately to catch Alex in her short sprint. "Get out of my way," Alex ordered. The officer moved for his cuffs. Alex's temper began to flare. "Get the fu..."

"Hey, easy there Kyle," Ferro appeared. "Come on, Agent." Fallon shook his head at the detective as he reached his partner.

Alex looked in through the large doorway and saw Cassidy sitting on the sofa, wrapped in a blanket and holding a glass of water. She froze for a moment and closed her eyes. 'Calm down, Toles,' she warned her own thoughts. Slowly she made her way to the woman she loved. "Cass?" Cassidy looked over as Alex closed the distance between them. Alex knelt in front of her and the teacher's tears fell as a smile of relief washed over her. Gently, Alex took the woman's face in her hands and Cassidy collapsed into her. The agent had no thought, had no care about who saw the exchanged affection or what anyone might surmise. All that mattered was the woman before her. "Cassidy, I'm sorry. I love you so much. I...I tried to...I..."

The blonde woman let the blanket fall and pulled back to lift a hand to Alex's cheek. "*Je savais que vous viendriez,* (I knew you would come)," she whispered to the agent.

"Always, Cass." Alex looked at her lover's wrists and closed her eyes.

"I'm okay, Alex. Dylan...where...."

"He and your mom are at Nick's."

Cassidy gave Alex a genuine smile through her tears. "Alex..."

Alex caressed Cassidy's cheek. "We need to get you checked out, love."

Cassidy shook her head. "No. I'm all right, Alex."

The agent looked at Cassidy's leg and felt a fury build within her. "Cass, this really..."

"It's just a cut."

"Yeah, I've heard that before," Alex answered. "Cassidy, please...honestly...you need to be checked out."

"I just want to see..."

The agent understood that her lover was anxious to get to Dylan. "I know. Let's just get you looked at, okay? Just humor me, Cass...Then we'll go to Nicky's. I promise."

"I don't want to leave you," Cassidy's body trembled as she grabbed for the agent.

"I'm not leaving you. Not leaving," Alex took Cassidy into her arms. "Not ever, really… maybe not ever…"

"I'm not taking you to the bathroom with me," the teacher said chuckling through a sob.

"Don't count on it."

Cassidy continued to cry and laugh at the same time now in the safety of Alex's arms. "I love you so much, Alex. I was so…"

"I know. It's all right, now. Come on, let's get this done so we can get to Dylan." The pair stood; Alex helping the smaller woman to her feet and wrapping the blanket back around her. As they began to move Cassidy stopped abruptly and grabbed Alex's arm. "Are you okay? Cass?" Green eyes tinted red looked deeply into the pools of blue above her and Cassidy pulled Alex's face to hers, kissing her tenderly. "What was that for?" Alex said as Cassidy slowly pulled back.

"I wasn't sure I would get to do that again," the smaller woman answered.

Alex bit her lip as she realized the fear that Cassidy had just experienced; not knowing if she would survive the sadistic Fisher's plans to see her family again. The agent caressed her lover's cheek. "I hope you spend the rest of your LONG life doing that."

The teacher smiled fighting against the tears that seemed to be endless. "Me too," she whispered.

***

Cassidy was markedly silent on the drive to Connecticut. Alex's thoughts were drifting back and forth between the woman she loved and the case that was still missing pieces. She held Cassidy's hand on her thigh and gently caressed it with her thumb as Cassidy gazed out the window in silent contemplation. It was in the agent's nature to see details in her mind and to continually

369

analyze them. She resisted her temptation to investigate the scene of Cassidy's torment earlier; knowing that the woman she loved needed her to be fully present. She was relying on Fallon and Ferro to see the details. When Fallon met them at the hospital with some clothes; Alex had gotten a chance to hear some of the more disturbing details and also some of Ferro's private theories about Fisher's death. Now, as their conversation played in her mind; she could see Cassidy in the kitchen, tied to a chair. It was like watching a bad movie run over and over:

"How is she?" Fallon asked.

"She's tough, Fallon. Not as tough as she wants me to think." *Her partner nodded his understanding. Alex looked into the room where Cassidy was getting dressed and then glanced back to her partner. "So, what did Ferro have to say?"*

Brian Fallon's eye twitched and his lips tightened. "Toles..."

"What is it Fallon?"

Through a heavy sigh Fallon expelled the detective's theory. "Two shooters."

"What are you talking about?" Alex was confused.

"Ferro thinks there were two shooters. There's only one entry wound. Two bullets."

Alex shrugged. "I'll call Brady. He probably fired twice."

Fallon shook his head. "Alex, when they do the autopsy we'll know for sure, but Ferro....He's pretty sure there are two different bullets. He found a casing near the counter that splintered the wood." Alex looked back toward Cassidy's location and considered Ferro's assessment. "You don't look surprised," Agent Fallon asserted.

Alex pinched the bridge of her nose and paced away from the door to the small room. "I'm not."

"Alex, it doesn't make sense though, I mean everyone thought..."

"No, it makes sense. He knew too much, far too much. Even with his background he had to have had help faking that suicide."

Fallon was confused. "Why would someone help him and then kill him?"

"Why do people do anything they do, Fallon?" Alex felt her stomach turning with the rage that had settled inside her. The knowledge that Cassidy had been hurt by anyone produced emotions within the agent she could not describe, anger, fear and anguish. She took a deep breath and exhaled it with force, rubbing her temples in frustration. The investigation, for Alex, would have to wait. Cassidy was safe. That was the most important thing. She stopped and covered her face with her hands. Fallon watched in amazement as his partner did the unthinkable. Alex shook her head. "Fallon, keep me in the loop, I'll call in some markers...but I...."

"Toles?"

Alex walked back toward the room and looked in the small window. Cassidy was fluffing her hair with her hands; clearly trying to get herself ready to face the world again. The agent looked at her friend and continued, "Brian, no one wants to get to the bottom of this more than me. I need you to be my eyes this week...okay? Dylan needs...and Cass is...."

"Don't worry about it, Alex. Hey, you know maybe this is...I mean maybe the suspension...it might be a good..."

Alex chuckled slightly. A suspension would do little to prevent her from investigating anything. Cassidy needed the agent right now and so did Dylan. For the first time in Alex Toles' life something was more important to her than the puzzle. "Just keep me in the loop, but quietly....All right?"

"You don't want her to know," Fallon offered.

"I want her to heal, Fallon. She got lucky, physically. That wall, it'll crumble. We both know that. The last thing she needs is constant reminders from me. Reminders of him...of..."

"Speaking from experience?" There was a great deal Brian Fallon did not know about his partner. He did know there were things in Alex's past that still haunted her. He'd seen the ghosts appear in her eyes during a few investigations.

Alex nodded. "I am. But, Fallon? I need you to keep an eye on O'Brien and Brackett."

"You don't think Cassidy's still in danger?"

"I think," she paused and pulled him away from the room, "that whatever he is into puts everyone in his life at risk. I don't think; I know."

"You don't...." he continued when his partner cut him off.

"No. I don't think Cassidy is in any immediate danger; or Dylan. Otherwise, Fisher would have succeeded. They would have made sure of THAT. Just keep an eye out; keep working that accident. Brackett thinks we've dropped it. There's something there, some link. If I don't answer, well..."

Cassidy was emerging from the room and Fallon watched the expression on his partner's face transition. He'd never expected to see Alex Toles like this. Cassidy clearly meant everything to his friend. It was written on her face more plainly than any evidence he had ever uncovered. He'd watched his partner on the plane earlier as she coordinated people and facts. Every time there was a moment of silence he would see the normally composed agent fighting just to breathe. Alex was a puzzle to him sometimes. She liked to seem in control, almost cool, but she was anything but hard.

Two years ago Fallon had been hit by a car as he pursued a suspect. His head injuries were severe and he spent five days in an induced coma. The recovery was slow and he was fortunate not to have any major memory loss or compromise to his motor functions. Alex took care of his wife, Kate, and his kids for three weeks. She made certain that someone was with them around the clock when needed. She drove the kids to sporting events and the hospital. He wondered if she had slept at all those weeks; working and taking over all of her partner's duties including caring for his family. Alex shrugged it off. Loyalty was one of his partner's most admirable qualities. Brian Fallon knew no matter what the agent said, Alex's sense of loyalty was born from compassion. Cassidy brought that into clearer focus. It was time, Fallon thought, that he return the favor. He smiled as Alex placed her arm tenderly around the teacher. "Fallon, why don't you come with us; stay at Nick's tonight. You are more than welcome," Alex offered.

Brian Fallon flashed a heartfelt smile to the women before him. "Nah. I promised Ferro a beer. Don't get to see him much."

Alex knew that was a lie. Ferro was likely still at the scene. She knew his type well and she knew her partner. "Okay."

As they began to make their way out Cassidy took hold of Fallon's hand. "You're a good friend, Brian," she said to him softly. "Thank you." Fallon smiled at the younger woman and when he looked to his partner, he saw it. There was an unmistakable tear running down Alex's cheek as she acknowledged him.

"Anytime," he answered as they took their leave.

"Cass?" Alex called gently across to her lover as she parked the car. "Hey…"

Cassidy sat looking out the window. "What am I supposed to tell him, Alex? He'll see…"

Alex tightened her grasp on the small hand that sat atop her leg. "I don't know. He's going to find out something; it's everywhere."

Cassidy threw her head back onto the seat and covered her eyes. "He's six."

Alex felt her body tense. Cassidy was right. No six year old should have to confront this type of harsh reality. Someone had hurt his mother. It was all over the television. It would be in all the newspapers by morning. He had just dealt with his father's accident and now his mother. The agent was seething and she didn't want Cassidy to see that. Alex knew eventually Cassidy would have questions. How did Alex know? And then, she would have to reveal that it was the congressman that tipped her off. He was indirectly responsible for this. She wanted nothing more than to nail his coffin shut right now. She wanted to bear down and root out who was responsible. And, she felt little need for mercy. Alex wanted to punish the people who caused this, all of them, the congressman, whoever he was involved with, Brackett, the press. But, that was not what Cassidy and Dylan needed from her now. They were her priority and they both needed to know that. She needed them to feel secure; to feel secure with her. She took a deep breath and gently kissed the small hand in her own. "We don't need to tell him anything tonight. He's in bed...let's just go in and see him...when he sees you are all right...he'll feel better. We'll figure out what to say tomorrow."

The smaller woman turned to face the agent. "And then?"

"I don't know....Cass..."

Cassidy's mind was racing and at the heart of all of her concerns was her son. "What about school? There's no way to shelter him..."

"Cassidy, listen to me. You are safe. He is safe and I will do whatever it takes to keep you both that way even from the press, even from school mates, even from...."

Cassidy let a smile creep onto her face as she looked into Alex's eyes; just a faint glow from the moon and the porch light gave Alex's expression away. "You're rambling."

Alex nodded. "I'm sorry. I just...don't....I won't let...."

"I know," Cassidy said seeing the pain in Alex's eyes. This, the teacher understood, had been painful for all of them. She couldn't imagine what it had been like for Alex to be so far away with so little control. And yet, she knew that Alex would find a way to get home; a way to get *home*. "Let's go," Cassidy said squeezing the agent's hand. Alex sighed. Another hurdle they would need to clear. Somehow, she knew that they would.

***

Rose could not contain her emotions as Cassidy and Alex walked through the door. She immediately embraced her daughter with her tears flowing freely. "I'm all right, Mom... really," Cassidy assured her mother.

The older woman looked at the agent and then took her into a hug. "Alex...Thank you...thank you for..."

The agent was still wrestling with her own guilt. "I don't deserve any…"

"Yes you do," Rose said stepping back and looking at the agent and her daughter. "I'm just so glad you are safe."

Cassidy smiled and looked at Nick. "He's upstairs," the man answered knowingly. "Alex…he wanted to sleep in the bunk beds with Cat. He did pull the bottom."

Alex shook her head and smiled. She took Cassidy's hand. "Come on." Alex opened the door to the room. A night light gave off a slight glow and the light from the hallway peeking in highlighted a small face in the lower bunk. She felt Cassidy's body begin to tremble and she tightened her grip on the woman's hand. Cassidy took a deep breath and quelled her mounting emotion as they approached the bed. "Hey… Speed, wake up," Alex gently called to him. Seeing small eyelids begin to flutter she continued. "Someone wants to say goodnight," she said.

"Mom?" He woke and wrapped his arms around his mother's neck.

"Hey, sweetie…I'm sorry it's so late… just a crazy day." She held him tightly to her. "I had to wait for Alex to come and pick me up."

"Why? Where were you?"

"You don't need to worry, sweetie…Okay?" In the light she could see that her young man was not so convinced. Dylan was a bright and intuitive boy. Cassidy ran her hand over his small head and ruffled his hair affectionately. Dylan looked at Alex; questioning her with his eyes. Cassidy watched and continued, "Alex is home now, honey…We're all okay."

Alex smiled and took a seat next to her two favorite people on the edge of the bed. "Get some sleep, Speed Racer. It's late. Tomorrow we'll all have breakfast together. Okay? We'll spend the day here with Uncle Nick."

"I have school," he looked at his mother.

"Well," Alex said, "not tomorrow." She smiled. "Tomorrow, we have other things we need to do."

"What?" Dylan asked.

"Ah....That's tomorrow, Speed. Get some rest." Alex kissed him on the head.

Dylan looked at his mother who smiled broadly at him. "I love you, Mom," he said grabbing onto her again and sensing in her that she was somehow sad.

"I love you, too Dylan, Alex is right...get some sleep. Okay? We'll be here when you wake up." She held him for another minute and then tucked him back in. Slowly she made her way back to her feet where Alex's arm swiftly wrapped around her waist and guided her to the door. She turned back and looked at the small boy already being reclaimed by his dreams. "God, Alex...."

"It's okay. We're all here now," Alex said closing the door and pulling Cassidy to her.

"I just want to..." Cassidy struggled to speak. "I don't think I can..."

Alex understood. "You don't need to go back down there, Cassidy. Come on."

"My mother....and I should really thank Nick and..."

Alex shook her head and lifted Cassidy's chin. "No. YOU should follow me. I will run you a bath. You relax. I will get our things. I will talk to your mother and you can see Nick and Barb tomorrow. They live here, remember?"

Cassidy couldn't help but smile. "What did I do to deserve you?"

Alex kissed the woman's forehead. "I think you have that backwards....Come on."

***

Cassidy got out of the bath and found sweats and a baggie T-shirt laid out for her. Alex was still downstairs. She was certain the agent was answering questions to keep Cassidy protected. The teacher smiled and climbed into the bed. She was exhausted physically, mentally and emotionally, but she was so grateful to be here. There was no way, she realized, that she could sleep in her own house right now. She didn't even want to walk back in there. A hotel would have been cold. Alex thought of everything. She rolled to her side and hugged her pillow, closing her eyes. The toll from the day captured her and her body gave over to sleep. Alex walked quietly into the room and threw on her long T-shirt and shorts. She slid under the covers next to the small figure in the bed and nestled her face into the long blonde hair. She inhaled deeply; the faint scent of Cassidy's shampoo invading her senses. "I love you, Cass," she whispered.

"I love you, Alfred," a voice barely managed.

"You're awake?'

"Not really," Cassidy admitted but rolled to face the agent next to her.

Alex ran her hand through Cassidy's hair and tucked it behind her ears. She was lost looking into the woman's eyes. Finally, they were completely alone. "Cass...I'm sorry that I..."

"Shhh..." Cassidy kissed the lips before her. "Don't you dare, Alex Toles." Alex had planned on comforting Cassidy. Now, holding the woman she loved, the agent began to tremble. Losing Cassidy frightened Alex in a way she could not fathom. She had held her emotions together all day. She had tabled her anger. She had buried her fear. She even fought to sequester the relief she felt when she saw Cassidy. There were so many emotions pouring over and through her now and Cassidy brought out every possible one. The feel of Cassidy in her arms was more than the agent could handle and her tears began to escape. All she wanted was to love Cassidy; to protect her. "Alex, I'm all right now."

"Cassidy....I'm sorry...I shouldn't be..."

"You shouldn't what? Have been scared?"

"What you went through..."

Cassidy closed her eyes and stilled herself. "Yes, but that doesn't mean you didn't go through something too. You had to deal with so much. Alex...I don't even know how you knew... How did you even get back so quickly?"

"Doesn't matter," the agent answered. "I would have stolen a plane if I had to."

Cassidy laughed. "I believe that, you know."

"You should." Alex kissed Cassidy's forehead.

"Alex? I don't think I can go back there..."

Alex already knew that. Unbeknownst to the teacher that was what she had been talking about downstairs. "You don't have to."

"Alex...It's home...I mean there's...."

"Stop," the agent said. She understood that this would be part of Cassidy's process. It was easier to deal with facts and realities than feelings after going through a trauma. But, Alex also knew that the less facts Cassidy had to confront or deal with, the less arrangements she became involved with; the sooner the teacher could begin to deal with her feelings. The sooner she did that, the better her recovery would be. "That's tomorrow's problem. And, I think I have some ideas."

"Is that right?" Cassidy asked.

"It is."

"Alex...Dylan has already missed so much school....And my classes...I...".

The agent stroked the teacher's cheek. Cassidy was amazing. The most amazing person Alex had ever met. This was not a diversion. Cassidy was worried about Dylan, about her students, and even about the agent. She always put everyone else first. "You are the most incredible person I have ever met, Cassidy O'Brien."

"What are you talking about?"

"You...worried about everyone else."

"Dylan needs stability...and those kids are..."

Alex ceased the woman's words with a tender kiss. "For once....Let someone take care of you." The words cracked the wall that Cassidy had been building all day and her sobs followed. Alex held her close and rocked her gently. "Let it go....I'm right here, Cass....I promise you....I am not going anywhere." Cassidy let herself go completely. Her body quaked with the fear and the anxiety that she had been holding in. Alex understood, completely. "You don't worry about all of those things. Let me take care of what I can...Okay? Please?" Cassidy nodded her head into the agent's chest. "I will take care of you and Dylan. I promise."

Slowly Cassidy's release of emotion began to calm and she looked back at her lover. "Alex?"

"Yes?"

Cassidy struggled to catch her breath. "I need to tell you something."

Alex went numb. She wondered if Fisher had done something Cassidy had not shared with anyone. Cassidy saw the agent's face contort and realized immediately what was passing through Alex's thoughts. "No...no...nothing about him, honestly. I told you everything."

Alex swallowed hard in relief. "What is it?" she asked softly.

Cassidy's voice broke as she began, "I need you to know," she hesitated.

"What, Cass? You can say anything to me...you know that."

"I do....I just," the smaller woman gathered her courage and continued. "I didn't know if I was going to make it out of there."

Alex closed her eyes, "Cass..."

Cassidy lifted a finger to Alex's lips, "Alex, please let me say this...Please?" The agent nodded. "I thought about you. I tried to picture you and Dylan; to hear your voice." She paused and took Alex's hands. "If anything ever happened to me. I would want you to take care of him...of Dylan." The teacher's nerves again took hold. "I know that's crazy and I have no right to...."

"Now *you* are rambling," Alex kissed Cassidy's nose.

"But, Alex, I understand…"

"Stop," the agent said firmly. "I know Dylan is not my son." Alex saw Cassidy's face drop and promptly moved to lift her face back to look at the agent's. "I love him. I love you. Both of you. You never have to worry about Dylan. I would do anything for him….anything."

Cassidy looked into Alex's eyes and knew that was the truth. "I can't lose you, Alex."

"Lose me?" She laughed and pulled Cassidy to rest on her chest. "That will never happen. I want you to try and sleep, okay? We have the rest of our lives to talk…about everything."

"When I saw you walk in today….I've never felt that way…I just…"

"I know…me too. Get some sleep. I promise it will be better tomorrow."

"Mmm…it's better now," Cassidy confided, feeling safe in Alex's embrace.

Alex chuckled. "I love you, Cass. I'm sorry if I keep saying that."

"Don't ever apologize for loving me, Alex. I don't know where I'd be anymore if you didn't."

"Well, that's okay because I'll be wherever you go. Go to sleep."

"Je t'adore," Cassidy kissed the agent's chest and held onto her tightly.

"And I adore you," Alex smiled. Silently she thanked everyone she could think of, even God, for the gift in her arms.

***

"NO!" Cassidy screamed and sat up straight. Her body was shaking uncontrollably.

"Cass," Alex gently put her arms around the woman. The agent was no stranger to nightmares. It had taken some time for her own nightmares to grab hold of her, but she had always suspected that was due in large part to all the medications she was on after the incident in Iraq. Cassidy had come home with a prescription for some anxiety medication but Alex was fairly certain that the teacher would avoid taking it if she could. The small woman collapsed against her and the agent could feel the thumping of the teacher's heart. "Cassidy, it's all right. Try and breathe."

The smaller woman shook her head and put her face in her hands. All she could see was her kitchen and *him*. Then she would shake that off and see the news trucks as Alex led her to the car. She was having difficulty catching her breath now. "Alex, I can't go back to that house. I can't be there. What am I going to do? How am I supposed to face my students?" Cassidy stopped and sighed. Alex was gently rubbing her back; listening and allowing her lover to release what was in her mind and her heart. "Those kids will be worried about *me*. I am supposed to be taking care of *them*." The woman let out a groan of anger and frustration.

Alex continued tenderly caressing the woman she loved. She spoke as quietly and as reassuringly as she could. "I know. We will figure it all out tomorrow. You need some sleep."

Cassidy's anger was rising. "I can't sleep, Alex. How the hell am I supposed to sleep? I start to sleep and he is there. Then I start to wake up and all these questions play in my head. Sleep?" Alex rubbed her temples and Cassidy's temperament and voice began to soften. "I'm sorry," Cassidy said as she stroked the agent's cheek. "You didn't deserve that."

The agent smiled. "Cass, it's all right. As I recall you've experienced my nightmares." Cassidy nodded and closed her eyes. "Listen. I know…I do. If you want to talk about this now; we will," Alex said.

"I just have no idea what to do, Alex."

Alex got up and positioned herself to sit in front of the smaller woman on the bed. "All right, Look…here's the deal… and before you say *anything*, I want you to hear everything."

381

"Okay." Cassidy nodded her agreement.

"I mean it Cass, everything."

"Okay," she assured.

Alex sighed. "I know that you love your job and I know that Dylan is in the middle of a school year..."

"Alex..."

"Cassidy...you promised me," the agent reminded her lover and received a nod. "All right, there are a couple of options. One...you can go stay with your mother and I will find some place nearby." The teacher's change in expression was immediate and she was clearly not pleased with the agent's first option. "Okay," Alex continued. "Two, we can find someplace together so that Dylan can stay in the same school." Alex gauged Cassidy's warmer reception to that idea. "Or," the agent paused. "Promise me you will listen?" Cassidy nodded again. "Or we move. Nick's old house in Westport is for sale. It's been on the market a while." Alex saw Cassidy's eyes narrow in confusion. "Look, it would mean that you would have to teach somewhere else and it would mean Dylan would have to change schools...and I know you want stability, for him... But there's the train...And we would be closer to Nick and you would be removed from..." Alex was cut off abruptly by a soft kiss. "What?"

"You're rambling again," Cassidy smiled.

"Cassidy, I'm not trying to take you away....Well I am, but I just think that if...and I know it's soon to think about us, well..." Another kiss interrupted Alex's thoughts. "Rambling again?" the agent asked awkwardly.

Cassidy laughed and kissed Alex again gently. "I love you, Alex Toles." Alex looked perplexed and the teacher chuckled. "I can't decide anything right now," she smiled.

"I know....I'm sorry... I just...I wanted you to know that...I want you to feel..."

A finger pressed tenderly to the agent's lips. "I know. And I love you for all of it." Cassidy pulled Alex back and put her head on the agent's chest. "I don't think I care where we are, as long as we're together...the three of us." Alex did not respond. "Alex?"

"I don't want to push you, Cass, and I don't want to...I just want you to be safe...and feel safe."

Cassidy held on tighter to the woman beside her. "I do, Alex. And, I don't think you are pushing. If anything...well, I realized today that I don't ever want to be without you again... not ever. I just need to sort it out...a little, you know?"

"I do," the agent said. "Do you think you can sleep a little?"

"Yes."

"Good."

"Alex?"

"Yeah?"

"That house..."

"Yeah?"

"Well...is..."

Alex smiled silently. "I'll take you to see it."

"Does it have a big kitchen?"

"It *was* Nicky's house...so yes. Why?"

"Well, butlers usually have big kitchens," Cassidy smiled.

"Is that right?"

"Um hum."

The agent grinned. "Even butlers with no culinary skills?"

"Yeah...they just do more dishes," Cassidy offered.

"Oh....I'll try and remember that," Alex kissed Cassidy on the forehead. "Get some sleep." There was no answer. Cassidy had already drifted away and Alex could hear the slow, steady beat of her heart as she finally relaxed. "You are something else, Cassidy O'Brien. Thank God you love me."

Chapter Twenty-Four

"It's everywhere!" Christopher O'Brien practically screamed. John Merrow sat behind his desk with a smirk on his face, holding the phone to his ear and trying to suppress the laughter that he felt mounting. "I should think you would be relieved Congressman, that Cassidy is safe; might I add thanks to Agent Toles."

"Of course I am."

"Interesting that Agent Toles put that all together. She is quite perceptive," he said; hinting that he suspected the congressman may have played a role in Alex's knowledge of Fisher. John Merrow was relieved that Fisher was gone, but his trust in the congressman was waning.

"Well, I am glad that Cassidy is safe, Mr. President....but this story...well..."

"Ah...you mean the story about Cassidy's kidnapping or the story about Cassidy and Agent Toles?" Merrow asked with some satisfaction.

"Cassidy has always been the all American girl, John....people love her. Now, this is not the distraction I need...trying to negotiate this bill and these..."

President John Merrow had little time for such nonsense. There were many things that Merrow had learned over the years. Everything he did had a purpose, everything. Everything he said had a meaning, no exceptions. He dealt with life and death in tangible ways every day. He had hesitated entering politics. He was strongly persuaded by some of his colleagues that his presence in the White House would be beneficial to their endeavors. It was made clear to him that a career in politics was expected. For years, Colonel Merrow worked to keep his country safe from threats, real threats. Who someone loved, where they worked, what color their skin was or how they worshipped were not concerns to John Merrow. That was the most honest part of his political platform.

Christopher O'Brien was a pawn in a large game of chess, and he was Merrow's pawn. It wasn't the president's decision to choose all the pieces for the chess board, but once they were in play it was his responsibility to keep them as assets and not allow then to become liabilities. The president respected Cassidy O'Brien. He was certain that she was, in many ways, the congressman's ticket to his current position. She was attractive but she was also intelligent, articulate, compassionate, outgoing and genuine. People loved her. He doubted that Cassidy's relationship with Alex was any threat to O'Brien; except of course to the man's never-ending ego. And, he did not want O'Brien creating drama surrounding Cassidy. It was contrary to Merrow's positions and the president needed consistency. Worse, anything that might hurt the congressman's ex-wife was certain to embolden Alex Toles. John Merrow could not afford the agent digging into anything that might lead to him. "Look, Congressman...You know the press, it's a seven minute wonder. They'll be bored with it tomorrow. My advice, Chris? Ignore it."

"I have already been asked for a comment. How do you think I should respond to my wife taking off with a female FBI agent?"

John Merrow cleared his throat. His impatience was mounting. Alex was far more than just an FBI agent to John Merrow and the congressman's off handed remarks were beginning to strike a personal chord with the president. "Last I heard, Congressman, Cassidy was your ex-wife and you were living with someone else." There was no response. "Be cautious, Chris."

Christopher O'Brien was not certain what that meant. The one thing he did understand was that image was everything in his business. "It's part of the game."

"Well, if I were you I would worry about Ways and Means, Congressman...and I don't mean Cassidy's."

✱✱✱

Alex excused herself from the kitchen table to accept the president's call. "Good morning, Alex."

"John....listen...thank you for..."

He interrupted the agent's pleasantries. "How is Cassidy?" he asked sincerely.

The agent looked back toward the kitchen. Cassidy was sitting with Dylan on her lap sipping a cup of coffee and talking to her mother. She was still quiet and Dylan was clinging to her. They hadn't told him any details yet and Alex knew they would need to tell him something. The boy was old enough and smart enough to know that something had happened and he did not want to be far from his mother. "She's all right," Alex took a deep breath. "Just all right."

"It takes time, Alex. You know that." The silence on the other end of the phone spoke volumes to John Merrow. "Listen, Alex...I hate to do this..."

"What is it?"

"I had a call with O'Brien this morning." Alex rubbed her forehead and cracked her neck. She had spoken to the congressman briefly while Cassidy was in the bath tub the previous night. It was a very short conversation only to tell him that the teacher was safe. "Alex? You there?"

"Yeah...I'm here," she answered with a stern tenor to her voice.

Merrow let out a sigh. Alex was important to the president. Things had gotten messy. He needed to protect himself but he had promised himself years ago that he would always protect

Alex. And, he had a deep affection for Cassidy O'Brien. "He's going to comment to the press."

"What?"

"Alex…The press is all over your relationship."

"Jesus Christ, John."

"I know. I told him to let it lie…O'Brien is…"

"A narcissist?"

President Merrow laughed. "Well…."

"John…he has no right to say…"

"Alex, he's impetuous and he's naïve…."

"She's been through enough. He's a selfish…" Alex interjected.

"Yes. He is. I just wanted you to know; in case you were planning on heading back. If I can do anything for any of you…."

"John…I don't know what I would have done without you yesterday, without Taylor…If Brady hadn't…"

"Well, be that as it may…..I met with Tate. Your transfer will be granted, but the suspension will have to stand for a bit, Alex."

Alex smiled and shook her head. "I appreciate that. Look, John…I'm at my brother's still. Dylan's birthday is Saturday…I just…"

"What is it Agent?"

"I think we'll stay away from New York. I have a place in mind, but Cass is…well…"

John Merrow laughed. "Alex, you can be very persuasive. I think I understand. I will talk to my people. We'll see if we can't spin something." The president was thankful for the agent's obvious desire to step away for a bit. It would give him time to regroup and he hoped, if the agent and the congressman's ex-wife could get some peace, maybe it would quiet Alex's need to dig as deeply. "Let me know where you'll be. I'll have Templeton talk to O'Brien's people. Step away, Alex, I'll handle the congressman."

"He won't like that."

"Well, his actions impact this administration. Just let me know…and Alex?"

"Yeah?"

"Have you thought about Taylor's offer?"

"To go back to the NSA?" she asked.

"Yes."

Alex pursed her lips. "Yes."

"And…"

"I don't know. Right now I just need to…"

"I understand. Keep me in the loop, okay?"

"Of course, Mr. President," she said jokingly.

"All right, Captain….Give Cassidy my best…and wish that boy a happy birthday for me. Is O'Brien coming…"

"No. O'Brien told me he will be in D.C.," Alex answered.

"Might be just as well, Alex."

Alex looked again to the family she had grown to love. "For me, yes…for Dylan…"

"Ummm," John Merrow understood. He had two children himself. He smiled. His affection for the agent now evident in his words. "Dylan's a lucky kid, Alex. He has you and he has Cassidy. I'm sure he knows that."

"No…I'm the lucky one, John."

President John Merrow nodded and looked at his phone. There was nothing he wouldn't do for his family. Alex, she was the most loyal person he'd ever met. She would do no less. She was his friend and yet she could become his enemy. He would need to keep her closer now than ever. "Understood. I'll talk to you soon."

"John?"

"Yes?" he asked.

"I need some time with them…but just watch your back." Her concern for him was apparent.

"What do you mean, Alex?"

"I don't like this whole thing. The accident, Fisher… Brackett…there's something…"

It was exactly what John Merrow expected. "Always looking out for me. Listen, I'll work with Taylor a bit…take the time you need, Alex. Trust me."

Alex smiled. "I do trust you. Thanks, Colonel."

"Anytime, Captain. Talk soon." Alex hung up the phone and let out a sigh of relief. She would have to talk to Cassidy about the press. They would need to talk to Dylan. And, now more than ever, the agent wanted to convince the woman she loved that a step away might be a good idea. She needed to step away too, just for a while. Knowing John Merrow was on her side made that much easier for Alex Toles. She had eyes and ears everywhere. She could afford to stay where she was. She was grateful for that trust.

***

"Mr. Krause."

"Gentlemen," Jonathan Krause greeted.

"*Il est bon de vous voir, mon ami* (It is good to see you my friend)," a deep voice called from the back of the hotel room.

"Edmond," Krause took the man's hand in a spirited grip. "You look well."

"Ahh…ever the charmer, Jonathan. Are you certain you are not French, my friend?" Jonathan Krause smiled. Edmond Callier was more than a business associate. He was a longtime friend and mentor. Callier was what every great agent, what every man hoped to be. He personified confidence. Standing an imposing 6'5, he had dark hair that served to accentuate his hazel eyes. He was extremely intelligent and personable and when he walked into a room everyone took notice, immediately. "Sit," Callier offered.

"Not to break up your reunion," a smaller man seated in a chair across the room interrupted. "But, we do have business to discuss with Mr. Krause."

"Oh, Viktor, relax. I am certain Jonathan is prepared for our meeting." Edmond made his way to a bar at the far side of the room. "Let's have a drink. We are among friends, here." As the tall man continued his rounds with the bottle of fine scotch he continued to speak. "So, we have some situations that need addressing. Our friends," he gestured to Viktor, "are concerned, Jonathan. Concerned about your president's resolve."

Krause accepted his drink and smiled confidently. "President Merrow has things well in hand. You do realize that the congress is largely out of his control."

"Yes...well...we have those issues here as well. However, we navigate them," Callier said as he took his seat.

"Even if the resolution were to pass," Krause began, "it would only slow our operations. It would not seriously compromise them."

"*Chtoby zamedlit' eto kompromiss* (to slow is to compromise)!" Viktor interjected loudly.

"*Uspokoit'sya, Viktor* (calm down, Viktor)," Callier warned before turning back to his friend. "Yes. That is true. But, Jonathan...now, right now, to have to regroup would be dangerous. Viktor is right. It would not compromise the operations, but it does, and you must agree with this assessment; put the clandestine nature of our efforts in jeopardy."

Jonathan Krause felt his muscles twitch slightly and the veins in his neck begin to pulse. "I assure you that suppression remains at the center of our efforts."

Callier chuckled, "I am certain." He stood and began to pace the room deliberately. "Syria, Pakistan...China...We have to be careful now. These....Well, the parties that we ally with can be....unpredictable. This is a tenuous time. We cannot afford to fail on a promise and risk exposure. Things... things have changed, my friend. Secrecy is not so simple anymore."

It was an indisputable fact. It was a fact that kept men like President Merrow awake many nights. Maintaining secrecy in a world that had become connected twenty four hours a day was no longer simple. It took finesse and careful strategy. Politicians and overzealous young journalists were the least of concern now. One wrong move, one alliance that was broken and everything could be lost simply from a video on the internet. "I understand, Edmond. I assure you, President Merrow is well aware. It's being dealt with as we speak."

"*A chto takogo kongressmena? On dazhe ne mozhet kontrolirovat' svoyu zhenu!* (And what of this congressman? He can't even control his wife)," Viktor slammed his glass down. "You expect us to believe he can motivate your congress?"

Krause's eyes narrowed and Edmond took note of his friend's response. The agent steadied his emotions as he was trained to do and calmly took a sip of his drink. "The congressman understands his role. He will deliver or he will be dealt with." Jonathan Krause took another sip and set his drink down. He calmly leaned forward to face his Russian counterpart. "*Chto kasayetsya vashego kommentariya. Kessidi ne tema dlya nashego obsuzhdeniya* (As for your comment. Cassidy is not a topic for discussion)." The severity in Krause's eyes was not lost on the smaller man in front of him and Viktor remained silent as the agent held his attention. It was understood that Jonathan Krause was not to be toyed with; not by anyone.

"All right," Callier said. "Viktor, if our friend believes things are under control, we must accept his analysis. He gains nothing by false pretense."

Krause straighten his posture. "I have another meeting. I am due at Technologie Appliquée in an hour. You'll forgive my need to excuse myself."

"Of course," Callier said standing to walk his friend out.

"It was good to see you, Viktor," Krause offered somewhat coolly before following his friend to the door.

"Don't worry about Ivanov," Callier assured. "He is impatient." Krause offered his friend a nod of understanding. "I am glad that Cassidy is safe, Jonathan." Krause smiled slightly. "*Je vois qu'elle a encore votre cœur* (I see she still has your heart)."

The younger man looked at his friend and took his hand in a firm grip ignoring the assertion but offering no denial. "Thank you, Edmond. I assure you, we will proceed as planned." Krause walked through the door.

"Jonathan?" Callier called after him.

"Yes?"

"Be careful." Krause smiled and walked away.

***

"What are we going to tell him?" Cassidy asked Alex.

"Well, why don't we try the truth, just a slimmed down version of it?" Cassidy closed her eyes. "Cass, he knows something happened. No details, just that it was scary for a minute and now we are all safe. That's all he needs."

Dylan walked in and looked at the two women on the couch. He stopped just shy of them and looked on hesitantly. "Come here, sweetie," Cassidy beckoned. Alex had already told her that the press was pouncing on the story of their relationship as well as Cassidy's ordeal. The agent had taken a few moments to go and look at some of the coverage. The press, it seemed, was painting quite a romantic tale. The agent feared the congressman might attempt to spin that a bit in the days ahead. Alex wanted to shield Cassidy and Dylan from the fall out as much as she could. There were realities to consider and she knew that. Dylan needed to be in school. He needed a routine and so did her lover. Cassidy needed to feel safe and part of that would have to be getting back to some kind of normal routine. Alex just couldn't see how that could happen in New York. Dylan sat between his mother and the agent and looked at his mother as she spoke. "I know you were worried yesterday, Dylan. The truth is that I was worried too for a while."

The boy looked at his mother's wrists which were still red from the ropes that had restrained them the day before. Cassidy caught his stare and Alex immediately saw her begin to crumble. "Dylan," the agent pulled the boy's attention to her. "Remember when I told you about that bad man that I had to stop a long time ago?" Dylan nodded; the fear evident in his eyes. "Well, Speed, sometimes there are people who don't know how to be good people." Dylan looked to her questioning her with his eyes. "I know," Alex said, "that's hard to understand. Some people don't know how to love. And sometimes they think that they can make someone love them, and they do things that you or me...well...we would never do."

"Like hit someone?" he asked.

"Yes, Dylan. Like hit someone or make them stay somewhere they don't want to...and that's sort of what happened to Mom yesterday." The boy looked again at his mother who offered him a comforting smile.

"But you stopped him," he said.

"Well, not exactly...but my friends did... yes."

"What if he comes back?" he asked fearfully.

Cassidy looked at Alex and let out a shaky sigh. "He's not coming back, Dylan," Alex said assuredly.

"But what if he does?" Dylan looked at his mother with tears in his eyes and Cassidy pulled him onto her lap.

"He can't, sweetie," she explained. "He can't hurt anyone anymore."

"Promise?" He looked at his mother. She nodded. He turned to Alex. "Did he die?"

"Yes, Dylan. He died," Alex said plainly.

The boy's small eyes narrowed as he looked at the floor. Then he raised his glance back to the agent. "I'm not sad he died."

Alex took a deep breath. "You don't have to be, Dylan. But...you shouldn't be happy either."

He looked at his mother who picked up the agent's train of thought. "Alex is right, Dylan. He was not a nice man. But, we are all safe and we have so much to be happy about. That's what you should remember. People like this man, they have nothing to love. We have everything to love."

"He hurt you," the boy said with anger in his small voice.

Cassidy looked again at the agent who smiled and then she took her son's face in her hands. "Dylan, listen to me. I am all right." She looked at Alex and a genuine smile began to take shape on her face. "Alex, Alex made sure I was all right."

"That's because she's our protector," he interrupted with pride.

"Yes, she is Dylan," Cassidy agreed. She looked at Alex and attempted to convey with her eyes where her thoughts were headed. The agent understood and offered a wink of encouragement. "Dylan, how would you feel if Alex lived with us?" The boy's eyes flew open and he stared at his mother. "Would you like that?" He nodded and Cassidy looked into his small eyes lovingly as she continued. "I know you love Alex…"

"Alex is my Alfred," he said.

The teacher chuckled. "I know she is…..I love Alex too."

"I know," he said.

Cassidy laughed. "So, I don't want you to think about yesterday, okay? We're going to spend a few days here with Uncle Nick until we decide what we want to do. Okay? The house is kind of a mess right now."

"Okay," he responded, happy to accept his mother's explanation. He turned and looked at Alex. "Are you gonna' get married?" he asked innocently.

Cassidy nearly fell over and covered her eyes with her hand, shaking her head, unsure whether to laugh or apologize. Alex was unflinching. "Why do you ask that, Speed?"

"'Cause when people love each other they get married," Dylan said as if she should already know that.

Alex chuckled. "I guess they do," she said. Cassidy looked at the agent in surprise. "Well, I think your mom and I have a birthday party to plan right now, don't we?" He nodded. "So, maybe we can talk about weddings another day," she winked.

He was more than satisfied with the agent's response. "Okay. Can I go help Uncle Nick now?"

"Yes," Alex said as he hopped down and trotted off.

"Alex...I'm..." Cassidy began.

The agent shook her head and giggled. "It was a perfectly valid question, Cassidy."

"Maybe...but I..."

Alex leaned in and kissed the woman. "Stop. It's fine. You're starting to worry me."

"What do you mean?" Cassidy asked.

"Do you have something against English butlers or just vanilla cake?" Alex joked.

"Funny, Agent."

"Cass...I'm glad he thinks that way."

"Really?"

"Of course. We've got lots of time. You need to stop worrying about scaring me away. Okay?" Alex kissed the woman's forehead. "How about we take a ride?"

Cassidy smiled. "Now?"

"Yeah...I think now is perfect."

***

"What the hell?" Fallon looked at Ferro.

"Definitely two....What did Toles say when you told her?"

Brian Fallon shook his head. "She wasn't really surprised."

"I think," Ferro pointed out into the yard as they traversed the short distance to the tree fort, "that one came from here. Probably the one that hit the counter." Ferro moved to his right and pointed off a short way. "The one that hit him.... from over there."

"Did you find anything? Fallon asked.

"Nope. Clean as a whistle," Ferro said as Fallon inspected the area. "Only thing I got was some Energy Plus truck was in the neighborhood."

"So?" Fallon asked.

"So...Energy Plus has no record of being in the area," Ferro smirked.

"Huh...really? Spooks?" Fallon asked.

"Maybe.....This O'Brien...what's his deal?" the detective asked.

"Don't know," the agent answered. "Toles is pretty sure he's into something."

"Well, yeah... that's pretty obvious," Ferro remarked.

Agent Fallon took stock in his friend. Pete Ferro was a good cop and he was both smart and perceptive. "You don't like the congressman much, do you?"

Ferro shrugged. "I don't know him....but no...not really. Pompous ass. Seen his kind. Only one thing matters to a guy like that."

"What's that?" Fallon asked.

"Himself."

"So, can we trace that truck?"

"Already in the works, Agent. Don't count on much. I have a feeling we might find more off of what Fisher left." Ferro winked with a sly smile.

"What did Fisher leave?"

"Just some breadcrumbs....but you know breadcrumbs, Agent, as small as they are, if you follow them they always lead you somewhere." Fallon was curious. "Ahh...Fallon, there were some handwritten directions in that bag. I suspect not his writing based on some of the notes and letters there."

"Traceable?"

"Everything is traceable, Agent...If you're willing to take the time," Ferro led his friend back to the house.

"You sound like Toles," Fallon laughed.

"Smart woman," Ferro complimented with a twinkle in his eye.

"Detective, do you have a crush on my partner?"

"Eh, I'm too old for crushes," he laughed. "I know a good investigator when I see one. She's sharp. I had a partner like that once, long time ago; and she's got good taste in women," Ferro smiled.

"Well, I can't argue with any of that." As they stepped back into the kitchen the agent's expression turned pensive. "We need to figure out who put this son of a bitch in play," Fallon said with an uncharacteristic harshness in his voice.

Ferro handed the agent a piece of paper and Fallon's eyes fixed onto it. He scanned it for several moments. "What the?"

"Ummm...follow the breadcrumbs, Agent."

***

"So," Alex started, "what do you think?"

Cassidy walked through the door and stared. The house was beautiful. It was smaller than the house in New York, but it was almost perfect. It was older and it was charming. It was so perfect that Cassidy wasn't certain what to say. It was set back slightly from the road and surrounded by large oak trees. The yard was beautiful and there was a narrow stream in back that Alex pointed out. The kitchen was large, just as Alex had said. It was completely modernized but the appliances were set amidst subtle brick and white washed cabinetry that gave it the feel of being somewhat antique. The teacher was breathless.

"Cass?" Alex called again gently.

"Alex...it's gorgeous."

"But?"

"No....no but....it's just...."

"You're not certain about a move?" Cassidy looked at the agent and then closed her eyes. "It's all right, Cass," Alex continued. "You don't have to decide now."

Cassidy nodded. "Can we look upstairs?"

"Of course." The agent led the teacher up the stairs and watched as Cassidy slowly moved from each room until they reached the last room at the end of the hallway. It was the smallest room with a slanted ceiling and a skylight. Cassidy stood in the middle of the room and looked up. "Are you all right?" the agent asked.

Engaging green eyes looked to the agent's and Cassidy smiled. "I love you, Alex." Alex seemed confused and the teacher let a soft laugh emerge. "I can't decide anything now." Alex nodded her understanding. Cassidy could see just a hint of disappointment in Alex's eyes that she knew the agent was determined to keep concealed. She made her way to the beautiful dark haired woman across the room and put her arms around Alex's neck. "I just need to breathe, so much is…"

The agent interrupted her lover's thought with a sweet kiss of understanding. "It's okay, Cass. Now you've seen it. You don't have to decide anything right now."

"Alex, this isn't just my decision," the teacher reminded the agent.

"Yes. It is."

"No. No, it's not. It's our decision." The words penetrated Alex in a way that she could not have anticipated. Gentle eyes caught the agent's expression and Cassidy took both of her lover's hands in her own. "I just need to think, before we can talk….about school, my school, about my students. Alex…and Dylan…I just need to…"

"I know," Alex said. "I don't care where we live, Cassidy. Whatever you…."

Again the teacher shook her head. "Alex, there is no *me* in this, it's *we*. Okay?" The agent started to speak and Cassidy stopped her. "I can see it in your eyes. I promise we'll talk about all of it. I promise. I just need to process all of this."

Alex kissed the woman's forehead. "I'm not going anywhere, Cass….We can stay at Nick's this week."

"I have to figure out Dylan's...."

"What if I told you I got Dylan's assignments for the week already?" Cassidy looked at the agent in surprise. "Mmm. What if I told you that Barb spoke to Cat's school and Dylan can go to the after school program the next few days? You know, so at least he gets to see some kids." Cassidy's eyes began to water. "What's wrong?" Alex asked.

"Nothing...nothing...I just can't.....when did you....."

"I had Barb make the calls yesterday." The agent answered.

"When yesterday?" Cassidy asked.

"When I was on the way to Andrews."

"The Air Force Base?" The couple had not truly had a chance to discuss the details of Alex's return in all of the chaos and emotion of the last twenty-four hours.

"Yeah...That's how I got here..."

"Alex...you're on suspension..."

"You forget. I have friends." The small blonde woman reached up and brought the agent's lips to her own. Alex gave over to the wonderful sensation that Cassidy's kiss and touch always commanded. "What was that for?'

"Just for being you."

The agent smiled. "Well...Why don't we head back? I'm sure Nicky will be back with Dylan from the restaurant and the beach tour by the time we get there."

Cassidy took a deep breath and sighed. "Alex will you promise me one thing?"

"Anything."

"Whatever *we* decide...we'll tell Dylan together."

"Of course.... Just be prepared."

"For what?" Cassidy asked.

"For him to send you down the aisle," Alex laughed. Cassidy shook her head and placed it against the agent's chest with a smile. There were so many things to consider she couldn't imagine where to begin. Somehow just that one sentiment; the idea that Dylan wanted them together; made the teacher understand that whatever was to come to pass they would be all right.

***

"Congressman! Congressman! Over here! Sir!" A barrage of questions and swirling voices all demanding attention filled the air.

"Over there...Rick," the congressman pointed.

"Congressman...how do you feel about your ex-wife's new relationship?"

"Well, Rick....Cassidy is her own person....as we all know," Christopher O'Brien joked.

"But...was that a reason for your divorce?"

The congressman pretended to ponder the question carefully. It most certainly was not a cause of his marriage's demise. If anyone knew the truth it was Christopher O'Brien. The press certainly was aware of his many infidelities, or at least the implication of those affairs. Cassidy had never made public comments about the marriage. That was not a courtesy the congressman intended to return to his ex-wife. "Well, Rick, I support Cassidy in her decisions." Snap and click the cameras popped off as more questions and similar cryptic yet interpretable answers were given.

"Jesus," Pete Ferro muttered under his breath. "Is this guy for real?"

Agent Fallon shook his head. "What the hell?" he said watching a clip from the news conference. "Why would he do that? After everything she's been through....I mean..."

"Guy's a prick. That's why," Ferro said turning off the television and reaching across the coffee table in Cassidy's living room for a piece of paper. "So, who do you think it leads to?" He looked at Fallon. "Other than that jerk," he nodded toward the television.

"Well, whoever Fisher met with on Sunday is the key. He met with that person here...in New York. So I doubt it could be Brackett and it can't be O'Brien either."

"Hummm." Ferro groaned. "Could it be FBI?"

"What?" Fallon snapped in surprise.

Ferro shrugged. "Well, Fallon...look at that. You saw it. Why would he have FBI credentials?"

"He was a spook, Ferro...I agree it's strange..."

"No, it's not just strange. It's a trail. He met with someone. He has an FBI badge he shouldn't have...if it smells like..."

Brian Fallon ran his hand back and forth over the top of his head. Ferro was right. He took out his cell phone and dialed. "Toles?"

"Hey, Fallon," Alex said lightly, glancing to Cassidy across the car with a smile of reassurance.

"Sorry," he apologized realizing that Cassidy was clearly nearby.

"No...she's doing better, thanks," Alex said.

"She's right there, isn't she?"

"Yeah...we're going to stay at Nicky's this week."

"I understand. Toles...He had FBI clearance...met with someone it appears in the field office on Sunday, and Toles the badge...the I.D. number? It looks like it was meant to get him...well, as cover."

"Wow." Alex said making certain to keep her tone even. "Well, I hope you can get back to D.C. soon. Kate's going to kill me."

"Look Toles...I'll work it the best I can but your contacts might...."

"I'll check in with you. Tell Kate I am sorry," Alex offered. "I owe her a dinner."

"I got it. Alex, I do hope Cassidy is okay...with the congressman's news conference and all."

Alex was stunned. "What?"

"You didn't know?" he asked.

"No."

Fallon sighed. "Shit, Alex...I'm sorry."

The agent sighed. This she could not hide from Cassidy. "What did he say?"

There was a brief and hollow silence before Fallon exhaled. "Nothing specific, and that said everything."

"Christ." Alex kept her left hand on the wheel and her right thumb moved to her temple. The woman in the seat next to her took notice and looked at Alex with concern.

"I'm sorry, Alex...I assumed you knew," her partner said.

Alex tried to press down her anger. "It's all right, Fallon. Seriously, though...get home to Kate, okay?"

Fallon rubbed his face in frustration. "Yeah. Alex, tell Cassidy...well...you know."

"Yeah...I do." She hung up and felt the heat of Cassidy's gaze on her.

"And?" Cassidy looked at her lover for an explanation of the conversation she had just overheard. "Alex...whatever it is..."

"He held a press conference."

"Chris?" Cassidy asked.

"Yeah."

"About what?" Alex stayed silent. "About *us*?" The teacher let out a sarcastic chuckle. "Of course he did, and he said nothing at all...which is exactly what will make them all think there was something to say, right?" There was still no response. Cassidy licked her lips and then shook her head.

"Cass..."

Cassidy laughed genuinely. "I don't care."

"Yes you do," Alex observed.

"Alex...I don't even want to talk about it. I'll look when we get back."

"Maybe you shouldn't."

"Oh no...I want to know." The teacher said flatly.

***

Cassidy paced the room that she and Alex were sharing. The agent could tell that she was seething, but the teacher was determined to maintain control as she waited for an answer to her call. "Cassie," the voice greeted with what seemed to be sincerity. "How are you feeling?"

"I'm fantastic, Chris. Being tied to a chair, cut with a knife by a sadistic freak that worked on your campaign was one of the more rewarding experiences I've had in my life," she offered with disgust.

"I'm sorry that you went through that," he said.

"Really? That's fascinating, Christopher."

The congressman took a deep breath. "Cassidy…I was worried about you."

Cassidy shook her head. "I'm sure."

"I'm sorry I can't be there for Dylan's birthday…"

"Mmm…well…we won't be home for Dylan's birthday anyway, Chris."

"Oh? Are you staying with Agent Toles' family then?" he asked.

Cassidy pursed her lips and gripped the back of her neck. "We're staying with family, yes."

He let out a slight chuckle. "I see….Well…if there's anything…"

"I think you've done quite enough."

"Cassie…what is this about?"

The teacher had officially reached her limit with her ex-husband. "You know, Chris…I don't really care what you want to say or do not want to say about me, about you, about whatever our marriage was to you; which right now, at this moment, I'm not certain ever meant a thing to you. But, I would've thought at the very least you would have considered Dylan."

He began to mount his defense. "I have no idea…"

"I'm sure you don't," she answered sarcastically. "Listen, I have some decisions to make."

"Decisions? About what?"

Cassidy smiled. "About my life and Dylan's life."

"What does that mean?" he asked her.

"It means what I said. I would appreciate it if you would be cautious about your actions for now. Dylan's been through enough with your accident and now this."

"Cassidy...Dylan is always my priority," he maintained.

The teacher rolled her eyes. "You know, the saddest part of that statement, Christopher, is I actually think you believe that."

"It's the truth."

"Well, Chris...You know...truth is just like politics, isn't it?"

"What do you mean?"

"All about perception. Right?" She let the pause linger. "Look, I am going to be out of state for at least the next five days. Just do me a favor and call Dylan Saturday."

"It's already on my calendar."

"I am sure it is. I'll be in touch." She hung up before he could answer.

Alex watched and spoke cautiously, "Cass...if..."

Cassidy held up her hand. "Alex...I need to take a walk."

Alex started to follow. "Okay...I'll..."

"No. I need to be alone, just out back...alright?"

"Cass..." Alex did not love the idea of leaving the teacher alone.

"Am I in danger?" Cassidy asked.

Alex closed her eyes. "No."

"Then I need to take a walk." Alex nodded. Cassidy tried to smile but her rage was sitting right at the surface. She slowly began to walk out of the room. She stopped, turned and took the agent's hand. "I love you, Alex. I need you to know that. Right now I have to..."

"I know," the agent squeezed the smaller hand and released it. This was the hardest part. Letting Cassidy go for even a moment after the previous day's events filled Alex with anxiety. This was something the woman she loved needed. The agent heard the edge in the generally gentle and compassionate voice of her lover. Cassidy needed time. Loving her meant giving it; no matter how hard that was. Alex took a deep breath as she heard Cassidy's feet hit the stairs and she lifted her phone.

***

"Taylor?" Alex began.

"Toles...How are you? How's Cassidy?" he asked with concern.

"We're all okay, Michael. Thanks."

"Well, I assume this is not a social call," Michael Taylor said.

"No. Fisher, he had FBI credentials on him."

"Are you sure?" Taylor asked.

"Well...I haven't seen them personally....but yes."

Taylor rolled in his chair. "Do you know where he...."

"I haven't seen any of it. Fallon says it looks like he was at the New York field office on Sunday."

He considered the new information carefully for a moment. "Huh...Okay, do you want me ....."

Alex needed her friend's help. For once, she could not place herself in the middle of the investigation; at least not yet. "Taylor...I need to be....things here are..."

"Yeah, I heard. Listen, Cap...I'll see what I can do. What about the colonel?" Taylor suggested.

"No...he's already put himself too far out.... I can't..."

Taylor pushed some papers on his desk. "I got it. Alex?"

"Yeah?"

"Think about my offer, okay?"

Alex sighed. "Yeah."

Chapter Twenty-Five

Cassidy sat down on a swing at the back of the yard and rocked it gently as all of her thoughts and emotions swayed within. "Hey," a voice called. "I don't want to intrude."

"No...truth be told I could use the company," the teacher admitted.

Barb sat down on the swing next to her new friend and held onto the chains. "The boys went with Alex and your mom down to the pond." Cassidy smiled and nodded. Dylan had been carrying on about catching frogs all morning. He wasn't interested in hearing that summer would be a better time for that endeavor and she was certain that her mother and the agent would have their hands full.

"Thank you...for everything," Cassidy said appreciatively.

"Oh, please, I am thrilled to have you here. Nick is so happy to have time with Alex, and Cat is excited to have Dylan to share his room."

Cassidy laughed. "I know. Dylan asked five minutes after Cat left for school this morning when he would be back. He loves it here." The teacher's eyes dropped to the ground and she sighed. "I know sometimes he is lonely."

Barb nodded. "Yeah, well, same for Cat. The only child thing."

Cassidy knew 'the only child thing' quite well. She was an only child and she always wanted a larger family for Dylan. "Not to pry," Cassidy began. Barb smiled and let out a sigh. Cassidy studied her. "Barb?"

"Haven't told anyone yet," she said. "It's early…"

The teacher beamed. "You're pregnant." Barb nodded. "That's fantastic. Nick must be thrilled. I know Alex will be ecstatic to be an aunt again."

"Well, we would have told you both after Dylan's birthday. I hadn't planned on saying anything with all the…"

"Nonsense. I could use some happy news. Looks like Cat will get to play big brother," Cassidy offered with a slight hint of sadness in her voice that Barb noted.

"Um, but he's eight. Big difference. I think he will prefer Dylan's company in most cases." Cassidy gave an appreciative grin to the woman. "So, what did you think of the house? If I can ask."

"I love it." There was notable stress on the smaller woman's face.

"Change is hard," Barb said.

"Some," she agreed with a sigh. "Can I be honest?"

"Of course. I enjoy our talks, Cassidy. I'd like us to be family. I don't have any sisters."

"Me too," Cassidy chuckled. "I'm worried about my students, walking out on them. So many of them already have abandonment issues; you know?" The taller woman listened to her new friend in amazement as she began to voice her concerns. "And Dylan and his friends… and school…"

"And?" Barb urged, sensing there was more.

"Whew," Cassidy let out an audible breath. "Alex. She's uprooting her whole life and taking on so much with us, and honestly, walking through that house…I just shouldn't be thinking…God, with everything that's happened how can I? But when I walked in that last bedroom I just couldn't help it… It's insane."

Barb laughed. "That was Cat's nursery." She understood exactly what thoughts were passing through Cassidy's mind and what fears.

"I don't want her to feel…"

"Uh hum…pressured?"

"Exactly," Cassidy confirmed.

"Cassidy, when I talked to Alex yesterday," the teacher looked at her new friend closely. "Alex was…Well, I've never heard her like that. She was determined that everything would be taken care of for both you and Dylan, but she was scared. She tried to hide it but I've known her almost fourteen years. She loves you. Last night, when you were in bed and…" the woman stopped and considered her statements.

"Go on," Cassidy urged.

"All she talked about was making things happier for you and Dylan. I think I heard her use the word 'family' more in that hour than in all the years I've known her. As far as moving, well, she was worried about getting you away from the stress, the memories, the press…but," Barb laughed, "she didn't want you to feel pressured."

The teacher laughed out loud. "Quite the pair, huh?" Her friend smiled. "It's crazy, if I think about it. It's feels like we have always been together. Yesterday, I thought I was going to die," she grew quiet as the thought passed through her. "Somehow I knew she would fight to protect Dylan, take care of him and I don't even know how to respond to that. It's been weeks, not years and I can't imagine my life…"

"Without her?" Barb finished the thought. Cassidy nodded. "Well, far be it from me to try and sway you," the woman rose from her rubber seat, "but selfishly, I wish you'd take the house." The teacher smiled. "Whatever you decide…well…"

Cassidy grabbed Barb's hand. "Thank you."

Barb nodded and returned the friendly squeeze. "Whatever you decide, you're stuck with us now," she laughed as she started to walk back toward the house. "God help you."

***

Alex and Rose sat on a large log watching as the two boys searched the edge of the water for frogs or any slimy thing they might discover. The agent was quiet, far more so than Rose had seen her. Alex had grabbed a long stick and was tracing circles in the dirt mindlessly as she kept one eye on the two boys who seemed determined to get in some kind of trouble together. They reminded her a bit of what she and Nick were like at that age. "You all right, Alex?" Rose asked. The agent let out a soft sigh and nodded. "You're worried about Cassie," the woman said plainly.

"I can't help it," Alex admitted before reprimanding the pair of small heads in the distance for getting too close to the water.

Rose chuckled. It warmed Cassidy's mother to see the agent with the two boys, and to see her grandson so happy in spite of all the upheaval in recent months and weeks. Alex brought something into their lives that had been lacking; love and stability. "She'll be all right," Rose said. "I suspect what she's worried the most about is you." The agent turned to the woman beside her with wide eyes, soliciting a giggle from Rose. "That surprises you?"

"I'm not the one who went through that ordeal," Alex said. "Worried about me? Why?"

"Really? Alex, you know Cassie."

The agent sighed and looked over at Cat who was just about to dip his sneakered foot into the water. "Christian Alexander! Don't even think about it!" He looked back sheepishly and then whispered to Dylan. "Lucky it's me here and not Cass," she muttered. "She'd have heard that." Rose smiled. The agent took a deep breath and looked at the older woman. Cassidy was a great deal like her mother and Alex adored the older woman. She was nothing like the agent's parents. Rose was witty and intelligent, but also gentle and compassionate. Alex enjoyed having her around. For whatever reason, the more time she spent with Cassidy's mother, the more she seemed to confide in the woman. "I don't want her to think that I want her to move here."

"But, you do," Rose smirked. The truth made Alex uncomfortable. She did. It was true. She didn't trust the congressman and she liked the idea of a fresh start; a start that would be further from his presence. She'd missed Nick and Barb. Family was something Alex never thought a great deal about until she met Cassidy. Alex had begun to realize how much family really did mean to her. Being here with all of them together seemed to promote a sense of home that Alex never experienced as a child. It wasn't something she had ever talked about and it wasn't something she intended to share with Cassidy, either. "Why don't you just tell her?"

"What?" Alex said with alarm in her voice.

"That you want to move here."

The agent shook her head. "I don't want her to do anything she doesn't want to do."

"I see. But, Alex; what about what you want to do?"

"I just want her to be happy," Alex said truthfully.

Rose looked at the two boys who were now throwing rocks into the pond. "He's happy," she pointed ahead to Dylan.

"You think so?"

"No. I know so. Alex, Cassie needs to know how you feel. I don't blame you…and frankly I think getting away from New York is the best thing for all of you."

"What about you?" Alex asked with concern.

"Why? Would you miss me?" Rose chided. The older woman was caught off guard by the response that she saw in the agent's eyes. Alex was strong, commanding and confident; not to mention she was a beautiful woman. It surprised Rose when the agent turned to her, to see the expression of a somewhat forlorn child looking back. Cassidy's mother suddenly realized there was a great deal about Alex she did not know. In a very short time they had all fallen into this unexpected family. They'd endured things in a couple of weeks that most people would never experience in a lifetime. Somehow, they all seemed to 'fit'. "Well, you wouldn't get rid of me that easily," Rose said. "I enjoy tormenting my daughter."

Alex laughed. "Rose? I saw her face in that house."

"Ummm," Rose tried to suppress her smile. Barb had shown the woman some pictures of the house and Rose was certain that Cassidy would be drawn in by it.

The agent shook her head. "But...I don't know...I feel sometimes like she's afraid that I...."

"She is. Alex, just tell her. I know my daughter." Rose laughed. "She needs you to tell her what you really want."

"It's too much," Alex whispered.

The older woman laughed as she beckoned the boys toward them. "I doubt that, Alex. You almost lost each other yesterday, just say what you need to." The words pierced Alex's heart. Rose McCollum had a way of speaking the truth like no one she had ever met. She had almost lost all of this, this family. Alex would have done anything to prevent that from happening. In a crisis, the agent was confident and assertive. Now, she faltered. Alex shook her head as the boys ran past them. Rose was right. "Tell her," Rose said as she placed a hand on the agent's back.

***

It had been a pleasant evening full of light hearted small talk and watching the boys play. Wrangling Dylan and Cat for bed had proved a Herculean effort. They were both wound up as tight as bow strings and it took Alex and Nick to physically lead them upstairs to calm them down at all. Cassidy sat on the couch with her mother sipping a glass of wine and smiling at the sounds filtering down from above. "How are you feeling?" Rose asked her daughter.

"Truthfully?"

"No, Cassie...Lie to me," Rose joked.

Cassidy laughed. "It's going to sound so strange."

"Cassie, I raised you, strange is something I've grown used to."

"Funny," the teacher responded. Her gaze drifted up as she heard Alex give a spirited command to head for the bunk beds to the boys. A heavy sigh of contentment escaped her. "I feel happy. Crazy...yesterday...I just...I've never been so afraid in my life."

Rose looked at her daughter and felt the gravity of the previous day pressing in on them both. She had been terrified. The thought of losing Cassidy was unbearable. They were far more than mother and daughter. They were best friends and Rose loved her daughter more than anything. They sometimes had a unique way of expressing their feelings, but both knew how the other felt. The older woman studied her daughter as she finally confided all that she had been thinking and feeling. Cassidy was remarkable and Rose was amazed at the younger woman. Not only had her daughter grown into an attractive woman; she had become a compassionate person whose intellect and personality only served to compliment her looks. Moreover, and Rose was most proud of this, Cassidy was humble, never seeing herself as others did.

Cassidy continued, sipping her wine occasionally and tracing the rim of her glass with her finger. "It is crazy. I keep saying that. I keep thinking that. But, I was sitting there...and he was over me...ranting and pacing. I would close my eyes and just for a minute I would feel safe. I thought...Well...when he pulled out the knife..." Cassidy's thoughts trailed off. She couldn't look at her mother. Rose was shaking but reached out for her daughter's hand. Finally Cassidy looked across to the woman. "I thought he was going to kill me then. I did. It was like in one second everything flashed and then everything was quiet."

"Cassie...I can't even..."

"It's all right, Mom," Cassidy gave a calm smile to her mother that surprised the older woman. The teacher took another sip of her wine and licked her lips. "All I thought about was Dylan,

413

and Alex...and when she walked in, when I saw her there..."
Cassidy couldn't control the tears that began to quietly fall.
"I knew I could never let her go. It was like; I can't explain
it. I don't know what to do with it, Mom. It's overwhelming...
it's...."

"You're in love, Cassie."

"I know, but it's more than that. How can I be thinking
about the things that...."

Rose McCollum laughed. "Oh, Cassie, you want a life with
Alex."

Cassidy's voice dropped to a whisper. "I do."

"So...what's the problem?" her mother asked pointedly.

"There isn't one...I just..."

"Cassidy Rose, I am going to tell you exactly what I told that
agent today." Cassidy looked at her mother in astonishment.
"And I want you to LISTEN to me. You need to just tell her.
I have a feeling you both want the exact same things. Now,
you just told me that all you could think about were those two
upstairs yesterday. That's certainly all they could think about.
So, if you don't mind me saying this...you're both being a bit
stupid."

"Mom...."

"No, Cassidy, I mean it. I was terrified yesterday. Terrified...
When Alex finally called, her concern was for Dylan...keeping
him calm, reassuring him. I watched Nick take Dylan into his
lap and tell him that everything would be okay. We got here
and Barb; she was beside herself worrying about you. I think
she was almost as worried as I was."

Cassidy swallowed hard. Her mother was always direct, but
now she spoke with an assuredness that Cassidy had not heard
in many years. It wasn't a lecture but it wasn't her best friend
speaking; it was her mother. "I...." Cassidy began.

"I'm not finished, Cassie. You always wanted a family. God
knows I thought he could give you that. I really did. I hoped
he would. He didn't and he couldn't. Not really. He gave you

Dylan and I know we are both forever grateful for that." Cassidy smiled. "But, Alex…She is the one that can give you a family; the family you want and need. I think she already has."

"She has."

"So, stop worrying and stop trying to figure it all out. You liked the house?" Cassidy smiled and nodded. "You like being close to Barb?" The teacher raised an eyebrow. "Um hum… so…What's the problem, Cassie?"

Cassidy began to spew her list of reasons, "Mom, Dylan is in the middle of a school year and there is still my students…."

"Cassidy, for once put yourself first. If you can't do that then put Alex first." Cassidy was stunned at her mother's words. "Dylan is six. He'll be happy as long as he is with the two of you. God knows he won't let her out of his sight when she's home."

Cassidy laughed. Her mother was right, AGAIN. "You think we should move."

"I think you deserve to be happy. All of you. That's what I think. And, I think you want to do it; so just do it, Cassidy." Rose stood and took her daughter's face in her hands. "I know you, but I am getting to know that agent of yours pretty well too. Don't underestimate how much she loves you both." She kissed her daughter on the forehead and began to take her leave just as Alex entered the room. Rose raised an eyebrow at the agent. "I'll leave you two to your evening."

***

"Where the hell did Fisher get FBI credentials?" John Merrow bellowed at the woman across from him.

"I had nothing to do with that," Claire Brackett said firmly.

Merrow guffawed and pushed a large binder aside on his desk. "No?"

"No."

"Claire…I had a contact call me from the NSA this morning. Do you have any idea how exposed we are right now?"

"What do you want me to do?" she asked defensively.

"I want you to find out...BEFORE Krause gets back, who gave Fisher that I.D. badge; who authorized it."

"I thought you wanted me to lay low," she said smoothly.

"Just do it. I've got Tate keeping Fallon in New York for the week. After all, we do need to close the case on Fisher....You have until Monday, figure it out. You helped to cause it, you're going to clean it. That's the way a collaborative works. We ALL play a role...now play yours."

***

Cassidy watched as Alex pulled the T-shirt over her head. "You know how much I love this?"

"What's that?"

"This."

"Me putting on a T-shirt?" Alex laughed.

"Actually, yes."

"You're silly, Cass."

"No, I'm not," Cassidy sat back against the headboard and propped a pillow behind her back. Alex laid down beside the teacher, propping herself up on one elbow, placing her other hand on Cassidy's thigh. "I didn't know if I'd ever see you do that again yesterday."

Alex sighed. "Cass...I'm so sorry that you..."

Cassidy stopped the agent. "No....it's over."

The agent thought it best to change the subject. "How was your walk?"

"Good. I ended up spending some time with Barb afterward."

"Oh?" Alex was curious. She knew Barb and she wondered what her sister-in-law had to say.

"Yeah. How was the pond?"

"Wet," Alex laughed. Both Cat and Dylan had come home without frogs but with wet feet in spite of constant reprimands.

Cassidy laughed and gently stroked Alex's hand. "Alex?"

"Yeah?"

The smaller woman sighed. Alex left her breathless now, just looking at her. Her eyes were so blue and they seemed to shimmer. The way that Alex was looking at Cassidy completely overtook the teacher. "God, you are beautiful," Cassidy whispered.

Alex smiled. "Where did that come from?"

Cassidy stroked the agent's cheek as her smile began to widen. "You know, I think I would like the master bedroom sage; it's calming." Alex felt her heart jump into her throat. She wasn't certain that she had heard what Cassidy said correctly, and she wasn't sure it meant what she hoped. Her eyes gave her questions away immediately to her lover. Cassidy raised her eyebrow. "Do you have something against sage?"

"I...uh....Cass–what..."

Green eyes twinkled and Cassidy leaned in planting a light kiss on Alex's lips. "I love you, Alex...I don't know exactly how to say this...."

"Just say it."

"I want us to be a family."

Alex smiled. "Me too. Are you sure, Cass? Because I...."

Cassidy stopped the thought with a kiss and pulled back slowly. "It scares me."

"What scares you?" Alex asked softly.

"Everything I want with you."

"Why does that scare you, Cass?"

The teacher sighed and continually caressed her lover's cheek. "Because I want everything with you. I've known that from the beginning, I think.....but after yesterday....and then walking into that house...and Barb telling me about the baby..."

Alex sat straight up. "The what?"

"Oh shit....I didn't mean to let that out."

"Barb's pregnant?" Cassidy tilted her head and shrugged, feeling badly that she had let that slip out. "Huh," Alex chuckled. "I'm not going to say a word. I'll act like a kid on Christmas when she tells me." Cassidy smiled. "It's not as big as your house."

"It's perfect."

Alex kissed Cassidy and searched her eyes. "I want you to be sure."

"I am sure."

"What about work?"

Cassidy shook her head. "Well, I suspect that is going to get a bit dramatic now, thanks to his highness and his comments." The agent had thought about that as well. All the press coverage would fade but it would inevitably complicate both Cassidy and Dylan's lives in the immediate future. "I think maybe I should just look at the fall."

"You mean take the some time off?"

"Yeah. Why; do you think that is a bad idea?"

"No, actually I think it's a great idea." Alex said. "And...I've been thinking myself..."

"About?" Cassidy asked. Alex sat up and her posture stiffened slightly. "Alex....what's wrong?"

"Nothing...honestly. Just Tate wants me back at the NSA and it might help...if I did..."

The teacher rubbed her eyebrow in thought. "Help with what, Alex?" Alex shook her head. "How did you know?" Alex looked at her lover with a touch of fear in her eyes. "Alex, how did you know I might be in trouble?"

The agent felt sick. A nice conversation was turning a dangerous corner. "Cass...."

Cassidy shook her head with a sarcastic smile. The answer was written across Alex's face. "Chris." Alex bit her lip. "Of course. What the hell is going on?"

"I don't really know, Cassidy...I just know he's into something...deep."

"Is Dylan in danger?"

"No...I don't think either of you are in danger, Cass....honestly....but I won't lie to you. Putting some distance between him and both of you...I know he's Dylan's father but...I just...I don't trust..." Cassidy was furious with the congressman but Alex's rambling was endearing. It was one of the things the teacher loved so much about the woman beside her. Alex could pivot from the most commanding presence to a rambling child in less than a second and Cassidy found it utterly adorable. She couldn't help but smile at Alex. "I'm rambling," Alex admitted and Cassidy nodded.

"Distance is good," Cassidy agreed. "I don't want to talk about him, not tonight." Alex smiled. "You know I will support whatever you want to do, Alex. I just want you to be safe."

"Cass, I am good at what I do," the agent assured her lover.

"I know that, but I can't help but worry."

Alex kissed the woman's forehead. "I worry about you. I guess we have a lot in common."

"I guess we do," Cassidy admitted and laid her head on the agent's chest.

"Let's do Dylan's party there," Alex said.

"What?" Cassidy asked in surprise.

"Let's have his party at the house."

"Alex...there isn't even anything at the house...there's no table, there's no..."

"Eh...minor details," Alex dismissed the observation playfully.

Cassidy laughed. "You're crazy, you know that?"

"Come on...we'll go shopping."

"Shopping? Alex, you hate shopping. You can't stand to be in the grocery store for five minutes."

"Different."

"Really?" Cassidy propped herself up to look in the agent's eyes.

"Yeah...Come on," Alex urged. Cassidy was delighted by the spark she saw in Alex's eyes. There was an excitement there that the teacher had not expected. The agent was like a small child getting a new puppy, wide eyed.

"Shopping for?" the teacher inquired.

"Stuff."

"Stuff?" Cassidy raised her eyebrows again.

"Yeah...Come on, Cass....Seriously...a FRESH start. What do you think Dylan would say about a Batman room?" Cassidy shook her head and kissed Alex. "What?" Alex asked innocently.

"I love you, Alex Toles."

"Good thing," the agent said.

"Is it?"

"Yep. Do you think we could make it Dylan's birthday present?"

"What?" Cassidy asked smiling.

"You know...the house...his room..."

"You really are Alfred," Cassidy laughed. Alex looked at her hopefully. "I think that could be arranged...yes...but I think," Cassidy kissed Alex gently, "that you," she pulled back and kissed Alex's nose, "might have some other things to worry about first."

"Really?" Alex asked. "Like what?"

Cassidy ran her hands up Alex's sides. "The lady of the house requires the butler's service."

"I already did the dishes," Alex joked. Cassidy looked at her and Alex took the woman into a passionate kiss. "But I live to serve."

***

Michael Taylor sorted through the large pile of files on his desk. "Jonathan Krause," he whispered. "Where have you been?" He leafed through a few papers before settling on one. He brought it closer and studied it for a long moment. He set it down and moved to his computer keyboard quickly typing in

some words, hit the 'enter' button and waited. "Well, well…. Admiral Brackett….and Major General Krause…What do you know? Old friends….Let's see…I wonder," Michael Taylor typed some more words and waited. He shook his head and tried something else as his tapping on the computer keys becoming more insistent. "Oh…. Fisher….Colonel Edward Fisher…fascinating…..What?" Taylor stopped abruptly and pulled his chair back slightly. He ran his hand over his head. "What is going on here?" Taylor picked up his phone and dialed. "Hey…Brady I need something."

"What is it?" Steven Brady asked.

"Well, what would you say if I told you that Claire Brackett's father, Carl Fisher's father and Jonathan Krause's father were all old friends? They all worked on a project together in the seventies."

"Weird. But not that weird…we all know service runs…"

Taylor stared at the screen in front of him. "Yeah…I would've dismissed it myself…if it were just Brackett and Fisher… but Krause?"

"What do you think it means?"

"Maybe nothing at all except that it brought them all together…but IF it IS what brought them all together, it would stand to reason that whoever is at the core of this mess with the congressman was part of that crowd too…Don't you think?" Taylor asked.

"It does. Is the congressman…"

"No, but there is a name on here that almost made me fall off my chair."

Steven Brady was curious, "Who?"

"Lieutenant General Anthony Merrow."

"As in?" Brady asked nervously.

"As in President John Merrow's father."

***

Cassidy woke up and heard the shower running. She groaned. Alex was already up and moving. The teacher threw the pillow over her head and grumbled some more. "What's the matter," Alex called playfully.

"Why are you awake?" a muffled voice answered.

"We've got things to do today," Alex said happily.

"Yes...couldn't we do them later, though?"

Alex laughed as Cassidy removed the pillow from her face and sat up slightly against the headboard. The agent leaned in and kissed the woman in the bed, her cold wet hair brushing the teacher's bare skin and causing Cassidy to shiver. "Awake now?" Alex asked.

Cassidy smacked her lightly. "And just what is on your agenda today?"

"Our agenda, Cassidy...We're shopping."

Cassidy shook her head. "You are serious about this party, aren't you?" Alex shrugged. The agent was smiling broadly and Cassidy was both amused and touched by Alex's plans. "Alex, we have everything Dylan needs at home."

The agent pulled a black sweater over her head. "Yeah, well...we can sell it."

"You have lost your mind, Agent Toles." Cassidy said half serious. When Alex turned to face her, the teacher could see that for whatever reason, this was important to Alex. "Alex... What is this about?"

"I just want it to be our house, Cass."

That sentiment was something that Cassidy understood and she expected that Alex would want to make the house their own. "We haven't even talked about affording the house, Alex. I mean, I own the house in New York. It was mine in the settlement, but it might take time to sell, particularly after the..."

"Yeah...I know. It's fine," Alex said as she turned to finish getting dressed.

"What do you mean it's *fine?*"

"I mean you don't need to worry about it."

Cassidy took a deep breath. "Okay...look...I am not going to have you..."

Alex laughed. "It's fine because technically I own the house in Westport."

"What are you talking about?"

"Nick needed to take out the loan for the restaurant. I took out the mortgage on that house for him. We rented it until three months ago. We put it on the market, but no offers that met my price...so, I've been paying the mortgage anyway."

Cassidy was stunned. "Alex...that house has to be worth..."

"Yeah...I know...good thing I am good with money, huh?"

"Alex..."

"Relax, Cassidy. My parents invested well for both of us. Nick's went toward the restaurant and this house. Me? I just kept investing. I'm not wealthy...not like, well, not like what you're used to...but I'm all right. Now, I can just enjoy what I've been paying for."

"Why didn't you tell me?" Cassidy wondered.

"I would have told you no matter what decision you made, but not until you made it."

"Alex..."

"Listen, whatever you want to keep from your house...that's fine. God knows I have nothing in the way of things to contribute to a house. I really want to do this with you."

"Shop?" Cassidy giggled. Alex shrugged. She looked at Cassidy hopefully. "This is really important to you?"

"Yeah...it is...I want Dylan to..."

"Dylan loves you; you don't have to impress him with things," Cassidy reassured.

"It's not that."

"Okay...."

"Look....I missed six birthdays." Cassidy was overwhelmed with emotion as she listened to the woman now sitting next to her. "He's been through so much, more than a six year old should....and he is still happy...I just..."

"Okay," Cassidy stopped the agent.

"Okay?"

"Yeah, okay." Cassidy said with a smile.

"You're sure that you..."

Cassidy chuckled. "Alex, my head is spinning. It really is." Alex's face dropped in fear and the teacher caught the change. "No," Cassidy laughed. "It's not a bad thing....just spinning. This is....you are....I just, well you surprise me....and then you....I can't..." She saw Alex trying not to laugh. "What?"

"You're rambling, Cass."

"Yeah? Well maybe it's contagious."

"Must be," Alex agreed.

Cassidy sighed. "Just promise me, not over the top....okay?"

"So...that truck cab and the 65" TV are out?" Alex said seriously. Cassidy just stared. "I'm kidding, Cass. Butlers don't make that kind of money and neither do FBI agents. I'm afraid you'll have to call Bruce Wayne there in Washing..." The statement was stopped abruptly by a kiss. "Or you could just do that," Alex said.

"Je t'adore," Cassidy reminded the woman.

"*Allez. Je suis impatient de rentrer à la maison* (Come on I am anxious to go home)."

Cassidy got up and headed toward the shower. "Me too," she said as she walked through the door.

"I hope you remember you said that," Alex muttered.

"Don't worry. I will," a voice called back.

Chapter Twenty-Six

"**I** don't know anything about that," Jonathan Krause said into his phone.

"Well, someone had to know," the president responded.

"You say he had FBI identification?"

John Merrow's level of frustration was rising by the second. "Do I need to say it in French for you? *Il aviat FBI identifictaion dons son sac.*"

"Yes, well…have you asked your *compagne?*" Krause sad flippantly.

"If you are referring to Claire Brackett she assured me she had nothing to do with it."

Krause opened a heavy wooden door to enter a large and elegant conference room. "John, I am in meetings today…. meetings with people whose support we need to preserve. My money is on Brackett."

"Brackett was here in D.C."

"I'll assume you have confirmation of that," Krause said.

"I do."

"First hand?" Krause said bating the president.

"Not exactly."

"Well, Mr. President….we both know that Fisher and Brackett knew each other since childhood and from what I gather, *intimately*. I'd get that confirmation."

"Brackett is committed. She has only one side to play," Merrow replied coolly.

Krause snickered. "Everyone has sides to choose, John... everyone." He hung up the phone leaving John Merrow to consider the words carefully.

"Keep your enemies closer," Merrow said as he gripped the sides of his desk. He picked up the large phone seated at the corner, "get me Claire Brackett."

***

Cassidy was thoroughly amused by the agent. They had only been together a short time but one thing Cassidy knew unequivocally was that Alex did not like to shop. The few times she and her mother discussed the idea, Alex cringed. The teacher secretly suspected that Alex's culinary abilities were better than she often let on, but she would never have a chance to *cook* because her idea of shopping entailed a five minute trip for macaroni and cheese. In the last four hours Alex had pulled the smaller woman to a host of stores. And now, Cassidy found herself walking through IKEA and losing the agent every five minutes. "I swear, Alex, the next stop is going to be to Babies R Us to get a tether for you if you don't SLOW down," the teacher called in mock annoyance.

"Awww....come on, Cass....come over here." Cassidy caught up to the tall, dark haired woman who was standing in a demo of a boy's room. "Check it out." Cassidy smiled watching her lover. "See...the table and the storage stuff is black. It'll look so cool with that bed stuff we found...and that clock."

"Who exactly is this room for?" Cassidy put her hand on her hip and smiled.

"What? Come on; it IS cool."

Cassidy shook her head. It was true. Dylan would love it all. Alex had dragged Cassidy to a collectible comic store and found some superhero things, a Batman clock, a lamp that looked like the Batcycle and some colorful things from Superman, Spiderman and some other characters Cassidy did not immediately recognize. Dylan LOVED superheroes and Cassidy was beginning to realize so did the agent. "Okay? So...How do you intend to get this all home?" the teacher asked.

Alex smiled. "I'll get it."

"Uh huh."

"This will fit in the SUV."

"Uh huh, and who's going to put it together?" Cassidy raised her brow.

Alex shrugged. "We will."

"*WE* will, will we?" Alex grinned innocently and Cassidy laughed. There was no way she could say no. Alex was already writing down the numbers she needed to purchase the items for Dylan's room.

"Okay," Alex reached for Cassidy's hand.

"Okay? Now what?"

"First we get this and then we have to make two more stops."

"You're serious," Cassidy rolled her eyes and shook her head. She looked at her lover and spoke softly, "Honey...I think he has enough." Alex's face lit up. "What?" Cassidy asked.

The agent shrugged and dropped her tone to a whisper. "I like that." Cassidy was completely confused and her face showed it. "When you call me that." Cassidy was perplexed. "You called me, honey."

Cassidy chuckled. "Yes, I did... *honey*, let's wrap it up."

"Can't."

"Alex..."

"Um um...Just trust me, please?"

Cassidy threw her hands in the air. "Fine, but just so YOU know...when I need you to go Christmas shopping I expect you to smile and carry the bags."

Alex pretended to consider the statement carefully. "Carry the bags?"

Cassidy began to pull slightly ahead of the agent's slowing pace. "Yes, Alfred. The bags."

***

"Chairman."

"Hello Chris," Chairman Stiller greeted the congressman.

"I am sorry that I have been out of the loop…this whole thing with Cassidy…"

James Stiller's brow narrowed to a point. "Yes, you must be relieved that Cassidy is safe."

"Well, of course," Christopher O'Brien answered gesturing to his colleague to accept a seat in a large chair.

"I must admit, Chris…I was surprised."

The congressman sighed. "Believe me, so was I. I can't imagine what Cassidy was thinking."

"Thinking about what?" the older man asked.

"This thing with this woman. I think the stress has finally gotten to her," O'Brien answered.

"I see. I was actually referring to your press conference."

"My press conference?" The chairman nodded. "You know how it is," the congressman said dryly. "They are relentless."

"Ahh…so you thought, feed the sharks?"

The congressman was growing uncomfortable with the conversation. "So, how do we look with that resolution?" He sought to change the subject.

Chairman James Stiller remained silent. He stroked his chin and considered the man before him. "Why the change, Chris…on this measure?"

"I thought that was clear, Chairman. The administration is concerned about the restrictions and its impact on strategic initiatives."

"But you don't work for the administration," the chairman responded. "You work for the people of New York."

The congressman responded coolly. "True, but sometimes flexibility is important. I have made commitments…"

"Hummm…interesting choice of words, Congressman." The chairman rose from his seat and stood looking at the younger man. "Loyalty is a precious commodity and allusive." He began leaving and then turned back to the congressman. "The resolution stands as it is. Please, if you speak to Cassidy, send her the best from both Ellen and I."

Christopher O'Brien felt his stomach twist. He offered the man a contrived smile, "Of course."

***

"Alex….No." The agent smiled and her eyes grew wide as she nodded 'yes' in disagreement with her lover. "We don't even know how long it will take to sell the house in New York."

The agent pulled the smaller woman down onto the sofa in the show room. "And…"

"And…I won't be working…AND you won't be working."

"I can see where we are headed," Alex smiled.

"What does that mean? I know," Cassidy chuckled, "that you are excited. But Alex we have all of this already."

"No…*you* have all of this." Cassidy sighed. Alex would have liked to have had them sleeping in the new house that night if she could. The teacher wondered how the agent was going to keep quiet around Dylan until the weekend. "Cass, the house will sell better if it's staged anyway," Alex said emphatically.

Hearing that statement conjured images of Alex in front of Martha Stewart for Cassidy and she chuckled. "I'm not even going to ask," the teacher said.

Alex smiled. "You love it…look at it…you love it."

"Alex…you have bought Dylan an entire new room, a new dining room set and a host of other things…paint and…"

"Cassidy…."

"Yes?" Cassidy smiled.

"Please let me do this." Alex decided to take Rose's advice and be direct. This was something she could do and something she wanted to do. And, she needed Cassidy to understand that. The little Cassidy did know about the agent's youth told her that *home* was something Alex had never really felt. That continued to be the one topic that Alex seemed guarded with.

Cassidy sighed and kissed the agent on the cheek. "I do love it," she admitted.

"I know," Alex beamed.

***

"Unacceptable," John Merrow said. "What exactly did the chairman say?"

Christopher O'Brien thought for a moment wanting to temper the situation. "He said the resolution stands."

John Merrow paced the floor. "Unacceptable....What else? Did you tell him that you were acting in part on my behalf?"

"I did."

"And?" Merrow said angrily.

"And he said I don't work for you. I work for the people of New York."

"Bloated...arrogant...Self-righteous son of a bitch," Merrow complained as he hurled insults meant for the chairman of Way and Means. "Why? What changed? What did he say?"

"That was it–other than asking about Cassidy," O'Brien explained.

"Mmmm..." the president began to put the pieces together.

The congressman, who was still miffed himself, spoke without thinking. "He basically accused me of disloyalty to her."

"What?" Merrow asked.

"Yeah...before he said to give her his best."

"You idiot," Merrow said. "Did he see that debacle you called a press conference?"

"I'm sure he heard the news if that's what you mean," O'Brien said. "She has undermined my..."

Merrow exploded in a sarcastic sigh that sounded like a groan. "His daughter is a lesbian." Christopher O'Brien looked at the president blankly. "You better just sit tight, Congressman.

Leave Cassidy alone; leave it be." He resumed his pacing speaking aloud to himself. "Maybe I can control this...I'll call Stiller...yeah...maybe Alex can..."

"Maybe Alex can WHAT?" O'Brien asked.

"MAYBE she can help me control your mess! If Stiller realizes that I am close to Alex, well..." The congressman let out a disgusted sigh. John Merrow walked to Christopher O'Brien and put his nose against the congressman's. "You wanted into this hit parade," he said menacingly, "so start marching in step. Car accidents are nothing."

***

"I have never seen Alex like this," Barb laughed with delight.

Cassidy rolled her eyes playfully. "Yeah...she'll sleep tonight."

Barb smiled watching out the kitchen window as Alex loaded Nick's truck with bags, boxes and tools. "She really dragged you all of those places?" Barb asked in amazement.

Cassidy let out a somewhat exhausted sigh and plopped in a chair with her Diet Coke. "And then some."

"And then some what?" Rose asked entering the room and taking a seat next to her daughter.

"Where have you been?" the teacher asked curiously.

"Did I forget to get my hall pass?" Rose joked, receiving a light slap from her daughter. "What did YOU do today?"

"Shopped. And Shopped. And shopped some more."

"I can't believe it," Barb remarked shaking her head. "Alex and Nick both hate to shop, for anything. The only time Alex ever shops is for Cat."

"Yeah...well we spent a good hour in the comic book store," Cassidy remarked. "But then we had to find the perfect comforter, the perfect lamp, the perfect desk and the perfect paint color to create the Batcave." Cassidy smiled thinking about how the agent was so determined to make Dylan's room perfect.

The last few days had been hard on them all. Seeing her lover so happy was worth it. No matter how much Cassidy protested, she loved it.

"Dylan won't leave that room Saturday for the party," Rose offered.

"Tell me," Cassidy agreed.

"You are in so much trouble," Barb said sitting across from her friend.

"What do you mean?" Cassidy asked.

"If she's like this now, imagine if you two ever have a baby." Cassidy nearly choked on her drink. Rose just lifted an eyebrow at her. "I'm just saying," Barb lifted her hands with a giggle.

Alex walked in from the back door and snuck up behind the teacher, "talking about me?" she asked leaning over Cassidy's shoulder. Again, Cassidy choked on her drink. Alex snickered, "guess that's my answer." She kissed the teacher's head and pulled out a chair.

"Busy day?" Rose asked the agent mischievously.

"Expensive day," Cassidy chimed.

Alex shot a teasing look of warning to her lover. "We got a lot done," Alex said. "Now, Cass can do the rest."

"The rest of what?" Cassidy asked.

Alex shrugged. "You have to get stuff for the party, right?" Cassidy covered her face with her hands. "Well?"

"I'm getting that tether," Cassidy said bluntly to the agent. Alex just shrugged again.

"What tether?" Barb asked.

"Come on....I have to do some things tomorrow....You three can go together. You all LOVE to shop," Alex said.

"Ummm," Cassidy replied. "What THINGS do you have to do?"

"Just THINGS." Alex looked at the woman she loved. They sat smiling at each other across the table, Cassidy lightly shaking her head but with great affection for the agent's antics.

Rose and Barb tried to conceal their amusement with the banter. Alex and Cassidy were adorable. Rose had never seen her daughter so happy and Barb had never seen the agent so excited about anything. It was almost impossible to believe that either had suffered through any ordeal. "All right," Barb finally interrupted the moment. "I am voting pizza tonight. You two made me tired. Too tired to cook."

Cassidy laughed and then looked at her friend. "No, I'll take care of dinner tonight," she got up and patted Barb's shoulder. "We'll go get what I need. Alex and I can pick the boys up on our way back." Alex looked at the teacher a bit surprised. "Well, come on," Cassidy offered her hand to the agent who stared at her blankly. "Let's go, Alfred–time to carry those bags."

"Yeah… you said Christmas," Alex replied grumpily but dutifully followed her lover.

"And I meant it," Cassidy replied as Alex followed her out the door leaving Rose and Barb to shake their heads and laugh.

***

"Why the hell did he keep that on him?" Claire Brackett threw her jacket across the room in frustration and slammed her keys on the side table. "Dammit, Carl!" The tall redhead stormed across her living room and plopped down onto the large circular chair that sat in its corner. She looked at the cell phone in her hand and groaned. "Shit." Letting out a heavy sigh of irritation she reluctantly made the call.

The voice on the end of the line was gruff. "Don't tell me what I DON'T want to know, Claire." The redhead remained silent. "You actually got him credentials?" The silence persisted. "Jesus Christ, Claire!"

"Those were my orders."

"Your what? On whose authority?" the voice bellowed.

"It doesn't matter. They were DOD orders," she answered. "I assumed that you would know."

"How exactly did you assume that? I told you to FIND him... You were WITH him."

"I had orders."

"From your father?" John Merrow felt a headache mounting. "Well, your father is not running this operation anymore, Claire."

"Neither are you, apparently," was her glib reply.

"I will deal with that. Now...you have NEW *orders*."

"What's that, then?" she asked.

"Christopher O'Brien," the president said.

"What about the congressman? Another mishap?" she smiled.

"No," Merrow answered. "I want you to use your *special* talents."

"Which talents are those?" Brackett asked seductively.

"Those. I want you to get close...keep him *occupied*. Watch him closely and keep him OUT of his ex-wife's affairs."

"What is it with you and Toles?"

The president rubbed his face and attempted to calm himself. "This is not about Agent Toles, Claire. Stiller is balking on that resolution. Krause is in France....and Stiller's motivation is O'Brien's stupidity when it comes to Cassidy.....I thought you liked the congressman," he said mockingly.

"Um...he has a, well....He has his purse; doesn't he?"

John Merrow smiled. "Christopher O'Brien has never been accused of loyalty...to anyone but himself. Get close."

"And then?"

"We have to regain control. I have to be in California this weekend for an event. Do whatever you have to. I want this thing moving in the right direction before I get back."

"It IS your ass," she said with mock concern.

"Watch it Claire. You're confidence if misplaced. You have assets on the line too. Don't think Daddy can protect you...and don't think people aren't watching, both of us." He hung up.

Claire Brackett looked at the phone in her hands again and rolled her eyes. She made her way to the kitchen and opened a bottle of Chardonnay. After pouring herself a large glass she made herself comfortable back in the large chair; draping her leg over the side and sipping the wine. Licking her lips she placed another call. "Congressman. Yes...I think perhaps we have some things to discuss.....Oh...I'm sure you'll find we have far more in common than you think....Tomorrow at eight? Ummm...Are you up to....it? Good. I'll look forward to it."

***

"You're not going running this morning?" Cassidy asked rolling over in the bed to see Alex putting on her jeans.

"Good morning," Alex smiled.

"Yes. It is," Cassidy raised an eyebrow. "So...why no morning run?"

"I told you," Alex answered sitting down to put on a pair of sneakers, "I have things to do."

"Yes...you did. BUT, you still didn't tell me what those things are."

Alex walked over to the bed and smiled at her lover. She tucked a strand of hair behind Cassidy's ear and studied the face before her. "You are beautiful."

"You," Cassidy smiled, "are avoiding the question."

"Umm...maybe I am," Alex kissed the teacher's cheek.

"What are you up to?"

"Nothing...You don't want to sit in an empty house and wait for furniture to be delivered, do you?" Cassidy pursed her lips. She didn't, that was true, but she knew there was more to this than just waiting for furniture. "I have a couple of things I want to do there is all."

"Alex....you know it doesn't have to be perfect for Saturday."

"I know."

The teacher looked at the agent skeptically. "I hope you do know."

"I do." Alex wanted to change the subject. "So, what are you thinking for Dylan's party?"

The teacher was beginning to understand that this was a losing battle. Alex was excited about the house and Cassidy was touched by her lover's desire to make everything special for her and for Dylan. It was clear that the agent was on a different sort of mission and Cassidy needed to roll with it now. "What were you thinking?" the teacher asked.

"About?"

"About Dylan's party?" Alex's face lit up and she looked at Cassidy in disbelief. "Well?" Cassidy asked.

"Superheroes...and THEN he can see his room," Alex answered.

Cassidy smiled and patted the bed for Alex to sit beside her. "Do you have any idea how adorable you can be?" Cassidy asked, feeling an overwhelming sense of gratefulness for the woman beside her.

"Really? Adorable?" Alex asked playfully.

"I'm surprised you don't want to make the master into Wayne Manor, though," the teacher laughed.

"Well...you are the mistress of the house...so the master is yours."

"Really? I kind of prefer butlers."

"Oh, well that's good, because you know...I've spent my life in service," Alex winked.

"Ummm...Always something to be thankful for," Cassidy said receiving a kiss on the forehead from the agent.

"I'll see you tonight," Alex smiled.

"Yes, you will."

"I love you, Cass."

"I love you too, Alex." The agent made her way out the door. "What are you up to Agent Toles?" Cassidy began to muse when an excited boy jumped into view. "Hi sweetie," Cassidy said as Dylan made his way to the bed. "Did you see Alex?"

"Yep," he said snuggling against his mother. "Uncle Nick is taking me to see ships today."

"I know. I heard," Cassidy said ruffling her son's hair.

"Alex says that some of those ships are older than Grandma."

Cassidy chuckled. "Much older, and I wouldn't share that with Grandma; I don't think."

"Mom?'

"Yes, sweetie."

"Can we stay here?"

Cassidy looked at the boy and bit her lip. "Well, we are going to be here all week, Dylan."

"I know," he said looking down.

"Don't you miss your friends?" He shrugged. "You like it here." He nodded. "I know you do. And, you know you will get to see lots more of Cat and Nick and Barb soon."

"'Cause Alex is gonna live with us," he said.

"Yes." Cassidy smiled.

"For good?" he asked.

"I hope so, Dylan; yes."

Dylan put his head against Cassidy's shoulder. "So....can Alex..." he stopped.

"What, honey? Can Alex what?" He nestled a little closer but didn't answer. Cassidy took a deep breath. "Dylan, what is it you want to know about Alex?"

"Well," he began shyly, "Alex can't be my dad." Cassidy closed her eyes and took in his statement. It was clear that Dylan was hurt by his father. He had not wanted to visit his father unless it was just for the day and in New York where Cassidy was close by. When he did have to spend longer periods away, he would cry for hours the night before leaving. Cassidy had to reassure him constantly. It wasn't until Alex came into their lives that the teacher discovered why. The reality that the congressman paid little attention to his son did not surprise his mother. Cassidy had fought that battle from the time Dylan was born. She had always hoped Dylan would bring them closer together but the opposite happened. It only served to pull the congressman and Cassidy farther apart. She listened closely as her son continued; knowing that he too had found something in Alex that he didn't know he was missing until she appeared. "...and she can't be my mom....you are my mom," he said. There was a touch of sadness in his voice. "And Alfred is Batman's so...."

Cassidy stopped him. "Dylan, Alex loves you very much."

"I know."

"And you want Alex to be like your dad...or like me." He nodded. "That's all right, sweetie."

He looked at his mother and Cassidy could see that he was afraid of hurting her feelings. "Dylan," Cassidy sat up and pulled the small boy to face her. She touched his cheek and smiled. "No matter what you call Alex, Alex will still be your parent....just like me and just like your dad." He looked at her hopefully. "So, whatever you and Alex decide...whatever you want to call Alex...Whether it's Alex or Alfred or I don't know... Po the Panda," he giggled. "No matter what you call her; she'll still be *your* Alex." He looked at his mother still a bit leery. Cassidy thought about her student, James, and the essay he wrote. She smiled. Dylan might always call Alex by her name but he needed to know that he could refer to Alex in whatever way made him feel comfortable. "And, I think whatever you decide is great, even if someday you want to call Alex your mom too. Okay?" He hugged his mother's neck tightly and Cassidy felt her heart swell. "I love you, Dylan."

"You're the best mom," he said affectionately as Cassidy felt a tear roll down her cheek.

"And you are the best Speed Racer. Why are you a Speed Racer?" Cassidy asked lightheartedly and with genuine curiosity.

"Easy. Speed's fast and cool like me."

Cassidy laughed. 'Another Alexism,' she silently thought. "All right then, Speed… let's see how fast you can get ready for breakfast." He hopped off the bed and ran toward the door.

"Mom?"

"Yes, sweetie?"

"Are we having cereal?"

Cassidy snickered. "Ummm....Why do you ask?" He shrugged. "How about pancakes?" Dylan nodded his approval and skipped off. "Too much milk," Cassidy chuckled to herself.

***

"*Il n'a pas le contrôle de la situation* (he does not have control of the situation)," a dark haired man sitting at the table said.

Jonathan Krause smiled. "Ahh….Andre. American politics are complicated. We always…."

The man stopped the statement abruptly, "*40 millions euros dans cette affaire, une Krause. Nous ne pouvons nous permettre d'interférence* (forty million euros in this one deal, Krause. We cannot afford interference)."

"You want assurances?"

A tall fair-haired man stood from his seat and walked toward Jonathan Krause. He smiled as he reached the American. "My friend," he said, "the message must be clear. If he cannot control this than we must control it."

"And how should we control it?"

The man narrowed his gaze and leaned into the handsome CIA agent. "You find someone who can," he whispered.

Jonathan Krause felt a rare chill travel down his spine. He stood tall and firm and clenched his jaw slightly. "What you suggest requires an opportunity."

"*Ensuite, nous allons créer* (Then we will create it)," the man said.

***

It was well past eleven o'clock when Cassidy heard the garage door close. Nick had spent the afternoon and evening at the new house with Alex but he had arrived home hours earlier; extremely tight lipped about the efforts. "Hey," Cassidy greeted the agent as she walked into the living room. Alex looked exhausted as she walked toward the small blonde woman. The agent sat down beside Cassidy on the couch where the teacher had been curled up with a book waiting. "You look like hell," Cassidy smiled.

"Ummm," Alex groaned a bit and Cassidy noticed she was wincing.

"Your back?" Alex didn't answer. "How bad?" The agent forced a smile. "Did you take anything?" No reply. "Alex...."

"It's okay," Alex said softly.

"No. It's not okay. Can you make it up the stairs?" Alex looked at Cassidy helplessly and somewhat embarrassed. "MMM," Cassidy shook her head and stood up. "All right. Stay right there for a minute."

"Where are you going?" Alex called after the woman.

"Just sit there," Cassidy called back.

"I don't have much choice," Alex grumbled.

"No, you don't," a voice answered as Cassidy entered the kitchen. The agent couldn't help but grin at the realization that Cassidy could hear a pin drop across the house. It was hard to hide anything from her lover. The agent moved gingerly and tried to bend over to untie her shoes when she felt a presence above her. "And...you would be doing what now?" Cassidy asked. Alex looked up at her with apologetic eyes. Cassidy had already learned that Alex became very quiet when she was in real physical pain. The agent was stubborn and pushed herself, but it was clear to the teacher that right now, her lover was in more agony than she was willing to share. "Take these," Cassidy handed Alex some pain reliever and water and knelt down to start untying Alex's sneakers.

"Cass, you don't have to..."

Before Alex could finish her thought, her sneakers were off and Cassidy was gently lifting Alex's feet onto the couch and helping her move into a more comfortable position. The teacher grabbed a throw pillow, put it behind the agent's head and helped her lie down. "Why didn't you call me?" Cassidy asked, running her fingers through Alex's hair.

"I was okay until I got in the car."

"Alex...you need to be careful."

"I'm okay," the agent smiled at her lover's touch. "I'm just tired."

"Well," Cassidy covered the agent with a blanket, "close your eyes and go to sleep."

"I don't want to sleep without you," Alex said almost like a small child.

The teacher smiled and kissed Alex's forehead. "Go to sleep."

"You..."

Cassidy smiled. "I'm right here...go to sleep." Alex struggled to stay awake. Her back was beginning to relax but it was sore and stiff and her eyelids would not cooperate. Cassidy watched as the strong, beautiful woman she loved gradually transformed into what looked like a peaceful sleeping child. "Je t'adore, my love," she whispered placing a tender kiss on the woman's cheek. "I never knew I could love anyone so much," she said softly as she made her way to the far end of the couch and lifted the agent's feet onto her lap. The truth was that Cassidy was still struggling with nightmares of her own and being close to Alex made her feel safe. "I couldn't sleep without you if I tried," she admitted aloud and stretched out to join her lover in sleep.

***

"Admiral....I understand....but this situation..."

"Jonathan...our friends in France are not wrong. I spoke to Edmond last night. I understand and this is not the course

441

any of us wanted but Ivanov is spooked. And, I just heard from the British Prime Minister. We have to get control back...send a message." Rear Admiral William Brackett was a large man with a commanding presence. At sixty-seven, he had spent the better part of his life in service to his country; much of that engineering delicate and intricate invasions and covert operations in Southeast Asia. He had served as an adviser to several presidents and was widely regarded within the intelligence community as a genius. When he spoke, people listened.

Krause took a deep breath. He was not looking forward to this next question. "Admiral...your daughter..."

"Yes, Jonathan?"

"She provided Carl Fisher with FBI clearance...Where would she get that?"

"From me."

This was the answer that Krause had expected and that he had hoped he would not get. "Why, Sir?"

"It's not always as simple as we would like, Jonathan. You know that. Edward Fisher was a good friend."

Krause stroked his jaw, "and so is John Merrow."

"That's true. But this is not my choice and it's not yours. I stalled this with O'Brien, made him the fall guy. That won't work again."

Jonathan Krause sighed. "When?"

"Saturday."

"Who?" Krause asked receiving silence at the other end.

"It has to be believable," the admiral answered.

"Very well...I will make the call.... Sir?"

"Yes, Jonathan?"

"About your daughter...."

William Brackett smiled. He adored his daughter but she frequently challenged his patience as well. Her affair with John Merrow had been ill advised as was her seduction of the FBI agent. "She's been sent to O'Brien."

"Is that really...."

The admiral nodded his agreement on the other end of the phone. "You take care of business...I will take care of Claire."

Krause hung up his phone and sat on the bench in the airport. He felt the spiral, a dangerous spiral. Nothing could go wrong now or everything would likely be lost, everything.

***

Alex woke up and still felt a bit groggy. She looked around and realized she had never made it to bed. As the room came into focus she saw that Cassidy was sleeping sitting up at the far end of the couch. Carefully, Alex maneuvered her legs out from under the teacher's grasp and got to her feet. Softly, Alex guided the smaller woman onto the couch and pulled the blanket over her. Cassidy grumbled slightly but then just shifted, never opening her eyes. "*Je vais passer ma vie à vous rendre heureux* (I will spend my life making you happy)," Alex whispered, planting a light kiss on her lover's cheek. The agent quietly headed up the stairs and peeked in Cat's room to see Dylan sprawled across the bed. She smiled. He was so much like his mother.

"What are you doing?" a voice whispered.

Alex turned to see the smiling face of her sister-in-law, "hey."

"You okay? Didn't hear you come in," Barb said shutting the boys' door.

"Yeah...Cass is on the couch." Barb looked concerned. "No, no...I was a little stiff last night when I got home."

"I'll bet," Barb said. "You know she doesn't expect..." Alex shrugged and smiled. "You are very lucky, Alex."

"I know," the agent said. "She's been through too much. They both have. I just...I want her to feel safe. To be happy."

"Well, I don't think you have much to worry about there. I'm going to go start some coffee. Are you going back to..."

"Yeah, can you keep her busy today?"

"She's going to be more than a little suspicious you know," Barb warned the agent.

"Fallon's coming. You know he's been in New York all week…so it's perfect."

"So you're meeting Brian?"

"Yeah…he's going to update me…and I have him bringing some things from the house in New York."

Barb shook her head. "You are too much, Alex. I think I can find something to occupy the Mrs."

"The what?"

Barb was already at the top of the stairs. "Oh, you heard me Alexis…don't even try to deny it." Alex laughed. Being accused of having Cassidy as a wife was hardly an insult. 'I should be so lucky,' the agent thought.

Chapter Twenty-Seven

"So, you're driving down to meet Agent Toles?" Detective Ferro asked.

"Yeah," Fallon answered placing some pictures into a box.

"About the case?" Brian Fallon looked at his friend and nodded. "What? Are you worried about telling her what we found?"

"No…it's not that. She wasn't surprised at the two shooter theory," Fallon admitted.

"Well, I didn't think she would be, but I didn't think she'd be happy about it either."

Fallon shrugged. "Toles…well she sees things, you know?"

"Yeah…she wasn't always FBI, was she?" the detective guessed.

"No…..but I don't know much about that. She has connections, powerful ones. I have a feeling this visit is about something else…not ballistics," Fallon said somewhat sadly.

"It's hard to lose a good partner," Ferro said. He guessed the thoughts in his friend's mind.

"Yeah, well…I knew she was planning on a move when she came down Monday. I have a feeling it's not just a change in field offices."

"Leaving the bureau, you think?"

Fallon nodded. "I do. She doesn't trust Tate."

"Why should she?"

"I know…I just wonder what we are into here," Fallon said.

"Nothing good," Pete Ferro chuckled soliciting a slight grin from his friend. "Look, Fallon...you're probably better off out of it."

"Yeah." Fallon continued gathering the things that Alex had asked him to bring. He grabbed the final box and walked out the front door, Pete Ferro following. "Thing is," Fallon said opening his trunk, "I'm not sure I want to be out of it."

Ferro nodded his understanding. "You know this is..."

"Yeah I do," Fallon said. "That son of a bitch O'Brien has something to do with all of this."

"Well, you let me know if I can help." Fallon shook the detective's hand. "You headed home after this? I mean not much left to wrap up here since we've had the lid shut on us."

"No, I'm actually taking next week off. Kate's coming with the kids tomorrow for a long weekend. Alex asked me to go to Dylan's birthday party on Saturday. Seems important to her.... Hell, least I can do. Plus, Kate loves Alex and she's driving me nuts every night about Cassidy," he laughed. Alex and Kate had become fairly close when Fallon was injured and his wife was more than a little bit curious about all the changes in his partner's life. "Listen, Pete, thanks for calling in that favor. How did you know they would rig the ballistics?"

"Well, I'd say call it a hunch, but truth is I've seen it before, a few times. You make connections," the detective conceded. "Just be careful, Brian," Ferro said as Fallon stepped into the driver's seat of his sedan. "O'Brien's a weasel...he's not the wolf."

"I will."

"Tell Toles..."

Fallon knew the sentiment his friend would share. Ferro liked Alex Toles and he respected her. Whatever she needed now, she had a friend in the NYPD. He smiled, "I will."

***

"I'm glad that Brian is coming to see Alex," Cassidy said.

Barb tried to suppress her grin, knowing that Agent Fallon was meeting Alex at the new house and not out for lunch somewhere. When Alex set her mind on something there was no deterring her. She wondered what Cassidy would think when Alex unveiled her surprise. The agent had already made all the arrangements she needed for her plan. Dylan would come to the party with Nick and Cat, and Barb and Rose would come over to the house early Saturday to help get ready. Tomorrow night would be all about Cassidy and Saturday all about Dylan. No amount of back pain or even the limited hours in a day were going to stop Alex. "I suppose it's silly doing this now," she said looking at a bedding set for a crib.

"What's that?" Cassidy asked.

"Looking at baby things," Barb admitted.

"I don't think so," the teacher smiled.

"It's just nice to have someone to do it with, you know? When Cat was on the way...well with my mother being gone... and you know Nick and shopping, he basically said *you buy it; I'll build it*," Barb laughed.

"So can I ask? Are you hoping for a boy or a girl, or does it not matter?"

Barb shrugged. "The politically correct answer or the truth?"

"Truth, PLEASE...I have had enough political anything for one lifetime," Cassidy rolled her eyes.

"Well...truth, I would love a little girl...but either way. What about you?"

"Me?"

"Oh, come on....I see your eyes in here."

Cassidy smiled. It would be a lie to say she didn't think about more children and it would be a lie to say Alex didn't make her want that more. Having Barb was wonderful. Babies were not something she intended to discuss with Alex in such a new relationship. "Maybe someday," she said softly.

"I would think so," Barb winked.

Cassidy blushed. "Barb? I'd really like to get Alex something…you know for the house. She is turning herself inside out to make it perfect for Dylan and me. I know she's up to something."

"Ummm…she loves you….And don't look at me, she's only let me know a VERY little bit and she has Nick sworn in some crazy childhood oath to secrecy. She figures you'll milk it outta' me," She was delighted to see Alex so happy and excited to have Alex and Cassidy moving closer. Family had been lacking and somehow it seemed that void was now closing for them all.

"I know, but it isn't my house, it's our house…it's just that she's just not…."

Barb understood. Alex was not a materialistic person. "Into things? No, she never has been."

Cassidy sighed. "I know…it's one of the reasons I love her so much."

"I can see that," Barb poked her friend. "Have anything in mind?"

"Only one thing. She lights up whenever they are at that pool table. I thought maybe…"

"She'll love that…she's a big kid, ya' know?" Cassidy laughed. "But she'll kill you," Barb laughed.

"Well, she'll get over it. Do you think I could get one delivered Saturday afternoon during the party? She and Dylan would just flip."

Barb gloated. "Actually, one of Nick's best friends owns a billiards store in Norwich. What do you say to lunch and a short drive?" Cassidy smiled and grasped Barb's hand in thanks. She was all too aware that Alex was up to something and she wanted the move to be special for them all. Alex was not the only one who could maneuver a covert operation and Cassidy intended to prove it.

***

"Thanks, Fallon," Alex said taking a box from her friend's hands.

"Holy shit, Toles." Fallon looked around the living room. "Does she know?" Alex shook her head. "You're really doing it."

Alex nodded and motioned for Fallon to follow her into the kitchen. "First thing I bought, coffee maker...second thing I bought on my way here, Diet Coke...take your pick."

"Coke."

Alex grabbed a can from the refrigerator and leaned against the counter. "So...two shooters it is." He nodded. "Shit. Damn spooks."

"You think so?" Fallon asked receiving a shrug in response. "Alex, what the hell is O'Brien into?"

Alex let out a heavy breath. "I'm betting some kind of arms deals. What his role is...Well...he knows more than he says, but he's not in any control. The accident proves that."

"So..."

Alex nodded. "I told Taylor I'm coming back. I'm going to call Tate Monday."

"Did you tell Cassidy?"

"I told her I was thinking about it. I hadn't decided until this morning when Taylor called. He was cryptic, careful. Said that there were some things that concerned him, connections, but that they would hold until next week."

"What do you think that means?"

"Don't know. I'll worry about it next week. This is way beyond the bureau, Fallon. Way beyond."

"Alex...what did..."

The female agent sighed. "I've worked on a lot of things, Fallon, a lot. Mostly investigating connections between people in our government, foreign businesses and intelligence. That's how I knew about your investigations into the laundering. I've worked with the Russians, the French, the Iraqis, the Israelis and MI6. It's deeply imbedded. I suspect that's what Taylor is afraid of…that it goes deeper than we once thought."

Fallon sighed. "Alex…I don't want to let it go."

"I knew you'd say that," she smiled. "Let's talk next week…. there are options….but now, I need to get THIS finished."

"Looks pretty finished," Fallon laughed. Alex smiled broader than Fallon could remember. He wondered how in a few days life could be transformed so radically. Just four days ago they were on a plane praying for Cassidy's safety. It seemed a lifetime ago now. "What about the stuff in New York?"

"Well, there's still things to settle, like school and…Well, Cassidy has to tell O'Brien."

"That'll go over well," Fallon rolled his eyes.

Alex shrugged. "He holds no cards. Let him do whatever he wants."

"Did you tell Dylan yet?" Alex shook her head. "Really?"

"Gonna' surprise him," Alex winked.

"Who are you?" Fallon laughed.

"Well…actually, Fallon, I've been wondering who I was."

"I just hope you know what you are getting into," he conceded. Alex looked at him with concern. "I don't mean Cassidy," he explained. "I mean this case."

"It's what I do, Fallon." He nodded. "I need to know," Alex said. "And I can promise you I will find out and when I do…. The person or the people that hurt Cassidy; they will spend a lifetime wishing they never met me."

***

"Hey," a voice called softly.

"When did you get home?" Cassidy turned to see the agent standing behind her looking tired but smiling.

"Just now. Is Dylan still up?" Alex asked hopefully.

A smile was followed by a shake of the head, "but I am sure he's still awake."

"I don't want to…"

Cassidy looked at Alex and searched her eyes. "Go…he missed you."

"I missed you," Alex confessed, kissing the teacher's forehead.

"Did you?" Cassidy asked sweetly. Alex sighed. "Go up and see him," Cassidy encouraged the agent. "Did you eat?" Alex shook her head and received a slight roll of the teacher's eyes. "Go see Dylan. I'll fix you something."

Alex made her way up the stairs slowly. She was tired and the stress of the week had finally begun to show on her. After Fallon had left for the evening, Alex started putting up pictures of Dylan and Cassidy from the house in New York. She came across one picture of Cassidy alone at the beach. The wind was blowing the teacher's hair back and she was squinting just slightly against the blowing sand. She held the picture for a long time, just looking at it. Cassidy was so beautiful. Alex suddenly realized how close she came to losing the woman she loved. It was a thought she had not allowed herself until that moment and she fell to the floor, tears pouring from her eyes and an agonizing stabbing sensation in her chest. The agent closed her eyes and tried to breathe, quieting her pain. She opened her eyes and looked again at the smiling face that she had placed in her lap and gradually felt love take hold again.

The eyes looking at her from behind the glass seemed to be speaking silently to her. Alex finished a few remaining tasks and placed the rest of the boxes Fallon had brought aside in the garage. This would be home and there would be time. It would never be perfect. She could not erase the fear or the pain that Cassidy and Dylan had felt, or even her own, not with paint or property. It would help. It might even bring some real happiness, but to heal; that required them to be together, not apart. Home was wherever they were together and that was not here, not yet. The agent made her way up the stairs and gently pulled the door to the boys' room open. Cat waved and Dylan sat up and stared at her. "Hey Cat," Alex called.

"Hi Aunt Alex."

"Hey there. How are you, Speed?" Alex smiled. The small boy just smiled back silently as Alex took a seat next to him on the bottom bunk. "How was your day?" He shrugged. Alex took a deep breath and nodded. She had barely seen him the last two days. "Did you go out with Grandma?" The agent tried to start a conversation. He nodded and then looked down. She sat for a few minutes wondering what the right thing to say was. "I'm sorry I wasn't home, Speed. BUT…think about it like this, pretty soon you'll be sick of me," she winked.

Dylan looked up at the agent and she noticed he was struggling with his tears. "Aww, Speed…What's wrong?" He shrugged. "I'm sorry, Dylan."

"Alex," he whispered.

"Yeah, buddy?"

"I don't want you to leave."

"Dylan, I'm not leaving. I just had some things to do. You know…somebody's birthday is this Saturday; and, can I tell you a secret?" He nodded. "I'm kinda' trying to surprise your mom with something," she whispered.

"Can I help?" he asked hopefully.

"Actually, Dylan, you can."

"Really?"

"Yeah…you can make sure all of your things are together tomorrow morning after breakfast."

"Are we going home?" He hung his head.

Alex took a deep breath. She had already changed her plans and she didn't want to give away the whole surprise. "We're not going back to New York, no." He looked at Alex curiously. "It's a surprise," she winked. Finally, he smiled. "Okay, Speed?"

"Alex?"

"Yes, Dylan?"

"Are you gonna' be my mom too? Mom said you can, if I want you to." Alex couldn't move. Dylan was so sweet and so honest. Her heart was suddenly in her throat and she wasn't certain what to say.

The agent had been gone longer than a usual good night warranted and Cassidy had crept up the stairs to see what was going on. She had just reached the doorway when Dylan finished his question. Alex faltered, afraid and unsure how she should answer. "Dylan, your mom…"

Cassidy had not had a chance to tell the agent about her conversation with Dylan the day before. Alex's back pain and then her flying off so she could catch up with Fallon had prevented that discussion. She bit her bottom lip as she watched and then decided to intervene. "Mom thinks that whatever makes you both happy is all that matters," Cassidy nodded to Alex.

Alex took a deep breath. "Why do you ask that Dylan?"

He shrugged. "'Cause," he hesitated and she leaned into him. "Cat said you can't be."

Alex rolled her eyes. "I did not!" Cat called from above, still awake and listening. "I just said she's just Alex. You have a mom and a dad. That's all I said."

"It's okay, Cat," Cassidy said softly as she made her way to Dylan and Alex.

"What do you want, Dylan?" Alex asked.

"Well…I kinda' want to call you Alex," he admitted, clearly feeling badly about the truth.

Alex smiled with relief. "Well, that's good because that's my name," she chuckled.

He looked at his mother and then at the agent and his voice became a whisper, "but I still want you to be my mom too."

Cassidy closed her eyes. His innocent proclamation overwhelmed her. He loved Alex. She loved Alex. Everything in all of their lives had changed so suddenly and yet it felt so familiar somehow. Alex put her hand on the boy's back as her own tears threatened to surface. "That's even cooler than being your Alfred, Dylan." He looked at her and grinned. "Who wouldn't want Speed Racer for a son," she winked.

"Yeah 'cause I'm fast and..."

"Cool," they said in unison to Cassidy's amusement. He sprang up a bit like a jack in the box and hugged the agent's neck. "I'll be ready," he whispered in her ear.

Alex smiled and looked at the boy. Her eyes grew a bit darker with emotion and she spoke deliberately and quietly. "Thank you, Dylan." He just smiled. Alex felt Cassidy's hand tenderly stroke her back. "Okay...into bed, Speed." He complied with a jump and Alex covered him lightly. She leaned into his ear and spoke so softly he had to lean closer to hear her. "You are the coolest son any one could ever have, Speed. I love you."

Dylan beamed. He looked at his mother, his eyes brighter than she had ever seen. Then he looked back to the woman he had only barely met, who somehow captured his imagination, his trust and his heart. "I love you, Alex." She winked again as her lips curled into a knowing smile.

"I love you, Mom," he said to his mother.

Cassidy moved in and kissed his forehead. "Love you too, Dylan...get some sleep."

"YEAH!" He cried out a bit louder than he meant to. "Surprises tomorrow!"

Cassidy cocked her head at the agent who answered only by opening her eyes a little wider and giving a shrug. "Ummm...I see," Cassidy chuckled. "Okay...good night boys."

"Good night," two voices answered as Alex led Cassidy from the room.

"Surprises tomorrow, huh?" Cassidy tipped her head and pursed her lips in amusement.

Alex sighed. "Come on," she said leading Cassidy toward the room they shared.

"Don't you want to eat?" Cassidy asked.

Alex shook her head. "No. I just want to be with you for a while."

Cassidy continued forward, following the agent through the door of their room. "Alex, are you okay? I mean with Dylan…"

"Just surprised."

The teacher walked to the agent and looked up into her eyes. Alex was tired and Cassidy could see the exhaustion. "You need some sleep," she said. The agent took a deep breath and kept her gaze on the striking green eyes that could captivate her in an instant. Affectionately, the agent lifted a hand to the smaller woman's cheek and brushed it lightly with her thumb. With her other hand she pulled Cassidy closer to her. "Alex?" Cassidy saw tears forming in the strong agent's eyes and she felt the firmness in her grip.

"I don't want us to be apart another day." Cassidy searched the agent for her meaning. "I almost lost you, Cassidy. I can't make that go away with a house, not with a…"

Cassidy took in a deep breath and released it. "No, you can't," she said gently. Her nightmares were still vivid and she dreaded the night.

"Tomorrow, I want to take you and Dylan…I want to tell him…"

"Alex…you were so excited…"

The agent stopped her lover's thought. "It will still be a surprise. No more secrets, Cass, not even little ones, not now. I just want to be with you both tomorrow, alone…spend the day…"

"You don't need to convince me," Cassidy smiled letting her hands caress the agent's back. "I just wonder what changed."

"Nothing, really," Alex said. She closed her eyes. "I just looked around and realized you weren't there. I want you there."

Cassidy grinned and stretched to kiss her lover. "You surprise me, Agent Toles."

"Yeah?" Alex asked. Cassidy nodded. "Well," Alex began, "I have to tell you something"

"What?"

"No secrets," Alex said firmly.

"No. What is it?" Cassidy asked.

"I'm going back to the NSA, Cass."

Cassidy closed her eyes and licked her lips. She was afraid of losing Alex too. "Is it…"

"Cass…I really am good at what I do. I need to keep you and Dylan safe…"

"I thought you said…"

Alex set out to clarify her meaning. "You are safe. But, I mean from…"

Cassidy leaned her head into Alex's chest and mumbled the name, "from Chris."

Alex swallowed hard. "From whatever he is into, Cass."

Cassidy pulled back slightly. "Are you sure that's what you want to do?"

"I am."

The blonde nodded her understanding and then took a deep breath. "Okay…no secrets, right?"

"No." Alex smiled.

"I went baby shopping with Barb."

Alex laughed. "That's a secret? I mean I know I am not sup-posed to know yet…but…"

"No," Cassidy giggled uncomfortably. "It made me think about it."

Alex smiled seeing Cassidy's apprehension in sharing her feelings. "Oh… Hum…"

"What?" Cassidy said nervously.

Alex laughed. "Cass, you already told me you want more children."

"Yeah but that was just in a…"

The agent kissed the teacher and let her kiss linger. She pulled away slowly. "You can tell me anything, Cassidy."

"I know," she answered sheepishly.

"Hey…" Alex lifted the teacher's face. "Vanilla cake first. Okay?" Alex winked.

Cassidy laughed. "You and your cake."

"Yeah well, I like cake."

"Alex, I…."

"Cass…no secrets. I love you. The only thing that scares me is losing you. That's all. We'll get there, past all of this…we will."

"I know," Cassidy answered looking at the agent. "But…. this is all so new…I never want you to feel like I am…"

Cassidy amazed Alex in every moment. The agent couldn't remember if she'd been with the woman a day or a lifetime now. Life before Cassidy was empty for Alex, in so many ways. She wondered who she was then. Now, she felt a part of something bigger. Being with her brother and Barb, watching Dylan and wanting to share the deepest parts of herself with this woman; it wasn't a choice. Alex didn't care what anyone thought. This was where she belonged and this was the life she had now. There was nothing she would deny the woman. She would move heaven and earth just to see Cassidy smile. "*Je vais passer le reste de ma vie en vous faisant plaisir* (I will spend the rest of my life making you happy)." Alex kissed the woman in her arms. "Come sleep with me. Let me hold you," she said tenderly.

Cassidy was breathless at the words as they fell from the agent's lips. She laid down beside the agent and let her head rest softly on Alex's chest. "Je t'adore," she promised.

"And I adore you," Alex smiled. She didn't care about anything other than holding Cassidy close and letting the world fall away.

"Alex?"

"Hum?"

"Don't ever let me go," Cassidy's voice was shaky, partly from her love for Alex and partly in fear of the dreams to come.

Strong arms gently pulled Cassidy even closer. If anyone understood the power of nightmares it was Alex Toles. "Never, Cass. I'll be right here, I promise. *Je vaisvous garder en sécurité, toujours. Je t'aime.* (I will keep you safe, always. I love you). No nightmares tonight, dream about tomorrow." Alex felt Cassidy release a breath in contentment and she closed her eyes. Tomorrow was a day Alex had never imagined and she couldn't wait for it to arrive now.

***

"What is it that you want, Agent Brackett?" Christopher O'Brien asked.

"Hummm…I'd say we have a lot more in common than you think," she breathed in his ear.

"How is that?" he asked.

"Ohhh…Well, neither of us likes rejection," she admitted. "And, both of us tend to cause…Oh, well, what would you call it? *Tension* in others," she cooed.

"And you think you and I can change that somehow?" he asked as he felt the woman's breath on his neck.

"I think I am quite adept at relieving tension," she offered.

"And, why would you want to do that?" He continued as his breath became shallower.

"Mutual interests should always be explored," Claire Brackett suggested. "Alliances are crucial in our work, Congressman."

"Are you suggesting, sleeping with the enemy, Agent?"

"Are you my enemy, Congressman?" She looked at him directly and saw the twinkle in his eye. "Ummmm….That's what I thought. Like me, whatever you need to be. I think it's time we explored all of our options." Christopher O'Brien accepted the woman's kiss. Brackett smiled. Her red hair fell onto the congressman's shoulder as she nipped at his neck and breathed her final words. "Know," she whispered, "I can keep a secret….and I will discover all of yours."

***

Jonathan Krause paced the floor of his apartment. He looked at the phone lying on the coffee table, wondering whether he could will it to ring. The knot in his stomach was not customary. His entire life was meant for these moments. It's what he prepared for, what he was taught, what he was literally bred to do and there were moments that he hated it. Maintaining distance was something the man had become a master of. Only two people had ever managed to bridge that distance. One was an unlikely young woman who had, within a moment in her presence, captured a piece of him forever. The other was the brother that had steadied him, encouraged him and taught him about obedience and resolve. Not a brother by blood. A brother born of a bond even thicker than blood. A man who shared the same reality and came to embrace it long before the man pacing now. A sound pierced the silence and Krause picked up the offending party. "Krause," he answered.

"It's set."

"Where?" Krause asked.

"Inside the hall. Should be about 20:00. Give or take. Only variable."

Krause closed his eyes and shook his head. His lips were pressed so tightly together they had gone numb. "Make it clean. Do you understand?"

"Understood," the voice answered. "Expect my call."

A breath escaped the tall, muscular man standing at the center of the room; a breath he did not realize he had been holding. "Jesus Christ, John," he lifted his gaze to the ceiling. "That's the best I can do now."

***

"And…"

"He will fall in line," the redheaded woman smiled slyly.

"I am sure he will," John Merrow replied. "Be careful, Claire. Christopher O'Brien's ego may just outmatch your gifts."

"I think I can handle the congressman," she smiled tracing the rim of her glass. "It doesn't bother you?'

"What's that?" the president asked. She stared harshly at him and he chuckled. "Really, Claire? We all have our roles to play and our unique ways to play them."

"When are you leaving?" she asked.

"Early tomorrow morning."

"Another speech?"

"We need to get Senator Blare and Congresswoman Collins' support on amending this resolution. It's the only way to sway the chairman. Your new friend certainly compromised us there," he said with contempt.

"You don't like the congressman much, do you?" she observed.

"I don't trust the congressman."

"Why? Because he's ambitious?" She said with a hint of admiration.

John Merrow moved closer to the young woman. He stopped just shy of her and looked directly in her eyes, holding her gaze in a silent dialogue before offering his thoughts. "He's not just ambitious, Claire. He stands for nothing. No loyalty. He believes in nothing more than *more*. He's a dangerous kind of ambitious. The kind that destroys everything around it," he warned.

"Hummm…worried about that agent of yours?" she cooed with dripping sarcasm.

The president took a deep breath in an effort to quell the anger in his voice. "Alex can take care of herself. But, yes…I worry about where he will lead her. You don't know Alex Toles, Claire…you just think you do."

"Jealous? I'd say I know her more intimately than…."

A roaring laugh interrupted the young woman's statement. "You think a couple of rolls on the mattress with Alex is intimacy?" Merrow shook his head. "You really are foolish, Claire. I've known Alex since she was younger than you are now. I've seen her give her heart once...one time...and that is to Cassidy O'Brien." He stopped and walked a few paces to the window behind his desk, momentarily lost in thought. "Alex would die for the people she loves, for the people she trusts." His voice became a hush, "even when she has no reason to trust them." He turned and looked at Brackett. For the first time the young woman saw in the president's eyes a hint of not just concern but sadness. "She will not rest now, not after Fisher... and THAT, Claire...That is what I fear. Not for Alex Toles...for you...for me."

"You give her a great deal of credit."

He smiled and sighed. "And so should you. Keep him close. Alex will follow; it's inevitable now."

"Because of the teacher?" She rolled her eyes.

He nodded and then shook his head. "Oh, Claire...you have a lot to learn."

***

"You're what?" O'Brien screamed through the phone.

"It's not up for discussion," Cassidy answered flatly.

"This ordeal has clearly effected your judgment," he asserted.

"I agree," she answered.

"Good."

"Yes, it's made me realize that our marriage was a farce."

"Excuse me?" he asked.

"Look, Christopher. This is what I need...what Dylan needs."

"Oh to take off on some lesbian excursion?" he shot back with malice.

Cassidy just shook her head and looked out the window where Alex was putting Dylan's things in the car while Dylan told her some story with great animation. She smiled and sighed. "It's not going to work, Chris."

"What's not going to work?"

"Your guilt trip, your insults or your threats. We are moving. Not that far; but far enough away for all of us. Face it. I have. We had separate lives for our entire marriage." The congressman collapsed back in his chair. Cassidy spoke now with a quiet confidence he had not heard in many years. She felt her body become lighter as she continued. "I love Alex. Dylan loves Alex. I hope you find that, Chris. I really do. This is *my* choice." She caught Alex's gaze as the agent shut the trunk of the car and felt her heart beat slightly faster. "If you care about us at all, you'll be happy for us both."

"Cassidy…."

"It's not a debate, Christopher. The call was a courtesy. I will talk to you later this week," she watched Alex bend down to her son, smiling broadly. "I have to go. My family is waiting," she said as she hung up the call.

***

"Where are we going?" Dylan asked from the backseat.

Cassidy giggled seeing Alex's face light up. Cassidy felt the agent tossing and shifting in the bed not wanting to disturb the teacher's sleep before the sun rose. Silently, she had reveled in the knowledge that Alex was so excited she could not sleep. It felt to Cassidy as if she were somehow being reborn into a completely different life. Alex's arms were around her. They were about to go home. It was an amazing feeling much like being a child again waiting for Christmas morning. She looked at Alex now and felt a gratefulness she would never be able to express in words. "It's a surprise, Speed!" Alex grinned.

"Are we almost there?" he asked excitedly.

Cassidy laughed. "It's not that far, Dylan." She reached across the seat and rested her hand on Alex's thigh. The drive would take about an hour and right now that seemed endless for them all.

"Can we play that game?" he asked.

"What game is that?" Alex replied.

"You know...where the cars are from."

The agent smiled. "Okay, Speed...keep your eyes open for those plates." Cassidy closed her eyes and took a deep breath. "You okay?" Alex glanced over at her lover.

"No," Cassidy said. She felt Alex's expression drop. "Better than okay." Alex exhaled and turned back to the road. "MAINE!" She yelled with excitement spotting the first plate.

***

"Where are we?" Dylan asked as the car pulled into the driveway. A gray house with blue shutters stood in front of them. Green shrubbery adorned the length of a front porch. "Who lives here?" Dylan asked as Alex opened his door.

Alex looked over at the teacher as she made her way to the pair. The yard twisted to the right and was dotted by several oak trees and a small tree perfect for climbing in the front. Cassidy nodded to the agent as she placed her hands on her son's shoulders. "Well," Alex said. She bent over to meet a pair of small eyes. "*We* live here." Dylan's eyes flew open and he tilted his head back to meet his mother's smiling green eyes. Cassidy raised her eyebrow and smiled wider. "That is if you want to," Alex said. A small talkative boy was rendered speechless.

"Do you want to go inside?" Cassidy asked. He nodded.

"Good," Alex said. She led them both onto the porch and to the front door where she stopped abruptly. She unlocked the door and put her hand on the doorknob. "Okay. Close your eyes," she instructed. Dylan complied immediately. "You too," the agent said to the teacher. Cassidy was puzzled. "Cass...close 'em," Alex winked. Cassidy squinted at the agent. "Please? Just trust me?" Cassidy sighed and closed her eyes. Alex stepped behind mother and son and guided them carefully through the door. "Turn," she ushered them to the left slightly. "Okay," Alex whispered. "Open them."

Cassidy could not breathe. She stood impossibly still as her eyes scanned the room. Over the fire place hung a picture of her and Dylan at the beach. The couch they had looked at was in front of the fireplace. The mantle stood adorned by small framed pictures of each of them; including the one that Cassidy had snapped of her and Alex the first day they had come here, standing by the small tree in the front yard. Everything was perfect. It was as if they had always been here. Memories already on the shelf awaiting even more. Dylan looked at his mother who had begun to cry. "Alex," Cassidy barely managed to allow the name to escape her lips.

Alex beamed. "Do you like it?"

"It's cool!" Dylan exclaimed snapping Cassidy from her emotional place.

"Yes, it is," she looked at Alex in amazement.

Dylan was almost bouncing. "Do you want to see your room, Speed?" He nodded. "Okay, come on," Cassidy followed as Alex led the boy up the stairs. The bedroom door was closed and Alex had a smirk on her face. Cassidy had no idea what to expect despite knowing some of what Alex had purchased. She wondered what the agent had truly been up to. "Are you SURE you want to go in there?" Alex joked. Dylan nodded with wide eyes. "Okay then," she opened the door slowly.

Cassidy shook her head. The walls were a light gray. Pictures of all of Dylan's favorite superheroes hung framed on the walls. Behind the small bed that Alex insisted they buy were decals that looked just like a city skyline and a figure of Batman soaring above. Many of Dylan's toys from the house in New York were already in the room. His rabbit sat against the large Batman pillow on the bed. The Batcave he had built right before everything had gone crazy sat in the corner of the room. Dylan ran in and jumped onto his bed looking around. "Is this really my room?" Alex nodded.

He ran to the agent and his mother with force. "So...you like it then?" Alex asked.

"It's the Batcave!" He said excitedly.

"Kinda'..." Alex beamed. "You know there is more to see, though."

"Can I stay here?" Dylan asked hopefully.

"Yes," Cassidy smiled. "You can stay here, Dylan." Secretly, Alex was glad that he wanted to stay in his room. There were surprises that she had for Cassidy and she had hoped to show them to her one on one.

"Okay...so...you and me?" Alex offered her hand to Cassidy.

Cassidy accepted the hand and gripped it firmly, her heart nearly bursting. "Where to?"

"Kitchen?" Alex suggested, receiving an agreeable smile. She led Cassidy down the stairs and into the hallway that led to the kitchen. "Close 'em," Alex said.

"Again?" Cassidy asked. Alex nodded. "Alex, am I going to have to close my eyes before I enter every room?"

"As a matter of fact, yes," the agent said with satisfaction. She had been waiting on pins and needles to unveil her surprise and she intended to enjoy every second of it. Alex gently escorted Cassidy into the kitchen. "Okay," she whispered in the teacher's ear.

"Oh my God, Alex...."

"So?" Alex inquired. She watched Cassidy slowly walk through the room. The teacher had fallen in love with this room the moment they had walked into it days ago. Now, it was unbelievable. There was a rustic table off to the left. On top of it sat a vase full of flowers. A small matching cart sat at the far end of the counter with a wooden bowl full of fresh fruit. The counter was sprinkled with all the necessities. Cassidy chuckled; not surprised to see a stainless steel coffee maker. There was a beautiful spice rack, full of everything she could ever need. Above her head the pot rack was now completely full with stainless pots and pans. She ran her hands over things trying to process all that Alex had done. The glass front cabinet was full of dishes; dishes Alex had caught her looking at on one of their many shopping stops. Nothing was missing. "Cass?" Cassidy turned and looked at the agent as tears fell softly down her cheeks. She had no words. "Please tell me those are happy tears?"

Cassidy's laughter broke through her tears which threatened now to become sobs of happiness. She walked slowly to the agent and placed her hands on the sides of Alex's face. "Are you real?" she asked softly. Alex just smiled, happy to lose herself in Cassidy's eyes. "Je t'adore," the smaller woman whispered, her voice trembling with emotion.

"Not nearly as much as I adore you," Alex answered.

Cassidy closed the distance between them. Tenderly guiding the agent's lips to her own. "You take my breath away," she confessed.

"I hope you always feel that way," Alex answered. Cassidy smiled. "Ready for the rest?"

"How about the master?" Cassidy raised an eyebrow.

Alex laughed. "Ummm…nope."

"Why not?"

"Nope…that one has to wait until LATER," Alex winked.

"Is that so?" Cassidy flirted.

"It is. How about a glass of wine on the deck. It's warm enough today," Alex suggested. "You know, to celebrate. We can show Dylan the…."

Cassidy laughed and caressed the agent's cheek. "You are not going to get him out of that room anytime soon. You'll be lucky if you get him out of there for his party tomorrow."

Alex beamed. "Maybe when he sees the family room," Alex gloated.

"Why is that?" Cassidy asked curiously. Alex shrugged. "Alex…."

"Oh come on. I want to show you that one together, later. Let's have a glass of wine," Alex smirked.

"We have wine?" Cassidy asked. Alex gestured to the refrigerator. Cassidy made her way there as Alex walked to a drawer and removed the corkscrew. "Alex...how did you?" Not only was there a bottle of wine but the refrigerator was fully stocked.

"Have to have stuff to eat, right? I mean we live here after all," Alex said as a matter of fact. Cassidy shook her head handing the bottle of Chardonnay to Alex.

"It's only eleven, Alex."

"So? You have other plans I don't know about?" Cassidy shook her head again. "All right then. Wine and then we will call Dylan."

The next hour was spent quietly on the stone patio in the back yard. Alex had not spared attention here either. There was a table and six chairs on the deck and a wicker patio set surrounded the stone fire pit at the center of the patio. Cassidy sat content to sip her wine and rest her head on the agent's shoulder until a small bundle of energy interrupted their companionable silence. "I'm hungry!"

Alex laughed. "Well, I wondered when we would see you," she said. "So...order a pizza?" He nodded.

The rest of the day was spent with Dylan asking endless questions and making endless discoveries everywhere he went. When evening finally began to fall, Alex suggested they watch a movie in the family room. There were only two secrets left to reveal; this and the master bedroom. Dylan entered first and squealed with delight. "MOM!"

Cassidy surveyed the scene and looked at Alex, shaking her head. "I thought we agreed?"

Alex shrugged. "Got a good deal," she explained.

A large flat screen television was mounted on the far wall. There was a reclining sofa and two beanbag chairs sat closer to the television. The agent had heard Dylan say that he wanted a beanbag chair for his birthday and Alex made certain he had two. There was also what Cassidy suspected was a game system of some sort and a tower full of all of Dylan's movies from the old house. "Alex...how did you..."

"I had Fallon bring some things."

It explained the pictures and the toys. "Why should I be surprised?" Cassidy smiled and Alex simply shrugged again. An evening of Batman and Spiderman ended with a small toe headed boy fast asleep in a beanbag chair. His mother lay half asleep with her head on the agent's lap. They were home.

"Cass?" Alex kissed the woman's forehead.

"Yeah?"

"One last surprise," she smiled.

"Mmmm...I know," Cassidy smiled without opening her eyes.

"If I take him up, will you put him down?"

"What are you up to, Agent Toles?"

"Well...." was the only response from the agent.

"Um hum," Cassidy smiled taking a moment to lightly caress the hand holding her. "Do I have to close my eyes again?"

"They are already closed," Alex observed playfully.

"Funny. You've been hanging around my mother too much."

"Maybe," Alex admitted. "Come on." Cassidy forced herself up and watched Alex scoop up Dylan. He groaned a bit. "It's all right, Speed," Alex assured softly.

"I've got it," Cassidy said taking over from the agent as she set the small boy onto his bed.

"In the top drawer," Alex pointed.

"Just like in his old room."

Alex smiled. "Figured it was easier that way....Knock before you come in."

"What exactly are you doing?" Cassidy asked.

"You've waited this long. You'll survive another ten minutes," the agent said making her way out of the room.

***

Cassidy took a deep breath and lightly rapped on the door "Who is it?" a voice joked from behind the door before opening it slowly. As the door opened a pair of blue eyes twinkled. Soft candlelight filled the room behind the agent. "Welcome, home," Alex whispered, taking Cassidy's hand and leading her into the room. The teacher almost didn't notice the room itself she was so consumed in the way that the soft light accentuated the beautiful face of the woman she loved. The reflection of numerous small flickers of flame sparkled in Alex's crystal blue eyes. "What do you think?"

Cassidy looked deeply into the agent's eyes. "Beautiful."

Alex smiled. "The room, Cass."

"Oh. Are we in a room?"

Alex laughed. "Look…"

Then it captured Cassidy's attention. It was her mother's old bedroom set. The one that Christopher O'Brien never wanted. The one she had loved so much and remembered crawling onto as a small child. She had hoped it would be the bed Dylan would run to when he had nightmares. "How did you know?"

Alex caressed Cassidy's shoulders as the teacher ran her hands over the bed. "Like you said…spending a lot of time with your mother. Couldn't have done any of this without her," she said with affection.

Cassidy turned to face the agent. "You are amazing…thank you," she said sweetly.

"No, you are amazing, Cass. The most amazing person I have ever met." Cassidy smiled as the agent's lips captured hers in a tender kiss. She felt Alex's embrace tighten and pull her closer. "Welcome home, Cassidy."

"You are my home, Alex."

The agent searched green eyes that now penetrated her soul. "*Et vous êtes tout pour moi* (And you are my everything)." Alex gently guided the smaller woman onto the large poster frame bed. Her hands delicately exploring the form beneath her, reveling in every sensation, every curve. Alex was enraptured by the feel of Cassidy in her arms. Her kiss found its way slowly over the teacher's neck. She intended to worship every inch of the woman she loved.

"Alex...."

Alex pulled away slightly to look into the eyes that could hypnotize her in an instant. She kissed Cassidy and gently ran her fingers over the softest lips she had ever known. "Right now, Cassidy...right now... *C'est le début de l'éternité* (This is the beginning of forever)," the agent promised. Alex kissed her way down the entire form that mesmerized her, drinking in the sight, the feel and the sounds that were uniquely Cassidy.

Breathless, Cassidy held onto the strong woman above her. Alex was making love to her so tenderly that Cassidy thought her body was being lifted from the earth itself. Every touch lingered for what seemed forever before continuing on; leaving a trail of love and desire that encompassed them both and carried Cassidy away. She struggled to find words as her hands ran softly through the agent's hair. Her body trembled and quaked and at the first quiver Alex simply held her tighter. Always a journey, seductive and sensual and wrapping them both in the safety and understanding of a loving embrace. "*Toujours ne sera jamais assez longue* (forever will never be long enough)," Cassidy professed as Alex guided her over the edge of sanity. "Alex, Oh my..."

The agent slowly placed a trail of kisses all the way across her lover until their eyes met again. "*Au-delà de amourng toujours, mon amour* (beyond forever, my love) welcome home," Alex smiled.

Chapter Twenty-Eight

"Cass?" Alex woke and was surprised to find that Cassidy was not next to her. "What time is it? Nine?" She grumbled and rolled out of the bed. She rarely slept past five or six. Dylan was not in his room either. Reaching the kitchen, she paused in the doorway. Cassidy was sitting at the small table sipping her coffee with Rose and Barb. The small blonde woman at the table looked up and smiled at the agent whose hair was still tussled from sleep. Alex just smiled back, finding it momentarily difficult to process the scene before her. They were truly home.

"Morning sleepy head," Barb joked. Alex just tipped her head, keeping one eye on Cassidy as the teacher made her way to pour Alex a mug of coffee. "You were the one who made us promise to be here by eight-thirty. Did you mean p.m.?" Barb poked again.

"You're a jack ass, and you know, there's still time to add pin the tail on the…" Alex's comeback was interrupted by the offering of a hot mug and a pair of green eyes that somehow instantly transported her. Cassidy raised her eyebrow and chuckled as Alex's arm wrapped around her waist. "Morning," Alex said to her lover placing a kiss on her head.

"So, agent," Rose snickered. "What are our orders?"

Alex laughed. "This one is all Cass." Cassidy looked at the woman next to her and shook her head. "Where's Dylan?" the agent asked.

"He's in the family room playing with that Xbox." Alex's face lit up and Cassidy tried to contain her laughter. "Just go," she said.

Alex bit her lip slightly, "are you…"

"Go," Cassidy repeated. "I'll call you when I need you." There was no doubt that Alex wanted in on the fun and Cassidy was more than happy to take care of Dylan's party. It already felt like home to her here and she could not remember when she felt so relaxed. For once she had spent a morning watching Alex sleep and she found herself musing that the reason she could not recall being this happy was because she never had been. It wasn't the house. It wasn't the things. It was the woman beside her. It was the small boy asleep down the hall. It was finally feeling a sense of home. She watched Alex walk slowly out of the kitchen and laughed aloud when the agent's pace quickened down the hallway. Turning back to the table she was met by two pairs of smiling eyes.

"So?" Rose asked.

"What?" Cassidy answered reclaiming her seat across from her mother.

"Well, how many things did you test drive last night?" Rose laughed. Cassidy poked her cheek with her tongue as Barb nearly spit her coffee across the room. "Oh…come on…I meant the game system and the television and the jet tub… honestly…you two have your minds…"

"My mind is a direct product of my genes," Cassidy quipped back. "And to answer your question; I have full knowledge of how *everything* in the house works." She raised her eyebrow, soliciting a fit of full blown laughter from all three women that would take more than a few minutes to subside. It was the beginning of what Cassidy thought might truly be the happiest day of her life.

***

Jonathan Krause paced the floor in his apartment, staring at the small flat object that lay just a few feet away. Eleven in the morning and he was already on his second scotch. He rubbed his hand over the top of his head and shook the ice in his glass. "Christ, John," he muttered under his breath. "How the hell did we get here?" A faint rattling disturbed his private thoughts and he very slowly reached for the offending party. "Krause," he said flatly.

"*Je suppose que tout est préparé* (I assume all is prepared?)"

"*Bien sûr, Edmond. Il sera toutefois soirée ici* (Of course, Edmond. It will be evening here however)," he answered.

"*Et Strickland comprend son rôle?* (And Strickland understands his role)?"

Krause felt his jaw clench tightly. "Everyone understands his part."

"Well, then let us hope that everyone can execute his part effectively. *Il s'agit d'une nécessité regrettable, mon ami.* (It is an unfortunate necessity, my friend)," Edmond Callier offered.

Jonathan Krause continued his pacing, considering the man's statement. He stopped at a small cabinet and set his focus on two photos that sat next to each other. In one, two young men stood side by side; one just slightly older than the other who had his arm across the younger man's shoulder. The other was a picture taken in front of the Eiffel tower; a much younger Jonathan Krause smiling wildly at a pretty blonde girl handing him a balloon. He took a deep breath and sipped his scotch, remaining fixed on the faces that lay behind the glass. He offered his response deliberately. "*Ce n'est pas une entreprise pour l'amitié. Attendez-vous à monappel* (This is not a business for friendship. Expect my call)."

***

"What the hell are you talking about?" Michael Taylor blasted through the phone. "What chatter?"

Steven Brady rubbed his jaw with some force. "It's just chatter."

"There is no such thing as just chatter, Brady. Either it leads directly to something or it is meant to lead us directly from something. Either way we need to know what the direction is. Timing?"

Brady shook his head and exhaled before speaking back into the phone. "No timeline in the communication."

Taylor rubbed his brow. "Location?"

"West coast," Brady repeated.

Taylor put his face in his hands. "What the hell is going on?" he muttered into his hands.

"Sir?" Brady asked unable to understand the words through the phone.

"Dig….And dig fast."

"What's the rush?" Brady said. "There was no timeline."

"That's what worries me…Dig now," he hung up the phone and tilted his head backward over the chair. "Shit, Colonel… what are we into?"

***

"Nope…sorry Speed!"

"Aww…come on, Alex…one more."

"It was one more like five games ago," Alex laughed, receiving a small pout. "We'll both be in time out if we aren't ready for your party."

"You're not gonna' be as much fun now, are you?" he asked with some seriousness.

Alex tried not to laugh. "Me? I'm Alfred. Is Alfred fun?" He shrugged. "Oh." Alex grabbed two small legs and pitched the boy over her shoulders. "We'll see who has fun!" She said to the sound of a delighted seven year old squeal.

***

"How many people does she think we are feeding?" Cassidy shook her head to Barb.

"She's a Toles. You get your genes from Rose, well wait 'til you meet Helen." Cassidy looked at Barb curiously. "Oh... yeah," Barb winked. "She might not be affectionate all the time but she sure as hell feeds us. I think that's where Nicky got his culinary obsession."

"Not Alex," Cassidy laughed.

"Nope. I think it would be safe to say that Alex and Helen are the human equivalent to oil and water."

"That bad?" Cassidy asked.

"Don't be too frightened. Remember, I endured that alone. You have me to protect you." Cassidy laughed. Her curiosity was now piqued about Alex's parents. It remained a subject that saw little conversation between them, even in the presence of Nick and Barb.

"Cassie!" Rose called. "You'll never guess who is here?"

The teacher made her way to the front door and was astounded to see Brian Fallon with his entire brood in tow. "Brian," she smiled, immediately taking him into a warm hug. "Thank you for everything," she gleamed, embracing him tightly.

Fallon tried to temper the rising blush he felt in his cheeks. Cassidy had a quality that he rarely found in others. She was completely genuine and unaware of how beautiful she was. It was a combination that existed in few people in his experience and he understood fully how Alex had lost her heart to the small woman. In truth, there was nothing small about Cassidy O'Brien. She was larger than life. "No need to thank me, Cassidy."

"And this must be..."

"Cassidy O'Brien, this is my wife, Kate."

Cassidy extended her hand to the woman beside her friend. Kate Fallon was an attractive woman in her own right. Her auburn hair fell at her shoulders and she had dark blue eyes that highlighted her fair complexion. Cassidy could tell just from her smile that she had an easy way about her. "Welcome. It's so nice to meet you. I'm sorry we have kept him away so much," she said earnestly.

"Comes with the territory," Kate said smiling sweetly at her husband and then back at the teacher. "You'll learn," she said jokingly.

Leading the group through the door Cassidy came even with the woman and returned the good natured joke. "After being married to congress I've learned how to do nearly everything by proxy." Kate laughed.

Barb stepped in and guided the Fallons' three children off to the family room to play. "Come on kids. I hear there is some cool driving game running in the other room. Better claim it now before Alex gets back." Cassidy laughed. There was some truth in that statement she thought.

The banter was quickly interrupted by the sight of Alex chasing a giggling Dylan toward his room. "No, Alex!" The boy was laughing so hard he could barely run.

"Paybacks Speed!" The agent called after him.

"No...Alex...."

The agent caught the small boy and picked him up in her arms. As she moved to tickle him she caught view of the small group watching in amusement from below and cleared her throat. "Yeah....Speed....Umm....sneakers," she placed his feet back on the floor facing the room.

"I win," he laughed running into his room.

Alex shrugged and smiled at the group below before following Dylan into his room. Kate looked at her husband in awe. "I told you," he said.

Rose broke the moment. "Ahh, still the honeymoon. Give it time. When she finds out how awful Cassie really is at yard work, it'll wear off...summer's coming."

Cassidy shook her head and Fallon laughed. "Thanks, Mom."

"You're welcome dear."

***

"Who's coming?" Dylan asked while making bunny ears with his laces.

"Well...Mom and me..."

"Doesn't count. You live here," he said.

"What?" Alex pretended to be hurt. He laughed. "So it's like that, huh?" He laughed again. "Well, Grandma and Aunt Barb and Uncle Nick....Cat and Cat's friend Bobby." Dylan looked at Alex and smiled. "And, Mr. Fallon and his family... he has three kids..."

"I know." Dylan said.

Alex laughed. She watched him finish his laces and thought silently how much she loved him. "You ready now?" He nodded.

"Alex? Will you be here when I am eight?"

Alex smiled. "I hope, Dylan...that I will be here when you are eighteen."

"That's old," he said.

"I guess it is, Speed."

***

John Merrow looked out the window and then down at his notes. "Mr. President," a young man in a suit approached. The president looked up from his papers. "We'll be on the ground in about twenty minutes. Is there anything you need before?"

"No, Rick. Thank you." The president returned his gaze out of the small window and then rested his head against the back of the seat he was in. He liked to watch the clouds when he was afforded the time. As a boy he dreamed of being a pilot. His father would take him to the air shows and his uncle, an Air Force pilot, would sometimes take him flying. It was not to be. There were other plans ahead for John Merrow. When he told his father, an Army General, that he wanted to attend the Naval Academy and become an aviator, the idea was immediately stamped out. John Merrow's path had been carved out long before he gazed into the clouds and dreamed of soaring through them.

Most people saw President John Merrow's life as charmed. He was a decorated Army officer, married a beautiful woman who had briefly had a career on film. He had two beautiful daughters and was widely considered one of the most intelligent and trustworthy people in Washington. It was not the life he would have chosen. It was the life he was given. It was not the woman that he fell in love with; though he had learned a great deal about that emotion from watching her with his children. Looking at the clouds he often wondered whose life he was leading. So many choices. So many directions. He was responsible for them all. Another day, another bridge that needed to be built. It seemed to him, looking into the clouds, that long standing bridges were crumbling now. Perhaps it was the foundation, he mused to himself. Perhaps the engineering was just outdated. He sighed and closed his eyes. It was no matter. Build the bridge. Mend the fence. That was the expectation. Failure was never an option.

***

Cat was leading a small contingent of eager climbers to master the small tree in the front yard. Cassidy had stepped out on the front porch to check on them and stayed to watch the scene unfold. Fallon's son, James, was eleven and he was helping the younger children reach the first branch. He looked a great deal like Brian, Cassidy thought, and he shared his father's kindness. "No...it's Dylan's birthday. He should go first," James said.

Cassidy stood smiling. So many nights she had wished that Dylan could have a life like this. She felt a pair of arms wrap around her waist. "Watcha' doing?" Alex whispered in her ear.

"Just watching."

"Ummm....that tree might end up being the best investment," Alex acknowledged.

"Maybe," Cassidy agreed leaning back into the agent and soaking in her warmth.

"Come back in," Alex said. "I promise he'll climb the tree again."

"I know."

"Hummm," Alex pulled Cassidy a little closer. "You're happy?" Cassidy didn't answer, instead placing her hands over the two that came to a point in front of her. "Me too," Alex said. "Come on."

"They won't miss us that much," Cassidy answered. The agent was more than happy to comply with the teacher's unspoken request. Standing here with this beautiful woman in her arms watching Dylan, the emotion Alex felt was almost more than she could fathom.

Rose reached the door to call the pair in and stopped. She pressed her lips together and wiped a tear from the corner of her eye. The tall, commanding agent was gently holding her daughter and placing small kisses on her head. She wasn't certain if Alex was saying anything, but the look in her daughter's eyes was unmistakable. Rose McCollum had one great love in her life, her daughter. She had never shared all the truths of her own struggles with love with Cassidy. Cassidy's father died when she was only ten and Rose never tainted her daughter's memories of the man that she had worshipped as a child. The older woman had always hoped her daughter would find what had alluded her in her own life: love. She kept silent watch now in the distance as Dylan made it to the first set of branches and she studied the expression of pride on both Alex and Cassidy as they watched. "MOM!" Dylan yelled "Look!"

"I see!" Cassidy called back.

"Hey...Alex is watching too," Cat waved to his aunt and Cassidy.

"I know!" ALEX LOOK!" Dylan yelled.

"Good job, Speed. Be careful," Alex praised and instructed. He nodded. "I think your son is having fun," Alex said. Cassidy turned in the agent's arms and looked into her eyes. She lost herself for a moment. "What?" Alex asked.

Rose took a deep breath as she witnessed her daughter's hand tenderly stroke the taller woman's cheek. Cassidy's smile grew and her voice carried with a confidence that completely astounded her mother. "I think," Cassidy said, "that our son is lucky to have you."

Alex closed her eyes as Cassidy's lips met hers. "Cass..."

Cassidy turned back in the agent's arms and held them around her firmly. "Talk to your son, Alex. He *chose* you; he got me."

Rose smiled and began to turn on her heels slowly. This was their moment. No jokes. No banter. No advice. "Oh Cassie, I love you," the words slipped from her at the same time as another tear fell.

"Mom?" Cassidy heard her mother's voice in the distance.

"How do you do that?" Rose waved innocently.

"Welcome to the family," Cassidy laughed taking Alex's hand to walk toward her mother.

"I'll take it," Alex said with a smile.

"I'll remember you said that."

"I know," the agent laughed as they walked back through the door of the house.

***

"I'm not sure," Brady faltered.

"Best guess?" Taylor demanded. There was an almost audible pause, the breath of both men heavy and strained. "Brady... Best guess...credible or not credible?"

Through a heavy release of air the younger man spoke into the phone, "I would not dismiss it."

Michael Taylor froze. It was the call no one ever wanted to receive and no one wanted to make. If he was wrong the fall out would be brutal. If he was right the consequence of not calling would be unforgivable. He steadied his breathing and laid his forehead on a closed fist. "I'll make the call."

"Sir…"

"Brady….I hope to God that you are wrong."

***

"Alex!" Cat and Dylan burst through the front door.

"What's wrong?" Alex immediately envisioned someone toppling from the tree.

"There's a big truck here," Cat said with Dylan nodding wide eyed.

Cassidy tried to fake a curious expression when Alex looked at her. She shrugged and the agent caught the corner of her mouth curling into a smile. "Cassidy?" Cassidy shrugged again and tried not to look at Barb as Alex made her way to the door. "Can I help you?" Alex asked the man now on the porch.

"I have a delivery for Toles?"

"I'm not expecting anything," Alex combed through her recent purchases in her mind. "No. I think…"

The agent felt Cassidy's hand on her back as the teacher pushed in alongside of her. "Downstairs," Cassidy directed.

"Cass? What the…."

"Oh so you think you're the only one who can keep a secret, huh?"

Alex turned to see the man unloading a large box and recognized the name Olhausen. "Cassidy…what did you…"

"What is it?" Dylan asked. "Is it a birthday present?"

Cassidy smiled. "It looks like your mom bought us a pool table, Speed," Alex observed. He looked at his mother hopefully and she nodded. After an energetic high five with Cat the boys followed the delivery team downstairs into the finished basement. Alex looked at her lover. "I can't believe you..."

Cassidy raised an eyebrow. "I expect you to teach me."

Alex raised an eyebrow of her own remembering their first attempt at that endeavor. "I think that could be arranged," she smiled and kissed the woman before her. "I love you, Cass."

"Yeah? As much as that pool table?"

"I'll let you know after the next lesson," Alex chuckled.

"I'm sure you will," Cassidy answered leading the agent off to the basement.

***

John Merrow stepped off the small platform and reached forward to accept the customary hand shake of his hosts. "Thank you," he said with a firm grip.

"We'll get it done," Congresswoman Collins whispered as he offered her a friendly hug.

"I know you will," he said pulling back with a confident nod.

"Sir," a voice broke into his ear. "We need to change the exit."

"No," Merrow answered.

"Sir, I am afraid I must insist."

John Merrow turned and faced the Secret Service agent. "No."

"There is..."

The president stood firm. "I appreciate your concern. I cannot change tonight's plan. Figure it out."

***

"Great party," Nick said. Alex smiled. "Alex," he continued. "Can we talk for a minute?

"Yeah, of course."

Nick pulled his sister aside. "I'm betting that you already know."

"What's that?" his sister asked.

"That Barb is pregnant." Alex laughed. "It's fine. I told her I was going to tell you tonight."

"Nicky, I am happy for you."

"Yeah, thanks. Listen, Alex when are you going to tell Mom." Alex felt all the muscles in her body tense. "I mean… she knows, Alex…it's all over the…"

Alex nodded. "Not now, Nick. Not today….all right?"

Nick sighed. "I just…"

The tension in the agent at the mention of her mother was palpable. "I know you want things to be different. I do. Right now, I just need to be with Cass and Dylan. Enough has happened. I don't need to deal with…"

"I get it," he conceded. "What do you want me to tell her?"

Alex shook her head. She looked across the room to Cassidy who was saying goodbye to Rose and trying to calm Dylan down at the same time. "Tell her….Tell her the truth." Nick looked at his sister. "Tell her I have a family." Nick sighed. "It's okay, Nicky…Tell her or don't. I'll call her next week. Just give me some time." He smiled as his older sister led him to the door.

"Alex?" Nick stopped.

"Yeah?

"She is great," her brother smiled. He thought the world of Cassidy and he understood this was his sister's time.

Alex chuckled. "I guess we both got lucky."

"Thanks for everything Nick," Cassidy began. "Dylan! No… No more pool!" She called down the hallway. Dylan was off like shot. "I'm sorry," Cassidy said grasping Nick's arm before beginning down the hallway. "Dylan James O'Brien!"

Alex laughed, "uh oh."

"Night, sis," he chuckled.

"Night," Alex smiled.

Barb reached out and hugged her sister in law. "Thanks."

"For?" the agent asked.

"Cassidy," Barb laughed.

Alex chuckled. "Yeah…it was all for you, Barb," Alex joked.

"I figured," Barb smacked the agent lightly as Alex let them out the door and closed it.

"Mom!" Dylan yelled impatiently.

"Dylan…" Alex noted the warning tone in Cassidy's voice. The excitement had finally hit its pinnacle. Dylan was wired for sound. The agent turned from the door to see Dylan stomping down the short hallway toward her and rubbing his eyes. "Over tired," Cassidy mouthed from behind.

"Hey Speed," Alex said gently. He stood in front of her wrinkling his brow and staring at the floor. "We're all tired."

"I'm not tired," he said indignantly.

"Mmm," Alex looked at Cassidy who rolled her eyes. "How about this…I promise tomorrow we will teach Mom how to play pool." She bent down and whispered to him. "And, I bet you can beat her." He looked up at the agent and sighed. His exhaustion was evident. "Piggy back?" He nodded.

***

Michael Taylor grabbed a hold of a photo behind his desk. In the center stood the colonel. He was handsome and strong and smiling broadly. To his left was a younger Taylor; he was thinner and he was sporting a Dodger's baseball cap. On the other side of the tall man was a young woman. Her hair was pulled back in a pony-tail. She had a soft, confident smile on her face. "Oh shit, Alex…what the hell is he into?" Taylor thought he might be sick. Something felt *off*. His gut was churning just like it did that day on Mutanabbi Street. "Colonel…."

***

"Is he down?" Cassidy asked. Alex nodded. "He was so tired," Cassidy observed.

"Well, maybe he will sleep in," Alex laughed.

"With that game system and that pool table? I wouldn't be surprised if he was sleepwalking down there," Cassidy joked.

"What about you?"

"I don't sleepwalk," Cassidy said.

"Hummmm...are you tired?"

"Why?" Cassidy asked playfully.

"You want a lesson?" Alex offered.

"What kind of lesson did you have in mind, Agent?"

"You said you expected a lesson," Alex reminded the teacher.

Cassidy smiled. "Well, given our history I guess that means we can just stay here."

Alex chuckled. "Really?" Cassidy shrugged. "Funny," the agent continued, "I seem to recall a very similar denim shirt."

"Not similar."

Alex looked closely at Cassidy, "yes it was." Cassidy shook her head. "Same?" Alex asked. Cassidy nodded. The agent pulled her phone from her jean's pocket.

"What are you doing?" Cassidy asked.

"Well, I am technically forbidden to work and I pretty much know where everyone is that I care to know about...So, I think radio silence is in order for the rest of this evening."

"Is that so?" Cassidy slowly walked toward the agent who tipped her head showing the teacher that her phone was off and tossing it aside onto the bedside table.

"That is so," Alex said.

"And what do you do when there is radio silence?" Cassidy asked letting her hands slowly trace the agent's sides.

"Sleep, mostly," Alex answered, trying to be serious.

Cassidy did not flinch. "Oh. Sounds perfect," she cooed and turned away from the agent. Swiftly she felt herself propelled back into Alex's arms. "Yes?" She asked.

Alex looked into her lover's eyes and lost all hope of continuing her playful game. "Cassidy?"

"Yes?" Cassidy raised an eyebrow.

The agent's expression became serious and she fought to swallow. "I need you," she confessed.

The smaller woman searched the agent's blue eyes. She could see Alex's need. There was an intensity in her eyes that Cassidy was not certain she had ever seen. The statement was not meant as a seduction; it was something much more. "Alex, you have me."

"I love you so much Cass. I can't even think of a way to tell…"

"Alex, you tell me every minute of the day. You tell me when you smile at me…when you play with Dylan, when you kiss me…." Her words were stopped by a soft, passionate kiss. "Come to bed," Cassidy whispered. Alex felt her heart skip as Cassidy led her to the bed they now shared.

"Cass…"

"Shh….I need to show you," Cassidy admitted looking down at the much taller and stronger figure beneath her.

"Show me what?"

Cassidy smiled. "Show you that I am yours…. *Je seraià toi pour toujours* (I will be yours forever)." She tenderly began to caress Alex's body and kiss her neck. Alex reached for her and Cassidy took hold of the larger hand. "Alex, *Laisse-moi t'aimer. Je veux que tu saches* (just let me love you. I need you to know)."

***

Krause set his scotch on the table and put his head between his knees as he lifted the phone to his ear. "Is it done?" He released his breath. "Is he?" He shook his head. "Where did they take him?…….Understood." He hung up the phone and looked over at the cabinet. "Jesus…How the hell did we get here, John?" He sighed and picked up the scotch, offering a toast in the air. "To brothers. Hard to fool, harder to kill."

***

"Cass?" Alex whispered.

"Hummm?" Cassidy answered through heavy eyelids.

Alex lay resting on the teacher's chest. Her fingers lightly playing over Cassidy's skin. "Thanks."

"What are you thanking me for?" Cassidy asked as she let her fingers run through the agent's hair.

"Saying that Dylan is my son....I never really thought I would have a son; you know?"

Cassidy smiled. "Don't thank me, Alex. I am thrilled by that, but Dylan made that decision all by himself. He didn't need my help to fall in love with you."

Alex nuzzled in tighter. "Cass?"

"Yeah?"

"You know, someday I might like to have another...you know..."

Cassidy felt her heart swell. There was nothing she did not want to share with the woman beside her. "I love you, Alex."

"*Je t'aime plus tous les jours* (I love you more everyday), Cass."

"Alex?"

"Hum?" Alex responded in a contented groan.

"Make love to me."

Alex immediately woke up at Cassidy's direct request. "Cass?"

"I..." Cassidy's voice trembled.

The agent smiled into the teacher's eyes and kissed the woman she loved. "I will give you everything, Cassidy."

"You already have," Cassidy said reaching out for the woman above her.

"Not quite. I think we'll leave the phone off for the weekend."

Cassidy smiled. For the first time she felt complete. That was the word she needed to describe this moment. She realized as Alex began to slowly explore her body and hold her heart, Alex Toles completed her. "Don't let go," she whispered.

"Never, Cass...never."

***

"Somebody get an ambulance!"

"Mr. President? John...John....." A voice continually called to the man now laying in a growing pool of his own blood.

"Alex? Sorry, Alex....Tell her that Dyl.....Didn't know.... Didn't know they would...Mutt..." a hand reached up and grasped the strong Secret Service agent above before falling to the ground.

"Don't talk, Mr. President....Jesus Christ! Hurry up!"

To Be Continued in Betrayal